I0635652

Chronicles of Sophron Book One: Seamus Chron

Written by Martin Poirier and Alibast Page

© 2025 Sophron Arts Productions www.sophron.art

Martin Poirier

Born in 1974, Martin Poirier is a professional screenwriter and author based in Quebec. He began developing the fantasy world of Sophron in 1996, as both a personal mythos and a creative playground merging philosophy, metaphysics, and narrative experimentation. After years of world-building and narrative refinement, he established a definitive model for the universe in 2012.

This novel, Chronicles of Sophron: Book One – Seamus Chron, is the first installment of the Babel War trilogy, a sprawling metaphysical epic where ancient truths, cosmic forces, and the fate of souls converge.

Alibast Page

The approximate time of Alibast Page's emergence into our world would place his birth around 356 BC. His essence first revealed itself to Martin in a series of vivid dreams between 1996 and 1999. Troubled by the wars, greed, and injustices ravaging Earth, Alibast took it upon himself to awaken Martin's inner vision — guiding him toward the hidden structures of reality.

Together, they began shaping the world of Sophron — a mirror, a warning, a sanctuary. Yet both remain bound by the subtle pull of the Greater Councils of Zendoria, whose designs may stretch far beyond their own awareness.

It remains uncertain whether Martin and Alibast are the true authors of these chronicles or simply characters in a story that was already unfolding before them.

For Emerald

Presenting the Ocorsurs

We carry it within ourselves — Beyond what the fleshed eye can see, past the limits of sensory reality. Worlds cradled within the folds of our individuality, spiraling far above the scope of eternity. These are the layers of the Great Entities. They move as one unified manifestation of truth.

We call it: the *pluriverse*. Seventy-two unique layers, divided among four primordial quadrants:

Matter, under the Ocorsur known as *Barbelo*.
The axioms of these realms forge solid ground — rock, ice, bone. Beings here project their existence through the bubbling depths of intricate neural foundations. Quantum laws govern a reality blooming as entangled certainties.

Life, under *Archeus*.
Beyond matter, consciousness unfurls. Biology becomes a field of evolving vessels. Worlds blossom into cosmic architectures, where life raises its eyes to the stars, questioning the expanse, daring to dream the unknown.

Thought, under *Logos*.
While mortals perceive in three or four dimensions, Logos-realms picture their existence in twelve. Matter vanishes like mist at dawn. Life fades into myth. Only thought remains, omniscient, shaping cities, beings, civilizations woven from pure reflection. Certainty sharpens itself until it approaches the edge of perception.

Void, under its eponymous Ocorsur.
Realms of absolute negation. Inhabitants — *hollows* — breathe blankness. Thought dissolves within remains of lost echoes. And yet, through blankness, quantum birth stirs anew, matter returns with Sophron's seventy-two domains

But if existence were that simple, wars would not rage across the layers. Selfish gods and dreaming titans would not manipulate truth. Some will seek conquest. Others, annihilation. The Ocorsurs — and the Great Entities who guard each realm — are drawn into the collision.

This chaos spills over to the Dreamers.

Some moguls of Gaia bought their ticket to the Void, rising into the stars. Billions watched — some with awe, some with rage, most in silence. They were Sleepers, heirs to brainless empires.

But the true road to other worlds exist by itself.
And it lies **within you**. As you read this novel in the comfort of your True Reality, you will find a door. And the pluriverse will open itself in your backyard.

Prologue:
The Dawn of a Storyline

The young student woke up in the middle of the night. They knew that a fragment of their master's favourite poet shone from under their pillow. Should they read it or fall back asleep? Looking outside their window, they saw the wonders of Athens, at a time when electricity only happened within a thinker's brain. Nature cohabited with the most important city of that era. The wind played with the curtains, teasing an empty street to the haunted student who dreamed of Sophron. Their dusty house would make them sick, but the papyrus under their pillow comforted them. They drew the lion from its claw.

The young trainee went straight to the master's teaching, soon after the first glance of sunlight confirmed that sleep would have to wait. Plato stood in the middle of the Parthenon, pausing for a few chosen ones to join him in the sharing of Great Mysteries. With his greyish hair revealing ages he keeps within his wisdom, Plato smiled more than the statues depicting him. The student held onto their fragment of a poem, reading it again, and trying to find the words that would convince their mentor that they had completed their homework. "What did Sophron mean, by that?" Plato will ask them. The idealess teenager kept silent. "It's something to do with cooking, I think." The pupil uttered. "Cumin is a spice, and ladle, you don't scrape with it, but."

Plato would keep his emotions to himself, reading the student's understanding of their homework through their eyes. Timid and a bit shameful, the apprentice viewed the six others, boys, girls and some devoid of any knowable gender. The pupil observed their entourage and they tried to interpret the puzzled look in those eyes. "How can we draw an animal from its claw?" they would ask Plato. "How can you scrape a spoon and slice cumin?" the teacher would reply. The growing child pondered for a moment. "You don't." they answered. The student thought and added:

"The lion eats to survive, but the artist will draw the beast for his own prosperity. Ladles give us nutrients, but they don't slice spices, so." Plato laughed to himself. "Perhaps you try too hard to provide a sense. Sophron's rhetoric never conveyed anything too deep, or too philosophical." The fellow grew more interested in the lesson. They wondered if Plato would elect this as a good time to display his master of ancient magical arts. Legend has it that the Great Mysteries formed a circle of powerful mystics. They understood reality beyond the fabric of our worldly illusion. The word among this elitist bubble involves enlightened minds who could create vast universes and project them into existence, using this very miraculous craft.

"Teacher?" the young one surprised themselves asking: "When will we be tutored about the art of mancing?" Plato paused for a long moment and explained: "You already know everything you need to master this form. If your time comes, I will provide you with the tools. Just let the story exist within you, and don't impose your will onto your characters."He smiled and invited his seven disciples to follow him in a cave, at the other end of the Parthenon. The light grew dim as they advanced inside this recluse area. A long corridor brought them across what seemed like the centre of the globe. The young student could feel a warm almost membranous thread forming around them as though they gradually stepped within a vaporous spider web. As they walked farther inside the tunnel, a blue gleam of feeble glow emerged, at the extremity. The shadow of their six classmates drew themselves.

Plato's silhouette led them towards that spark. While their eyes grew accustomed to this lack of clarity, they could see the walls built out of pure metal. It appeared the whole place was carved within a huge block of shiny iron. When the group arrived at the opposite end of the corridor, they witnessed the presence of a floating orb, the size of a melon. It emitted enough light to expose the entirety of a gigantic room, devoid of any art or furniture.

The crystal ball shone solo in this huge chamber. In a solemn manner, Plato stood across from his pupils, on the other side of this magical sphere. When the teenaged student brought their eyes upon it, they perceived thousands of images entwined onto one another. "A good mancer will acknowledge that each and every pixel that form those floating paintings, inside the orb, produces its own sovereign universe." He seized the object and offered it to the inquisitive young one who requested to see this marvel. "Take it." Plato instructed, before adding: "And now, you will tell us a story." The student grabbed it. Thousands of millions of existences instantly filled them. It felt like a shock that struck their conscience. They thought for a moment, and uttered: "I sense the presence of a tale. It involves gods and their reflections. It begins in a city that some will call Montreal, yet for me, it sings the last whispers of Thebes. In it, I warn you, a wise man will die of his own accord. Pain, you see, that agent of destruction, calls him. You shouldn't let it bring you to any tomorrow."

"But he did?" asked Plato.

"Yes, and he died." Frightened, the student left the spherule alone and walked away from it. "I could feel the reality of a boy, around my age. This novel displays a different existence of mine?" Plato caressed the orb, as though trying to quiet a passionate cat, and agreed: "This explains why I believe you are ready. Sophron isn't just the name of a beloved poet, you see? It is how we call the One True Reality. Now, give your story another trial. We are listening."

8

Fear made them question their desire to pet the lion again. Still, the student approached the sphere. They closed their eyes and put a hand on top of it. At the centre of the crystal, a few words appeared:-We are pixels of illumination and darkness, on a blank canvas that knows of no good or evil.

The student opened their eyes and looked deep inside Plato's orb. They saw buildings made of metal and concrete, stone, and swords, they thought: *What are pixels? How can they illuminate and remain obfuscated?* They tried to get attention from their teacher, but they realized that the assignment implicated floating images in the middle of a crystal ball. Why would they involve a wasp and an owl? Why is the student feeling compelled to express pride and prejudice? *Focus on the tale that inhabits you.* They thought, and don't hate what you fail to comprehend.

Ancient wisdom will always try to survive the vileness of greedy avenues. No joy remains in greatness. None outside those who stood before us. Only peace finds itself in improvement when we experience prestige like none of us has witnessed. "Don't let words repeat themselves." the teacher said, then added: "Pay attention to the usage of your verbs to Be and to Have. A true calling implies self-abandonment." the student pondered for a longer moment and whispered: "I think the main character is an ignorant prick."

Journey into the Hourglass:
One

I met Martin at a bar in Avalon, where I grew up and made a living as a poet. He'd get drunk there weekly, reminiscing about someone because the barmaid reminded him of home, Earth. Feeling sorry for him, I'd often help him after he passed out and let him stay at my place. Over breakfast, we'd talk about his failed writing career in Toronto. I encouraged him not to give up.

"You know, Martin." I would tell him. "Failure doesn't exist, until you give up." *Maybe we could write something together.* He responded. "Sure. What about we write your story, and how your consciousness awakened and travelled all over Sophron?"

We decided to tell tales of other souls on their journeys to enlightenment. We created characters like Seamus Chron seeking redemption; William Francoeur, who would follow an arc of self-discovery, after finding himself on the other end of the Veil; Nempty, who would discover virtue, after caring for an android daughter; Ishtar searching for her beloved Indra's lost soul; Marduk intent on conquering Sophron, and Sekhmet and Melpomene two powerful characters, caught in these tales.

Chapter One:
Seamus the Narcissistic Prick

To the universe, life is but the sigh of an ant at the feet of
Mount Olympus. I have been travelling through almost every layer
of Sophron, and I saw marvels unheard of, from ordinary folks.
A mere mortal, but my job puts me at odds with cosmic entities.
My name is Seamus Chronenberg. I protect the Veil.

As you read these words, you may see me as a rugby captain in
Leonard Cohen High School, in Westmount, at the heart of
Montreal, Quebec, Canada. If you look up that institution
on Google, you won't find it. It exists in a possibility you may have
never heard of. If Google means nothing to you, then I take off my
hat and salute you for having discovered this novel. We find
ourselves advised about possibilities: Dreams of what could have
been if only we did this or that at that or this moment. I tell you;
they are all over us, all the time. We can only harness one, at one
given instant, and let the billion others escape or evade our trials
and errors. It requires several lives to realize how we can go from
nothingness to true light. I wish I could fully understand, but I'm
merely a traveller. So, they said.

I always considered myself separate from the world I grew up in. I would often take the metro and contemplate the crowd that filled the train, and I felt like viewing a scene from a movie. If I were to shout, people would look at my estranged self and would try to avoid me. The film I would watch would continue, with my crazy intervention having left a mark. Everyone would soon forget my face, and I would become a speck of dust on their daily story to tell their loved ones. But I swear. I feel all their existence and their conscience the same way my lungs would feel the smoke of a thousand cigarettes. This would explain why shouting tempts me in the first place. You and I share a layer in the vastness of Sophron. We may never see one another, as, to you, I play this character in the novel you hold in your hands. To me, your existence seems even more remote and abstract. But we have a moment when you read the words that some Author chose to put in my mouth. If I were to describe me, now, you would see this tall youth with a pranking grin across his face. A mop of dirty blonde hair partially concealed my eyes and broad shoulders. I like to wear black t-shirts with incomprehensible logos of famous death metal bands.

You would picture this, and now I live in your soul. If you were provided with the gift of journeying through the worlds and the possibilities, you could find either me, or an alternate version of me, somewhere. The minute this encounter would happen, I would cease to exist as a novel's protagonist and narrator in your mind. This is how Sophron works. In fact, you meet visitors often, and unless they are awakened and aware of the realms and Dreamers, they would remain oblivious to you growing up in a different dimension. We all travel through Sophron and form endless alternate possibilities, clashing with the many layers, on a regular basis. Life, as we all understand it, lasts a moment that doesn't attach itself to the past or to the future but creates the future and saves in your mind recollections of a past. The only difference between us is the fact that I can alter my surroundings, so I may voluntarily distort my reality. When having a quest as a group, we share this rearrangement.

My story begins long before I knew how to apply this gift. Growing up as an anglophone in a city where French shines as the main language tends to make you feel a bit alienated. Westmount is, however, a rich ghetto. It's like Beverly Hills in the middle of a working-class metropolis. My father, this renowned surgeon, moved to Montreal from London, after falling in love with a French-Canadian singer. I attended French schools at a young age, because my parents always intended for me to speak two languages. I was deemed the popular kid in school. I can modestly say that I am good-looking. Not that I wish to fall into some narcissistic phase.

I wouldn't be considered awakened. If having gorgeous girls getting into fights over me were any indication that attractiveness ran in my blood, then I would recommend that you take my word for it. Have Tom Holland mixed with Justin Timberlake, and you'll find my lookalike. I never felt like I belonged to any gang or group, but I always preferred to surround myself with the cool cats. We have, in high school, an ecosystem that separates the fresh from the creep. When you strive among the elitist segment of popularity, you can't be seen befriending a freak. I took five years of my time to rise to the top of the chain, and many douchebags want to ridicule me in front of my fans. So, it is of great importance that I hunt the loners, the weirdos, the nerds, to establish and secure my territory.

I often heard people say that they dreamed of me as their best friend. When this happens, I simply smile, reminding myself that only those adored can aspire to great power. And while two minorities share the views of the masses, only the one that has properly demonized the other, while gaining the community's affection, can rule. In high school, I was a legend. The nerds, well, their intelligence won't bring them admiration. Success, will. And grades aren't an indication of achievement, when you're a teenager who wants to fit in with the ladies' men. I delight myself in a school's appreciation and requests for advice on how to win a woman's heart.

13

This loner haunted my campus, William Francoeur. He's the omega to my alpha male thing. Short and skinny, with an unbuttoned shirt and a preppy college vest he wore above his purple pants and belts, he looked like a clown. Bullies would often pick on him. They loved to throw his thick glasses in the trash, and I didn't care at all. I once saw two muscular guys grabbing him by the elbows and throwing him in the garbage, before resuming their walk in a sea of laughter. At the cafeteria, people would voluntarily leave their seat, after he would have joined their table, pretexting that their new neighbour had some serious body odour problems.

It wasn't true at all, I find William to have an exquisite fragrance coming out of his perspiration and lack of showers, but maybe it's just me. He would sit there, alone, and eat his meal. I didn't feel it in me to get along with him. In fact, most of the time I just ignored him. Otherwise, I would pick on him in front of a crowd to protect my popular image. Heck, it became one of my duties to make his life miserable.

Associating myself with a loser would taint my reputation. Sure, it feels awful to see him covered with spaghetti every other day. Having his lunch money stolen after a deluge of kicks and punches troubles me. Seeing his homework put to flames by jealous dunces horrified me, but what could I do? The world doesn't belong to the sympathetic who cares for a vulnerable soul. Bullies rule us! Nurturing intellectuals brings death in a war. By the middle of our last year in high school, I had decided to make William my insurance. The more I would personally torment him in front of everybody, and the more I would alienate others from him, the more he would feel lonely and isolated, and the more popular I would become. I couldn't just call him names or throw insults at him. Creativity calls! Making his life a living theatre of humiliation could achieve it. I once persuaded one of my groupie girls to pretend to fall for him, just so she could convince him to get closer, and smooch in a dark room. I would turn on the light and have all his bullies laugh at his sorry self.

At first, he declined the offer, telling the girl that someone else owns his heart. Oh yes, this make-believe fiancé, a model he met in Toronto, who would become his wife, one day. Emerald, he said, she was called. But even the most faithful teenager will break when a girl removes her bra, from under her shirt, and hands it over to him. And project humiliation was a big thing. Total success! Ever since I encountered William, I felt this strange connection that prompted me to get to know him better. Although I didn't have a great deal of respect for him. I never followed my instincts to the fullest. When I felt I could take my picking on him to the next level, after this masterpiece of a bullying operation, I would rather leave him to his loneliness and go back to my life as the school's celebrity. Day after day, I watched William's morale beaten and dragged. Awful monsters harassed him, and I could feel agony growing silently behind his sad eyes. He would look at me with disdain and resentment.

If he ever tried to approach me, I would ridicule his move. It is painful to see someone in distress and choosing to leave him to his despair, knowing that he drowns right next to you. Unpleasantness is what we need to overcome if we want to get stronger. I guess my motivation to ignore him, and at times make his life miserable, grew hand in hand with my addiction to this feeling of adoration. I met Ishtar the night that followed my first encounter with William. It happened in a dream, my first revelation, my first experience with the Sophron paradigm. Have you ever been through the stress of sleep paralysis? I woke up at around three in the morning, or so I thought it was. I froze. I couldn't move any limb. My open hands drained my sweat, next to my hips, palms against the mattress, eyes wide. I felt a presence, and my neck became hypersensitive, as if someone tickled it gently to the point of annoyance. When, at seventeen, a few months shy of your eighteenth birthday, you go through this Calvary, considering you had seen everything, it puts your thoughts in perspective. Ishtar appeared at the tip of my bed, looking like a geyser of pure blue light, with the contours of a very sexy young woman.

She walked into my room slowly, and I could only perceive her approaching from across the corner of my right eye. Her flawless face of a porcelain doll emanated light, chiselled with patience and eternity. Her dress fused to her skin, and it was impossible to tell where the fabric begins or ends if I saw nudity or not. She seemed to float towards my bed, but I could see her feet moving, definitely.

"You have to protect William." she whispered. "A glancer has to protect the mancer he will work with. Like the eyes need the hands, and the hands need the eyes." She vanished just like she appeared, and I was able to move an hour after she left. I returned to school the following day, and I observed William's calvary under bullies. In my mind, I dreamed horribly. Maybe my accumulated guilt held my subconscious and exploded into this sort of nightmare.

I shook it off and resumed my daily routine. It consisted of nagging teachers in class, pretending to some thuggish rebel title, if only to get the ladies' attention, and watching the girls bite their lower lip to find the courage to whisper: "hi." Was it written on my face that I was a rich kid from Westmount? Did this contribute to having so many ladies pursuing me? Mom didn't want to send me to a private school. She grew up in an average family, and easily convinced my dad that my education would benefit from public schools. I chased Alexandra Sicard ever since I entered this school.

She's this tall and enigmatic girl, dark hair with the prettiest face you could expect. She wasn't into any sort of fashion, but it appears she preferred black for her clothes and her makeup. She could fit right in with the goths, she would fit just the same with the preppies, the geeks and the hipsters. She was my equivalent in popularity, minus my attitude. She would never return my flirts, or my flagrant display of bravado. She wouldn't smile. Not even after I had just told the funniest joke in my repertoire. Often, I would wait for her at the end of a class, and I would hand her this paper flower I made while I ignored the math teacher. "Cute." she'd nonchalantly express.

16

She appreciated talking to William. Not only this, it seems the two of them were only able to smile and have fun when they were together. What worked for him and didn't do for me? You ever felt your ego getting infected by murderous ideas? Heck, they came to me out of some dark part of my brain without me ever summoning them, and always when I saw the two enjoying their life together. I would rather side with the bullies, sometimes, than I would take William's defence. William would never retaliate to the wrongs I or others would do to him. He kept all that stress to himself, looked down and tried to forget I had just thrown him in an empty locker and shout: "Stay in the closet!" Alexandra and I didn't make love that night either. Oh well. Victoria Picard, the most stubborn of them all, would wait for me at my locker.

She talked about that one date we had, and why I would never return her text messages. Though I would ignore her, she would follow me in the corridor and beg for a second date. "We didn't even have sex! We have to make love!" she would shout, in the worst English I ever heard, and everyone would stare at us. "We held hands," I responded.

"That's nothing, Seamus. Hands mean nothing. You're not my boyfriend. We don't sleep together." I inhaled deeply and looked her in the eyes. "I'm not your boyfriend, Victoria! Get lost!" she would go and scream. Back the same day, she repeated the same scene. This one time, however, William looked at us and I felt his pity for me. "What's your problem, loser?" I asked him. He directed his eyes to the floor and left. Alexandra and Victoria are BFFs in case you inquired. And I learned a lesson, here: don't try to sleep with your true love's best friend. Later that day, Victoria would gossip about a so-called sex life that we shared, if only to sound more important than she is. She would invent dates and events that never happened, like the time I took her to the Mount Royal, and we kissed in the park, while we listened to the beats of a thousand tam-tams. For some reason, I wouldn't mind her behaviour.

I would follow William down the hall, intrigued by the smile that he had shown earlier. Was he laughing at me? I spent the entire lunch hour in the library, watching him from a distance. He felt at home with books. I imagined that if he had friends, they would meet on weekends to play Dungeons and Dragons, or some sophisticated board game. I always wanted to try these.

By the end of my stalking experiment, I felt like he knew of my presence. He closed his eyes and, again, he smiled. He didn't say a thing, however. He left the library, while I looked interested in a book about migratory birds. I left fifteen minutes after him, and that made me late for my gym class. I walked down deserted corridors; questions filled my mind. Would I see the ghost again tonight? What was her connection with this marginal? I skipped every class this afternoon, as I felt compelled to wander by myself behind the school. I looked at the sky and, I think, I tried to summon Ishtar, but it never worked. A strange sensation of detachment from this reality wrapped my mind in numbness. I could feel the wind that caressed the trees and the plants as though my skin became the scene of this aerial molestation. I could drop out and wander the streets, beg for money, it would mean nothing compared to the bit of awakening, then.

I looked at the building, on the other side of a fence, beyond a soccer field, and I could still feel William's presence. It was stronger as I walked farther away. I sat on a rock, and I closed my eyes to recollect my thoughts. The entire universe spun in my mind. I observed nature, the same way I observed William earlier. Birds weren't aware of my existence, or if they were, they played their ignorance game well. I could have grabbed one as though I wasn't there. I was a ninja. Something else got to me, beyond my thoughts, but connected to them, just as my life was to my matter. Words I heard in my mind, for a second or less.

You were dead when I found you.

18

I shook my head and looked at the school. Was I the loser for leaving the premise, understanding that William just wanted good grades and not be bothered? Ishtar! What do you mean when you speak of eyes and hands? I roamed farther away, knowing that I would reach rails that could take me home. I walked across these tracks, sometimes stopping to make sure no train would come out by surprise. I would resume my trek forward, shocking myself as I looked down and I smiled for no reason.

When I got home, my mother was cleaning the floor. She didn't question me as to why I was back so soon; she just contemplated her chore and grinned. "Did you skip math again?" she asked. "No, Mom, I skipped gym." I answered. She lost her smile. I went to my chambers and looked for weed I hid under my pillow, like a friend you want to keep close whenever your dreams become strange. I sat down on the floor and patiently, painstakingly, destroyed the small cocoon of green goodness. Metal music haunted my room, and Mom knew she best should leave me to my youth. I was in front of my laptop, selecting the song of the moment: Cannibal Corpse, Festering in the Crypt. In it, the singer talks about a decaying cadaver, and how the flesh turns grey, and melts away from the bones. I would light up my bong right by the first chorus, and inhale, store the induced slow motion deep in my lungs, and exhale as my mind becomes blank. The trials hardly bring anything, only smoke and a few coughs, but the magic happens when four minutes forty-four second of songs feel like the entire night. It appears I had put that song on a loop. It would restart just as I would get higher.

Or perhaps I was travelling in time to the beginning of the opus as THC clustered my brain, more and more. I enjoyed Void and life. Well. It flew. Have you ever noticed how your intellect remains quite awakened, day and night? When you slumber, your neurons shape their own reality, because it requires one to sustain its need to feel its conscience.

Maybe, when it's daytime and you don't sleep, the world creates a system that gives your mind tools. Like those that make you aware of its existence. It doesn't need to dig beyond this illusion. Movies, sports, video games, work, tax, politics, religion. Freedom exists within, my brother, my sister, and my soul sibling. It's within.

"Have you talked to William?" I heard Ishtar from inside my own voice. "I'm getting there." I replied and inhaled another puff.

"You have to talk to him! Don't let Void take him away!" *Void is my friend*, I thought to myself, he'll be just fine. "Promise me you'll talk to him tomorrow!" What is he to you, anyway?

"You are too young to fathom the story I would tell you, so don't ask me this question." So, he's nothing to you. He's a loser if you must know. "He must be something to you, Seamus! You both need one another, do you understand?" I don't. And I don't worry. He can die, for all I care, really. A burst of electricity got into my veins, coming out of nowhere, and it was so strong, I screamed in agony. It felt as though my entire body instantly disintegrated, then reformed, and disintegrated again, over a million times in one second. I caught my breath with great difficulty. My mom opened the door and looked at me, I was still in pain. "Are you okay, there?" my mom asked me. "Fine. Fine, I'm okay, Mom." I complained.

"Get your shit from a better dealer, boy." She laughed and left.

"Talk to William!" Ishtar ordered, before vanishing. Void was then my only friend. Anxiety has its way to get to your brain from your nerves when you lose it over a greater unknown. The music expanded chaos. The inebriating smoke had no effect. I just had adrenaline surges the size of Mississippi.

I looked at the ceiling, as I tried to hold my breath, and, I never felt the presence of axioms, these tiny dots of reality, before. Call me existentially challenged, in this moment. Who brought Simon and Garfunkel's hippy lyrics in my head? I swear I put an all metal and hip-hop playlist! I felt an urge to tell the world that I loved it, but my loneliness kicked that gut instinct in the balls. Me! The victim? No! The whole universe, as I know it, revolves around me. Neither Alexandra nor Victoria would understand the chances they left behind. They could be sisters, or strippers for all I cared, they never had this rush of life for so many times in such a small window in.

William, my twin soul from another cosmos, let him be my eclipse. As my drugged mind stepped farther into this mystical state of existence, I could clearly see every one of Sophron's seventy-two layers. I could sense every single one of the quintillions of sextillions of possibilities, all happening at once.

"After your training, you will be able to achieve this level of consciousness without any sort of chemical or natural support."

Ishtar appeared to me in her actual demeanour. Tall and slim, like atop model, she wore ancient Greek clothes. Kindness populated her eyes, and peacefulness in her soft gestures. Whenever she spoke, it was as though a breeze of calmness brushed away dust over my shoulders. "Where am I?" I asked her, seeing that my room had disappeared, and an immense chamber made of glass took its place. She approached me and put a hand on my left arm. She looked me in the eyes and smiled:

"This layer is known as Saguenay. I brought you here, so we could discuss away from the stalking ears of Void's agents.

"And who are they?" I spoke.

"All will be explained in due time, Seamus Chron. For now, you must understand your place in the Greater Schemes of our beloved Entities. You were born on the layer of Gaia, in the possibility of the Maiden Crone. We have known each other in a past life, same layer, but in a Dreamer far away from your current one. Your ancient self-died at the hands of Marduk, devotee of Void, before you could master your gift. Marduk decided to haunt your reincarnations and make sure that you never reach your true nature, or else you would present a threat to his life. He just can't make you experience what is called The Final-Vanishing, the one that prevents your essence from discovering its way into a new being. He became stronger. More with every passing era, finding the means to make you taste your finality, so you must train as soon as possible, and you must protect William at all costs."

"Who was William to my ancient self?"

"A friend at a time of war with my people and my lover. You were known as Tristan, during the Babel Wars."

I perceived old memories that didn't belong to my current being. Indra? We fought together. Enlightenment kept me still, and I hardly felt any effect from the cannabis I inhaled. I walked around this bubble of a place, and I looked beyond the transparent walls. Colours running wild. They reshaped everything that I accepted as real. I could never describe them to you. I had no idea if I was observing a landscape or a visage, a crowd of faces or a single tree.

"Can I sober up, now? Please?" I begged Ishtar. This is not my place. The more I attempted to understand the reality I was in, the more seasick I felt. "Ishtar? Are you still there?" She left, obviously. I shut my eyes, and I forced them to close as hard as I could. I hit my forehead with my palms a few times, then with my fists. I repeated "Wake Up, Wake Up!" in my mind, as much as I could, but when I opened my eyes, I was still in this immense crystal chamber.

I walked like a hamster in a gymnasium. I wandered to find a door, a window, an exit, anything. Every time I came closer to a wall, the room expanded, and I faced a new, far away, wall. I had to find a way out, or else I would die in this dream. The more I panicked, the closer the walls got to me. The more I breathed, the calmer I got, and the ramparts kept moving far. A vision flowed to me. It will happen the next morning, at school. I will wait for William at the cafeteria. He will show up, and I'll try to engage in small talk. He will ignore me. When I try to get friendlier, he will leave. Later that day, I will defend him against other bullies, only to find myself ridiculed. I would then face an imminent challenge: losing my popularity or doing what the blue lady says. I searched all around the crystal room, and that vision of my near future was all over the walls, playing like a movie.

William would leave me to the douchebags, and I would have to do some damage control to restore my reputation. I would spend the rest of the day, and the week, looking for a way to make William cool in the eyes of others. We would have to find someone else to pick on and make his life miserable. I vouch for Yvan Schmidt: very small, thick glasses, and not very bright. I would guide the bullies towards making fun of him, and when they'd follow my lead, I would convince William to join the pleasure. He would punch me in the face and leave with a tearful Yvan. Was this vision really what was coming? Is it too late to rethink my next moves? I stayed in this room for what felt like many months. Ishtar would show up just to teach me a thing or two about the pluriverse they call Sophron.

World within World, within individuals, the cosmos shaped like Russian dolls, existing in an entanglement so complex, every Dreamer who has known enlightenment connect with their reflections. If I wake up, I will see my other selves, and perhaps one day I will be able to have all of them act as one, as I. The essence flows in my gift. I am a glancer.

The four Powerful Beings mentioned. The Ocorsurs: Void, Matter, Life and Thoughts. My ancient self-remembered. Patience births space in the process. Will breathes life, and kindness shapes oxygen. I could still   see through all the layers. I could feel through all the possibilities. I would become whole and all as I have always been, but my frantic attempt at defining this weird experience kept me away from this basic revelation of my current reality. The more I got to think about it, the more it made sense: I was in a reversed sleep paralysis state. Ishtar appeared to me, only this time, for that reason: Pour a positive image! I had seen her in her negative image before. I guess Life and Thought axioms constituted the layer of Saguenay, since she wanted to keep us away from Void. Regardless of the likelihood I was in, I just had to figure out the right map and wake up in my original one.

Axioms are like atoms, on a greater scale. I'm a glancer, I can see through the Veil, as I see through the eyes of my past lives. I am baked as hell, somewhere down this image and that feeling, and this is the possibility I need to reacquaint myself with. Baked as hell. My host would say as f***. He would laugh at the sensation of cursing. He would watch his mother look at him with perplexed eyes of laughter or disapproval. "Are you hungry, now?" my mom said, as I tried to recollect the pieces of this hallucination I just felt.

"Yeah, I want pasta. Please." I murmured. And in that moment, I realized I had left the crystal room in Saguenay and found my mundane reality in Gaia.

First Intermission:
The Student Sees the Veil

Shocked and awed, the student let go of their grasp over the orb.
They stepped aside. To their left: two fellow students observed the
events in great astonishment. On their right, four more were divided
between an awkward sense of admiration and a fearful one. Plato
smiled and asked the class: "Why do you think Seamus should be
considered a prick?" Nobody dared an answer. The teacher looked at
the student and waited for them to respond. "I don't think he realizes
that he harms others." they explained. "With the correct guidance, he
could be a hero. With the wrong influence, a villain."

Plato acquiesced softly and walked among his pupils. "Are the
characters in your story either heroes or villains?" he inquired.
The student pondered for a moment and explained: "They all show
the right intentions but interacting with others can lead to hurting
without realizing it." The wise man kept mental notes of what was
discussed, and turned to the others: "What do you think about that?"
he asked them. One voice stood out, from the back of the room:
"Perhaps it is required of Seamus to undergo a journey."
they guessed. The student smiled and added: "It would be a
transformative odyssey, yes! He would discover his own path towards
enlightenment." Another disciple participated in the discussion:
"We need to know about his past. This is how we'll tell what made
him into the prick that he is, but also why he would feel the desire
to better himself."

The teacher enjoyed listening to this collective creation. While they did, the orb would gather all their thoughts and project those axioms deep within its core.

"What is stronger?" he asked them. "Love or shame?"

Trick question! The student felt like they knew the answer, but to formulate the proper response proved unimaginable.

"It takes a lifetime to tell." Plato added.

"Jealousy!" the pupil affirmed. The teacher was listening. "If gods can create entire worlds, but they destroy them with no disgrace. Just out of pure envy. Then love isn't strong enough."

"What about love of a brother?" the wise man asked. His eyes looked deep into the student's confidence.

"Or a sister?" The trainee raised the stakes. They felt like they could put the teacher down to shame! Certainly, right now, they knew better than all the Great Mystics combined.

"Or a sister." the mystic agreed. The learner had no more refuge to reply. They looked to their classmates for some sort of approval, but some of them were already thinking about other things. Nobody dared to participate in this debate.

"I think." The apprentice struggled to form a comprehensible thought. "I think."

Plato listened and saw no reason to affirm his superiority over anything that manifested itself, right now.

"Maybe. Humility is good?" the learner finally said. "

"Perhaps. Why don't you tell us more about Seamus Chron?"

"I think. He's with his mother, now. She was a prostitute? I'm not certain."

The student felt those beings living in his soul. It was as though billions of little ants appeared and crawled against his neurons. When they singled out one of them, they felt the worlds that existed inside that character's mind. If this fellow focused on a god above, they would perceive Sophron above their head. Think: Looking at a god, like mirrors facing infinity between their shared gazes. Was the student writing them a story in his psyche? Were they merely a spectator retelling tales they witnessed? The mother wasn't a prostitute. That's impossible, but her existence involved pleasuring the flesh.

"She danced for a living." they said, while looking at Plato for a sign of approval. The Montreal that they created in their brain was a city set in the far future. Over there, men would pay women to undress on a stage. The class listened to every word, capturing the essence of every character. The tale revealed itself differently to each one, forming many new beings inside the collective mind. The student closed their eyes and continued shaping this storyline. Soon, they could hear Seamus narrating by himself.

Chapter Two:
The Strange Man and the Wasp

Mom had a wildlife, before she got me. She worked as a stripper when my father encountered her. He travelled to Montreal, from London and met my mom at the bar l'Olympe, on Saint-Denis Street. He would return to that club every night, just to be around my mother. With Dad well in his thirties at the time, and Mom who had just turned nineteen, they formed an odd couple.

Never married, and without any children or a girlfriend waiting for him back in London, Dad knew he had to seduce my mama. Justine Grégoire was known by her stripper's name as Gemini, and he felt compelled to marry her. When Arthur Chronenberg has an idea in mind, nothing can stop him, except my mother's attitude. She played hard to keep, at first, but she managed to leave him her number, before he flew to England. They would converse online, and on the phone, for several months.

Mom sent him videos of her singing, alone in her room. So, my dad chose to invest in giving her a stage, in some obscure bar near his workplace. He started her career abroad, and she became an instant sensation over there. She remained with my dad for seven years. Then they both elected to use their combined net worth to acquire a nice mansion in the heart of Montreal and move back, so they could give birth to a child.

They had me two years later. Mom put her singing career aside. The stay-at-home life called, and she raised me the best she could. Dad would have preferred to see her bloom as she made her dream come true, but I guess I became her new passion:

This seventeen-year-old stoner just came back from the weirdest trip ever. I stared at my plate, like watching a David Lynch movie. My macaroni made up most of the plot. I would spend the rest of the day in my room. I don't like my dad seeing me like this. They would ground me, but Mom was cool.

"Why did you scream, earlier?" she asked me. I didn't answer. Hunger kept me silent. And as I binged down my plate like an ogre who hadn't devoured any meal in weeks, Mom sighed and ate her share. What was I supposed to say? Hey, Mom, I was revealed truths about the universe that you could never have guessed on your own. At times, we just can't allow ourselves to fall into impossible conversations. "Did you smoke just pot?" she insisted. Checkmate. I just hummed, or maybe I growled and that prompted her to think I took something much more potent. "Seamus. Tell me what you had. It's okay, we can discuss this." I looked at her and. Nothing. Void. A beast. I turned into pure matter. My life and my desires remained non-existent. My feelings were peeling off my mind like flaky skin, after a sunburn.

"Mom."

I complained. It took me everything to pronounce a word. I returned to my meal, and I tried to forget she was there. The rest of the dinner became even more surreal. The more detached I went, to prevent the complex sensations that prompted my gift to provide some sort of certainty, and the more I could understand my mama's truth. She had hard drugs, in her past, but she witnessed the death of a loved friend. To her, cocaine reigned as the most extreme type of opioid she could accept. We narrowly know what comes out of illegal laboratories. She never told me that story, yet, as I gazed into her frightened eyes, I saw the entire scene.

It happened a few weeks before she encountered dad. The club shone with emptiness, with far more strippers than clients. Mom was sitting behind a table, looking deep into her smartphone. She remained oblivious to her future.

Her life turned around after she'd meet a tourist, four months, and three days from then. She was obsessed about her mother punishing her for having found a bag of cocaine under her pillow. Justine never took that stuff. Only when she had to. Not when she felt like it. This guy, at l'Olympe, Svens, had the solution to a stripper's problem. He even sold to the staff and many clients. You can't have everything you wish for at once. I mumbled: "Sensitive detachment, Mother." I had no idea what came out of my mouth. "Talk about this to your dad. He's the brain; I'm the means." I nodded, I had to eat, at some point.

My father is hardly at home these days. His job demands a very chaotic schedule, as he must work in the middle of the night. He remains ready to answer highly delicate emergencies. My recent travel through the Veil brought me a different version of this story, and yet I decided not to venture into this possibility and find out. If I come back to my senses with the realization that my dad cheats on my mom, but I have only this gift to rely on, catastrophe would bully us. Also, I still have no idea if I imagine every bit of this, or an existence shine beyond our modest understanding of the universe. What about a multiverse? I think I heard someone, somewhere, during my recent hallucination, calling Sophron a. Pluriverse. I ate my vegetables with the hope of cleaning my brain of all these questions.

That night, I felt a deep and strong state of calmness inundating all the fibres of my flesh and my soul. I no longer felt drugged or high or anything. I was, how do we name it, Zen? I could see myself at school the next day, just as though I had some sort of camera in my tomorrow cognition, and this current state of consciousness experienced it from a distance. I was right between wake and sleep, and this is where I best tune myself into Sophron.

I walked down the hall, and every time my future self encountered another mate, I could see the realms and Dreamers through that person. Both our universes then connect, and the pluriverse, as we know it, expands. If I say one word to that person, my inner layers interact with them, and both our possibilities get affected. Did Ishtar manage to put me in that state?

Or did she only awaken my powers? Was I only able to view my tomorrow being? I tried to visualize my past self, but zilch came of my attempts. For some reason, no matter how vivid was the memory I attempted to revisit, I faced a locked door. So, I guess a rookie glancer can only see in the future, or in the extended present. *While I was at it,* I thought, *I might as well try to find William and see if I can peek inside his layers.*

I recollect the vision I had of that day, and how I would finally get a chance to approach my brother in arms, amend the wrongs I did to him, and start a new relationship. While the things I pictured inside the crystal room were clearly projected against the walls, I had rather blurry hallucinations. Years of practice call me before I get an HD resolution, but, eh. It's better than nothing. I roamed past a corner, and there she smiled: Alexandra! Oh, boy, dude, eh! I must not lose the chance to peek into this one!

"What do you want?" she said, as she looked straight at me with an annoyed face. "Quit staring at me, creep!" she insisted, before trying to go away. Okay, how does this thing work? I walked back in front of her, she stopped: "Seamus, are you high?" My later self couldn't speak. Maybe my present self holds the keys to that. I projected a thought, and a few words came out of my future self's mouth: "We need to talk!" I let go. She sighed and looked away, I could see tears in her eyes and there, right there, the Veil opened itself to her universe. I could picture her childhood, in France. She fell victim to abuses several times by a drunk uncle before she turned eight. This explains why her single mom decided to move with her to Montreal.

31

"I don't like boys who play games, all right? Go back to Victoria, she misses you." Her words flew in the air, but my entire self glued onto her consciousness. Call me a gentle parasite, a remora to her shark of an existence. The first time she visited a French-Canadian school, she panicked. At twelve, she got into a private party, and older teenagers convinced her to smoke pot. They raped her. "Look, Alexandra, I was an asshole. I treated you like a less than nothing. Truth be told, I am happy when you are around, and I want to learn how I can make you pleased. I don't know, maybe you had it rough with men and boys before. But I don't intend to, listen to me, I don't try to hurt you. I wish to do everything in my capacity to make you happy. And I will make it up to you."

She hugged me so tight and cried so hard, I imagined myself dropping my breath. Even my present self couldn't deal with so much emotion exiting her realms and into my soul. I could map her Logos-Archeus quadrant, and I saw that her life was flooding her thoughts. She was losing her grasp on her matter and void layers, so I concluded that a lot was going through her mind at the time. "Seamus Chron. Get out of my head!"

She said, or did she? Did I imagine this part? Was I hallucinating the whole thing? She vanished, just like in a dream, and my current self had some difficulties maintaining contact. It was as though she realized that I attached my soul to hers. I had to find William and talk to him. I had to see if he was as attuned to Sophron as I was. I inhaled deeply to calm down and project axioms to strengthen the union between my two selves. Before I could find the right state of being, Victoria appeared in front of me. She was like a ghost at first, but the more I concentrated on my efforts to see and feel this future moment, and the clearer she was to me. "Why did you make my best friend cry?" she asked. This one seemed easier to peek into. She spent her entire life as a spoiled brat who considered friends as assets to support her supposed popularity. She chased me because of mine.

32

"She's not your best friend, you use her vulnerability for yourself." I scolded her, and she did not appreciate these words. "You're a monster, Seamus!" I fought the desire to say anything beyond that. I just walked away from her. William. Locate. William. That's all that mattered to me.

"You were dead when I found you." Who said that?

"Your sight flew beyond your body." I could hear this voice from all over the place. It had a sombre and sinister tone. As though some narrator wanted to recite an obituary and creep its audience out. "If you look for William, my friend, you won't find him here." the voice said to me. The freak spoke to me directly! And I couldn't respond. "The one you seek just died."

"Seamus?" It was Alexandra. "Seamus!" I had frozen in both time and space. I shook my head and looked at Victoria. Oh, she snapped me out of it.

"Are you okay, my love?" she inquired. "No, I! I don't know." Words evaded me. "William is dead."

And then I fell asleep. Well, my current self did. I have no clue what occurred to my future me. The following day, my mom woke me up in a hurry. "You'll miss school, Seamus!" she shouted. What if I missed school? Will everything that I visualized the night before just never happen? Would this prevent William from dying? Mom opened the door with such violence, I had to exit the mattress: "I'm not writing you a sick note, boy! Go to school!" The power of a mother's authority. I left my sheets with this groggy feeling I went to bed with.

I took the subway with my backpack, and a death on my conscience. Or maybe, I was hallucinating again. Of course! I should quit drugs and get help. I looked at the passengers that shared my ride. This homeless guy slept on the seat in front of me, except he wasn't vagrant. He's a successful businessman who wanted to scrap everything and just get drunk for two weeks, sleep in parks, like an economical masochist who would have the whole society to act on him as his sadistic dominatrix. He will return to work, in two weeks, resume his practice, and pretend that none of this ever happened. He meant to understand the life of a crackhead, without smoking drugs, and he missed the track. He would brag to the board of investors that he had twelve amazing days in Cuba, but never speak of the night he spent with a runaway Cuban teen.

When I exited Namur station, I saw another hobo man. He looked at me, and I felt his name: Nempty. He had a pet wasp he played with. If he had a racoon, I guess I could consider, but a wasp? "Do you have change for a coffee, mate?" he would ask. He asked everyone! *No, my dad gives me money. Ask him.* I never had the gut to express these words, but I'm sure he'd understand. Nempty stood up and looked me in the eyes; yet he froze. "Sorry, sir, I have to go to school." I apologized.

"You found her, you son of a bitch!" he shouted before I deeply inhaled to get the courage to leave.

"Take me to him! Get me to William!" he insisted, but I ran as fast as I could. When I looked behind, he was gone. I sighed and scratched some time to catch my breath, then I turned right on the following street, and I returned to the school. Why do I find all these imaginary friends asking about William? I looked both ways, and the street seemed eerily empty. The more I walked towards the building, the farther it appeared to be. I stopped to observe the scene around me, no sound. This quietness reminded me of some haunted boulevard in a horror movie.

"It's called a limbo. Sorry I had to drag you into this, but you and I need to talk."

The homeless man came out of my shadow against the street, and it looked as though he turned my silhouette into black smoke. He rose in front of me, and he certainly wasn't very tall. He had a hump, but that didn't stop him from standing straight, with his long grey hair falling down his back. He wore denim and an old Hawaiian shirt, yellow with red flowers all over. He didn't have any shoes on. He kept his hands behind his back and looked me in the eyes, then he uttered:

"When you see William at school, today, tell him Nempty has the boat ready. I could use his mancing skills on board. You should tag along; he will need your gift."

"Where are we going?" I asked him. "I'm looking for Indra." He replied. "The Indian god?" Surprise hit me. He smiled: "This wasp is linked to him. How did I find out? Millions of trapped Walkers told me. What's that, you ask, boy? It's you. It's William. It's, well, it's complicated. There are things the enslaved ones know and understand that I don't. That's because I'm a little bit dumb, and I don't know how this jumbo-mumbo."

"Mumbo-jumbo."

"That too. When you find William, make sure he's safe."

"Ishtar asked me to protect him. Why should I trust you?"

"What does the little girl know about the war we got ahead? No, you go fetch William, and you contact me. I'll take you both to my boat. I'll be waiting."

"How do I contact you?"

"I'm not the glancer; you figure it out!"

35

He evaporated the same way he emerged. Before I could realize what happened, people appeared on the street. Cars that had vanished made a comeback. The whole environment changed colours, getting rid of that boring grey that mirrored the dwarf's hair. I shut my eyes, trying to put myself in a state that would intertwine me to Nempty's essence, but. Nothing. For some reason, even though we were in a different layer of Sophron, or maybe a bubble within Gaia, I felt a strong presence of axioms. I couldn't connect to Nempty's possibilities. A car brutally HONKED at me, and I had to shake this up. Then return to the sidewalk.

When I arrived at school, I relived the exact same scene I had envisioned in my awakened dream of last night. The long corridor was crowded. I looked around me, I tried to grasp the lives of everyone I encountered, but it appeared my gift didn't work. At best, I felt the presence of these layers and possibilities, but I couldn't peek into them as I did in my dream. Even when I confronted Alexandra and Victoria, their inner universes seemed far to reach. I guess my gift only functions on my approach into Morpheus' arms. Do I need a nap, later, if I intend to contact Nempty? Or should I practise some form of meditation? These questions haunted me all the way to my history class.

I sat at the back, not hearing anything the teacher said. My mind was wrapped in a fog of thoughts, and I tried to fall asleep to see if I could channel my gift. It didn't work. The entire room seemed plunged in a state of grief. The teacher sat on his desk, his eyes red, and he looked at the floor, while attempting to explain something to the students. All I could hear was: "William committed suicide, this morning. An ambulance found his body down a high path. With a bullet in his head."

Journey into the Hourglass:
Two

Introducing Seamus Chron as a selfish bully seemed like a good idea. He would learn to become selfless, but only after Ishtar would confront him with the consequences of his acts. I think we need a bigger bully. Martin came up with this idea, one morning. Someone who would threaten all of existence, and he would become Seamus' ultimate villain. "If we already have Ishtar, then we should stick to the Mesopotamian myths." I suggested. *What do you think of Dumuzi?* I thought about it, and I wrote down this idea. Something didn't add up. "Wasn't Dumuzi her husband" *Maybe Indra could be shown as having taken the Dumuzi name, according to our story.*

"And let's have a jealous Marduk in the lot." Martin liked that idea. So, we added Marduk to the Chronicles of Sophron. Something about mixing two cultures and mythologies sounded fascinating. *Perhaps Sophron could be a vast sandbox where various gods and goddesses compete to gain the trust and affection of Greater Entities? Marduk would have fought Varuna, in ancient times, causing a major catastrophy. It forced the councils of Great Entities to banish them, although Marduk escaped.*

"Yes!" Martin agreed. "He killed one of them, and now he threatens to destroy all of Sophron. In his mind, it's like purifying reality so that he may reshape it in his name."

Chapter Three:
Marduk the Conqueror

A bright and sunny day shone over Akkad-Lazuli, a vast and modern metropolis in Nibiru's northern hemisphere. Its pale blue sky with black and grey clouds projects a gloomy feeling over its tall and thin buildings, like metallic plants that scratch Heavens' bottom. The streets of Akkad-Lazuli are plated in gold, with billions of lights, sensors and Anunnaki technologies that make people fly or float, using only their legs as means of propulsion. In the centre of this immense capital, we find the Genghis-Maal, a palace so enormous we could fit the Grand Canyon in it and find room for the Rocky Mountains. When Marduk ordered its construction, soon after the end of the Babel Wars, his intention was to inspire fear in anyone foolish enough to think they could conquer Nibiru.

The severed head of an Entity sits on top of the Genghis-Maal, in reminiscence of Marduk's most celebrated achievement: He killed one. The skull covers one tenth of the roof's surface, but a simple mancing spell ensures that the head appears as big as the palace. The Entity, a Logos-Archeus Chimera, growled within a powerful Dreamer. Not long after winning the Babel War, Marduk looked at this Gaia world he had just invaded and declared:

"The Great Entities have challenged me! I stand victorious before their trial! Hear me! I shall bring to this world a great conqueror, and more! I shall create these human warriors, in my image! They shall be enslaved to their blinded desires of submitting all that do not speak their name! Enlightenment will come to those who conserve their traditions and diminish ideas of openness and forgiveness!" Marduk trained and led generals, on Gaia, from Genghis Khan to Napoleon, and many more. He claims the Great Entities defied him, but historians support the hypothesis that Marduk's ego challenged them.

It is a fact that his uncontested reign which lasted for billions of years brought much wealth to Nibiru, and particularly to his palatial city, Akkad-Lazuli. Sophron worlds have a limited number of axioms. Creating and owning others" reality shows a sign of achievement, especially for a god of his kind. Invading realms to establish a funnelling system that would redistribute pixels to the conqueror's beliefs bears the fruits of power.

Perhaps Marduk had other ideals in his agenda, however. He unshackled his layer, after having obliterated another. He ensured that this would reflect throughout the myriads of Dreamers and Sleepers. It was as though he wanted to draw constellations of his design. To what end? Would he gain enough power to alter his state of awakening? The entire Babel Wars were fought to prevent humans of Gaia from attaining such a state of enlightenment, and Marduk contested hard not to allow it. He won. Every now and then, a human would achieve that coveted state of existence, and he, she or they would turn it into either prophecy or poetry. Marduk had left that layer, since, concentrating on his other occupations: Sint-Holo, Saguenay, Phaeton-Tiamat. Recently, he coveted Athanor and Tir na n'Og.

That morning, the Hound Lord of Nibiru examined his modest map of conquered worlds. He then looked at the reports of axioms he properly channelled into his gains, going through floating images and numbers, as though swarms of mosquitoes, drawn to his sight, but remaining immobile.

Something wasn't right, he thought.

"Haslem!" he shouted. "Haslem, show yourself!" he insisted. A giant rat with the head of an owl timidly opened a door. Haslem bowed in respect, pulling a heavy boulder that prevented him from flying away from this servitude, and showed up in front of his master. Marduk looked at the charts, the floating images, and pointed at one in particular: A blue angel sitting at the end of a bed.

"Is she alive?" Marduk asked.

"Please, Lord Marduk, Let's not get into this."

"I asked you a question. Is she alive?" The enslaved owl-rat closed his eyes and thought for a long moment. "I have no knowledge of her whereabouts if she is, I swear on my mother's soul."

"I ate your mother's soul on pancakes. If Ishtar lives, then so is Indra. Do you want the Babel Wars to see a round two? We don't need that. Find me Indra."

"Master, I don't think this would be wise."

"Would I be wrong to destroy your world? You will do as I say, or there's a Sphinx Entity in Ker-Ys I can decapitate next." Haslem suddenly opened his eyes and looked at Marduk in disbelief and fear. "You can't just declare the death of an Entity like that!" Marduk moved his hand over Haslem, slowly, tightening the chain until the bird-rodent coughed and spat blood. Marduk loosened his grip and smiled.

"Your home world's Entity is a drunk lunatic. I see less of a challenge there than the chimera ever was. Find me Indra."

The owl-rat bowed in respect and left the throne room. Pulling his ball and chain through a very long corridor felt painful and excruciating. Never mind the artwork depicting Marduk's invasions, the Lords he killed, the entities he tortured. The saddened eyes of Haslem throne as the most difficult thing to watch. He carefully conquered every stone that covered the mile-long floor. Once he arrived in his room, the door would shut and disappear. The ball and chain would as well. His prison cell bore the most freedom he could ever experience.

A small room, but Haslem had managed to create a limbo, next to the toilet, where he would sometimes escape to taste a semblance of liberty. Marduk knew of his sage's scheme to evade in a makeshift world, but he let him do so. Perhaps a limit to his cruelty opens to a beginning to his empathy. He made the most powerful glancer in the Ker-Ys layer prisoner. It happened after a militia supporting Varuna had tried to confront his special police, in Phaeton-Tiamat. After Marduk personally intervened, pulverizing the militia, he scanned the essence of every rebel and found that Haslem masterminded this operation. The tiny nymph thought that Varuna should have won the Babel Wars. Humans should have achieved enlightenment, and Logos should overcome the Void. Marduk crushed Varuna's army. The sky god, then, found himself imprisoned. The hero may have fallen, but ideas live on.

Haslem has access to every essence of all he encountered, within three degrees of Dreamers. He could feel his sibling's presence within a Sophron that existed in a Sophron above or beneath him, as easily as he could sense his brother's spirit in the possibility he inhabits. Or Sleeper, we can never tell if the host of the inner world we live in is awakened. Marduk knew that Haslem, Ishtar and Indra's friendship survived the test of time. Keeping him alive carried an asset.

When Haslem sat on his uncomfortable bed, a rigid mattress with stinking sheets, he shut his eyes. Connecting with essences comes with difficulty, even for an eighth rank level two glancer. Uncovering one link among the quintillions of selves within novemdecillions of possibilities was like going through a library that had a near-infinite number of books to find one phrase. Haslem loved Indra. Dearly. If his soul still existed, he knew he had to locate it and find a way to protect it from Marduk's greed.

The first thirty days of his meditation proved unfruitful. He scanned many realms and essences and tried to connect them to the one he sought, but he unearthed nothing. Oh, he saw the image of a brain with a bullet stuck inside, coming from the mouth. He saw a black unicorn turning the world around it white, and he thought that a white unicorn could turn the world around it black.

What a beautiful scenery! The stench of his bed, the feces he let out, would sometimes disturb him. But he's been through worse. He had to find Indra. What connected with this picture of a suicidal brain? Keep going. Keep on living. Haslem wished to say to that image's host. But that wasn't Indra, so he had to search further. He saw Garuda! As a child, Haslem would watch this giant warrior fight other gigantic monsters in arenas, and Garuda would always rise to the top of any championship.

He adored this creature! When he later learned who inhabited these juggernauts, he decided to develop his gift, until he could pilot his iconic biomech. But the Babel Wars broke out. He had to lessen his dreams until he could join a rebellion. He meant to tell Marduk that he couldn't just get away with killing worlds. Marduk got away with destroying one. Haslem must find Indra's essence.

He focused for another forty-two days. During that time, he saw many images of strip clubs. He observed this vision both from a Logos and an Archeus perspective, thoughts, and life, two ends of a same thirst. When he looked away as though using some virtual reality goggles, he perceived Void and Barbelo fighting. A corpse saw its soul evaporate. *Someone just died*, he thought. *And that someone had a connection with Indra.* He can locate it and warn the essence before Marduk finds out. Who was it? Haslem focused further and saw an introverted human, a teenager, holding a girl. She's nude. She's asleep, and he doesn't know how to wake her up. That was the closest he has ever been to an unclothed woman who just shared with him her entire life. *Noises*, Haslem thought, *Indra's essence is in this human.*

He focused closer into William's soul and felt the inner Sophron he held. He also heard Marduk's footsteps coming closer. If Marduk finds out, he'll kill this boy and continue with his agenda, just as he did whenever he suspected having seen Indra's psyche in somebody. Haslem knew that the saviour's soul did cohabit with that William person. It does! Maybe Marduk will inspire someone into making that kid's life miserable, until he kills himself, and then Marduk will expect his afterlife and simply split the two and kill Indra again. The Master was getting closer, so Haslem had to act fast. He could transpose Indra's essence into a different organism, and lead William into Marduk's arms. He would save the next uprising and let some extra die for nothing. Well, for the greater good, of course.

"I sense that you found him, my rat." Marduk grumbled.

"Almost, my lord!" Haslem replied. He had to uncover a way to create a diversion. Indra's soul was in Gaia, so he could project a reflection of it within another being or organism. A rat? A human?

"Present me the essence." Marduk insisted, entering the room.

"I will if I can find it. Wait a few more days, I beg of you!"

A prehistoric insect! He could quickly conceal the tiny bit of the existence he detected within a DNA strand, but he had to choose a simple animal. This spell, Temporal Nucleosyl, allowed him to combine specific axioms, known for holding the essence he wishes to protect, onto others, and back in time. The temporal side of the spell felt too difficult. He could only successfully perform it by aligning his focus on a specific possibility and trace a moment on which he could perform the graft.

Indra's soul shows a level of complexity that compromises a maneuver at high speed. The only organism in Gaia's prehistoric past he found looked like a wasp. While observing the timeline, he saw the passing of this presence onto various other creatures, as the wasp would feed, hand its genes to its descendants and die. As the chronology unfolded, he completed the delicate operation. He meticulously practised an incision in the creature he had summoned out of Gaia's Jurassic period. He then saw trillions of other animals possessing bits and pieces of Indra's essence. Until one specific individual, a human, ended up with the bulk of the god's existential emanation.

"A human boy?" Marduk questioned, as he stood tall and menacing before his prisoner. "In Gaia, of all places."

"Yes, my Lord."

Marduk thought for a moment, he mediated as well, then ordered: "Bring me that boy."

"My Lord. I can't!" Marduk hatefully looked at Haslem.

"Show it to me. Show me where."

Haslem hesitated for a very long moment. He closed his eyes and cast a spell of forgetfulness onto himself. Marduk sensed that he attempted to hide this information at all costs. He swiftly convoked a blade out of his right hand, letting it grow until it pierced through the rat-owl's flesh, forcing the prisoner to open his eyes in a stupor. Marduk used this element of surprise to read the dying bird-rodent's soul. "So. His name is William."

Sensing his last moments approaching, the walking nymph battled far and wide to escape. Weak, it was impossible to gather enough energy to do anything. He used the last parcels to fulfill that spell. Sure, the end was near, but the bird-rodent could smile. He successfully brought a real game changer, long before a new war would erupt. The next campaign was inevitable. New players were already called to the front. Poor Haslem would have loved to fight, once again, with his old friends. But in this story, his part would be very limited.

Marduk wouldn't wait to see what could come next.

He no longer had any use for this prisoner. He already milked everything he needed. Keeping him alive, knowing that Indra roams within these worlds, would be a mistake. Without any emotion, the Hound Lord of Nibiru grabbed the nymph's head with both hands. He swiftly pushed his thumbs deep in Haslem's eye sockets, popping his eyeballs like rotten cherries. The god's fingernails grew deeper, until they reached the prisoner's brain. Haslem screamed in intense agony. The pain was so potent, it was now impossible for him to think of a spell. The Lord cracked the nymph's head open and threw the carcass against the wall.

He then summoned a floating image of his fleet. Next to it, a lemur in combat uniform appeared, awaiting orders.

Marduk proclaimed: "I want spies in all layers, looking for this William, or anyone in close connection with him. And prepare my fleet! We're going to Tir na n'Og and pay Sekhmet a visit."

Marduk left the bird to die in the most atrocious pain imaginable, right after casting a spell that would prevent other emanations of Haslem, in different possibilities, intertwining. Haslem would perish everywhere, just as he does here, now. Billions of iterations, all succumbing to the same fate: eyes popped, brains smashed, skulls crushed. Corpses lying on the floor, souls evaporating, falling in total nothingness. This is called a Final-Vanishing.

Journey into the Hourglass: Three

"What are we doing with William?" I asked my partner, one day. "If we have him acting like a goal for Seamus to redeem himself, we might as well tell the story of his soul." Martin didn't feel inclined to give William too much screen time. It's not his story, Alibast. He told me. Let's keep it between Marduk and Seamus. If we write too many stories, we'll lose our reader's interest. Okay, so Martin is the professional screenwriter and I'm just a poet of Avalon. But I don't like the idea of pushing a character down to his demise, without doing anything to save him.

"I'll let you write the Marduk parts, but, please, let me develop William's storyline." I asked him, very politely. You speak like you cared about them. He rolled his eyes. They're just characters!

They don't exist! We create them, and we can do whatever we want with them. They are tools, Alibast! We are their almighty Authors! That hardly convinced me. If they exist in a book, then they exist in some universe. There's a possibility that they develop a consciousness of their own. If this is the case, then we must protect them.

"They exist, Martin! They deserve rights and we must respect their freedom!" I stood my ground. I know I'm correct with this. My co-author growled and got himself another beer. Okay, fine! Write William's part, and I'll write Marduk's.

Chapter Four:
William's Decent Into the Abyss

You were dead when I found you. Your sight flew beyond your body. You had no tears or fear, you had but my hand leaning towards your mind. You bathed in silence like a newborn about to leave their mother's womb. You couldn't quiet the voices that carried you to this desolated place, however. A few minutes earlier, William, you stood up, alive, and contemplating a decision you can't reverse. So many memories of a life spent in challenges and depression drew a line between then and now. You could have avoided this. You could have just allowed yourself to scream, yell, shout and walk away. It would have been okay to cry. You know what? It's normal to look at your daily life with intense fear. It cripples you from the core of your being.

Life designed itself as a difficult riddle. From your first breath to your last, Agents of a Greater Ordeal provide every organism with trials that define their path. Every second brings a new array of choices. Each one leads to more love and light, wounds, deception. It's about the glare, the darkness, how you cope with both. In the end, fruits flourish from an inner peace built for you, everlasting nights pour misery over your hopes and dreams. Interactions with others, and whenever you formulate a thought that will become speech and action, you offer yourself to Agents of Progress. Or you surrender to Goons of Destruction.
You chose the latter.

What does it bring you, now? Did you think your quest would
end with the final moments of your life? I didn't elect to see you
part from your loved ones. Look at them, William. Alexandra
holds your hand in the ambulance. She stood by your side under
some mystical call. At your school, even those students who never
spoke to you flooded their cheeks in tears. They mourn someone
they failed to acquaint themselves with. The bullies who made
your life unbearable can't live with their own conscience. It doesn't
mean you tormented them. This isn't payback; just one step too far.
We never have to bring ourselves to this. Solutions exist, William.
For a given unthinkable action, millions of alternatives thrive, each
the more enlightened. You picked the one that should never come
to anyone's mind. Now, everything bathes in pitch darkness.
Blank over nothingness, all. Absolute stillness. You can't sense
your limbs. Your organs rot like dead meat. You lie there,
with your eyes wide open. Now, an inanimate object, covered in
blood. And then you woke up!

We stood in darkness within darkness, silence within silence,
and light without light to show you the day prior to the third week
of your conception. Peace, is it not? You leaped inside yourself,
your innermost one. You used to call it existence, yet this time, it
lacks your senses to give a biological meaning to it. You were
in you, where I have always been, and you saw me. All exists and
doesn't in me. You had to visualize my self to perceive my soul.
You pictured a tenebrous chamber in the middle of a starless
universe. Torches floated to the east, if you had a Sun just waking
up, but you didn't, and dark flames consumed the west. That's
where you found me. The sun rises to the west on Judgment Day,
doesn't it not? Welcome to my world. I stood still within the grim
robe and the armour, half black and half white, that you envisioned
for me. Absolute vacuum iced the interior of my Victorian hood.
I didn't imagine you, because you were, in any event, in any form,
that tall and skinny, light-brown hair, intelligent-looking William.
I just take away and you do your best to take back or take anew.
A table was between us. A papyrus stood in the middle.

"Ishtar!"

You shouted! And tried to fathom some air. You had no operational organ to do so. You grasped imaginary air with imaginary lungs. But you did.

"Do you think you can find her here?"

I replied. You looked at me with eyes that seemed to doubt the truth standing before them. Skeptics have the habit of dreading uncertainty, but it never lasts; I tend to nod, just before they finish fearing the loss of what they used to call reality. Your time has come. You didn't believe in my nemesis, the one you called Archeus. He was my reflection. You didn't consider his genesis. You don't really believe in me either, is that correct?

"Where is she?"

"She was never by your side. You may now follow me."

"Take me back to her!" you cried. Tears feel awkward. What should it be? I call it me, and that's it. "Take me back." you insisted. I hate to see my subjects drown in their cries. Usually, they just exhale a big non-breath and accept whatever ordeal I call upon them. After all, I am all, and none.

"Let her be, William." I said, in a gentle voice. You had to give up, and I had to show you that last respect.

"Just be and let her be." I insisted, as I took that long, black, grim Victorian robe you imagined away from your sight. I walked farther in front of you.

"I can't even feel myself anymore." you sighed. Don't even try.

"But I have seen you before!"

"It should be no surprise to find me by your death." I mildly said, as I roamed to the end of the corridor, towards a great altar, a black-on-black piece of amazement, engraved in one block of solid ozone. Faces seem to appear from nowhere and melt as the gas evaporates, only to freeze again, and more visages carve themselves.

"Death?" you whispered. I kept silent. I wanted you to enter this room, at the left side of the altar, and give your past a pass. Let it go. And go.

"For a certainty, this name that too many would seek to award me, suits only my light side. If only to oppose a world of the living and pretend to an absolute being. Yet, I stand beyond life, ashes, biological manifestations of existence."

"God?" I had to laugh. I couldn't. I would love to appreciate the title, but no. A mere Ocorsur, you see? A Great Entity within this Dreamer you would have called God if you believed.

"Void! Emptiness. Lonely nothingness." I whispered, almost annoyed, and then I raised my voice:

"When God dies, I'm all around. When God sleeps, I'm all over. When He lives, I am all within. I am. I truly am."

Your face froze, like the many more all over my altar, and you asked: "Void?" On which I nodded.

"And so are you. Now, follow me." I walked away from your conceptions, and you drove yourself closer to me. Came a hallway of anarchy, with order to arise, and chaos stemming back. The walls surrounded us. Came a drowning new beginning. You followed me down that funnel and tried to talk your way out. "What took me here?"

"You did."

"I never asked for that end."

The corridor swirled. Nowhere and everywhere fought for this moment. I stopped and gazed in your direction. You wore that different robe, it made you look like an Egyptian priest, or a third-century alchemist: the jewels? Egyptian, most definitely. You have blue eyes and brown hair, William, William. You know what I will say, but I said it anyway. You listened, half there, half in your dreams within dreams. "It ate you from inside. You just had to cry your wounds and abide to the farthest extent of your pain."

"Emerald."

"How can you love anyone while maggots lick the last remains of flesh and muscles, like moist, on your bones?"

"Take me back! "

"Walk with me."

You stood in front of the altar. The ozone shines from the darkest depth of the faces' eyes and it reflects onto your own. The room advanced, slowly as to invite you inside. It growled. You were motionless but defiant. Tremors shook every fibre of your being. You had your head down, a tear about to stream as you feared aloud this dream, and you finally mumbled: "You didn't hear what I said!" I had to sigh on this one. But I, somehow, am a gentleman. Call it my whatever nature. "Did you repeat yourself?"

"Take me back to her!"

"Who? Emerald?" I walked closer to you. There, all around, the breath, the breeze you felt, the coldness of non-life? Yeah, me. I whispered, from deep within my cloak, and you could hear me scream in your head: "Who keeps you back?" You heard a voice that spoke through me but wasn't mine.

"Tell, what do you see? What was her name? This soul of beauty. Tell me, William, who holds the essence of Ishtar? William loved too many and couldn't stand still! Tell me, where is Ishtar?"

You stood silent. I chased the ghost away and you attempted to formulate a thought. You couldn't. You didn't know who this Ishtar was, yet you shouted her name when you woke up in this world. Balance? Are we talking about someone who would make your existence in equilibrium with mine? I'm sorry, but you hold on to pain, right now. Didn't you jump off a bridge? Or was it a high path? Didn't you shoot yourself on your way down? It hurts, doesn't it? Or what does? For whom?

"I don't know." you whispered back. "Thank you."

I politely said, as I took your hand and brought you to that room of forgetfulness. You entered it with your conflicted mind. You couldn't remember anything, as if reason felt suddenly afraid to follow the will of passion. It had to live. It had to live on.

Spasms. Did you feel spasms' grasp over your brain? Death withering through your veins. You hold on to life in vain. Thoughts. Images. And thoughts. Your temporal lobe triggered emergency tremors. It soothed the crude reality that got you when your heart struggled. Neurons just wanted to handle another breath. Just one. Just. Spasms. Thoughts. Images. Spasms. And that taste of Void in the wake of Sophron!

53

What's the only feeling as powerful as passion in the endless moment of love? Pain in the aftermath of a loss. We can't sense the one we miss, but we mourn from the yearning of the one we lost. You skinned your Muse alive. Fleshed to the marrow, you couldn't let it heal without. Touching the wound from the inside out. You can't forget her smile, and all the while, you tried. Where did you meet her? Do you remember? As you descended, Emerald carried your ascension. She knew, yet she left you to bleed, infatuated. One day, can you recall this one day? She named you the one who would put lotion on her body, as she sought some sort of comfort. You would only borrow the time she would allow you, and the touch? Just one. A gentle one. Down her neck, and up her back, your sight on her legs, the butterfly tattooed on her lower back, the one you could never catch. The beast covers innocence like a cocoon of death around the most precious pearl of life.

You let your desires rot beneath a crust of good manners. You brought her presents, cried for her presence, the one she deprived you of. Moving back to Montreal brought you despair. Why couldn't your mom leave you in Toronto? For the months that followed, the thought of Emerald haunted every second of your miserable life. You were, once, lovers. She played no teaser; you would convince yourself. Unlike those who lure with a cleavage and a whisper when we salvage a tender bliss or the savage blister of a kiss. You fell for her?

The evenings you spent for that entire month, you would observe every one of the two hundred pictures, taken from her websites, and you would imagine constellations from the almost invisible beauty marks on her face. You hold close to your heart every photo you took on your mobile phone. Each one tells an amazing coming of age story. Your first kiss, after an entire evening at the movies. You didn't know if the time was right, but you were afraid to impose your desires. She had to be ready, and she had to consent. How wonderful did it feel? Her tongue lost every ounce of resistance as it swam across your mouth. Oh, William! Nobody in your new school ever felt this sort of love.

That entire day you spent together, at the mall! Look just how happy she was holding your hand! You promised one another you would always be there. If only those bullies who pressured you could feel the happiness you felt, then. They would have been jealous. What about this picture? You snapped it at a Dragon Boat race, on Toronto Island, correct? Oh, my friend, those eyes speak of marriage. If only you had stayed in the Queen City.

"And what about now, William?"

I asked you, seeing how you couldn't let your sight leave that altar of mine. I know your world within. It called for your resurrection. Sadly, for them, and I was there to remind all of you, salvation only means the essence born of the selfless. Your sacrifice stinks of absolute selfishness.

"If I were." You finally whispered. That world within summoned you, more and more. Your Muse. Emerald. The girl exists for you to love and to breathe her affection. The woman that meant, for you, an eternity spent in the comfort of her remembrance, as you sensed the Siamese twin that shares your soul. He, too, lost a desired one. You whispered: "If I were the dust of a thought at the back of her hopes. I could live in someone, and you would have nowhere else to take me."

"Dream, oh Dreamer!"

"I will fight you with every living cell of me!"

You stood mid-way between pride and fear, and I was there. If I had a face, you would see me grin.

"Welcome to your world." I calmly said. And it all went blank.

Chapter Five:
The Hound Lord of Nibiru

The Great Lord, killer of entities, was born on Nibiru, ten thousand years in your past. He had shown an interest in war and battle at a very young age. Legends have it that he mastered the sword and various martial arts before he could speak. Of course, those are tales that old Anunnaki tell children to put them to sleep. The true story is that Marduk attended a military academy at age twelve. Military school requires attendees to reach fifteen years of living, on Nibiru. After seeing him fight other kids in a back alley, Lady Marl-ures of Alibastat, an influent political figure at the time, took him under her care. She would mentor him in the ways of mancing, and she would get him to join her own army as the youngest lieutenant that ever walked on Nibiru.

With the body of a lioness and the head of a top model stolen from Playboy, Marl-ures displayed as much beauty as the fear she provoked. As powerful as she may have been, we talk about a self-taught tyrant. She could never master magic. No orbs would have made it into her hands, and yet so many mighty Walkers died under her strangling grasp. Her armour merged with her flesh, and that, reader, always comes as a political statement.

Before reigning as Her Majesty's protégé, he was Gil the bald. To name orphans after certain attributes of theirs, with one syllable to designate them, becomes common practice. After leading armies into merciless battles both on Alibastat and on Nibiru, his mentor chose to adopt him. She titled him after herself: Lord Mar-dukes of Nibiru. He carried over the vengeful arm of his lady for thousands of years. Some believe that, as Marduk became a tall and handsome Anunnaki, the two of them shared a secret affair. This was unlikely, since Lady Marl-ures prefers the comfort of other women but seeing them so close to one another triggers the imagination. When Gaia first showed signs of enlightenment, with Neanderthals and Homo sapiens evolving as self-aware organisms, Marl-ures was among the first to send scouts. Other Neymlisses with ideas of conquest quickly followed, forming premature civilizations that would come, rise, and fall overnight. Perhaps the most significant example we could think of touches the fabled Atlantis, with a history we find all too familiar: it sank.

But the fearmongering Queen of Alibastat spun a different idea. Instead of inspiring sedentary cultures, let's encourage the strong hunters and gatherers to rise. Marduk positioned himself to lead those prehistoric tribes. He did it so well, we got to see cavemen burning entire cities to ashes. A feat that would have dwarfed the conquests of Genghis Khan, have your modern historians held a clue. Around that time, the Hound Lord of Nibiru met Ishtar. She sat against the beach of the river Styx, on a quiet morning. Twelve naked apes gazed at the goddess' beauty, while she cleansed her hair. Not too far from her oasis, a tall general, bald with a grim look, took six of his entrusted advisors to inspect the area. Nobody prepared him for the magnificence that followed his encounter with the young Anunnaki princess. He walked near her and offered her a towel.

"Alone and naked with the savages?" he asked her. "You attract trouble."

"If you call them savages!" She raged at him. "Then you and I have little ground to share. Show them respect and you might earn their respect." Of course, Marduk wouldn't show any form of appreciation for primitive organisms. He could have felt outraged by her comment. How can royalty such as herself act in weak modesty? He should scold her! Have someone to remind the maiden that those primates worship her. They should! Those mindless animals' only purpose is to die for Marduk's conquests. Or for his pleasure. He sat next to the goddess and put the towel around her shoulders, covering her breasts.

"I was informed that you would be on this world, Lady Ishtar of Nibiru. I wasn't prepared to confront a breathtaking beauty."

"Compliments mean nothing, from a brute. You have been in this realm for two centuries, and all you accomplished was decimating early societies and brutalizing gentle nomads."

"Treating them like your children would be any better? We are here to punish our enemies and take away their land! Must I make you remember?" He calmed himself, seeing how he unsettled her away from a peaceful bath.

"I didn't choose a side in your conquests, Marduk. I'm sorry we had to meet like this. I would have preferred an occasion where I wouldn't end up despising you."

She sheltered her body under the long towel and left the river. She gestured the men and women who waited on the beach. They unceremoniously left the scene. Marduk didn't bother to see her leave. He joined his own entourage, they resumed their walk.

The years passed. Marduk and Ishtar participated in the creation of Mesopotamia. The Lord would encourage this aborning civilization in the ways of battle. Ishtar would prefer the teaching of love and wisdom. The two of them seemed clearly incompatible, but an uncontrollable feeling blinded Marduk. He would shower her Grace with gold and jewels. She would provide strength and freedom to the slaves who brought those gifts. He would name entire cities after her magnificence. She would put wise men and women in charge of bringing light and peace to those regions. The more he would attempt to seduce her with his might and power, and the less attracted she felt towards him.

Meanwhile, not too far from Akkad and Sumer, other powerful gods, and some Neymlisses, taught entire communities the ways of Sophron. They were, at the time, a small House. They had travelled all the way from Svarga Loka to visit Gaia. Word made it to their palace that humans grew a brain capable of performing kindness. Telling right from wrong, entering the long karmic journey towards enlightenment, those lifeforms evolved to meet Varuna and his heavenly House of brightness. With fifteen drops of Logos for three drops of Archeus, their home world showed more thoughts than their garnished life. Beings who evolve on that layer embrace immateriality. We find essences over substances of any kind. Therefore, angelic creatures who explore the Barbelo-Archeus quadrants must incarnate in one manner or another.

The body that Indra favoured dressed him as a blue-skinned humanoid. Gentle eyes stood out, but a strong grip to his ironlike hands showed just how powerful he could be. A warrior if needed, Indra preferred the ways of selfless care. One morning, while visiting the vicinity nearing Mesopotamia, Indra confessed to his best friend and teacher, Varuna:

"I have seen the most amazing form of beauty, bathing by the river Styx." he told him. "I believe she saw me, but I was too intimidated by her presence to reveal mine."

Varuna sat on a wooden bench near the humble palace they built by the Ganga River. "Son, don't fear your own feelings." the elderly sage replied. "Stay true to your altruism, and those selfless principles we hold dear. Provide her more listening and attention than any manifestation of desire, hunger, and thirst you might build from within. Don't chase her! Let love find you both, at its pace, in its time." He lit an oval-shaped pipe and cleared his mind of any longing. Indra reflected on those words and acquiesced.

The following day, the young prince from Airavata returned to the river Styx. As expected, he saw Ishtar bathe naked, among her disciples. This time, he found the courage to mingle with the flock of humans, turning his gaze away from the goddess' intimacy. "I sense a divine presence with us." she said to herself. Indra heard, but he chose to remain quiet. "Have you been sent by the Hound Lord of Nibiru?" Seeing that she was onto him, he spoke: "My Lady, I apologize for my intrusion. Say one word, and I will disappear. However, I felt kindness emanating from your essence, and it felt rather. Attractive." Indra covered her naked body and left her bathing activity to discuss with her visitor.

"You hardly sound like those gods whose main purpose involves invasion and subjugation." she concluded. Indra smiled, without daring a look in her direction. "A civilization maimed and controlled with terror is a diminished one. My House and myself believe in the empowerment of Gaia's humans. Let them be strong and free! Let's share our gifts with them! They deserve to walk as our equals! We will build much stronger heralds than we would if we kept them small and fearful." the blue royalty spoke words that reached her soul. "Why aren't you looking at me, oh prince of Airavata?" she asked.

Indra kept his eyes away and replied: "I never got your consent, my liege." Convinced, she took his hands and gently caressed his palms and fingers. "I authorize you to look into my eyes." Hearing these words, Indra closed his sight and turned his head to face Ishtar's. He then uttered those words: "I thank you for this privilege, princess of Paradise. I will allow your gaze to merge with mine, let it stand as we will remember it for all eternity."

When their eyes finally met, time and space found itself encapsulated in a moment that reflected true infinity. Silence fell upon the land. The force of attraction between these two deities brought tremors that shook the heart and spine of all living beings. "I believe I am expected in my palace." she whispered. "I wouldn't dare keep you by my side." he murmured back, but she ushered a powerful: "No! Of course, I didn't mean to say." He smiled and let her hands leave his grasp. They spoke no other word, that day. Ishtar returned to her quarters, and Indra was in love.

Chapter Six:
The Lost Boy

If we could send a satellite to probe the layer of Athanor, we would see clouds that looked like foggy membranes. The minuscule lightning of a silent thunder poked at the almost non-existent sky, right before vanishing. Past the flashes, down where a lonely gloomy purple sun shone from a mythical distance, mountains of flesh shared the stage with oceans of liquid bones, forests of chaos, fields of harmony. The Temporis continent, and its borders with the next territory, Berellumec, would hardly stand as visible. This strange layer shifts its weather more often than a rock star swaps clothes in a show.

South from this supplement of an area, you could find my legions. My darkness obscures the middle eastern portion, in a struggle to reach that occidental ideal and the far-oriental memory. Temporis covers a much wider surface. Muses and nymphs of Athanor had been at war since the time of your birth, billions of years ago by their calculation. When I struck, with the power I had in hands, they forcefully put their differences aside and fought back. Prophecies had it that a saviour would come. The Dreamer would embody himself as a nymph, or a muse, or a form none could ever comprehend, and bring salvation to the land, resurrection to the worthy, punishment to the wicked. Pockets of towns and villages waited. And waited, fought hollows, waited.

From a distance, armies of hollows by the billions seemed like a starless end of the universe. A closer look and we would see a monster without a shape. Mind you, I find them rather pretty, that's a highly subjective statement. To the many organisms afraid to die, my pets embrace the bodies of demons, the mouths of cannibal sharks, the jaw of sabre-toothed tigers, times fifty, and the eyes of terror. The nose of a wolf atop a bear's neck. Arms would stretch to expand the reach of nine claws, seven fingers, four paws and no shoulder. How a highly subjective sight.

These hollows were born in the layer of True Void. Their flesh sucked life more than an absolute vacuum, while their mind projected ideals of life. Most hollows lack a static form. As we advance in the cycles of Sophron, within the Void-Barbelo quadrant, hollows tend to allow matter to dictate a form. Life, here, to those creatures, is a metaphysical concept. Where I come from, my children tend to remain unstable, as winds battling over mandalas of sand and salt. Before you woke up, you could hear waves against a beach. Seagulls laughed, reminding you of Chekov's play and how you could have written it so well. Ishtar. With your eyes closed, you could picture that bright sunshine of her youth. A pale blue surrounded clouds, like grass of white steam, and a yellow star. You smiled, as you tried to espouse this image with every ounce of oxygen left in your brain, as if your mind could live forever in that dream. Let it be more than that.

But you had to. Open an eye. A dark black moon shone above. Far from a fantasy, and you knew. Your chin and left cheek could feel the icy bricks, just as your ears could hear the wind that broke in the freezing arms of a breeze, away from any beach. That brick you looked at, as your sight gradually parted from the dream state you were in, had wrinkles. As if you could immerse yourself in one of them and find yourself on that sand that you missed so much. Imagine the cloudless blue sky through which the sun hammered the white sand with heat and light.

"Are you awake?"

A gentle voice asked you. You blinked. You did not move.
You turned your head, as if your nose better took you down that
crack in the road, but you could only feel that rough brick against
your face. You stayed like this for a long moment, as you
attempted to figure out if any of this sounded genuine. You shut
your eyes and tried to picture an idea if you could. That beach,
again on Toronto Island. Just a thought. You could easily compare
it with the paved cruelty and tell of the true reality.

"Maybe you are hungry."

The boy's voice said, piercing your silence. That felt tangible.
Perhaps you should face your guest and speak. You turned around
with your sight closed. The moon shone through an even darker
sky. Wasn't the astral sphere white? It's supposed to be. You opened
your eyes. Nope! Black.

"Here!" the young boy said. "It's the last one I have." There
was a tiny hand, maybe a nine-year-old kid, that tossed you half of
a pomegranate. You could guess the age by the shape: slander,
fragile, a small round head atop a slim long neck, and short blonde
hair, and yet. The blue skin showed fiery-red flesh. This yin and
yang water and plasma caught your amazement.

"It's the last one I have." He apologized. A delicate face, a
bright face, in harmony with that soothing voice, looked at you.
He smiled under a deep purple set of eyes.

"Don't chew the flesh. Just suck the seeds. Just the juice.
We don't have any more apples, I'm sorry." He wore jeans and a
white T-shirt with a bat drawn on its front. The surroundings
seemed more like a Victorian village with light poles gathered in a
long line to nowhere. The buildings were tall pyramids with square
doors marked by wooden Xs.

"Thank you."

You slowly said, as you sat down against that metallic pole. You grabbed the fruit and sucked these seeds with appetite. "What nation are you from?" The boy asked you, then joined your side to better observe your facial traits. He could notice your pale beige skin, your light-brown hair, your blue eyes. Obviously, nobody had ever seen any nymph, or maybe a muse, like you.

"I beg pardon?"

You gravely inquired. Your tongue battled the flesh of seed stuck against your teeth. "This is the village of Grief. It used to be a muse's city, but, since the invasion, it became a mixed haven. I'm Touch, from the nymph nation of Amiben. Are you a muse?"

No. You were not amused. He assisted you up and proudly uttered: "It doesn't matter, now, or here. I guess I should bring you to our Grand House." You struggled to stand up, but gravity kept taking you down. You observed around you, tried to gather sense of these tall and thread-thin, grey light poles; you couldn't.

"Did I die?" you asked him. He didn't reply. He just aided you, again. You surveyed around, once more: Three pyramids and a thousand pillars, all extinguished, in front of you. A thousand more stood behind, all lit up. You saw more pyramids until your eyes could no longer perceive anything.

"We don't have too many strangers." Touch told you as he grabbed your helpless hand. You looked at this curious black moon, again and again, at that weird blue hand, red flesh deep within, holding yours.

"Not in a long time, and I'm too young to remember that far back. They say if you don't leave your haven, hollows will leave you alone. So, we gathered anywhere we could to fight in any way we could. I'm not told much. They claim that it's for my own good if I just occupy myself with light poles, setting them ablaze as fast as I can, and go to bed."

"Is that all they taught you? Can you count and read?"

"I'm a nymph, sir."

"So?"

"I just take care of light poles. I was told I would do that since I was five. Before that I was too busy playing, but I don't remember what it was like to play. They just told me."

"Who told you?"

"The muses, sir. This is an ancient muse city. I don't know what it's like in a nymph's city. But I wouldn't dare to leave this home of mine. I don't want to get caught by the hollows."

"How old are you?" Touch frowned and lost himself in an intense thought. "They never told me." he pondered, as he slowly approached a light pillar. He extended a long stick, letting the farthest end ignite sparkles onto gasoline-soaked clothes. Drops of water quickly formed around the ball of fire and made the sphere atop the pole resemble Touch's flesh and skin. You observed the boy walk his way towards the next one. You didn't know if you should accompany him or try your way out into the mystery.

Confusion cloaked your thoughts. "We shouldn't stay outside for too long." he sighed. "But I have to finish my job, or we will lose more streets, more houses."

You let him perform his work and followed from a shy distance. You went down a long, narrow trail and crossed many paths. The surroundings were at their darkest when they stretched towards horizons deprived of any light. All the buildings, the roads, the entire landscape stood out as a copy of a copy. It all looked the same. When you checked the sky, all you could see hardly portrayed what you could feel: These membranous clouds and those tiny pixels of brightness, born dead as if they never existed, mocked you. Or if only for one intense moment.

Crows with dark flames covering their eyes and their feathers, like phoenix transformed into hellish birds, observed you in flocks on every house's roof. Mice ran a crazy marathon along the road. They zig zagged around your legs. You danced to avoid them, and when you accidentally did step on one, the black creature swiftly turned into gooey tar under your foot. At the far end of the main street, seventy-two white grapevines shone, the virgins, purest fruits among the purest of fruits. They stood entwined to one another and formed only one. Only one huge plant. Temporis, the land of God. This is where Joan of Arc met the Deity, and where Paul encountered Christ on his way to Damascus. It is also where Dostoevsky wrote The Gambler.

You walked through the immense vegetation as if it weren't there. Another cloud, perhaps, although you could sense the grapes tickling the hairiness of your skin. The journey across the bush felt like an inner crusade, one you would share with the symbol behind these ghostly vines. Suddenly, every war that had ever stormed the surface of your previous life raged within you. It was like one immense battle, your very own. Your heart hammered the inside of your thorax in a rhythm that compared with the drum rolls of ten thousand helicopters. Light flashed before your gaze. You felt an eye for an eye. A light for a light, a throb for a throb, and your whole dizzy world went blind.

As you almost collapsed, Touch grabbed your hand and took you out of the tree of knowledge. Numbness. Darkness punctuated with millions of bright dots, as if each one projected a soft needle against your balance. You won't fall, you will stand, but you can barely see clearly. Can you breathe? Can you try to walk? Try, just this once. Sir? Can you hear me?

"Sir? Can you breathe? Sir! Can you hear me? Walk, it will go away. I'm sorry, I should have warned you."

You gradually regained your sight. When you turned your head, you saw the grapevines fade away. The flaming crows seemed to laugh at you from a distance. You had no idea what was going on, but you sensed that something was off. A silhouette manifested itself on the horizon and walked in your direction: One big guy, with wide shoulders. An orb floated in front of him. Before you had time to realize what was happening, light came out of the flying sphere. Everything blurred. You could manage to see Sherlock Holmes appearing from the crystal ball. Well, it was more like a zombified version of the famous detective. The literary hero turned monster ran in your direction, all fangs, and teeth out. Touch froze in panic. You had to do something, and quick. You seized the first object readily available to you, a rock, and tossed it at the walking cadaver. It fell right in front of you.

Your head hurts, now. How can you possibly fight? Sherlock Corpse jumped on Touch. You could hear your friend scream in agony. You shook your head, grabbed that rock again and threw your weight at the beast. You smashed his face with more strength than you thought yourself capable of. Enraged, the zombie left Touch alone and looked at you. Drooling blood. You never fought. It wasn't in your DNA. In a different time, a different space, you would have allowed this creature to eat you alive. Did our encounter trigger any spasm of survival? You screamed louder than Sherlock did. You jumped on him and smashed his head with the rock you now held with both hands.

You shattered it again! Again! Again! A lifetime of rage manifested itself in your berserk move. Before you could calm yourself and recover, two giant bats appeared behind you. Touch ran away and left you alone to fight this new threat. A bloodied rock was all you had. Just as you turned to smash a monster's head, you heard the other one shriek. It dug its teeth deep in your skull. It hurt so bad, you felt intense electric shocks down your spine. You dropped the stone, wrestled the winged mouse to the ground.

Your hands grabbed both ends of its jaw, ready to tear its face open. The beast's claws said otherwise. Razor sharp, they planted themselves deep in your torso. Its companion used the moment to join the fun. You carved the animal a wider mouth, blood flooding the land. Before you could pull any further, the other bat took a huge chunk of flesh out of your left thigh. It hurt so bad, you screamed until your entire being went numb. A good time to die, now, right? No. It's not. Just fight! You finished the first monster, tearing its head in half, revealing a brain that fell next to you. But the other one was still clamped against your thigh. With all the strength you finally gathered, you ignored the agony. You bit the bat's neck, willing to eat it up like a hot dog after a long hunger strike. The creature screamed! It yelled! You swear it feared for its life. No time to rest, you tore both its wings off, a demon choosing the fate of an angel. The feat was demanding. You lost your hold on to the wake. Exhausted, you passed out. The last thing you saw was the wingless bat's open mouth. It descended to eat your face-off. And you blacked out.

Journey into the Hourglass:
Four

I found Martin reading my manuscript, one morning. He spent the entire night up, drinking. I hate seeing him like this. I made myself eggs, while he turned the pages violently. When I sat down at my kitchen table, he sat in front of me. His breath smelled like old beer. Did you? He stuttered, burped, and continued: Did you just write William into a path of enlightenment? "Yes, I did." He sighed: Good, okay, so now we need to write him a solid backstory! I ate my eggs slowly, trying hard to wrap my mind around the fact that having an enlightened character displeased him. Sure, we want Seamus to find his power, and wake up. But why can't William do the same? "We'll just find William a decent mentor and we'll have two main characters who awake." I defended my ideas. We'll have too many characters, Alibast! He vehemently objected. "What about we write ourselves in our story?" I smiled, but he didn't. What part of too many characters you don't get? We can't be involved!

But what if we could? I trusted my gut feelings. Seeing how Martin suffers, the way he spoke about his failures, I thought I could do him a favour. "Regardless, Martin, I will defend William's right to achieve enlightenment and wake up in his inner universe. Also, trust me, let me write the next chapter. You'll thank me later." He finished his beer and opened another one.

Chapter Seven:
The Victorian Author

Transylvania, but in the middle of Times Square. New York after an atomic bomb. This version of Gaia exists in the soul of a very deranged Dreamer: the possibility of the Devastated Duck. Horrors invaded Earth, in this possibility. The tall buildings that once defined Manhattan rot as gothic ruins, now. The streets are loitered with burned cars and wrecked buses. Trucks covered with moss and the remains of corpses. Ponds of blood gathered on every corner. The gloom became so heavy, the most lighthearted optimist would fall into an incurable depression, just looking at a picture of this place.

At the other end of Time Square, a gigantic castle was erected. It stood out from the rest of the scenery. It felt like a UFO had landed. A bulky silhouette walked slowly, trying to advance cautiously. Zombies could very well jump by surprise to spill his blood on the paved roads. Anyone who was born in this reality knows how to live alongside perpetual danger. Nobody grows up very old, in these parts. They were approaching the tall palace when crows flew over their heads. The birds could attack at any time, but the silhouette stood ready to give them a fight. The goal, however, was to reach this tall and dark building at any cost. They ran to enter the weird facilities. The front doors opened automatically, letting the brute inside the rustic interior.

Armours eaten by rust, weapons on the verge of collapsing in dust, the corridors projected the looks of a medieval library left for dead. The silhouette kept its pace, dashing to the other end. It quickly turned to embark on a long descent, down tight stairs. A wooden door waited. The shade could hear screams of agony coming from the other side. A guttural music, almost cavernous, played in the background. The door opened. The guest entered. Beyond the gate, the sight was even more depressing. Walls made of lungs breathed. Thousands of them, breathing air in and spiting blood out. The shadow walked carefully. The heavy atmosphere and the stench were too much to bear. A green river of mucus gathered at the bulky shade's feet.

Another silhouette populated the room. At the far end, a black chair stood behind a dark laptop. The lonely light coming out of the screen glowed in the castle's centre. The guest walked towards the master of the house, head bowing down, in reverence and respect. Or in fear. "I wasn't expecting you so soon." the man said. His voice made the walls tremble. The silhouette stopped midway and genuflected, still looking at the floor. "I visited the possibility of the Maiden Crane." the shadow replied." I was inside William's innerverse, my lord.

As you asked." They found the courage to raise their eyes and added: "You were right. He did manifest himself in his own soul." *How could a Dreamer end up in his own inward world?* The master pondered. "Did you engage him in battle?" another voice, a grave one, responded. It came from everywhere, and nowhere. This frightened the valiant warrior even more.

"He fought my creatures, but I sensed Melpomene's presence. I can't face a Great Muse. They weren't supposed to take sides in those wars." The silhouette was awaiting their execution. It could come from either the Lord sitting behind a screen, or the graver voice without a body of any kind. It was difficult to tell who was more intimidating.

The Lord turned his chair to look at his guest. A thick beard covered the lower portion of his face, while scars deepened the upper one. "Melpomene can't take part in this." he let out. "I already made sure Sekhmet would yield."

"About that." the hulked of a shadow uttered, knowing it would enrage both of his interlocutors. "She's also investigating William's death."

"Are you certain this is her motivation?" the hauntingly grave voice asked. The master behind his computer seemed unfazed, but the third presence made itself felt with a sour tone.

"She surprised me while I followed a lead into the mind of a different Dreamer." the agent explained. "I can only deduce that she's after William as well."

"That makes sense." the Lord of the castle uttered, in a solemn but aggravated voice. "If she is, then Marduk is probably observing the same lead. He must have found out about William's remarkable feat before her. In my story, she spies on the Hound Lord of Nibiru."

"It doesn't mean anything!" the ghost said. "Stop! You are being paranoid."

"We can't make as though he fails to know! Come on! Do you want to face a god on our own battlefield? I spent too much to conquer this world. We don't want gods to interfere!"

The silhouette stood up, almost in a defiant manner. "If you allow me, Lord." they suggested. "I may have found a way to turn those tides in our favour." The master turned his back on his visitor, focusing on the screen. He looked at a few words he keyed in, earlier. "What do you have in mind?" he asked. The guest approached the chair but stopped short of stepping into the Lord's inner circle.

"When I was investigating William's manifestation, I came across a Dreamer who imagined the entire scene. This is where I battled with Sekhmet. I don't think she realized that she had strayed from her Sophron. Unless she acquired the means to elevate herself beyond her initial state of awakening, but the Egyptian gods have yet to learn what Buddha invented."

The master seemed a bit annoyed, but he kept on listening. The shade continued: "Can you write my essence in her storyline? I will manifest myself, and I will lure Marduk and Sekhmet away from our goal."

"I don't feel like my novel should go over there. I'm sorry." The invisible voice interjected at this very moment, causing the lungs to shine. *That's a good idea!* The entire room thought. "I'll cast you over there right now."

"No! Please. Let me finish the chapter I was working on. Come on! I'm supposed to do this sort of work. Don't play a Hollywood exec stunt on me, okay? I'll do my best, and we'll see."

"Like you're in charge of your own inspiration! Your lackey comes up with the most brilliant plan, and you downplay it because you want to write your novel? Come on, Martin! You know better than this." The master looked away, as though he meant for everyone to disappear. It didn't happen, so he claimed: "My only concern is William. I don't care about Sekhmet! And I don't care about Marduk! William should be dead!"

"I'll be working on this." the muscular shadow whispered. "I just need more power." The creature begged for a divine intervention of some sort. Neither the Author nor the mysterious ghost seemed to bother. Disappointed, they left. "I don't believe this should be a concern." the voice uttered.

The Lord sitting behind his laptop computer was lost in deep thoughts. He looked at the ceiling and claimed: "I am interested about William uncovering a life that was should have vanished long before I started writing this novel." A window appeared, embracing the shape of a sphere. Light emanated from this circular piece of glass, bursting into a flash of orange and white. The blast lasted three seconds, and then bizarre forms and figures drew themselves. In the middle, on the lower section of the incoming painting, a curious hole stemmed into existence, as white as the fragments of crystal. Like pure ice showed up all around it, covering the upper two thirds of the abstract picture. The rest appeared to be the ground surrounding that round entrance. The voice came from the other end of that hole.

"You shouldn't have written his demise." the painting said.

"Did I? Did he call upon himself to do that jump?" he replied.

"You know you have the ultimate freedom, Martin. You are God to those characters."

"You have no idea what it's like to compose anything." Martin left the comfort of his chair and walked past a puddle of puke. Darkness covered his steps as he approached a small refrigerator. He could hear the voice in his head, as it attempted to return to its former glory, all around the room. "Did you cast me out? How mature of you! Can't handle a bit of opposition?" she whispered.

"I need time on my own." Martin replied. "You have no idea how compromising this is."

"Just rewrite William's chapters. "

"I can't."

"You can't? You stupid! You're in charge!"

"I didn't write them. They ended up in the final draft. I can't just rewrite what's in the final draft."

"Who wrote them? Marduk?"

"He's not awakened enough to compete with an Author. He still thinks that Sophron only has Sleepers and Dreamers."

On a side table, an orb floated next to a grey mage's robe. Metal pins kept the upper end of the fabric closed, while the lower one appeared as a veil over the void. "I created him, you see? Back in nineteen ninety-six." Martin opens the fridge and grabs a beer.   It reads: Ishtar's Bitch, on a purple sticker.

"The biomechs, well that was Alexandra's, but the whole thing That was me."

"Why did you create William?" the voice insisted.

Martin couldn't answer. His heavy head fell, just like a boulder over a veil of feathers. The lungs, around him, showed incompetence to breathe. Some coughed, others spat mucus. "I don't know." The Author shrugged. Silence came back. Solitude landed on his shoulders, and he felt the necessity to sit down behind his computer to compose a few words.

"Maybe it's time for you to write William's destiny." the voice uttered, haunting the room once again.

Martin was out of ideas. He drank his beer and considered logging onto some video game. He felt unsure if it meant to prove his supremacy over characters in his mind, or players without a life. The Author was unable to get the better of this challenge, so he closed the laptop and his eyes shut.

"Okay, I see what you want. I'll give it a try,"

Chapter Eight:
The Brave Young Light Bringer

You woke up under the care of your small nymph friend. Deep wounds covered your entire body. I can assure you, William, life was still with you. Touch attended to your every need, making sure that you were getting better.

"I'm sorry you had to go through this." he told you. "I never saw creatures like those, before." When you closed your eyes, you felt more strength. You opened them, just to look around. The beast that tried to eat you was blown into pieces.

"Did you do this?" you asked your friend. "No, sir. It was them." He apologized.

"Them?"

"Yes. Are you good, now? They are ready to see you."

"But who are they, Touch?"

"They're just one. Can you stand up?" You could, but it was painful. Keeping your eyes closed sounded like a better option. You returned to your blackout. After what felt like a second, you woke up. Touch dragged you to a very long distance. The poor guy really wanted you to meet his friend. You opened your sight again, and your energy returned. You inhaled a profound breath and found the will to walk on your own. Touch was relieved to see you gaining some independence.

Before you, now, as your eyes grew accustomed to this new sight, a palace arose: deeply white, almost crystal bright, and a hundred times beyond the height of the Great Pyramids. Touch stood by the main door and waited for you to brush this amazement off your wide-open surprise. The middle tower held the shape of a forked asparagus atop a temple, like two halves of a disc that held the structure's foundation. Every following six buildings looked like beer bottles, with long necks and short, fat bottoms. They surrounded the fundamental tower like a six fingered hand over a column. Beyond this sensual architecture, the Cothurni Towers, or great houses, had a deeply tranquil aura. From a specific angle, the palace recalled the sight of a meditative angel: the central enclosure acted as the body, and the others around it shaped the folded wings.

"It's here, sir!"

The boy shouted. The ground slowly attracted you, as you advanced closer to the entrance, your heavy head down. A growl, or was it om, flooded the corridor. The indoors enticed you, more and more. Reflections of gold and silver, parcels of mystery against the wall, led you into the narrow way in. As you approached, the nuggets embraced the shape of ancient artwork, animals and humans sculpted in platinum and diamond. Enlarged Sumerian eyes, long, rectangular beards. Statues of men with both hands over lengthy sticks, and women with a finger inside vases, guarded your every move, at every corner. They showed different forms as you walked farther. There, a Babylonian cherub mounts an Egyptian sphinx, surrounded by Christian angels. Here, it's a tall Egyptian pharaoh instructing a naked Greek athlete, frozen in the rock. The growl seemed to intensify. When you pivoted your head to look behind, you saw the main door, the gigantic door, shut. Everything, every piece of art, made into nuggets, and mere dots of gold and silver on the wall. Right next to you, on both sides, immense statues stood still. In front of you, on both sides, you saw paintings of all kinds. Prehistoric origins turned into Roman frescoes, scenes of hunts and banquets.

The growl, too, evolved, to become the songs of a thousand organs, hundreds of thousands of violins and cellos, all as one. You heard drums of every nature, and billions of voices, angels and demons alike, that offered your ear Gregorian chants in the purest harmony. Finally, the long walk ended at the feet of two steel gates. Touch kneeled before them and embraced the floor. The doors opened, painstakingly slowly, to reveal an empty room as wide as a whole city. Fresh air kissed your cheeks, and it suggested that some environment, and a micro solar system, allowed the room to suffice to its own light and atmosphere. The sun, however, sits at the centre of the place. The ecosphere lay there, a green carpet of grass-like fur, mounted by a ceiling as high as it was blue. Creatures that existed, here, exalted pure thoughts.

One step of yours covered half the distance between your initial position and the middle of the room. A second stride took you towards half that remaining interval. The centre of this new universe expanded beyond your belly button. Three steps, however, were enough to bring you at speech distance from the owner of this magnificent palace.

He sat on a black and silver throne made from his cape. It elevated him halfway above the floor. Aside from that leather cape and chains, the hulk of a man-Muse didn't seem to wear much. His lower face was hidden behind a hand that could easily cover your entire head. His index finger on his nose almost touched his right eye. He looked down, where an elegant nymph stood by his side. Her skin turned to a brownish purple. She wore the wings of a moth as a coat, and she held his arm with great love and affection. I present to you Sthenele, the Princess of pain, Superior Nymph of Temporis, Moth Queen of Athanor. The mammoth with tanned skin and shoulders thrice as wide as his thorax projected fear. I will present you Melpomene. The Muse, William, of your tragedy.

"Do you bring me the Dreamer of this possibility?" Melpomene said, in a grave, solemn voice, like an earthquake.

"He isn't, my lord!" Touch swiftly said, before he prostrated in fear and respect. "I apologize for this interruption, my lord, but. He is simply a lost wanderer."

Melpomene didn't bother to reprimand Touch's insolence. He walked away. The throne turned back into his gigantic cape, and he approached you. Touch rapidly gestured you to bow down in reverence, but you didn't. The air that surrounded Melpomene changed into streams of water in zero gravity. Sthenele lit the air around her in fire as she stirred clear from her lover.

"Have you found what you were looking for?" the Lord asked you, then he sniffed your neck, your face. Touch trembled against the floor. Every move that Melpomene makes suggests an immediate decapitation. The powerful Muse could, at any time, grab his sword and chop Touch's head, or maybe Touch's new friend's. He lost so many this way. One word. Touch knew that if he says one word, the Lord might respond with a silence and make it his last. But his boy must bow down! Touch couldn't find the courage to say anything. He can only fear and stay quiet.

"I am not this Dreamer of yours." you said. He smiled:

"You are lost?"

"Most likely."

"Have you found her?"

"Her?"

"The goddess who breathed, from within her soul's womb, the life of muses over the land of Athanor."

"That goddess never existed!" you said promptly, and with a defying voice. I laughed. It is sad you weren't that confronting in my presence. When quiescent, it is easier to oppose a friend than it is to face a foe who wants you dead. How sad that you are that weak, William.

Melpomene stood back and smiled. "She never existed? William, be serious."

He whispered. Obviously, you said these words without thinking. He asked you a question you couldn't answer, so you responded with the same tact he used for his query, minus the intelligence.

"Or you can't remember? In a past life. Oh, of course, you haven't encountered your glancer. He would have told you the whole story, or most of it. Think, Willy boy, think!" It hit you like a spasm and a ton of bricks. Melpomene walked behind. It allowed you some space to ponder. The waves of steam and floating water that covered his entire self, and followed as a gown or as his cape, espoused his moves. They showed you vague images of a high tower, the CN Tower; this is Toronto.

"How sad that you both had to die before your love transformed into one universe. Has to be the biggest tragedy in all of your existences."

"The biggest? What about what I just did?"

"You did it for her? You sacrificed the lives of so many beings inhabiting you for her?" Did you? Indra, you couldn't! Oh, I just find this highly entertaining, but these people take it more seriously. Either you did or not hardly bothers me. I will exist, if we call it that, with or without you. Still, it's your struggle we should talk about. So, was it her? Is she the one who keeps you away from me? And who was she? That Victoria Sicard you seemed to get along well with?

It must be her. She's the one holding Ishtar's essence? I might pay her a visit and have her dead by next week. Tell me. She made you jump? Didn't she? Tell me! Let me know the name of the girl who embodied the attraction of this god within you. That Emerald, you mentioned. Both of you got very close. Did you jump because of her? Do you try to save her from something? Was it for someone? Are you saving her from you?

Ishtar!

You thought. Sure, you did it for Ishtar. But we want a different essence. Her images got blurrier than the sound of her voice against the edges of your skull. The last time you saw this beauty, Winter fell over Alibastat. A blizzard raged on over this layer of Sophron. She had left the comfort of Babel's remains, where both your souls had decided to spend eternity laced into one another, like Siamese doves.

You vowed to be the first conjoint Entity that had ever awakened. They call it the process of leading mankind to a Greater Enlightenment. Adream you cherished soon after the fall of your last human tribe, in Gaia. The Roman Empire had found keys to dominate this tiny world from behind the Veil. A secret that Far Eastern Neymlisses, those warriors, had learned. A highly holy entity taught Paul of Damascus what the Romans would only understand after years of persecuting the vulnerable within their land. Pagan tribes and their guides would die under the behemoth of an arisen Empire. Many more cultures would crumble under its foot. Without Varuna, these small clans couldn't survive. Alexandria, the last standing column against the Roman Empire, saw its vast library destroyed. A Neymliss would awake in the Middle East, few centuries after Ishtar and you had left Gaia. Following this satori, humanity would rely on ideas concealed within literary work, poetry, to connect with Sophron.

Theocracies would prohibit further wakes from happening, suppressing mancing and glancing. Sophroning would be outlawed and forgotten. Only dancers and fencers remained. Far Eastern Neymlisses would hide inside Buddhist monasteries and Hindu temples. The Western ones would project their own rises onto a legendary representation of the mancer that started their movements. As you watched this humanity from a fair distance, Indra, you thought it would be pointless to even aspire to a revival of the Babel ideal. Tribes and Empires battled to impose views and laws. They did everything to prevent mass awakenings.

And so, you forgot all about these creatures you had grown to cherish and fought to protect. The Greeks you inspired with an Indian touch. The Celtics you carried under your arm. The Norse you loved, despite their taste for violent conquests, ideal missionaries for the new Roman Empire. You trusted that the Sons of Babel left enough of an essence to shine into the buried gnosis of this entire humanity. Let them recall the basics that lead to this greater enlightenment. Recollect, through the fables and legends that retold ancient history, the coming and the departure of these gods and goddesses, the spiritual benefits behind self-renounce and reciprocal admiration. Little did you guess that their animal tendency towards corruptive power would spoil it for you.

Did you remember Marduk's rage, like a mad soul, right after the Sapphire Council pronounced his sentence and enforced the truce? "These spiritual vehicles need to submit to an awakened one, or else they will always let aliens bring discipline and will never know the value of self-abandon and mutual respect." His sermon aimed at the Councils that condemned both him and your mentor. It may have risen as prophetic, since Marduk would have known he would return or never truly leave.

The Councils' Great Entities hardly budged. Left behind with only fragments of memories of a time prior to the fall of Babel, humans scattered around Earth. When they stood as one Entity for a greater good. After that time, when they formed smaller groups that each tried to salvage the little mastery and wisdom left, they would fear or oppose one another to this ideal of a world community you cherished.

The one Marduk despised. They would confuse the core message that, once, existed among all cultures. They mistook it with the fragment they kept within ancient words that only timidly defined their cultural individuality. Stories mean more than essence. Varuna and Marduk were both exiled, after Babel's fall.

Ishtar and yourself, without the presence of Varuna, with Enki also gone, decided to only practice greater altruism. As time went by, you would have counted three thousand years on Gaia, five hundred on Alibastat, you realized that Ishtar had grown more and more distant. You had mutually evolved to the point of seeing this conjoint Entity dream at reach, but she had different ideals.

Gradually, one lack of confidence after the other, the embrace as strong as eternity when you both made it your sole reason to exist and be as one, Ishtar wished to be herself again. She grew melancholic, a poison for any soul that had tasted enlightenment, and searched for her roots. You followed her all over Sophron, until you encountered her in tears, in the middle of a blizzard that painted Sint Holo blank.

She had borrowed the body of a very tall nymph with blue skin and purple flaming shell, under an indigo robe and silver hair. You had the flesh of a fair folk, imposing and passionate, yet reserved and in reflection. She understood you too well not to realize your presence, even if you kept it concealed behind the whitened walls of wind.

84

You knew her too well, aware that she uncovered your hideout. She calmed down, then, and looked in your direction. Did you do it for her? For Emerald? Did you do it for Alexandra? Which one hosts Ishtar's soul? "I did it because my life was pointless without her. It became an existential nightmare, when I was left by myself in that school, and her best friend failed to protect me."

"What about Ishtar? Did you find Ishtar?" he asked.
You looked away and sighed. "I don't know who you are talking about." you answered. Melpomene scratched his chin and proclaimed: "Your glancer should have brought you to her. Unless the two of you join forces, you won't be able to stand up against Marduk and his army."

"Marduk?" you asked. Melpomene closed his eyes and breathed: "Varuna respected his sentence, after losing the Babel Wars, but Marduk rebelled against the Great Council, and left his exile.   He chose to destroy Sophron, and no longer just conquer and enslave Sleepers. He killed an Entity with his bare hands and all his anger. Without Varuna to confront him, Sophron degenerated.   This takes place within a Dreamer above you. When you are ready, I will get you there."

"And how can I find my glancer?"

"When you exit my lair, follow the ways of the Veil. It flows alongside the poet's inspiration. Should your path cross the Author's, you may ask him. I don't know the identity of your glancer, William, but Indra's friend was Tristan. If you find Tristan's essence, you will uncover your man. If you find your dancer, you will unearth your man. If he finds your dancer, he will also unearth you. This is as far as I can be of assistance."

"And who is my dancer? Didn't you die for her?" *Emerald*, you thought. But where is she? Did she perish and then she ended up in this world as well? Does she know really your glancer?

"Show me, oh Great Muse. My destiny." you murmured, in a solemn and grave voice. Melpomene walked towards you, a triangular screen floating around him. He laughed, mildly:

"Your destiny awaits. Please, allow me to display to you the past of this soul that inhabits you. The essence of the one that will ignite flames in this war. Close your eyes, William. Conceive that your name is Indra. You existed thousands of years ago, in the ancient cities of Gaia, now in ruins. You loved Ishtar, and together you built a short-lived empire: The Kingdom of Mitanni."

Marduk loved Ishtar as well. They came from the same people, and they both learned the secrets and magic of Sophron, back in the realm of Nibiru. In his quest to conquer layers and enslave their inhabitants, Marduk found himself in your world, around the time early Mesopotamians and early Indians cohabited. You had vowed, with your mentor and friend, Varuna, to protect this world, you also know as Earth. When Marduk's imposing army arrived on Earth, your pantheon fought day and night to repulse the invaders. One morning, as you approached a splendid lake on which you could bathe, you saw her. The most beautiful being you had ever encountered. She found you as well, and she didn't blush. Ishtar! The strong and emancipated lady warrior.

Second Intermission:
The Student's Homework

When the class ended, Plato signalled the student to stay, while the others would return to their homes. He looked down, as though reflecting on the right words he could use, and then pointed his gaze into the pupil's eyes. "I want you to take the orb with you, tonight." he instructed. "Those characters now live within you. Their story will depend on your feelings, your thoughts, your desires. Do you believe you can continue with the exercise on your own?"

The student felt honoured, and afraid. This humbling request brought some pressure, and they weren't ready to handle such a demanding task.

"Of course, teacher." They bluffed.

Relieved, Plato let them take the crystal sphere and leave. The disciple observed their new toy with awe and apprehension. What if the story they tell isn't good enough for the great philosopher? Sure, you have Seamus who teased William, but he was supposed to protect him. William killed himself, and after that the student isn't sure as to what happened. Should they ask Plato about it? No! Of course not. They must learn on their own.

"Can I ask you a question?" The words came out without your reasonable approval. Plato turned and looked at you.

"Of course. What do you need to know?"

The student thought they heard voices. They stopped for a moment, took the time to recover from this frightening sensation, and wondered: "Will there be an exam tomorrow?" That wasn't what they meant to ask. But it didn't matter. Plato smiled with all the kindness in his world. "This, is your exam."

Chapter Nine:
Old Enemies

Marduk and Varuna were once engaged in the most destructive battle that Gaia had ever been through. You both escaped this violence and vowed to teach humans the ways of peace. You meant to keep tutoring mankind in the values of love, science, and philosophy. You couldn't stay under this warring sky, so you gave this task to the primordial prophet, Prometheus of Olympus. In the course of three thousand human years, Prometheus brought up the now fabled Atlantis. They learned of the various technologies and gifts. Atlantis has known the very first human Walkers.

When Marduk learned that, somewhere on Earth, his slaves were getting as powerful as his men, he chose to sink Atlantis. Varuna stood against him. Zeus, who sided with Marduk, chained Prometheus in the Open Door, a hellish world in the Void-Barbel quadrant. When Ishtar decided to join your fight against her own people, to protect mankind and allow for them to enhance their awakenings, Marduk killed her. This was the cruellest experience the Hound Lord of Nibiru ever lived. Having to kill the one he loved, for the greater good of his ambitions, was more painful than a thousand deaths.

You wandered, lost. Heartbroken. You knew that true vanishing only happens, for enlightened beings when they achieve the Final One. Her spirit, you thought, must have been someplace, in some other layer and, or, some possibility, in some Dreamer. You sought her everywhere! You shouted her name in all languages existing in your soul. She never responded. You visited the Fates, one morning, a hundred years after she departed. They hide in Elysium and share their time between this layer and Hades. To find them, you had to confront Kerberos, the three-headed wolf who feeds on the anxieties of Sleepers. Yours had grown anew, and Kerberos knew. You feared never seeing her again, regardless of which name she'd perceive you as. You worried about spending infinity in time and space without her.

You feared so vehemently. You wrestled the wolf who stood taller than a mountain. You fought with every ounce of desperation that intoxicated your fright. You dislocated his left jaw with a moon you conceived and threw. The canine's claws penetrated your Archeutic axioms, leaving the flesh of this soul you inhabited scarred. The pain you felt did not match the one you carried. Of all the entities, the Fates were the only ones who would know how to find her. And you hurled yourself at the second head, not afraid to die from this Final-Vanishing. You gathered every pixel you could find within your pluriverse and grew to become twice his size. You decapitated his middle head with both arms locked on his neck and your legs' propulsion. He fell and had to retreat, to regrow his lost skull.

You let your adversary escape, while the river of blood collected at your feet formed a new ocean. You kept your eyes shut. Her scent inhabited your nostrils, the same you had searched in every other woman. The one that took you to venture all alone, in Toronto, homeless at fifteen years old. The one that took you back to Montreal to finish your high school, a year later.

"We have a visitor."

90

You felt Clotho's essence growl in a raging whisper. "We never have any visitor." Lachesis replied, like the mother of zephyrs over a quiet plain. Atropos remained silent. As their voices haunted the surroundings, a cave appeared all around you.

You walked into the cave like a spirit, with heavy footsteps that brought their remembrance of life with matter. Stalactites as stalagmites made this wide chamber resemble a grinning demon's mouth. The three ladies had merged with every axiom that comprised Elysium. You knew you couldn't approach them unless you became part of the psyche and axioms they gathered, the essence they weaved, the reality they cut in layers. You stood in front of the Great Sisters in a quest for answers. They simply entwined the pixels with the souls without much of a look at you. Humbled, you genuflected and paid your respect:

"I apologize for my presence."

You solemnly said. They never moved away from their work or even acknowledged you.

"But I come to you as a god in distress."

Clotho's eyebrows showed you a sign of interest. That is if god and distress were words that shouldn't be together without the rise of a concern. Clotho stood as the tallest of the three, looking more like a thread herself, with thin arms and legs, almost like an impossibly skinny skeleton. She had the visage of a horse, with distinctly human features down the nose.

Lachesis seemed very short and fat, a toad, with a head twice the size of her body. She could hardly stand on her tiny feet, and her limbs could never go very far around her. She handles the threads of reality in an almost mechanistic manner. Atropos had more proportionate features. She looked like a sweet grandmother about to bake chocolate cookies, but her face resembled that of a hummingbird.

"I have lost the most precious pearl of my life." You gasped,
they took a deep breath and then you let out: "I need to understand
why someone who was given eternal life would suddenly desire
Final-Vanishing?" They waited for a longer time to answer,
and this nourished even more grief within your soul. You remained
calm and you remained patient. Three hundred years on Gaia
would have passed between your question and Lachesis'reply:

"Until you have felt what she tasted, you will not know.
Until you have savoured what she experienced, you will never
understand." And there she appeared to you as a glimpse of the
Fates' Orb, the blind entities sole sight over the true being
of the Dreamer. Her long brown hair embraced shades of blonde
with hints of mist. She looked at the world with hungry slanted
eyes, filled with a thousand lives over a single strain of wisdom.
Petite and with a white tank top that spelled Ramones in bright red
letters, you couldn't help but notice a floating picture of her, sitting
behind a flash of light. Her thighs wide open showed a fishnet
under a black and red skirt.

Emerald looks professional even when she sleeps. She walked
to tables and either danced or served beers, you could hardly tell.
The image was blurred, once more. You encountered her in
Toronto, William, during that year you spent on the streets.
Was she the one you now seek? How can you meet her again?
Her eyes were focused on the narrowed world around her steps.
You tried to clarify this memory, entangled with Indra's, and with
the blind Fates. All you could think of, however, was Emerald.

"Love songs float in her jazzy gaze." you told Melpomene,
then you added: "Her smile, even when hidden behind a serious
frown, beats the drum of a loud lullaby. Her laughter could destroy
armies in a wake pf absolute cuteness."

High cheekbones that invite the looker's eyes to glide gently from an earlobe, shy behind silks of hair, down to her lips that support the biting of cherries' flesh. A constellation of beauty spots, on and around her nose, forms a Trimurti of quantic beauty. Only this muse beyond all those who gathered the Author's heart could radiate with this light. This magnificence, the one that travels through your eyes, only to tear your heart with reality's butcher knife when you know you will never be with her. This agony reached its truest meaning with Emerald.

"She made you jump?"

Melpomene insisted. The green carpet brought you back. You stared at the dark water that formed his cape. You found yourself on your knees before him. He was like an emperor and held your head up, only so you could see the scars through his pupils. Your wounds. Your sight. You stood up and walked away. You thought, once again, and whispered:

"That was one year ago."

Melpomene grabbed a globe. A perfect sphere, although if you looked at it more closely, you would perceive facets the size of microns. This is an orb made of flawless crystal.

"Perfect attraction never fades, Indra." he said, almost with my voice, almost with yours. "If your suicide were in sync with an ideal universe, we shouldn't be fighting this ordeal. Was your appeal, back then, as unblemished as your realization of a right moment to die?"

He did say suicide. How creepy does it sound when pronounced by someone you could mistake for Conan the Barbarian? Melpomene isn't famous for his diplomacy, but rather for his crude factual statements. Yet, around Sophron, without an awakening you remain invisible. Just the other day, I saw Einstein sell hot dogs in Ephemoria. It's a very fragile layer, not too far from Nirvana, and they make awesome burgers too. Not to lack any respect for Einstein, but this shows just how fame means little in the realms of absolute awakening. To his credit, his essence knows more happiness, there, than it had when the atomic bomb was invented. Einstein's essence of wisdom never lied. And, besides, nobody had ever thought of fast food in that world before.

"She wasn't the one?" you asked. Afraid. He left the orb in your hands. A brain, your brain, with a bullet near the temporal lobe's nucleus, floats in that sphere. Is that your brain? "Where did the bullet come from?" You wondered. Melpomene heard that. The orb heated your palms as it emanated energy. The blue lights that cover it would slowly evaporate, and I savoured the moments.

"I am both your creation and your creator, William." he said these words with a solemn tone. The head you held attracted your gaze. He roamed through the room, while the splendid moth queen seemed to avoid your curious gaze.

"Just as you are the Dreamer of this world and its dream. You will find me in other possibilities, and I will remember you just as I conjure you now." When he walked back, another orb formed itself in the palm of his right hand. He looked through it and then claimed:

"You have much to learn before we can consider yourself awakened, William. Yet, we need Indra fully enlightened. We need you on our side." It felt like a cold breeze went down your spine. "A battle? Is there? Is there a war coming?" you asked the Muse. "Days of darkness are ahead of us."

His response caused you to reflect on your existence. Why are we calling you Indra? Why this Ishtar character comes to you as highly familiar? You cannot recall having met her.

"I'm sorry, my name really is William. I don't know any Indra, except perhaps in Hindu mythology, and I'm Canadian."

"Interesting."

"But if this is true, and if this is my new world, now, then maybe there's something I can do, right?" Melpomene sighed while he summoned a finely chiselled crystal cup and, with an upward movement of his index finger, poured wine out of thin air.

"You just found yourself an unlikely centre of attention, William. You will have to choose a side. And let me warn you that those who side with Void may not like you very much, although some of them are fond of this Indra character." He summoned you a glass of wine. You drank his every word, then looked at Touch who remained motionless on the floor, venerating the great Muse. You observed this mute beauty, at the other end of the room. Sthenele showed you eyes of attraction that left you repulsed.

"I do have some feelings, like."

You attempted to reckon. You tried to produce a memory, and whispered:

"Some feelings, as though I knew who you talked about."

"Ishtar?" he inquired.

"Yes! Yes, Ishtar! From a distant past, I think. I guess I was indeed in deep love with her. This is all I can vividly remember."

Melpomene laughed while he drank. He put his cup away and observed his orb.

"They'll want to break you open like a crab, Willy. They're not interested in you. They just desire the fragment of the essence you hold. If you think you experienced death before, wait until you see what Marduk and Varuna are capable of."

It got you go hummm. I'm kind of happy it did. "What is that. That they're capable of?" You had to ask. Melpomene approached you and Touch. He whispered a few words you couldn't hear or understand. Touch stood up, slowly. He could hardly look at the Muse, so he kept his stare very low. Melpomene kneeled to let his gaze confront the frightened boy's. He laughed so loud, you felt it down your spine, then he allowed his hysteria to impose silence. Touch stood there: as immobile as stone. You can now see the boy shiver.

The Muse put a hand on his head, one on his shoulder, and stripped Touch naked, while every axiom that composed his clothes suddenly vanished. Humiliated, the victim cried. His tears soon became screams of intense pain while his flesh flaked away, summoned out, called to disintegrate, very slowly. You couldn't oppose him, though you wished. You couldn't stop it, and you kind of enjoyed it. The thought of seeing another creature suffer made you feel perverted. The boy howled more. He squealed while Melpomene robbed him of his matter except for a skeleton, a heart, a brain, and vocal cords so he could yell his agony even more while the heart pumped blood and brought oxygen to the neurons.

Melpomene looked at you with questions, and you observed the spectacle, fascinated. With a few more gestures, the Muse further stripped the boy of his matter until he could only retain axioms of life and thoughts. Then he merged all the organs and let them fuse until they became a solid shell. Melpomene held the carcass in his left hand and violently threw it on the floor. You saw a bright light in it. He grabbed the glow that seemed to beat like a heart and showed it to you. With the snap of his fingers, it disappeared. Don't worry. He acts more tragically than sadistically.

He enjoys putting on a show, but Touch's essence gets reincarnated in a same organism, as we speak. The young boy will never remember what just happened. Before long, he will be back on the streets to light the poles of Athanor.

"You have twenty-seven hours to exist. This sounds like your only chance to escape the same ordeal, while whomever catch you will keep the fragments of an essence more valuable than your entire life." He looked at Sthenele who seemed possessed by a desire to touch you. Her muteness made her suffer even more. Melpomene smiled a very sadistic grin.

"You have Marduk who must be making a pact with Archeus as we speak. You'll be safe with us." Melpomene returned to kiss his moth queen, seeing how hurt and terrified she appeared. Tears fell down her cheeks.

"Shhh, now, my queen, shh. You thought it would be easy?"

"What should I do?" you asked. He looked at you and smiled:

"You can't stop the formation of this destiny that wants you either dead to save Indra or have Indra falling into Final-Vanishing to save you."

"But I don't want to die."

"Sure, you don't. You should have thought better while you were alive, Will. Now it's a bit late to have the easy way up. You'll just have to swim among the enlightened powerful beings and pretend you know your path." You'll grow to understand reality, and then perish as planned. Take it as my ephemeral gift to your courage if I allow you to oppose me like this.

"Were you properly introduced to the mechanics of Sophron?"

Melpomene asked, coldly. He won't help you much. "I..."
You stuttered, watching the orb. It opened to a universe of brilliant
colours. Your brain shone in the middle, with the bullet in its
temporal lobe: that was you. A greater dot, around a pellet, stood
not too far from there. Darkness spread quickly. That was me.

"I don't have time to teach you. You should hurry." He sat on
his cape, and it gradually became his throne. Sthenele rested at his
feet and licked them, gently. You would have asked the Muse a
few more questions, but Melpomene was lost in a trance as
Sthenele's hand went to his chest. You felt pressure to leave. You
wanted to stay. You wanted to learn more. You expected
Melpomene to tell you everything. You thought it would come to
you so simple? One of your problems, William: you always had it
easy. You supposed death and rebirth happened as effortlessly as
switching channels on a TV? Did you really? Where are you?
Aren't you suffering? Guess what? I own that remote control.
I can let it last an eternity if I want. Do you find it easy, now?

You checked that crystal ball. It looked back at you. They say
you know a mancer by his orb. Yours doesn't seem very bright.

"I have to locate Emerald." you uttered. As you put the orb
away and walked out of the room.

How many times? "How many times?" Melpomene shouted
from a distance, greatly annoyed. You turned around to see this
lady moth fly in your direction. Something urged you to join her.
And as you observed the other end of the corridor, you couldn't
find a way to the exit.

"How many times have you claimed an infatuation to be your
soulmate?" the Lord asked, calmly. You heard it through the flaps
of Sthenele's wings.

"I know when it hurts."

You said, as you bravely faced the incoming fangs of a moth
queen about to haunt your grief. You didn't have to look at the
other side to know that the exit stretched over a long way ahead.
You confronted the lady-creature, ready to suck your blood.
You smiled. "I died once. You think I'm afraid to do it twice?"

"Come on!" you shouted. And yelled: "I'm not going to fight
back! You bitch! Hurt me, come on! Eat me alive. Make it slow.
Bitch! Tear my flesh apart! Ha! I have seen the worst in worse."

Then time stopped as she landed in front of you. She looked at
you with so much passion concealed within every breath, you
wondered if she meant harm or not.

"So, how have you been?" She seemed to ask you through her
eyes. You remained of stone, suddenly at loss of words.
She examined you with a frightened sight that almost whispered:

I've missed you so much. You have no idea. I miss you, still.
I miss you too much. Then she walked in front of you and guided
you through the exit door. You observed her brown back with
beige stains, some seemed blacker, others appeared whiter.
Her wings covered her entire body. Her breasts prominently
embraced the air with a thirst for milk. Something in her made you
feel quite alive, once. Something, you have no idea what.
What did she try to tell you? It appears her eyes and lack of
apparent mouth could only speak to herself. You followed her and
remembered the old saying: "If you love someone, let go."

And you left the palace, unsure. You thought of her in tears,
but did you really know that she cried?

Journey into the Hourglass: Five

After the enlightened William incident, Martin and I part ways. He couldn't keep up with all the various directions I gave to our many characters. We must keep it simple, Alibast! What are you doing? He would scream at me like a lunatic. "It is simple, what are you talking about?" I confronted him. "We have William on Athanor. Marduk prepares some big invasion. Ishtar looks for her beloved Indra! Now, we have the Great Muses, with Melpomene." I really liked where those intertwined stories were going. *Dude!* He shouted. The name of this book is, drum roll, please.

Seamus Chron!

Oh, yeah! I totally forgot about this one. I wonder if characters evolve on their own if Authors stop looking at them. After all, they have their own existence. Maybe they're like photons. They have their freewill, and they exist in all forms and aspects, until a creator measures the length of their consciousness, and exercises their own will upon them. "Yeah, you're right." I conceded. "I'll check Seamus out." I went to grab my laptop, but Martin wouldn't buy my concession. I'm going home. He announced. "On Gaia?" Yeah! I built myself a nice castle, in the middle of Time Square. "Wow! New York?" He nodded and picked up his things. We kept in touch, mainly through our dream network. In Sophron, these works like Internet, but for awakened souls, connecting every layer, all the worlds.

Chapter Ten:

Regrets and Amendments

I spent an entire day on my bed, looking at the ceiling. William died. Maybe I killed him. I pushed him, I bullied him, he's gone. I attempted to impose myself a state of awakened dream, or sleep paralysis, anything to have Ishtar in front of me. But nothing worked. I kept my room's door locked, and I would only go out to buy weed or eat from the fridge without alerting my parents. I skipped school and my social life. I evaded everyone.

My mom was the least concerned. I would hear her try to discuss the issue of my isolation with my dad, and she would convince him that I was only going through a phase. My father wouldn't buy it. I smoked to recreate the state that awakened my gift, but nothing happened. After two weeks in that self-imposed state of unending highs, paranoia became my only company. Weeks soon turned to months. What got to me? Why am I so wounded? I didn't even know the guy!

I remember seeing my dad standing straight, like an army officer scolding a cadet. I could recollect his small moustache on a frail jaw, his solid eyebrows and square shoulders, a football player turned concerto pianist. "I won't have a junkie living under my roof, do you hear that?" he would shout.

"You have one week to clean up your act or I'm having you detained in a youth centre until you become eighteen." Dad would never say such a thing unless he intended to carry on with his promises. And I defied him as I was forever intoxicated.
I'm waiting for the voices, Dad. I would complain, unsure as to my sobriety status when these words formed themselves in my mouth. I wouldn't dare explain to him the nature of my gift, it would have prompted him to steal my bong for his own use. He would mumble his strong disapproval and shut the door on his way out.
Two months and three weeks passed since the partner I failed to protect chose to leave us. I would easily smoke to the point of delirium, but my powers wouldn't manifest themselves.

Two days had gone by, after Dad made clear he would treat me as a delinquent unless I became a clean and perfect teenager overnight. I would stand up in front of my window and watch pedestrians. I would shut my eyes and pretend I could get into their heads, tap into their lives, see what they see, but blankness roamed all over. While I did so, my smartphone would often ring and vibrate, from underneath my bed. I haven't looked at it for the last month that I wasted in my room. Who cares about such primitive technology when I can connect my mind to the universe's Wi-Fi? In five days, I would be locked in some juvenile prison. For some awkward reason, the anxiety made me perceive the unavoidable event loud and clear. Every moment, every second, at every given instant, I saw myself walking down a long corridor with my belongings in a packsack. At night, this event became vividly real. Was fear the trigger to my powers? Such as when I dreaded Ishtar's strange encounters? When have I worried about the unknown of my mission with William? My dad's promise of locking me up pushed me into anguish. And I knew it would happen. *I might as well spend my last moments with my family high as hell,* I thought. But then, three days before the fulfillment of papa's prophecy, I blanked out.

The blindness felt like an eternity, and my mind had grown numbed to the point of total oblivion. I recall flashes and images, comparable to those I had, when I last successfully performed a connection with my future self. Only, this time, my essence found itself linked to a thousand possibilities, all over the seventy-two layers of Sophron, and through at least a hundred Dreamers and five thousand Sleepers. The amount of information that my brain caught all at once weighed too heavily for my rookie neurons to hold, and my entire mind collapsed. From what I remember, I perceived a black unicorn and a wizard rider. The horse's name was Karkadan. I saw a frog with a cat's skeleton as its conjoint twin, and some sort of floating boat. Another ship, a bigger one, with three living dragon heads in front, flew across the Veil. An entire fleet flew behind it, and this boat belonged to a very dangerous and powerful being. I heard a name, like whispers that some wind blew in my mind: Don't go to Tir na n'Og. For some reason, I felt a strong connection with the cat-frog and his boat, the Barracuda.

I had seen it before, and if it weren't for the numbness that kept me paralyzed, I trust I could make this image clearer, until it becomes my new reality. The captain. I know this guy. He asked me for money in that limbo the other day, and her kept a wasp with him. He seemed different then, with those two animal heads, but the essence remains the same. When I woke up, I was in a small chamber, connected to machines that probed my life signs. My mom sat against the wall, facing my bed. The room had this hospital stench that made me sick, and boredom proved already an issue. I could hardly lift my head. My entire body ached.
"Get more rest, Seamus." my mother softly expressed.
"Your father is coming back soon, he left to eat some snacks."
I meant to apologize for this trouble I had put them through, but I couldn't say a single word.

When my dad returned in the room, holding a coffee cup,
I could sense his profound shame, mixed with some sort of sorrow.
At this point, it was easier for me to connect to my dad's fear and
to his mind than it was for my voice to produce a sound.

"Don't think you'll celebrate your eighteenth birthday home,
son!" he growled. Mom promptly turned to face him, with
disapproval in her eyes: "Arthur!" She melted. He sipped his
coffee and looked down, before adding: "They'll make you follow
a strict regime to quit that habit. It's the only reason I'm having you
attending that youth centre. Break it before it breaks you." He left
the room right after saying these words.

Mom went straight to my side, holding my hand with all the
love a mother felt for her only son. "It's for the best, Seamus. I was
against, but I think it's for the best. It's only three months, after
that, you will be an adult. Please, be a responsible one." She kissed
my forehead, and her fear was all over me. I could see through her
eyes. I felt through her senses. Here's me, pale and naked under a
hospital gown. My lifeless sight lost its gaze over my blue mouth,
lacking blood. I experienced a profound affection coming out of
my mother's soul, as it merged with mine. If I closed my eyes, she
and I would find our conjoined selves in a crystal corridor floating
above a supernova: my own doing. This process allowed both our
psyches to cohabit in the same space. With a twist of my mind,
I could give a certain shape to my mom's essence, so I chose to
turn it into a computer.

I could also mutate myself into any hallucination that could
populate my head, but I had little control over this ability. I ended
up looking like a cockroach on two feet. I walked towards the PC
in a very clumsy manner. In my mind, I felt like Charlie Chaplin
making a movie. In the Author's mind, I was a hyperactive squirrel
impersonating Buster Keaton.

Who cares? I finally found a connection between my gift and my mom's past. Whose author, anyway? That Greek student who looked at me when I got high? They really thought they could escape my gift? Ha! Wait until I get into my mother's womb. Back to where it all started, right? Right. How do we go on the Internet with a Commodore 64?

This cockroach was losing it. The whole hierarchy of music. The who's on top? Who makes the decisions? Who wrote this story? Hold on! I'm stoned. My mom is giving me some affection. Maybe I can hack into this dinosaur of a computer with all six feet on the keyboard. Even the best binary hacker wouldn't stand a chance against quantum computers. Unless. I let go of this illusion. It's all about the essence. I couldn't find Ishtar when she tested me because I tried to. She spoke to me; I should have just listened. And what about my mom? Maybe I could give it a try.

I did. My mom was at her most vulnerable, fearing I could die at any given moment. I tried to get into her mind, like an opportunistic nerd who just realized he could wow a woman. Wow. I think I know William better, now. But hold on. Is my mom crying?

I should have had an abortion. I heard her thinking. Hold on, no way! No! Why don't you tell me how to use a Commodore 64 instead? You would have been better in a different world.
You deserve a better family, Seamus. Mom! Okay, I need to calm down. We're both panicking, so one of us should quiet down those nervous energies.

"Mom." I felt, as I let that smile bring an ounce of peacefulness. "Mom?" I asked. She looked at me with tearful eyes. She grabbed both my hands with so much vigour, I thought she wanted to tear my wrists off my arms. "Yes, my love?" she responded. I took some time to ponder, and then I asked: "Did you have a Commodore 64 when you were little?"

Her brother did, of course! Uncle Jonathan is a forever virgin who only lives for computers! Okay, so I found the connection. She loves her brother like a second father. He could never find the right words. And he never had the muscles to protect her, but his heart was always at the right place. And I was a cockroach! I could access videos showing her childhood, her adolescence, or easily sneak into more hardcore stuff, with my dad, but I kind of refrained from going there. A channel appealed to me. I read: "Wicca" under the file. When I retrieved it, I could see images of my mother, between the age of thirteen and twenty-five, dressed like a witch in harmony with nature, practicing incantations to summon greater forces.

In this video I gathered significant interest in, Mother was with three other friends of hers. All the ladies wore goth clothes. A pentagram stood in the middle of a forest, with lit candles all around it. I heard chants in a strange language, before they all cut their hands with a razor blade and let blood stain the base of bigger candles. The wind caressed the leaves, then a burst teased the fire, before dying at their feet. Silence came soon after. The flames turned into bright lights that rose above the four girls' heads until it expanded to become a second sky. Forms danced against that new firmament, and I could tell that they had just summoned the Veil to surround them. On the other side, above their skull, a different world exists, perhaps Duat or Hades. At this point, my cockroach self-understood more about this phenomenon than my mother ever had or ever will, although it seemed like more intuitive knowledge from my part. A ghost appeared in the middle of the pentacle. The spirit projected a feminine shape, with a blue light that emanated from its core. *Ishtar*, I thought. I quieted this realization as I observed the video further. Then, the trees around my mama and her friends changed colours, looking more like purple, blue and yellow plastic plants. The ghost approached my mom and extended a hand towards her:

"Justine Pascale-Grégoire, daughter of Armand Grégoire and Viviane Pascale." Ishtar almost chanted. My mother froze on the spot. The vision continued:

"Five years from now, you will give birth to a great hero, savior of worlds. The Four True Entities of Sophron decided his path. Protect him, for malevolent forces will want him dead. Protect him, for beneficial forces will also want him dead. I want him to live and fulfill the destiny of the Beyond."

The spirit vanished right before touching my mother's forehead. Her three friends looked at the scene in disbelief. The Veil soon disappeared as well, leaving my mom and the witches alone in a spooky forest. They all observed one another, promising never to say a word about this.

When I opened my eyes, I felt an inner serenity that was beyond any peace I had ever experienced. I caressed my mother's cheek, and she could clearly see sparks in my sight. I smiled and kissed her hand, as she fondled my cheek in return. She smiled, and then I whispered: "You never told me." I was weak, and it pained me to utter these words. Waiting for her response felt like an impossible burden.

"Told you what, my love?" she replied.

"Magic, Mom. When you were my age, you did magic. -- Ghosts." Her face turned pale.

"Seamus? What are you talking about?"

"It's okay, Mom. The blue lady. I saw the blue lady."

She cried, either fear, terror, or joy. Her essence clearly felt conflicted. It all came back to her, and she must have know that this day would arise, sooner or later. She tried so hard to convince herself that her friends and she collectively hallucinated the whole scene. After the group stopped seeing each other, Mom forced onto her the idea that she imagined this event. She hugged me so tight, my aching muscles hurt like crazy. The following morning, I received the visit of Alexandra and Victoria. I must have regained some energy, as I spent the rest of the day, after my parents left, and the entire night after meditating, but the numbness remained. I could hardly speak without losing my breath. Victoria stopped at the door and looked at me with tears in her eyes. I could feel a great deal of fake in those tears. My immediate reaction would have been asking her if she cries because she craves her popular pseudo-boyfriend by her side. A genuine sadness floats, somewhere, beyond her troubled ego of a crazy lady. Perhaps if she had been in better control of her narcissistic passions, I could have fallen for her. Or maybe if I hadn't been such an asshole myself.

"I miss you, pumpkin pie." She smiled, as she rushed herself to kiss my forehead, my cheeks, my scalp again, stopped at my lips because I just had to turn my head. I tried to make eye contact with Alexandra, but she looked away.

"Hey you." I let out, but Alexandra exited the room. Victoria hugged me so hard, I sighed and almost vomited on my pillow. "Why did you try to kill yourself with drugs?" Victoria asked me. "I didn't! It was the pot!" I told her. "Oh, stupid, is it because of William?"

"I didn't try to kill myself!" I insisted.

"But all the kids at school they say you did, and some claim you were secretly in love with William, and this is why you skipped class after he died. Is it true? Are you gay?"

"No, Victoria! I have superpowers. I attempted to trigger them with pot, so I could find William, and tell him that a ghost lady wants me to protect him, so we can travel through space and time to save a bigger universe."

"You are gay?" Her frightened eyes made her look so cute.

"Yes, Victoria, yes. I am a homosexual sorry if I, just now, tell it to you like this."

"It's okay! I'm bisexual, maybe we can work something out."

"I need to speak to Alexandra."

"She doesn't want to talk to you. She just gave me a ride."

"Tell her it's important." Alexandra erupted in the room at that point. She listened the whole time. She looked at me, and I could see she grieved. I could sense that we both did, for the same soul. I closed my eyes to project my feeling into her, and she cried. I did as well. "Can you leave us alone?" I asked Victoria. She nodded and left the bed. She sat on a solitary chair, while Alexandra stood next to my face. "Hey!" she welcomed me with.

"I know you dream about him." I told her.

"How do you know?" she inquired. I looked at her and I smiled. Her grief opened a door to her soul and her memories. "You dream that you find yourself in the ambulance, and he dies in your arms. You two talk about me, and you try to make him forget that I even exist." She cried and grabbed my hand.

She ushered: "I have that same one every night. Every time it happens, I pray the angels, sometimes the demons, so that he hears me. He should feel me. We both must !" I kissed her hand and I whispered: "He is still alive. I know, and I'll find him."

Three days later, I was dismissed from my hospital stay and welcomed into a maximum-security facility for troubled teenagers. A long and white corridor stretched open. I had nothing but my packsack to carry. Even though I wore my favourite jeans and my Morbid Angel t-shirt, I felt naked, or dressed in a prisoner uniform. I walked to my room in a slow fashion, trying to calm myself, so as not to connect my gift with all the wounded souls that surrounded me. Two guards took me to my chamber, a very small one with no TV. I present you my *solitary confinement*, as they put it. I had to stay there and reflect on the reason why I would finish my adolescence in jail. Every morning, I would meet with a counselor, a man in his late fifties, almost bald, with huge glasses, and dressed like a hippy psychologist. "Do you know why you are here?" he asked. I kept silent. I knew this was not where I belonged. He would insist:

"Do you assume you are ready to act like an adult?" I would look at him and spit: "What's an adult?" He would calm down and replace his glasses, before inquiring:

"What do you think will make you work well with others, when you have a job, when you have finished your school?"

"Magic !" I rushed him.

He sighed and scribbled some notes. He observed me and waited a bit before formulating his next question: "Why did you confine yourself in your room to smoke pot?" I looked at him and asked: "How else can I save the world?"

"You want to save the world, Seamus?" I was passed his series of queries, they annoyed me. I went as blunt and clear, as frank and honest as I could, I looked at him again, and I stated the obvious: "If the Greater Dreamer dies, we all do. Marduk and Varuna act as agents of Void and Archeus, respectively, they both think they can protect the Beyond. How wrong they are. I need to find my friend, and Nempty, so we can build a team that will oppose the two of them, in their millennial war, but we are weak, and I guess this is why I smoked pot."

Bernard, as I recall, I never cared to remember his last name, observed me with a funny smile.

"We have a poetry and literature club, and we also allow our visitors to play Dungeons and Dragons, would you like that?" *Yes, I would like that, of course,* I thought to myself. I sighed and looked away. Back in my room, I realized that I could easily connect my essence to any random inmate's and make my own movies. The first couple of nights, I would try to find a sexually wounded girl, and picture the events that brought her to rebel. It ended up far too monstrous for me to keep up with this. I kind of assumed that most youths in this building were heavily hurt, and it further enforced my decision that I just didn't belong here. I had to leave, escape, somehow, somewhere, maybe being held in this crappy place could allow me to practise my gift, though.

I had to find myself in such a state of calmness that I could connect my psyche with others' suffering without letting it lose my cool. I tried with Gwen, first. I saw her, this morning, at the cafeteria. She was molested by her grandfather when she was five. A successful banker who had millions in estate to promise his two sons and two daughters. This garbage of a creep kept dark secrets. Gwen's mother was also sexually assaulted by her egotistic daddy, but she left the family to live poorly.

She only returned after becoming a single mom and heard of the vile patriarch's cancer treatments. She wanted what was best for her girl, and the monster didn't disinherit her for parting from the family when she turned sixteen. When her mom learned about Gwen's aggression in the hands of that perverted piece of shit, she was left with two choices: Either she denounced him to higher authorities, or she convinced her daughter to go along with it. Normal, it's okay, the troubled mom chose the path that brought Gwen here. As for grandpa, the violence she unleashed, with a butcher's knife, onto him left deep scars and fragile lungs.

111

I located her room, at midnight, as I travelled from one essence to the next until I recognized certain patterns, and elements of her story. She was visited by the same nightmare. Always that   of a fat man eating her from inside, topped by a picnic where the grandfather would appear naked, and all the family would look away while he forced himself on her five-year-old body. At thirteen, now, I sensed the wounded fiver would remain all her life. Whenever the bastard would enter her dreams, it felt like when I saw Nempty's boat in my blackout. I could just summon myself in and I just don't know how.

The following morning, I waited for her at the cafeteria. She would always sit alone and eat her breakfast without looking at others. She reminded me of William. I would observe the scene and take notes, it would often end up with Sabrina at her table, throwing Gwen's bowl of cereals to the ground. Why are there so many jerks in this world? Gwen was being pushed towards her self-hatred, I sensed. Sabrina just wanted to feel alive.

The following night, I connected myself to the bully's universe. When still a baby, her dad left her mom. Her mother could never find a job outside of the sex industry, and Sabrina always dreamed she would grow to become an astronomer, someday. Seeing her junkie guardian sniffing drugs and please clients, often three at the same time, scared her.

She wanted Sabrina to learn at a young age that sex was good. She just had to master her inner resilience, her attractiveness, so she could earn money by promising old men with a feeble spirit that they could fall in love with her. It disgusted Sabrina to no end, so she took that frustration away on weaker girls, at school. She couldn't understand how her mom would find actual pleasure in this world of total depravity. She thought that her mom created a strong persona to conceive her suffering in the eyes of rich clients with fantasies of abuse and dominance. I realized that Sabrina and Gwen shone as two extremities of a same string. And I always wanted to be alive.

When Bernard welcomed me to his office, a month after I first entered this facility, two after the other end of my thread died, I attempted to bring these stories to him, but he wouldn't listen. He would still assume that I imagined everything I shared with him. If I tried to shake him up with a revelation out of his own secrets, I failed, every time. The man was obviously at peace with his life, and with all around it. No pain, no suffering, damn! No gossip for me.

"Did you want to ask me a question?" Bernard inquired. I froze! *Don't go to Tir na n'Og!* I heard, but I had to shake it away, and I dared: "How can you be so calm when surrounded with so much agony?" He drafted some notes and thought for a long moment. He smiled, looked at me, and wisely uttered:

"Seamus, you make your own agony."

Three months went by since we learned of William's death. I just turned eighteen. My parents waited for me at the exit. I had my packsack in my arms, and that hellhole at my back. I was ready to move on.

I arrived home and could hardly face my father. Everything in this house made me feel fear and grief, fear of the unknown, what happened to their only child? Grief of the past they must leave behind. I couldn't confront my mother, she just kept silent, stuck between defending me in front of the love of her life, and reprimanding me, to avoid hurting her marriage. When I got to my room, that night, I felt like returning to my stoner times, so I could go through another day with my conflicted parents. I didn't have a job, so I couldn't just move out and find an apartment. I couldn't wait in this environment. I couldn't exist in this polluted habitat. My own fear grew to such an extent, I connected with my inner universe, and it created strong feedbacks. I felt as though I could end my world in the blink of an eye. I couldn't breathe in this state of pure chaos. I had to leave, I had to stay in the streets for some time, until I could restructure myself, get on my feet. But the mere idea of nesting in the boulevards frightened me as well.

"You are afraid to live your life, agent of Archeus." I recognized that voice. I could sense her presence, but since she wasn't the cause of my fear, I didn't feel paralyzed. I just looked at the end of my bed, and I saw her blue light shine. She observed me and smiled. "You missed me?" she asked. "That gift is getting out of control." I replied. "It's time I gave you some teaching."

She put her hands together and created an orb, perfectly balanced and floating between both of her palms. My eyes were so focused on that enigmatic object, I didn't realize that my room turned grey. *This is a limbo*, I thought. "Yes, Seamus. But not our final destination." I looked around again and trees as tall as mountains surrounded us. The soil resembled liquid, but whenever we would put our feet on a certain spot, it transformed into, I don't know, it was hard for me to assess, but I would say spongy dirt. The sky would switch from cloudy to sunny in instants, depending on where I would lay my eyes on. I tripped on a rock, and when I looked down, the stone grew wings, and an angry face without a mouth. It quickly flew away, then let the wings vanish, and it fell to become a stone once more.

I gazed in front of me, unsure if any of this came from a dream or a hallucination. For the record, I have remained sober for three months, minimum. And I know I didn't fall asleep, so this was real.

"You are in Lemuria, Seamus." I heard Ishtar's voice, but I couldn't see her. "I am one layer away from you, either on Litooma or on Athanor. You have until sundown to locate me."

"Or what?"

"This is a simple task, given how developed your gift must be right now." Sundown? How can that happen on a world where the weather has no apparent order or form, or anything? "I need to connect to someone's fear, or it doesn't work!" I shouted. Silence! "Ishtar?" hush, then I thought, for no reason, about how I would make a girl fall for me.

Victoria did rather easily, especially after I ignored her, after having spent some time complimenting her, making her draw some rushed-to conclusions that I would neither confirm nor deny. It all operated in her own imagination, and as long as I wouldn't step in to interfere with the world she would create around us, she would either find herself in love or frightened. I liked to think   she was genuinely in love, like Eugenie, the poster girl for our school's chess club.

She was drop dead gorgeous. Yet she decided she would live a happy existence as a single, and young feminist, woman. She hung out with the rejects to learn board games with the nerds, perform at it, and work towards her ambitions as an attractive intellectual. I know that none of the geeks ended up in her bed, and that must have provided her some insurance. But as the perfect count Valmont that I was, I played the dangerous liaisons and I won, only to send all the nerds in that club pictures of her giving me a blowjob. *Sundown*, I thought. I looked around me and saw nothing but tall black and purple trees. Perhaps this realm was connected to my inner version of Lemuria. Maybe all these layers forming what we call Sophron are all intertwined, and this is how I manage to peek into worlds of complete strangers.

I link with my own, and I find a domain we both share. At that given moment, and from there I open the Veil and feel that Dreamer's entire life, makes sense. How would this theory of mine, if correct, could allow me to locate a ghost? "I'm not a ghost, Seamus!" I know, but work with me, Ishtar. This world is linked to my perspective, but it has a truth of its own. If I observe the firmament and see clouds, it doesn't signify that the actual sky is hazy. When I looked at Eugenie and meant to speak words she would enjoy, I would do it to build trust. That demands time. I had to play the detached essence who would give a "whatever" when the timing asked for it. I must become the attached soul when I felt she needed some approval to her own narcissistic quest at becoming the most perfect feminist out there. Sundown doesn't happen until I say so! And Ishtar, you are in Athanor!

"Why am I in Athanor, love?"

"Because I declared it." The whole world melted before my eyes. We returned to my room, and I saw the blue spectre staring at me with desolation in her face. I must have been the worst student she ever had to deal with. My quarters didn't change, it was as though all of this only lasted five seconds. Ishtar approached me and looked down. I felt a bit confident, mostly afraid.

"We never left Gaia, you can't tell if an essence parted from the world it was in." Yet, we moved.

"Seamus, you did. I brought you to another dimension, that's all I did." But you said.

"So, what if I said? Seamus, you have too much life that needs to be dealt with before you can get the first glimpse at even thinking you earned enlightenment. I'm not about to teach you this. You must decide right here, right now, what it's going to be."

She vanished as she came, as always, leaving me alone. The reality didn't change from last time. I kept the fear to face my parents and I felt frightened to confront my demons. I wasn't ready to look for William. I already failed him once, and I can't fail him again. I examined my room's door, as I heard my begetters arguing about my fate. If I open the door, I will find myself in the middle of a divorce. If I stay in my quarters, I will discover nothing but reasons to contact my drug dealer. My only way out was through my window. Living my life meant roaming the streets. I could always find money and get enough to rent an apartment.
I would call my parents once I settled, and I found my independence. I'm an adult, after all. I can work, I can survive, and I have a gift, a superpower! That will help me like nothing else.
I opened my window, and I grabbed the last pocket change I had left on my table. If I outlive this night, I will be fine. I walked.

Chapter Eleven:
Marduk Visits the Fairies

Assembling an armada to visit House Sekhmet of Tir na n'Og wasn't an easy task. Hundreds of captains shouting orders. Thousands of lieutenants, for hundreds of thousands of soldiers, disposed to fight at the Great Warlord's instructions. This is how Marduk conducts diplomacy: talk with the biggest gun in his hands. His own personal warship is known as the greatest among all Houses. In one corner of the assembly platform, thirty special agents get ready to storm in the silence of the night. They are called: *The Squall Squad*, recognizable by the black uniform they wear.

Their mancing division is made of five powerful spellcasters, with tiny orbs on their fingertips, with which they can coordinate axioms and summon creatures in a highly agile fashion. Five glancers always support the mancers. Ten deadly dancers practise advanced martial arts that they blend with their gift of Veil manipulation. Ten fencers controlling the Ether, within the Veil, complete the force. Marduk is also known for having the most impressive army of biomechs that anyone has seen. A biomech is a synthetic organism, sometimes a mix of biotechnology and cybernetics. Some will bear artificial flesh, muscles, and bones. Most lack a functioning brain, however. Theirs is made specifically for hosting a soul that exited its body. A skilled mancer will manipulate pixels within the world he or she inhabits to design an item, a beast, or an energy.

A master mancer, such as Marduk, will summon axioms from layers and import them to his location, creating objects or creatures, or some complex phenomenon.We can't conquer a realm based only on this gift. Having a weaponized army and the right vehicles to transport it becomes handy. The largest spectre boat in his fleet was nicknamed: *The Layer Killer*. Its actual name was the Nomicon. As massive as an average city, it could even provoke eclipses, on certain worlds. Its front is shaped like a cigar, with three immense dragon skulls pointing out of holes. One such skull would cover an entire neighbourhood, and legends have it that Marduk destroyed these beasts himself, in the realm of the Open Door. Others argue that Varuna did the feat when Marduk tried to invade Heliopolis, and that would mark the time when the Sumerian god decided to jump into the technological age.

The Layer Killer is so huge, it is almost impossible to map its exterior, and get a description of its shape. If the front resembles a cigar, the back is sculptured like a diamond with immense wings. Also, there is an actual government, and a population, existing within the ship. Its sole purpose was to maintain it, repair when needed. Alterations to its shape vary from time to time. It does too from one administration to the next. The overall people of this ship were well over three million souls, most of them belonging to Marduk's army or private guards. Marduk didn't like the name Layer Killer. He called his dear possession Venus, because it reminded him of Ishtar, the love of his life. Right after Venus, you had two lesser spectre boats, Yuan and Gong, with populations of half a million each. Five thousand house-sized vessels stand behind them, with fifty passengers.

Inside the Layer Killer, we uncover a vast complex of corridors and chambers. At first sight, we could almost compare it to a hive with thousands over thousands of rooms. They were annexed to one another via a maze-like system of tunnels, secret paths, bridges. It is impossible to find our way to the biggest space, the Lord's apartments, from anywhere.

To get there, the visitor needs to access a pocket dimension that only Marduk can enable. Once in it, however, we may witness the most amazing spectacle that technology and spellcasting can provide. At the far end of the room, a giant screen acts as a window, showing what the three dragon skulls could see. The ship itself is being navigated and controlled by ten airmen, in a different chamber. Marduk can, at any time, grab the wheel, so to speak, from a gigantic chair. Several wires float above and around it, waiting for the Lord to sit and order the living cables to connect with his mind. He may then upload his conscience, as he would do if he wanted to drive a biomech and pilot the entire vessel on his own. Nobody comes close from bettering him at soul-maneuvering. Marduk's archoid, Humbaba, has made quite a stellar reputation. While battling in an archoid-arena tournament, Humbaba demolished over forty opponents at the same time. Humbaba is an archoid capable of performing spellcasting.

These biomechs have psyches of their own, and only allow specific other consciousnesses to share their space. Humbaba also interacts with Marduk's secret chambers, standing tall next to an indoor waterfall. It turns into a river that flows across the room and returns as the same waterfall through a mind-blowing optical illusion-like sculpture. White with bestial features, the biomech resembles a yeti, with three pairs of condor wings attached to his back. Laser canons and torpedoes are fixed to both arms. As with many archoïds, the rockets, biological missiles and bullets are generated by the mechanoid's organs.

Marduk stood in front of the gigantic screen, examining his platform, while everybody busied themselves with putting up together a vast army, ready to fly away. While it remains impressive, it only constitutes one tenth of Marduk's entire military. And as he contemplated his force, a familiar face appeared on the monitor.

Sekhmet, with her panther-like features, harbouring a pharaoh's crown, looked at Marduk and snarkely smiled: "I was told you wanted to pay me a visit. Why would you need all this force? We are not at war."

"We have located Indra's essence. This arsenal is merely for self-defence, or protection, call it as you will."

"You have just found Indra? Marduk. I have been on his case since young William was born."

"Concealing such information from your closest ally?"

"You had nothing of interest to provide in exchange. I am glad you found out his whereabouts by yourself." Even if he wanted to hide his frustration, Marduk's silent growl became apparent behind his aggressive frown. Sekhmet added: "There is no need for you to come to Tir na n'Og, Marduk. Please, stay in Nibiru."

"I will accept orders from no one, friend or foe. For our alliance to continue, I will ask for your cooperation in capturing this William individual and handling him to me. We sail in three days, and I would recommend you not to convince me to turn this diplomatic envoy into an invading faction. Otherwise, Tir na n'Og will not be the only layer I will conquer next. Duat will also be on my plate."

"You threaten like a true emperor, dear friend. Please, be my guest. I will throw a welcome party for you, in Arcana."

"My presence, Sekhmet, shall be kept secret. I have already set a plan to lure the rat to your place."

"And I have means of insurance. I am not your common idiotic house cat, Marduk. The threat you pronounced against me has been duly noted." Sekhmet's image disappeared from the screen. The warlord observed, once again, his minions getting ready to deploy and travel through the Veil. Next stop: Tir na n'Og.

Chapter Twelve:
William Visits the Naked Truth

A flock of flaming crows circled your moves, ready to dive and bite off your liver, were you to find yourself handcuffed to a rocky cliff. You kept on, with each step further conquered until the streets were no more. There was scorched grass, maybe a field or a valley. Perhaps a garden or a forest, you could never tell with all this obscurity. The murders of dark phoenix gathered more and more above your head. They covered the sky with absolute blackness. Their incessant laughter smothered the sound of your agony.

Your cautious steps felt real. Where will they take you? I could hint you on an imminent threat, a danger unlike anything you have ever endured before, but that would bear no fun. I still need my own entertainment. Now, watching you suffer amuses me. Blind. I see you blind. You stretch your arms and wave your hands around, in every manner possible and to all directions knowable, and. Oh? Did you panic? Or was it a surge of adrenaline? Maybe both, but. I don't think you are ready to die. Hey! You will, on all levels, how funny is that? Very funny, Mr. Void. Why, thank you, Mr. Void. Anytime, buddy.

One more step, careful, I need to be careful. This one you kept it in the air. You first tried to grasp something with your hands. And showed up, from the other world, your previous home, a cold object that pierced you through your brain to allow liquids to flow out. And came, almost instantly after, a huge cloud of oxygen that filled your lungs. The dark as absolute whiteness, no better for your immediate total blindness.

The crows died, some managed to become flaming doves; you still couldn't perceive anything around you, except, maybe, blinding flashes. A cloud blackened your sight. Some transparent grey, some beige, left you disoriented. Stars hit your mind like needles. Numbed! Your head hurts, but it's numb. You can hardly see, you can't have any sensation, and yet you know what's going on.   You can hear cars that move fast on one side. The sounds of larger trucks followed them. You can feel your skull completely turned to the right, a perfect ninety degrees, yet you could breathe, that's a miracle by itself. God wants you to live! Why don't you?

The intense white gradually faded to grey. And the pitch blackness won't take over. For this next segment of your odyssey, you forced yourself to see in black and white. A war movie, how ironic. Your ghost wanders in Baghdad, a reflection of the devastated capital, only this city is in your head. Buildings hardly stand as they used to. Some are in ruins; others barely stand under a crumbled roof. Bodies of dead children cover the streets. Mothers in tears hold on to the corpse of their lost ones. You float around that sight of despair like a remorseful spectre because you know you made it happen. You left them so you could live with Ishtar. The truce never mentioned you, Indra! You could have further pushed the imminence of world peace inside a corrupt politician's mind.

You could have inspired humanism as to let it take over theocracies and failed democracies. Why did you choose the love of a single soul more than that of a creation?

122

Leaders who decide these wars, and who count collateral casualties as mere numbers, think in much the same manner you did when you premeditated that jump, William. Only the immediate outside matters. The rest doesn't exist. What we don't understand or suddenly experience leaves us unscarred.
Still, reality stood a chance. It did for someone just like you, whom you knew, who loved you, who only now shall see how difficult life is if, in lieu of you, questions subsist.

"Hollows!"

You heard a father scream. This is not Baghdad, only the burned-down city of Self-Grief, a few kilometres from its sister village. When you turned around, you saw five flying hydras, or a hollow version of the mythical creature. They each displayed seven heads, all black. They spat fire or a highly flammable venom. One landed on a tall skyscraper, teared all the floors it could grasp, and ate the nymphs and every muse it could find.
It left nothing but blood and guts drip down its seven mouths. You materialized yourself just as this other one was about to engulf your ghost. You could barely react.

You just stood there. You waited for the teeth to rip your head off. The beast approached quietly. It looked at you, then at itself. Silence. The hydra ran towards you, as if your connection wanted to be tamed. You moved aside. You didn't see the warrior, a male with a muscled torso and huge arms, dead. The monster walked forward, as its seven craniums merged into one, and it strolled slowly. It spat flames in a sneeze, ejecting air and fire through its nostrils. The reptile's feet and body also embraced the form of a nightmarish horse. The animal stood humbled in front of you. The whole village now observed the scene, perplexed, not sure if they should fear you more or praise your presence. The muse, or nymphs, who could tame a hollow. The beast of oblivion approached even closer.

You walked backward, only to stumble over the carcass of the warrior nymph, dressed in tight leather pants and a metallic coat that espoused its skin perfectly. You lost balance and fell.
Your hand hit the corpse's back. The light that your palm emitted soon covered the cadaver's entire body, and life was breathed into the male nymph once again. He woke up, as you had, earlier, and he shouted.

"Ishtar!"

Just as you once did. He stood up and ran away. That little miracle brought you the whole village's attention. You could almost hear the air filtered through whispered words of amazement and awe. You sat on the ground, then. The four other hollows joined the scene. They circled you. You couldn't move anywhere. Five horses that now looked like pitch-black unicorns put a leg down, as if in a respectful genuflection.

Their heads were down, their noses touched the ground. As you slowly arose, the five beasts combined into one. It was difficult to say if they ate one another or if they mated, or simply merged like drops of mercury on a mirror. The animal that faced you shared its height with Mount Everest's. You would have thrown a lance into its skull, and it would have done nothing to prevent it. The beast lowered its head to meet yours. Slowly, gently, you put your hand on its forehead, near the immense lonely horn that shone in pitch-black. You have encountered her before. A female.

She comes from far away in your childhood, the earliest days of your infancy. A time long before you could be exposed to speech, the voices of others. As your grammar, it consisted of only one word: "Om." Certainly, Indra, you recall Karkadan.
The animal flew away. A sandstorm built under its feet, as gigantic wings sprung out of its back and it painfully whipped the air, repetitively, until it could ascend or float towards the sky.
Stones followed it. They formed clouds and cloaked the beast.
Peace finally settled in Self-Grief.

124

The audience that gathered down the streets, survivors, elderly people, mothers, fathers, children, sang a welcoming roar for the saviour. You felt them all in you, as a part of you. When the chants, the tears and shouts of victory reached a peak, you sensed the most desolated you have ever been in all your life, the one prior, the one within, the one without. Seeing how none awaits after. And you rejoiced as the hero at the heart of his present life's most beautiful day. How can your loneliness remain that pronounced? Your lungs hurt. The light that surrounds you, as it seems, appeared more electrical and less natural. You walked away from the audience, you ignored them, and you focused on your wounded lungs. Someone, a voice tried to awaken you far from this world.

"Can you hear me?" you heard. "William?" You heard again. You knew that voice. "Say something, please, please, buddy. Say something!" A growl rumbled. It was as if it came from you, but you hadn't felt this type of life in the longest time. As if you could pump the air in and it would allow your speech to embrace the wings of sound waves and be carried into the mind of another, merge with that mind's voice. You growled, yes, it was you.

"I'm sorry."

You heard. The high path. An ambulance. The face of someone you hadn't seen in forever. "How." you stuttered, as you borrowed the same lungs to project a mutilated oration.

"How is Seamus?" you uttered again. You couldn't quite distinguish the visage that looked at you. As if you could perceive her soul better than her matter. You could hear an ocean of pain thrown out of her tall self. More storms, more stones, more sand, more wind, more wounds. You calmed down and tried to breathe. You could clearly see two men working hard to keep you alive, and you could feel a hand holding yours. If you pushed yourself in this world, you would sense Alexandra in tears.

"Who cares about this asshole?" She shrugged. "Okay, talk to me, okay? How are you? What happened to you? Why did you do that? Okay, talk to me, talk."

And came the end of it. In an instant, you were back in Self-Grief. You walked on a huge boulevard that stretched far into the horizon. *Those cubic houses scattered on both sides could shelter a family of rabbits,* you thought. You came across a few that seemed like immense specimens, like a palace, most of them black. Some went for the shades of grey.

The street took you to a tiny club, almost a cave carved within a square, or two pyramids joined by their base. It stood on one of those peaks. The entrance also matched that summit against the soil. The discotheque's sign was mirrored on the ground, like lights that came out of the cube's own shadow.

Systems of Belief written in intense red and purple letters. Platonic Strip Joint written underneath. A platonic strip joint? What does that do, anyway? A place where only the truth gets naked? You entered the cave through the very narrow stairs. They took you down, down, to hell, perhaps, but down. Farther down, laughs flew to your ears, first. Then murmurs. And music, someone played an Andy Williams' classic on a piano and strings, as if the crooner personified an opera singer. A techno beat supported the chant in the background.

Silence. Torches lit you the way. Their aura fornicated with the shadows produced on the wall of bricks and moss. Before long, the stairs you left behind were ancient memories of a legendary sun, with its nonexistent light. You reached the first floor, near the centre of the Earth, and heard cheerful laughter. Wasn't hell a place of endless torments? Why happiness? Torches seemed to provide the only source of sight, even as you passed through a curtain of prayer beads and rosaries, as if someone decided to conceal this joy under chaplets and repeated blessings.

126

There, people chained to the walls. Priests hid behind television sets through which the prisoners could watch nicely chiselled shadow puppetry performed. They all saw the same theatre but benefited from different angles. You had, thus, Catholics on one side, Orthodox on the other, Protestants, yet, on a separate rampart. They felt happy for as long as they could share the same illusion.

As you walked towards the middle of the room, the place shifted. The walls merged and stood behind you. In front, nothing existed beyond smoke and light. There, a different audience discussed the new theatre they watched. What made the smoke and how did it become a screen? How they could use it to perfect the shadow puppetry that kept people numb and happy. Perhaps a new form of television could be developed.

Still, for them, the sun bore ancient history and its glow became legendary. This smog was all there had ever been, that barrier, and the laser that drew shapes and brought lives within it. Past the smoke screen, you saw a wider room. Only those without chains could access this hideout: The bar. Tables full of drinks, beer, wine, and ashtrays packed the place. Shadows sat behind blue fog, at each table, and watched the ongoing performance. Some chat with their peers. Nymphs sat among muses, a few souls and spirits, scarce shifters, one interesting crowd.

A stage opposes the fourth wall. It seemed as non-existent as the other three, at the far back of the room, where philosophers
and scientists were still closely fixated onto the smokescreen and lasers. The rock band that performed on the scene must have come from a sci-fi film. Look at the filiform singer, a black worm with blonde hair that covered his tiny face. He wore jeans and a leather jacket, and he held on to the microphone as if about to eat it, slowly. He danced suavely, smoothly, and seduced the crowd with his other four hands that moved all over his body. His lead guitarist appeared like a small beefy elf, almost a dwarf with pointy ears.

He played on a human spine and a waist three times larger than him. He held a fat instrument, curved, like a harp, with bones of a giant and seventy-two cords. Let's call it a harp guitar, although, over here, they call it Rumi's rose thorn. The piano took the whole background. You would have numbered three hundred and fourteen trillion one hundred and fifty-nine billion two hundred and sixty-five million three hundred and fifty-eight thousand nine hundred and seventy-two keys. If you could count that fast. The huge circular piano monopolized most of the scene. It stretched from wall to wall.

Maybe a lesser entity, or a reflection of myself, still the player had nothing but void to fill his entire being. The piano's music was what gave it a form. One that changed, adapted itself, evolved, devolved, all the time into a complex dodecahedron. At times you would see a fruit worm at other times, a caveman, a rockstar, a metal god. It was me all the time. You sat behind the only vacant table you could find. A vixen of a Ki-Rin lady materialized herself next to you. Her cleavage prevailed to her low and quiet speech, as you had no idea someone had asked you a question.

"I'm sorry?"

Was your instinctive answer. She cleansed her throat and repeated: "Hi! Welcome to System of Belief, a platonic strip joint, can I take your order, please?" Confused, and with no menu at hand, you ordered: "Can I have a beer?" A beer. Here, William. Sure. "I'm sorry." she replied. "But you will have to be more specific." Do you know how many kinds of alcoholic beverages your world has? Times it by as many keys you'll find on my piano, and you'll start to get an idea as to how many labels of beers they have, here. You checked her cleavage, you forgot she had a face, but you did remember that you heard strip joint at some point.

"Hmm, what do you recommend?" you finally said, hoping you could add that one to whatever brand she would list. "Sir, beer is but a word to define a gross spirit. May I know what your immediate being is like? And I may suggest a more refined manner of altering its state." Why is it that she would have won you over with a stout? Beers taste awful, over here. Unless they use the word with a different perspective.

"OK, I'll have that." you finally said. She rolled her eyes and left. You smirked, you almost smiled, and you moved your gaze around. You tried to figure out what a platonic strip joint was like. Like a regular strip joint? Muses and nymphs wandered all over the place, yet you could see them as animals on two feet. A cat, here, with two female human breasts pointed out of a very loose piece of black lingerie. She had long blonde hair, and a shy tail that wiggles in sync with a loud girly giggling voice.

She sat next to this gorilla and put her arm around his neck. Her eyes penetrated his eyes, almost as if she considered French kissing him, but she remained calm. Two lama women, a platypus and an onyx lady, a walking jewel, gathered to chat and laugh. A human-male muse who looked a lot like Mozart spanked the strippers. He made them laugh and then he ran away. He chuckled and sat behind a table. The precious gem lady joined him. She sat on his lap and examined you prior to a smile.

She had no hair or features, except for perfect round butt cheeks and a body chiselled by an absolutist. She whispered in Mozart's ear, who giggled and kissed her belly. He played the trumpet with her navel, then licked it as if we could taste a blown raspberry. The lama women and the platypus rallied right in front of you. They gossiped and laughed before they left.

A chameleon lady, minus the reptile's infamous repugnance, walked among the small group of strippers. This one's skin changed its colour as her emotions did, from intense blue to deep yellow to light green. She had a bird face and breasts as big as oranges under a long white night robe. She would look at you and touch her breasts, lick her lips, and, hmm. The sensual muse would leave you motionless. To your left, on the stage, not too far from the musicians, a more humanlike dancer walked from one end of the stage to the other. She wore a bikini and black high heels.

"Can I sit here?"

You heard the chameleon beauty from your right. You could feel her heat and smell her perfume. Her skin glittered under the black light, and her profound dark eyes projected the sparkling brightness of faraway galaxies. She had no pupil, only that intense lack of radiance you would gladly immerse yourself in. Why don't you? She smiled. She was now beige, more to your liking, almost yellowish. Her breasts seemed larger than before. When she crossed her legs, you could see her thighs made from the very flesh of Heavens. It formed slight curves that ended with the three bones of her knees and returned as long straight limbs.

Her smile lost a few feathers when you remained unable to pronounce any sound. She bit her lip and leaned her head down, her eyes up, with a gaze that spelled: "Well, didn't I?" The Ki-Rin waitress showed up with a beer mug that almost looked like a Martini glass. "Foolish! I love foolish beer!" she giggled. "Yeah. Me too." you spasmodically stuttered. She put a small towel on your lap and sat. "That thing will make you relax." she whispered, before she licked your lobe. "Can I have one?" her puppy eyes asked you. The Ki-Rin waitress sighed:

"I'll add it on your tap." To this moment you still have no idea what a foolish beer is, but you'll find out soon enough. She moved her palms up and down your back.

"You are so stiff." she whispered, though she didn't know half of it. Then she grabbed your hand and shook it.

"You can call me Kiya."

"Will, William." you stuttered. She repeated it, as if she memorized a poem, and smiled.

"Nice to meet you, Will, I am. I like it." She went down your shirt to massage a nipple, and she laughed again. A gorgeous bird lizard never molested you, before. She bit; she almost licked her lips. It made you feel more in control, more confident, so you tried to find the right way to put your hands behind her back. You didn't intend to lose your respect for her, but you wanted her flesh so bad. Then you sensed her leg as it teased between yours. That you experienced, hmm. You blushed like a teenager in hormonal appetite. Isn't that what you were before you jumped?

The waitress came back with Kiya's cocktail. She put it on the table, next to yours, and left. Kiya grabbed her drink, you took yours, and she raised her glass to cheer. She binged down a long sip. You followed. You thought it would quiet your beast; it was only beer. You felt the scorching alcohol with scorns of licorice, as it tore the flesh off your cheek, from inside, then your palate, your tongue, and your throat, all the way to your stomach! And it burned. So bad. "Wow!" she expressed, as you tried not to reveal your immense pain.

"A man who can drink foolish beer like that must be quite the solid one. I enjoy that!" Your face turned red. Your eyes turned to ponds of tears, but you toughened up. Like you never thought you could, as you said, in a choked voice:

"I used to use a funnel. In college." Too proud to admit you were in high school. And you coughed and coughed. She had a second sip from hers and kissed your cheek. It felt soothingly good. The music reached an end, so she asked you.

131

"You want to do it now or we wait for another song?" Right. You are in a strip club, after all. You held on tight and, confidently, asked: "Are there VIP rooms, here?"

She smiled and grabbed your hand. She pulled you away from your chair. Mozart kissed the onyx and the platypus, then laughed so hard it haunted you until you reached the closed little cabin. You sat on a very comfortable leather couch, and she stood under a sensual light, right in front of you. You knew what was coming, so you opened your legs. You lowered yourself down the cozy furniture, kept your arms and hands ready to grab her breasts. If she doesn't allow it, you apologize, but feel happy you have tried. While she is all over you. She sat on your lap again and she played with your hair. "I love them!" she shouted.

"So fine, shiny, so beautiful. They flow between my fingers like water, and they are dry like wheat in the sun." You could hardly wait for the next song to begin. "You can commence whenever you want." you announced and hoped she would start now. She put the tip of her thumb on your lips, and she licked it. You remained calm, but it ate you from inside. You must have her! And the new song finally began, smoothly at first. She then stood up and danced. You smiled and closed your eyes.

You waited for the skin to come your way. "Give me the flesh!" The more this thirst of yours grew, the more you felt a presence sneaking behind. As though that Ki-Rin waitress chose to spy on you. You'd be lucky if she decided to join the trio. However, she seemed rather silent, back there, as you impatiently felt the strip was about to start. Getting close and intimate with a lizard-lady felt kinky. "I had a tense relationship with my dad." she uttered, quietly. *Her dad?* You thought. Who cares about her dad?

"I didn't really know mine." you said, pondering about your stepmom who raised you, while your father gambled at the casino and spent nights with hookers.

132

"You know Spinoza? When he refers to God as a being, you think he means a creature or a concept of being?" You had no idea. You opened your eyes and saw her. She sat next to you with philosophy books in one hand and glasses in the other.
You attempted to grasp her fingers, but she wouldn't let you.
You apologized and felt cheap you had tried.

"My dad never liked Spinoza. I do. And this is why he disowns me. Ever since Mom passed away, he started treating me like a second wife. He also touched me, once. I slapped him so hard, he cried. This is when his depression worsened. I had to walk elsewhere, get on with my life. Now, here I am, revealing myself to complete strangers, and it doesn't always feel clean, but you. You look like a gentleman." You took a better posture, one that would allow you to listen. She won't even authorize you to hold her hand? Your stepmom was about your age, but she raised you like a kid brother she never had.

"What about Hegel?" she asked again. You had no idea.
But you wanted to tell her about your mother who killed herself, and the morning when you saw her hanging in the backyard.

"His belief of 'Being-in-and-for-itself,' as the essence, you think it's connected with Spinoza's concept of God, like, Hegel's absolute would be the same as Spinoza's god? And you think they talk about a construct or a creature? And with the Bible that

"Maybe." you whispered, disappointed, struck by a migraine. You tried to peek through her cleavage, at least. The song finally ended. You stood up. You will not stay for another one.
She followed your move.

"That's going to be a hundred praises." she explained.

"For one dance? Not even one?" You were beyond yourself.
"What do you mean, dance?" She opposed your interrogation"

133

"This is, hello, platonic! It's twenty-five praise per revelation, I revealed to you about my father, my dead mother; plus, we discussed Spinoza and Hegel, that's four. One hundred praises, payable to the stripper, cash. Thank you." Oh, it gets funnier. Just wait until you tell her you actually are without any kind of monetary resource. "Hmm." Yes? Say it. "I don't know what's praise like?" She didn't want to hear what was coming. "You have no cash with you?" she spat out like venom. She struggled not to strangle you. "Who's going to pay for the drinks, huh?" She shouted. "What's your problem, coming in a strip club without any money? What's your problem?" You earned it. Heck, doesn't it feel awful to be treated like that by women in your real world?
And now in your inner layer? Oh, William, poor guy.

She rushed you out of the VIP room. She followed you closely, then asked two bouncers to watch you: A tall and wide Minotaur and a bigger werewolf, both in a clean tuxedo, black pants, and shoes. She returned with more strippers and a supervisor, a goat lady, as old as ugly. "Kiya has told me you ordered two drinks and four revelations with no money." The manager cringed.
You timidly nodded. "How would you like to pay us back?"
She inquired. You couldn't answer that one.

"We'll have to keep you for our amusement until the debt is cleared, plus interest." She smiled. "What. What amusement?" you asked. She kept silent and waved at the two goons. The strippers looked at you. The onyx had a pitiful face, compassionate, while the lamas and the platypus laughed. A few more birds, insects, gathered on the floor above the stage. You saw that floor for the first time and the place suddenly seemed like an immense Victorian palace.

"They'll strip you down and try all sorts of devices on you, some are rather sharp but others tickle." A masculine, almost heroic, humble, voice said from behind you. Everybody turned to witness the entrance of a tall and slim black frog. The corpse of a cat, almost a skull with sporadic flesh and skin, acted as his second head. He wore a dark and purple cape, a high hat, crossed with a Stetson, and held a silver cane with a diamond orb. He walked to the manager and handed her three offers of a hundred praises each, then offered a hundred praises to each goon and stripper. Mozart joined the line-up, hoping to get one as well, and he did. The frog turned to you and whispered: "We have about fifteen seconds to get out of." The supervisor looked at the coins she had just received. She studied them for a moment and shouted:
"Hey! Those come from Tuurngait! They're worth nothing!"

"And I suggest we run." added the frog, right after he grabbed your hand. He walked faster, before you could voice the question that burned you within, and you had to keep up. When all went black, you heard his cane as it tapped, like a blind man would seek his path, and you sped as the sound got farther. Soon, the cave would be behind you. However, the real surprise waited for you at the exit. Two immense gorillas, and I mean actual silver-furred apes, stood in front of the door. They had their arms crossed, and they didn't look very happy. In fact, they didn't appear pleasant at all. Your saviour held his cane with both hands and tried some diplomacy: "Gentlemen, I believe it may be in everyone's interest if you allowed my friend and I to leave this premise. There is no need for us to get violent."

One of the goons laughed while the other grinned and uttered: "Maybe we want this to get violent. Who knows?"

"Would you like to hear what else I bring from the marvellous world of Tuurngait?" the frog asked. He faced you with a "tsk, tsk, now" look in his eyes. He closed them, put his gaze away and pulled a very thin bastard sword out of his cane, then gave you the weapon's cover. The gorillas jumped on him.

With finesse, almost dance moves, your new friend evaded their goofy charge. One quick maneuver from his agile wrist scratched the belt off the closest brute. Another finished the humiliation, throwing his pants down. The frog returned the blade back in its cover and signalled you to follow. "Son, I would encourage you to catch up! We don't have all day!" he sighed. The first bouncer pulled his pants up, while the second one charged once again to tackle the annoying amphibian. By now, you seemed to realize that a dead cat's head bopped back and forth against his shoulder, while he smiled and swiftly evaded every punch and every kick that came his way. That kitty skull was getting your attention. Were they Siamese twins? There's no way he could have grafted another animal's head to make a fashion statement.

While you pondered, the curious stranger was back to the action. Well, what a bizarre word since he didn't appear very animated. His opponents, however, were losing their patience. The more they hammered him with their fists and their feet, the easier it was for the frog to bow, then jump, land on their back, and jump again. He leaped and dodged more than he fought. It was getting obvious that this battle was far from an equal ground. He outsmarted every charge they made. When the homo stupid us finally gave up, having lost too much energy, the amphibian inspected his cane and resumed his walk. You followed behind. You could hear the manager scream: "Don't you ever come back! Yeah, you! Next time I see you, I callback my goons!"

The frog in a black cape ushered outside, and you had to run to join him. "Oh, good! Here he is!" he joked. You frowned and replied: "Did you come for me?"

"We could say that. I have unfinished business, and they include you." You remained as calm as you were puzzled. You observed him, his elegant posture behind the purple cape that barely hid the decayed cat head.

You uttered, quietly: "Yeah, I guess." He left.

Journey into the Hourglass:
Six

Connecting William to the frog character seemed like a natural order of things. I liked that new character; I called him quid. I imagined another goofy friend; I would call him Nunc. Do you get it? Quidnunc! Quidnunc! It's Latin for What Now? Often used when referring to gossipers, and I loved the poetry behind this choice of names.

Martin hated it. Too many characters! He texted me. You're killing our story! I mean, come on! At least give a smiling face emoji and a thumbs up. It's hilarious! "And what about that student?" I texted him back. Every awakened soul knows that the wise Entities of Noesi de Vel named our purgatory Sophron as a reference to the Greek Mysteries. But to include a Greek character? No way!

What student? He texted back. And what fragment of what are you talking about? Rogue photons, that's what all of this must be. We're writing a story, while our characters develop their own consciousness, and they challenge us to earn their freedom. Not only this, but the book itself is alive.

"We really need to cast ourselves in our own story, Martin.

"I warned him. You're stupid!" He confronted me, looking for a fight.

Third Intermission:
The Story Thickens

The student looked at the orb, while reflecting on how their main persona could further develop into the ideal hero they were meant to become. Plato thought it would be wise to let them take this tool back to their home and practice. Sitting on their bed, observing the sunset, they mused on what they had just experienced. Telling their story as it unfolded inside their psyche, and now living it, as though they incarnated every character that comprised its narrative. The sensation was inebriating. A grin shaped itself across their chin, and they dared touch the crystal again. *Gently*, they thought, *as to not disturb the bond that formed between the Dreamer and the object.* Deep within their mind, they could say that these voices existing beyond the fabric of the sphere called their name. Were they author of their lives or a spectator?

Feeling intimidated, they left their bed and walked around their tiny room. The globe floated and remained firmly planted in the centre of their privacy. Could they find a way to strengthen the bond? They thought about this question for a long moment: if these characters and their stories exist within their soul and should the orb act as a channel through which that universe could be projected, then the answer is also inside their head. They cleared their mind and focused on the window that showed an empty courtyard. The sky was darkening, with a few stars already apparent. Somehow, they felt a connection with this Seamus figure so strong, they could sympathize with his current struggle.

What can they do to facilitate his quest? Were they, as the active Author, participating in those characters' lives? If William were able to manifest his existence within his own dream, could the student do the same? Those interrogations fell over them like a thousand bricks. Perhaps it was safer to question Plato about these. Or maybe it was better to experiment with this magic by themselves. They turned around and gazed at the gleaming ball. Certainly, the teacher trusts them with keeping this precious treasure at home. They were instructed at a young age to let their curiosity roam free. Fair enough, they supposed, let's see what happens if they open their awareness further. Approaching the orb very slowly, the student closed their eyes. Words manifested themselves at the back of their conscience. They carried images retelling the tale of a selfish hero embarking on a journey to atone for a grave mistake. A tree appeared as though a phantasm came to display within their thoughts the connections those characters shared. They were promised a fantastic odyssey.

The student pondered over the nature of this journey, just as they opened their eyes and looked at the fortune-telling bubble that seduced them. At its core, they saw a bench on which a magical man slept. This odd and wonderful realm called Montreal fascinated them, with those autonomous chariots and people curiously dressed. This character could provide guidance to a lost *Seamus*, they thought. How could he shape a link that would show the hero the way to become more than he ever was? Perhaps the stray man knew the gods and their battles across the seventy-two layers of Sophron. The student imagined a creature that could follow this sage across urban nature.

Could he carry a small cat? No, a wasp! Waving their hand over the orb, they recalled what the owl saw, while in captivity. This insect will set a wonderful adventure in motion.
They envisioned long wings, almost like those of a dragonfly.
A tiny abdomen could have made the creature look more like a bee, but the head was that of a fierce predator.

Soon, the Dreamer had nothing else in mind but this modest art project. They let their finger glide over the crystal, drawing a park with amazing flowers and tall trees. The wasp would enjoy its flight away from the busy street. They envisioned a statue overlooking the bench, where the homeless man slept. Bystanders would look at him. Nobody could have guessed that a special bond linked the elderly sir to this fragile-looking beast. The student, however, knew. All of this was born from their creative mind. Oh! Surely, Seamus would have to see this connection as well. If all of this takes place in the pupil's head, or in a vast and complex universe that inhabits their innermost self, then those characters would have to shelter the same kind of inner world.

Obviously, to the student, Seamus also practised mancing, or some sort of magic. The wasp would convey a miracle within its very existence. The more they thought about it, the more this concept made sense. After all, why did they choose this majestic pest to carry out such an important task? Because Seamus acts as vermin in his own respect, they guessed. Both would orbit around this wise man sleeping in a park for the same reason: self-awareness of the wrongs they did, and the salvation that shines from this man's presence. The yellow stripes that appeared on the flying monster contrasted so much with the black ones, day and night alternated their shift around it. When investing their attention on one line on its abdomen, the student could see a whole other world. There, they recognized the landscape of Sparta, and valiant warriors defying giant creatures, under the leadership of one powerful Marduk. Biomass? As the disciple recalled. Did the wasp's soul fight the legions of the mad god? He did, yes. That owl, Haslem, did succeed! Oh, the apprentice enjoyed it! Indra survived, but he can't confront his greatest enemy, just yet. Maybe something they could perform would protect Sophron from the Entity Killer. It all made sense, in the trainee's mind. Marduk wants to achieve a state of absolute existence. This explains why he murders entire worlds, within this storyline. Indra must have given his life to protect the pluriverse. What if all of this took place beyond the limits of the student's mind? What if it happens as they conceived it?

140

So many essences and existences depend on the pupil formulating the correct choices. *First,* they thought, *let's project the right set:* **"The first night I spent in the streets of Montreal was the scariest."** Just came to their mind. There had to be more they could do. Could they write themselves in their own story? I could also link myself to the wasp! They considered. Maybe that insect doesn't only carry Indra's essence. It conveys the student's very fabric of consciousness as well! And why not? Who will stop them? Nobody's witnessing the existence of this story, right now, except the tale's creator.

Just as they closed their eyes to project their being within their dream, the orb moved. It was like three or four rapid tremors, at first, but it grew stronger with every new prognosis that the disciple's mind made. Animation got to the wasp's wings, and the student felt that coming out of their own back and shoulders. Is it supposed to hurt? Maybe they could push the envelope a bit farther. They could renounce their immediate consciousness and embrace the essence that called them.

Inhaling deeply, they cleansed their mind of everything. Their small brain couldn't even consider the events about to happen, so they had to let go. They had to abandon the very notion of interpreting their existence. The world around them could no longer define who they were. Only the one within made any sense. They took another deep breath, and they shut their mind off, once and for all. Only to hear, at the farthest end of this emerging reality, Void speak.

"Ah! Here you are!" the Ocorsur said. "Two Dreamers dreaming their way too hard in the same story? Wow! And I thought about telling Alibast to write me off, out of boredom."

141

Chapter Thirteen:
Seamus the Homeless Rookie

The first night I spent in the streets of Montreal scared me more than all I've been through in my life. Every car that seemed to slow down sounded suspect. The strangers gazing at an eighteen-year-old fugitive had eyes that carried piercing blades. Every step I pushed forward weighed more than the ones I left behind. I walked over Montreal's Mountain and approached downtown, determination and uncertainty fighting the crowded space in my mind. By the time I reached Square-Philipps and searched for a bench to sleep onto, I had run across some other homeless people.

Many came to me, begging for some change, and I realized that I didn't quite fit the part. What am I supposed to look like? Should I tear off my clothes? Should I dirty myself on purpose? That would be wrong, I guess. We don't become stray from one day to the next. And I won't be awakened that fast either. We are only as fulfilled as we are at the time being, and any direction, up or down, only nears our grasp one morning at the time, one effort or one abandonment at the time. Could I experience both homelessness and enlightenment? What if I wasn't deserting my family, but, instead, I was leaving everything that kept me from reaching that achievement? I had to replace them with better options, I guess. What about that frog with a dead cat's head on his left shoulder? Ever since I imagined this image, it haunted me. Like the vision tried to pull me into a floating boat or something.

I sat on a lonely bench, and I looked at the stars. I observed the bright constellations, and I thought to myself: I leave behind my fortune, and the laziness that grew with it. I substitute it with empty pockets, and a soul ready to learn. That idea felt so right. What else was I evacuating? My friends? No, I was abandoning my attachment to others behind. Replacing it with an inner strength, I had yet to discover. This line of thinking removed so much pressure, I had to continue, but I couldn't force it either. It had to come as obvious as the light that shines over my path. "Are you going to eat that?" I heard a voice near me. When I turned around, I saw an old man, covered with a grey cloak, pointing at the remnants of a poutine that someone forgot on the bench. I shook my head, opening the way for him to sit next to me and binge down these fries, gravy, and cheese curds like a famished nomad. "I just left home." I explained. The elder observed me and smiled.

"You'll be back to your momma and poppa before tomorrow. You're not the bum type." he concluded. I looked at him wolfing through his meal at such speed, it made sense that he hadn't had any decent one in days. "Hmm, by the way." he added, "You haven't seen any hobo guy with, say, a pet wasp?"

"A pet wasp?" I wondered. "Who chooses an insect for a pet?"

"Just asking for a friend." He finished talking and resumed eating his repast. This elder wasn't an ordinary homeless. He knows about Nempty. Perhaps he knew that I knew, and wanted to make known that I now knew that he knew that. You know where I'm going with that, right? I spent the night on that bench, and I could hear the old man snore from a nearby one. He had removed his shoes, and the stench that came out of his naked feet disgusted me. I didn't sleep. I just watched the stars and wondered if the planets that I saw, with Ishtar, existed in that space. Athanor, Saguenay, Tir na n'Og, Duat. I perceived only a handful of them, but something in me wanted to visit them all. Was it that past life who knew Indra?

143

Does Tristan still reside in me? The same way the Hindu god shares a presence with William? These questions haunted me the night over. When the sun rose to the East, it was time to think about getting breakfast. I examined the old man. He sat on his bench and coughed. He then put back his dirty socks and ancient shoes.

"Why are you looking at me like that, mate?" he asked. I didn't realize I was fearfully surveying what I could become.

"Oh! Are you concerned about food? Damn, mate, may I take you to the Ritz? I heard they have golden eggs. I never had any. Just the green stuff with ham. Can I have fancy bacon with that? With a side of I don't give a crap, please. If you want to survive, just follow me. Or go back to your family." I stayed quiet for the rest of the morning. I accompanied the old man down Beaver Hall, across the financial district, and in Old Montreal. He didn't beg, ask for money, or anything. He just walked. And walked.
And sometimes he would stop, and look at the sky, and smile.
He would then walk again. And walk. Again. And walk. By noon, my feet were killing me. He didn't pause. My back hurt, I needed to rest. He meant to see if we could cross the Champlain Bridge on foot.   I opposed the idea, because it's a "car only" bridge, but that didn't stop him from trying. Do I wish to survive next to a suicidal fool? And I didn't want to return home either. He perceives something. The pet insect, he knows! When we reached Longueil, after having evaded a few speeding vehicles, heard several horns, and he managed to dance in the middle of the road. I asked him.

"Sir. What about the wasp?"

"What about it?" he inquired.

"Do you know? About. The other worlds?" He chuckled when I said that. "The other worlds?" he questioned, and then he walked away, laughing. I had to find out, but I couldn't just connect my power to his essence. What if I shared my presence with a much more formidable gifted? He stopped in a park and observed the Saint-Lawrence River flowing. I sat next to him, and I wondered.

"When do we eat?" I asked.

"You have any money?" he replied. I looked at my pocket change. I had enough toonies and loonies to cover fifty dollars.

"Not much." I sighed.

"Then, you go your way, you find money, and you locate something to consume. And I go my way, I do the same, and we pretend we never met."

"Where can I find you? If I need you, I mean."

"You did now. Stay with me and you won't lose me."

"But I'm hungry, and I don't even know your name!" He got up and left. I surveyed around, concerned about what other bystanders might think. A small family, I gather dad, mom, and a toddler breastfeeding, on a nearby bench. They looked at us, and I felt the stories they projected in their mind. A rich young boy insisting on grabbing the attention of an old penniless man. He was getting away, so who cares? I hurried to find him, and as I approached, I asked: "How did you know about the wasp?"He didn't even look back at me. He just kept on walking. "Do you know Ishtar?" I asked. He didn't respond."And what about Indra?" I insisted. He stopped and lectured me. "Do you know that Ari Krishna white boys who sell you books, and just try their best to find peace, are more admired by the Hindu community than you appreciate Indra by babbling about Ishtar, right now?" What he just explained made absolutely no sense.

145

"It's a cult, they're in a cult! Why do you say that?"

"Are you hungry?" he asked.

"Why do you talk about a cult and Indra?" I felt puzzled.
"Let's go have a poutine. I'm buying." he told me. We stopped on a
busy boulevard, and the elderly fool would stay there, looking
pitiful whenever he made eye contact with an old woman, or a
young man. Sometimes, I could sense empathy connecting the
two. That's when he would smile: "I haven't eaten in days, well, I
had a decaying feast of gravy, cheese curds and fries. I was sitting
on a bench last night, and this brave rich young man is hungry.
I want to repay him, show him my gratitude. I don't do drugs!
I don't drink, I'm just homeless. I need your help." Most often than
none, people would walk away. They would listen to his story, and
they would leave midway through, when he mentioned me.
He spoke in all honesty. He managed, still, to collect about fifteen
dollars, over the course of five hours. He pleasured in spending
money on a poutine I would eat alone. He would just watch me
with thankful eyes. I could have paid for it myself, but he was glad
to reimburse me for the piece of crap I let him eat next to me, last
night. I felt bad. I meant to give him all my change. I could never
pull up the show that he did. I felt too scared to talk to strangers,
and tell them I had no money, or I hungered for that. "Is it good?"
he asked me. "Delicious, thanks." I expressed. "You want some?"

"No, it's all yours. You're hungry, not me."

"But you haven't eaten all day."

"It's all about balance. I'm sure you'll discover yours." Yeah,
I'll fetch mine. I need to find William. I can't use my gift to journey
anywhere. Nobody can help me get to where William is. I smiled
at the old man. He knows something. Perhaps he's a traveller too,
like Nempty, or what I'm destined to evolve into. Maybe someone
sent him for me. I just have to remain with him a little more.

Possibilities are what you could have become if you decided differently. And they all exist within your mind, in your spiritual self. I just need to peek into his inner world to find out.

"Are we going back to Square-Phillips?" I asked him. "Only if you dance in the traffic." And I did. I wasn't even drunk or high, but I knew that inhibitions are what kept me away from my gift, and   I had to let go of those. No time to fear death. I can't destroy my clothes or get them dirty. Cars would pass through me and honk. Motorists would yell:

"Get out, stupid, you'll be killed!" And I would reply: "Don't do this at home!" The old man would walk right behind me, letting me lead the way. It felt good. It felt liberating. I wonder if William felt the same way, right before he fell and saw the traffic coming. And I no longer felt like dancing. We reached Square-Phillips by the time the sun was about to set. As we walked back to the place we met, I observed the old man and pondered on his name, his story. I couldn't connect to him; he wasn't afraid of,anything.   I guess this fact explained why I felt safe with him. When we sat on that same bench to look at the stars, he grabbed a poutine that was left there, and he binged it down just like before. "See? Here's another one." he uttered. He ate it as fast as he did last night, and the only thing that I found disturbing, then, was having him sleeping without his socks, near me. "There's a war coming, I heard." I replied. He looked at me, with a fry halfway in his mouth, and smiled. He swallowed his huge bite and grinned: "Only if you fear for it. Damn, I love poutine!"

We slept on our respectful benches and, this time, I dreamed. I saw an immense library, with books about everything. There was a beach, and an ocean that caressed the sand with great tenderness. The old man was holding a wasp at the end of a stick, forcing it to grasp pollen out of giant flowers, and into other plants. Was it the same wasp? Is he forcing Indra to pollinate a dead world? I looked at the stars and tried to name the constellations; I heard him snore.

147

Chapter Fourteen:
Marduk's Diplomacy

Hydaspes exists one minute behind Tir na nOg and one layer after Saguenay, in the Archeus-Logo quadrant. Because, at this point, the thought axioms dominate over the life pixels, this dimension resembles a vast hologram. For Marduk, a native of Nibiru, where elements of the mind don't exist, and life energy is intertwined with matter, the use of either technology or mancer magic is necessary to occur. He is seen as a very powerful mancer. He could, at any time, summon clones of his other selves from thousands of various possibilities. Normally, the nexus rule states that not two same consciousness, from parallel universes, can co-exist in a same dimension. Marduk found a loophole in that natural law.

His clones would all have the exact same knowledge, creating in the process an army of himself. He performed this feat, once, while engaging Varuna's troop to conquer the layer of Tabriz. This, however, soon went against him, as each and all copies of Marduk battled one another rule over this Tabrizian realm. It gave a much-needed momentum to Varuna's legion, as they were on their way to utter defeat. As powerful as Marduk could be with his gift, he relied much more on technology. To travel through worlds and Dreamers, he used spectre boats. While fairy-vessels can take you from one layer to another in three months, spectre boats take only three days.

It might be important to mention that days, in Sophron, hardly follows the movement of a planet around its star. The laws of time apply themselves differently to various worlds. One brilliant glancer, in Duat, found a system that makes it easier for travellers. If we consider Gaia's time, with its planet Earth as the basis, then we have these twelve months or fifty-two weeks that you, the reader, knows best. Another foreign globe in this layer would have a varied scale, but highly irrelevant for Sophron. A traveller can't rely on this when he visits a different realm. So, that glancer, his name was Thoth, discovered that axioms have a lifespan of their own. Pixels in the Void-Barbelo quadrant had the exact identical existence as those in the Archeus-Logos one.

Much like when we throw a feather and a bowling ball in a vacuum, they will hit the floor at the same time. When we isolate two elements from different layers and put them in a limbo, they will bloom, live, and die at the same rate. We call it the orderly core within a chaotic pluriverse. Thoth later determined that an axiom's lifespan equalled one day, which translates into six days, seven hours, and twenty-eight minutes where you live.

If you could film them within the Veil, as they make their way to Tir na n'Og, Marduk's armada must fly over Hydaspes. If you were on this world and looked up, you would see the Veil appear, and you would see this gigantic caravan of flesh and metal drifting like cells in amniotic liquid. The cavernous sound that these bio-machines make, however, feels creepy. A fairy-boat, when it floats in the Veil, almost sings its way through. Heavier spectre vessels, as they advance towards their target, seem to wound the very fabric of Sophron, forcing the pluriverse to scream and cry. The Layer Killer produced a much scarier sound. Some argued that Marduk had a sacrifice chamber. The release of souls on a regular basis fuelled the vessel.

Marduk loved the control room. Located on the largest of the three-dragon skull's forehead, it was big enough to gather two hundred elephants. Arts from all around Sophron richly decorated the place. Axioms that Marduk had collected from his first conquest covered the floor. We found, basically, the flesh, bones, energy, and soul of two billion beings from Biarmaland. It looked like a giant TV screen, and the word pales against its actual size, with faces reaching up for air, some grieving, others tortured. It really seems tremendous, for a goth punk observing this art from above, without any idea that consciousness suffers under your feet.

Marduk stands like a ruler, a great emperor, peering out through the dragon's third eye. He sees this membranous grey that swamps his ship, like a vast ocean with no land in sight. He's a tall and bulky bald guy.

"The Dreamer killed himself, my lord."

The voice came from a small lemur. While a hero and a legend among his people, he looked at Marduk with fear. He did point out how Marduk tried to conquer a dying world. If the Hound Lord of Nibiru killed all his other selves to stand supreme, then he just can't accept that this possibility could just fall in forgetfulness. The lemur knew he could perish the moment Marduk would hear his news. Marduk observed the greyness in front of him with some sort of wisdom, but mostly despair.

"Did he have an aid?"

The animal looked further down and suggested: "We think he was bullied by his aid, my lord."

"Great! What are we fearing, then?"

"My lord, we can't invade a dying Dreamer."

Marduk shut his fist and summoned razors to badly wound this small bringer of bad news. Scarlet blood stained the white feather. The animal's head rolled to the Lord's feet. Marduk didn't have the will to laugh, but he smiled.

"I don't conquer worlds. I conquer love."

At the other end of the room, a gold and grey shadow lurked against the wall. Marduk saw the shade spying over him. He signalled it to reveal itself. The silhouette embraced the form of a glowing blob floating, as it gradually espoused a humanoid type. It grew limbs, when it reached a space, midway before being in front of the Entity-Killer. Arms soon followed, but the head remained formless and bright.

"Jarov! What have you uncovered on Gaia?" Marduk asked.

"Good Lord, we have located a boy who has seen the wasp." The creature answered.

"How do you know if that boy realized how important this wasp is?"

"Lord, we don't, but we will find out. We know that he has some sort of affinity, perhaps to essences."

"A glancer?"

"Yes, Lord, but a newcomer at his gift."

"Show me." The spy projected ink out of a floating page. Some letters formed sparks of blackness, as they became words:

We reached Square-Phillips by the time the sun was setting. As we walked back to the place we met, I observed the old man and wondered about his name, his story. I couldn't connect to him; he wasn't afraid of anything. I guess this fact explained why I felt safe with him.

"Who's that old man?" Marduk asked.

"My lord, we believe he is a powerful Walker. We don't know where he came from, but he seemed to find his way into Seamus Chron's life at specific times. So far, only the existence of the wasp connects them."

"Alibast Page."

"I'm sorry, my lord?"

Marduk fought hard to keep his cool. He thought for a long moment and summoned his crystal ball. It flew deep within his pupils, then appeared next to him. When he closed his eyes, he could hear a voice: "Are you sure William should die? Why don't you write his destiny?"

Marduk looked at his orb, floating around him like an electron. He recalls the time when he assassinated a powerful Entity that guarded Alibastat. When slicing the being's throat with all his might and magic, he perceived the presence of a powerful existence, with deep connection to the world he had just annihilated: Alibast. "How could you tell?" he asked his spy. "Name me your sources."

The shadow remained calm. They tried to think it over but couldn't find the words. They felt like freshman students with the hopes of becoming a powerful politician. They were stuck in the rhetoric of a teacher too bitter to let go of a failed destiny

"It could have been a mistake, My Lord." We find no error when the Golden Ratio chooses a side to lead nature on.

"I don't think so." Marduk replied. Some Dreamers will try and make sense of mathematics, even in realms where numbers never existed. For the tiniest form of a sentient being, infinity stands all mighty beyond a conscience. Marduk calls it Monday.

"Who envisioned William's death?" he asked the genderless.

"Seamus Chron was the name brought to us, Lord."

That didn't mean anything. No! It couldn't be. The night that followed the fatal blow, Marduk felt the existence of dimensions beyond this one. The chimera died. And just as Alibastat was becoming a sterile world right before his eyes, enlightenment gave the Lord strange sensations. He felt as though someone had scripted his life. This epiphany didn't stop him from pursuing more conquests. But when he returned to this barren layer, thousands of years later, he met a curious old man. A quiet monk, brown beard, blonde hair, dressed in a grey robe, who would wander all over this dead realm to ensure that flowers would grow, and beauty would remain. He wore thick glasses on top of a very peaceful visage. That's Alibast. When the Hound-Lord of Nibiru engaged in a conversation with this hermitic gardener, he encountered a great wall of silence.

When he tried to dispose of him, seeing a threat in someone who attempted to give life back to the world he had just destroyed, Alibast simply summoned a winged dozer, like an angel, to protect himself. Still, just pollinating flowers and planting seeds all over Alibastat. Marduk realized that he couldn't compete with this Walker. He had encountered the most powerful gifted in all Sophron. And he was just attending some botanical activities. The Lord left and never returned to this land.

But what if Alibast decided to interfere with his plans, now?
Heck! He barehandedly murdered a Great Entity! He certainly can
get rid of this nuisance. He observed his servant and ordered:
"I want the boy killed. Don't engage the old man." The creature
bowed down and left the scene. Marduk wandered alone, in his
throne room.   He sighed and sat on his magnificent seat.
He summoned a book, looked at it for a long moment, and closed
his eyes. Words appeared: *There was this eye. Halfway closed,
halfway proud.*

He felt pain as he tried to forecast more phrases onto the novel
he held. Were they coming from him? He convinced himself they
were from someone else. He projected more paragraphs:
*A glimpse of a tear. The light that shone by the brow. There was
this eye, and the cheek underneath, as wide as the eternity that
handled the birth of this universe.*

He searched around him, fearing that somebody might observe
him, or look at what he was trying to accomplish. Several aeons
passed since he summoned spells this way, the archaic way.
Why did Alibast prefer the old practice? Marduk didn't know, but
if the foolish monk wanted a fight, then the Entity-Killer would
give him one on his ancient grounds!

He shut his eyes and meditated further. more words appeared
on the book: It looked at me, unaware of another eye, just like this
one. A nose that broke through space, gently chiselled as it offered
itself to a clear and white forehead, but refined, near the labial
beauty that shaped the object of my desire.

"I recollect her hair as long as endless fields of silk. It reigned
over the smoothest shoulders this side of Creation." he whispered.

Journey into the Hourglass: Seven

One morning, I woke up to find a flood of emails from Martin. He had overindulged and was talking to himself, like a sleepwalking soliloquist. "Hey, are you okay?" I asked. *No!* He replied. *We're not okay! Indra appeared to me in a dream, and now I'm having a panic attack.* Indra symbolizes a goal for many characters, ultimately for all of them. Sekhmet secretly loved him, but he married Ishtar. Marduk hated him, envious of this marriage, which led to war. We infused Indra's essence into William's soul, and now the Hindu god is haunting us?

"He's a central object, Martin, right? Not really a character." I tried to follow his screenwriting-like structure. He's a total mess! Martin panicked. *We need to connect his awakened soul to advance Nempty's arc. Nempty's role is to bring Seamus to William, so his arc involves gaining a virtuous quality.* "I think Nempty wronged Indra before," I suggested. "Lucretia gave him a reason to wish he knew right from wrong." *Why? Because she's a sex doll?*

"No! Because she's an innocent consciousness forced into a doll by vile entities." *Nempty realized this after purchasing her.* "Exactly! She's just a child, Martin. Nempty knows that. Maybe Indra made him aware of this wisdom before, but he only understood it after getting Lucretia, and his paternal instinct kicked in." *And now?* Martin asked. "We have Nempty pursue a wasp."

Chapter Fifteen:
Nempty finds a Wasp

There was this eye. Halfway close, halfway proud. A glimpse of a tear. The light that shone by the brow. There was this eye, and the cheek underneath, as wide as the eternity that handled the birth of this universe. It looked at me, unaware of another eye, just like this one. A nose that broke through space, gently chiselled as it offered itself to a clear and white forehead. Yet refined, near the labial charm that shaped the object of my desire. I recollect her hair, endless fields of silk. It reigned over the smoothest shoulders this side of Creation. She had a skin slightly pale with a shade of twilight. Her high cheekbones demonstrated her latest form of reincarnated beauty: halfway Chinese or Japanese and almost French. In the beginning came Ishtar.

My Perth, a pole that stood straight and strong to keep two parts of an X separated. Two halves drawn to one another, against a tall spine that would never bend. A table or a jar, depending on how the rune would fall. A squared C with both extremities flexed inward, then out. I loved her not for the need. It was for the features she had that reminded me of a time before I even came to be. One, most certainly, I would rejoin when I'll die. I loved her for the goddess she was to a circle other than mine, yet I felt her as true as myself. We belong to a layer of Sophron made for us, but one that, our many existences over, has waited for our return like an orphan world hoping for a Sun.

We may have been born of the same crux, I often thought.
I wondered, though, if she erupted out of me or me out of her.
Every time, every life reborn, every new chance created, our paths
crossed, then something in the form of somebody forced us astray.
Every time, every love adorned, I have found her essence in the
most unexpected hosts, and yet I realized only too late. What and
who was I to her?

This question always presented itself to me when a first glance
made its way between us. I felt that I existed only through her
vision on me. I often sensed that once her sight looked away, I
became the ghost of some fleshless thoughts in need of her body to
carve a meaning. So many names shone against her identity,
reported in books by her wrath and jealousy. Goddess of love and
war, my home, my cherished Queen Sachi. We had circles of
believers at our feet, with countless minds to project us this eternal
life we both enjoyed.

It had been demonstrated, in the world I came from, how
existence breaks itself in equal parts of consciousness, linked to
our very being one with the entirety. Substance joins a spirit
through a complex mechanism of flesh while an ether connects the
psyche, in meditation, to a soul that mothers the essence as though
a womb would bear the very infant of reality.

We are, individually, Sophron. We hold all seventy-two realms
reflecting the seventy-two layers we reside in. If one collectivity of
kingdoms makes a possibility, then it is correct to say that
Dreamers dwell within Dreamers, probably to infinity, although we
have yet to journey beyond a fixed recollection. The farther away
from a source, an essence, our home dimension, in the Dreamer
that saw us being born, and the more difficult, the more hazardous
it gets to travel in worlds within as in worlds without. Perhaps only
entities exist after these borders, but until one truly awakes past the
last enlightenment, one will never know.

The essence stands as our most valuable part. The flesh may rot, thoughts may no longer procreate, void may no longer float, but while minds carry an essence, a soul lives on. Cults, sects, religions, various cultures, appeared in poems, hymns, stories, films, to allow circles of believers to carry our existence further away from a Final-Vanishing. I keep close a last memory of her embrace: Warm and comforting, her breath against my shoulder, with promises of a never-ending heartbeat.

I vaguely recall visions of our world. She is there, however, all over, whenever I project this last embrace. I do not know if my essence speaks through this book or my soul. I know I must inhabit some host, somewhere, in one form or another, and he, like me, must think of someone he loved and will never see again. If only. If I could better manifest myself through his creation, then I would reunite with a circle of believers, and my conscience would carry on. Where is she?

Where is she? Under the curtains of sorrow, within the painful unknowns, I sense a breathless desire of wholesomeness. One spirit, one soul, one. And we stood for mankind with the affection of a thousand gods. Ishtar! How I wish flesh could host this "I" that would flood your cheeks with the tears of a million oceans, billions "I miss you."

I know from the words that this Author lays down, story begins for me in the awakening of my substance, having kept a partial portion of my reality intact in a piece of amber. A primitive insect, you see, that retained it within its DNA. Prehistoric at the time for the people of Tir na nOg, but for mankind, in Gaia, we look at a wasp that currently flies in central park, Manhattan, on a splendid summer of nineteen-seventy-four.

Tir na nOg lies beyond what we consider True Archeus, or the realm where we physically uncover only axioms of life and no more of matter. Beyond True Archeus, we approach the hemisphere of Logos, and the worlds are populated with fairer folks than wraiths, and more nymphs than muses. With its wide prairies of sand, rivers of grass on which ferry boats, those immense wingless dragonflies with masts that taunt the purple sky, sail like wild winds. It is hard to find a more exotic dimension. Perhaps Athanor, located a few layers closer to True Logos, could seem stranger. The main attraction that makes Athanor unique, compared to Tir na nOg, is how its background constantly changes with the weather. Here was a sea; now it's a desert. There was a forest, now its a mountain. As we approach the Void quadrants, reality swims with chaos. In Tir na nOg, existence remains as stable as what we can know of those other worlds that form the Barbelo and Archeus hemispheres.

At the time of this story, however, Tir na nOg hosted the battleground of an important war. It happened when House Abraxas of Duat invaded House Ossian of Tir na nOg. The fairy-boat floats on the river of grass. It approaches the ruins that once sheltered King Ossian, forced to an exile when the troops of Sekhmet destroyed every village. She killed every faerie that formed Ossian's necessary circles of faithful believers.
She established a new reign for incoming societies of Duat to make herself further awakened. Worshippers nourish a lord with axioms. While people contemplate someone, Logos will mirror matter over these thoughts. Powerful Neymlisses and Walkers have good use for these religions, since they provide them a solid ground on which they may create their own existence. When various circles come together to reflect the same Lord, we call this ground a House. Sekhmet grabbed the throne of Wells from Queen Anastasia's reach and weakened Ossian. After Duat's influence vanished from the corners of Gaia, following the crumble of an ancient Egyptian empire, Sekhmet's ambition has been to establish a House for herself. She forced Queen Anastasia to exile.
Wells became her seat of power thereafter.

We, gods, are destined to live on through the ages and every layer of Sophron. Our ideal intends to achieve several stages of enlightenment until we may evolve into an Entity. We may also become a powerful being representing one of the four Ocorsurs. Grow until we may finally break free from the bondage of realities and transition into a singularity.

Sekhmet's Master represents the great Void. She served under Barbelo long enough to acquire skills within fields of mancing, manipulating axioms of matter. She grew in importance amid the various circles of Asyut, Badari and many others that gravitated around believers in ancient Egypt. That importance is notably attributed to gods and goddesses imprisoned in limbos. They were apprehended for their parts in a revolution, soon after the last battle for Babel. Among Varuna's sympathizers we found Horus, Serapis, Bast and Anubis. All of them, alongside Ra, were missing from their cliques of faithful disciples. Their vanishing left Marduk and his legion of Neymlisses and Walkers. All free to enslave humanity into a new era of theocracies.

I heard that Varuna and Marduk, too, found themselves judged by the Sapphire Council. I could only hear parts of the actual story, since the end of the Babel Wars meant no connection for me to share with either mankind, my House, or allies. Nempty called his flying building: Barracuda. On that fairy-boat, we found treasures taken from every corner of Sophron. Lapis-Mol dari from the realm of Kyöpelinvuori shone behind a thick glass that contained their highly volatile axioms. Their radioactive properties were, once, created bombs that could force an entire continent to implode. Lapis-Mol dari remains illegal under every sky.

Behind the threatening element, jars filled with honey wine from Kaamelot, on Avalon, triggered many an appetite. Farther to the left, beer from Akeldama, in Jeruselah flowed from a fountain. Look at the back of the room to find spirited liquor from Cognac, in Nirvana. Now, I know you might want to tell me about this nectar getting its name from a French region, but I assure you that nirvana has a village of the same name. Next to the jars of liquor were vaults packed with jewelry and fancy clothes, armours, shields, swords. On the upper level, the safest place in all the boat, there are priceless items used for alchemy and mancing.

Nempty once laboured at the bridges between Gaia, Duat and Hades. Known as Charon, then, he took souls from all three worlds and passed them to the next. That was until the Babel Wars. He has since been working as a merchant, and a smuggler. He was very successful with both. A very small number of enlightened beings earned the skills to manipulate axioms, through alchemy. Unlike Walkers, Neymlisses will never develop the skill to control pixels and change the fabric of reality. For them, sadly, the journeys of higher wisdom will end there. Nempty knows that he will never truly know enlightenment. He may act as a powerful Neymliss with no hope of shaping up as a mancer. He doesn't seem to mind.

Rather small and scrawny in size, he hides his skeletal frame inside a darkened cape, black jeans, and a leather coat. The sea of grass opens in front of him. He leaves his boat, the crew of over a dozen faithful followers, and the cargo worth an entire planet behind him. His clouded eyes with no pupil seem like chasms into a grey soil. He is paused, reserved. Little facial features define him, other than a long scar that mingles with his small mouth. A cross between a grey and a nymph, Nempty roamed as a freak among his kind. A freak, perhaps, but no longer the servant of gods, goddesses, not even of those influential human organizations that took over, on Gaia. No church or bank would own his soul.

He observed waves of grass. They seemed to have been spat out of powerful currents, only to die against the hull and resurrect as they reach the bottom of the sea. He looked at the winds that appeared to gaze back at him. No one scares him. He survived not only multiversal battles, but, also, world wars in every one of those layers. He did by with loyalty to his cause: himself, his own vitality. He rewarded all the friends he made, along the way, but they always required faithfulness to each other. They allowed him their alliance, as they knew how powerful Entities respected him. Others just knew better than to consider Nempty a leader, a foe, or even a comrade. But Nempty never had any true mate. He only trusted constructs to help him on the boat. Two treefolks, nine golems and two androids assisted him on board. They don't require a salary, they rarely complain, they leave him alone.

The captain faced every tempest and feared nothing. He died, a Primordial Death, so often, that not even pain and intense agony shocked him. Once, he fought legions of merchoids, these tiny orchids the size of any given common being. They beat him and left him for lifeless in a jungle at the farthest end of Agartha. He suffered the most horrible forms of torture imposed to him by nature. All this, as certain beasts were sent to feed on his skin while his soul remained conscious, for weeks. Until an unknown mancer would pass by and reshape his flesh. Only then did he realize what his existence meant.

"If I should die, let me die prosperous."

He convinced himself and the Dreamer that may have heard him, then. And so, he perished for a last time, and was resuscitated before he could find the wreckage of his fairy-boat. He travelled until he could regain his old self, his own strength, and his pride. Thousands and thousands of Sophron cycle past since this resurrection. Nempty became one of the most influential merchants. He stood as the richest, the most powerful! And, one morning, he made an unsuspected discovery.

162

The Babel Wars had been over and forgotten for millions of years. I died, and so did Ishtar. Should anyone go by the words of legend, the entire House Indrashtar fell. But Nempty was known for his ability to tell an essence from an ether, and a substance from a spirit. Not only that, but he could also recognize previous hosts, and the same for soul particles. Because he has travelled so far, has seen so much, it is possible to assume he did confront Dreamers that not even Anu, Amon-Ra or YHVH would have encountered on a bright sunny day. Yet, Nempty could not manipulate these axioms he knew so well.

There was this wasp, and a baby boy that had been born, only two months prior. Nempty's decision to visit Manhattan in the seventies almost came by chance. He stubbornly showed his desire to meet The Crone and ask for advice. Nempty has long since wished to understand further awakenings, but nobody ever, had even hoped to help him in this quest. When he learned of Void's sole daughter refusing to become one with her father, he knew she would teach him well.

She wandered in big cities, all over Gaia, herding cats or pigeons, depending on her mood. He walked through that park and tried to spot mammals or birds, and he would later confirm them according to their proper specie. He saw only insects. Humans let their bug pet bark at others. Some had to grab insect feces into small bags, but most did not. How could he have found a cat or a pigeon, he wondered? As he wandered in the park, in search of The Crone, or any sign that could lead him to her, he heard tiny wings that broke through the air with a brave natural persistence. He turned around and saw a wasp, about to land on an oak tree. Forgetting his selfish journey, he approached, observed the beast.

"*I know this DNA.*" he thought to himself, just as the bug was parting from the bark. The beast flew towards a good-looking duo, landed on the arm of a baby boy, in a crib. "I was married, once." the dad, behind the cradle, told the young Afro-American student.

163

"I'm sorry. I grew up as a lone child with my mother.
I understand." she said, then kneeled to wave at the sleeping baby,
unaware of the perverted look the father gave her miniskirt and
thighs. Nempty observed the wasp, only the wasp. The dad saw the
dwarf who seemed to beg for money or food, but he ignored him.
The wasp! The midget knows it! Where did he see it, before?

"It's not that bad, but. I do need a new baby-sitter." The child
yawned, but only Nempty noticed. "Sir." The father could have
seen it coming. He just laughed once she'd reject his approach.
She looked at him, deep within, through his eyes and scolded him:

"Sir, I think your infant deserves a mother more than you need
a daughter. Thank you." She left the park, insulted. While Nempty
observed the wasp landing on the baby's forehead.

The sun reflected through the creature's wings like sprinkles of
night on the shadow of dawn. It stepped very gently on the child's
delicate skin. The beast strolled near the eye and stopped.
It cleansed its head with both front legs like a fly, and then went
over its mouth. It stayed there for long seconds, on the edge of
leaving or attracting more wasps. Using a pocket device that
looked like a jewel box, Nempty unveiled a gate to an abandoned
limbo that allowed him to walk closer and unnoticed. Until he
could further observe the insect. "I know you, boy." the Neymliss
said. "Do you remember me?" Baby opened his mouth to yawn.
The wasp got its sting imprisoned between two shadows of a tooth.

"You know? Some people really miss you. You could make me
earn big money."

He gently tried to grab the beast. Though the Veil between both
worlds did not exist. He failed magnificently. The bug stung the
baby's tongue and flew away.

The baby cried like his life was about to end as quickly as it started! And he didn't want that. But it hurt! So much! He cried, because he couldn't reason, think or say anything, and it hurt so much. Nempty watched the wasp fly away. He observed the father who tried to quiet a two-month-old child wounded deep for a first time in his life.

The Neymliss chased the flying menace throughout the park. He held a pocket travelling staff that a mancer built for him, and with which he could swiftly journey across layers, piercing the Veil. He walked past trees, cars, and buildings, created poltergeists as he pursued it even faster beyond a convenience store! Scared customers and perplexed shared the floor with tons of candies, cigarettes, and magazines to pick up and put back on their shelves.

All the way until time stopped. And time almost did. When a minivan entered the bridge. Nempty, despite his fragile shape, bravely jumped behind the bug, right before the vehicle would hit the wasp. Nempty had to think fast if he wanted to avoid the crash to leave little to no chance of recovering the insect's DNA. Were he a mancer, none of this would have been an issue.

He faced the traumatized look that inhabited the driver, an African American father of three in his mid-thirties. His wife sat next to him. His youngest daughter, three years of age, slumbered at the back of the minivan, between her older brother and sister. The car halted. The insect landed on their windshield. Casually, Nempty climbed the front of the car. He bore a much-annoyed look on his face while he walked to grab the wasp and imprison her in his right palm, gently shut. Just as nonchalantly, he walked away from the cute little family. They experienced difficulties coping with this scene out of a horror movie.

With an immense grin that demonstrated much pride, Nempty thought that this catch deserved to breach the Veil. Now, he must find a way to preserve that DNA and allow it to survive the passage through many layers of Sophron. Being a mere traveller forces the Neymliss to use some creativity. The first flash that got to his mind in the form of an idea involved amber. He drifted through the Veil, passing the nearby realm of Hades. He didn't pay attention to the river Styx. It still roams around the limbos all over Greece, across Hell and Akeldemach. He reached Hades, and then walked through the Veil again to end his trip in the mountains of Santiago, Chile, in the middle of the night. While travelling with the Ether-Stick seems fast, it has nothing to envy the long travelling on boats. Any trek involving magic allows for quick bursts in and out a different layer, or superficial visits of said realm.

He hates the South Americas. Every time he breaches the Veil, there, he ends up on every local newspaper with badly shot pictures and big letters that read: Chupacabra! El Vampiro de Moca. He finds this whole craze silly, and it's not like he can find better goat milk in other parts of Sophron either. He felt the insect barely alive in his hand. The animal wasn't prepared for the stress of a quick in and out past the Veil. The pressure threatened its life. Nempty knows that unless we preserve the DNA to survive through millions of years, none will believe what he found. Imprisoning the beast inside amber became his best option.

Chapter Sixteen:
Sekhmet is not a Fairy

The dark and dry throne room showed a lone window, at the far end. It displayed pale landscapes that almost projected light as in a dream. Tir n'a nOg resides in the Archeus-Logo quadrant. Over there, matter and void only exist in legends. For a goddess like Sekhmet to exist in such an alien world, it requires a great deal of magic. We can reprogram axioms to behave as their opposites. In this manner, Sekhmet was able to reshape her entire being so that Tir n'a nOg would consider her one of its own.

When she meditated, she preferred keeping as little light as she could. Her chamber was immersed in shades and darkness, with only the throne to shed a gleam around itself. So many ancient thoughts visited the cat-goddess, it was rather complicated for her to cleanse her mind. She recalled having introduced opioids from Hydaspes to turn many fairies into junkies. This would result in throwing the fairy population into apathy and depression. It would make the whole invasion much easier, with less bloodshed.

Her biggest concern, now, was seeing a return to the times of the Babel Wars. She lost control over her Egyptian empire when this last happened. Horus gained charge of operations, with Thoth acting as his beloved advisor. Sekhmet's influence on Gaia highly diminished with time. It compelled her to concentrate her efforts on different worlds. It would take the intervention of more subtle deities to restore mankind on the path to enlightenment.
The ancient gods and goddesses, forced into retirement, left Gaia's humanity slowly develop into their own Houses. With Indra possibly coming back, and should Varuna escape from his imprisonment, the conflicts with a warmongering Marduk would bring Armageddon.

It was imperative for Sekhmet to choose a side, perhaps. It may as well benefit her to remain neutral, but she would have to become the power that can shift the balance to one end or the other. Any tactical decision would require a reasonable plan. This process would have to begin with a short trip within her inner pluriverse. Hence why she ensured that nobody would disturb her while she meditates. She closed every door and shut all windows in her immediate vicinity. She peacefully installed herself on her comfortable throne, and she brought absolute blankness to her mind. Her possibility was once mapped under the name of The Cat-Fish Supreme.

The proper manner of entering those realms within start with renouncing our essence attached to the world without. The body's empty shell remains, while the soul gradually detaches itself from the illusion. Images processed by our eyes lose their colour and shape. The sounds turn to empty winds. Taste, smell, and touch no longer defines the hell in others. Sartre himself would lose his references on what existence is or should be. This is when the subconscious becomes the only vessel to carry the self. If the sojourner wears a sock, the inside becomes their dreams, hopes, desires, and the outside connects with the world. That sock, turned inside-out, would best represent the innerverse.

168

Every trip within differs from one traveller to the other.
For Sekhmet, the process carries colours and fractals. They slowly
merge into one another until order appears. A landscape surfaces,
then a sky, a ground, horizons. When she opened her eyes to look
at this novel scenery, she saw an empty street made with white
bricks. She walked this ground dressed in a long white robe.
She borrowed the traits of a young maiden, dark-skinned,
reminiscing about her black fur. At the far end of her sight, small
holdings appeared. Right in front of those rustic structures,
children threw leather balls at one another. *This is Greece.*
she thought to herself. Why do my dreams take me there?

She walked past the kids, the farms, and considered searching
for a certain building made with stone pillars. She found it in the
middle of the ancient city. She stopped in front and observed
its wide stage, surrounded with circular benches. She looked at
the sun and thought to herself: *My friend should be in his cave, at
this time of the day.* She entered the Parthenon and walked directly
to a carved-in tunnel, as though she had made this trip often
before. A long corridor took her to a wide chamber. There, she saw
seven students and an old wise man, surrounding a floating orb.
One of the disciples was telling his flock a story. The elder smiled.

Sekhmet stood in a shadow, as to not disturb the class.
She observed the small group and pondered. What connects them
with the struggle? When she cultivated her reverie, her motivation
came to transcend the current flow of events and connect her
essence with a stage beyond. For some reason, her old friend Plato
acted in this unfolding play. However, he doesn't choose sides.
He never wielded his knowledge of sophroner magic to fight.
He would rather use it to teach humans how to escape the
smothering illusion. His implication in this battle makes no sense.
If she appeared here, there must be another reason.

Someone else must be producing these thoughts, as she witnessed the materialization of a tall and muscular silhouette. It stood only two feet in front of her, its eyes aimed at the group of young boys, girls, and differing genders. Sekhmet swiftly realized that this intrusion wasn't as peaceful as hers. Whoever appeared, just now, bore ill intentions. Before she could contemplate any further, the block of flesh grabbed a crystal orb and summoned an intense blue flame. He could be about to throw all of them, Plato included, into a Final-Vanishing, for all she knew. No time to process any thought, now. Time to act! She cast her own sphere and swiftly tossed a limbo to separate them from the group. Her incantation came too fast, however, and even for such a powerful sophroner, she couldn't find time to make it perfect. Greyish walls surrounded them. It was still possible to see the group on the other side. The brute could easily uncommon her magic and resume his vile act. She had to use the element of surprise to cast another spell. Blades first came to her mind.

Five swords blasted out of her crystal ball, thrown directly at the shade's back. Her foe had enough time to turn around and block them with a shield that emerged from nowhere. Swiftly, the panther goddess caressed her orb. A giant cat-bear appeared. Her adversary sent a hulking zombie to fight back. While the creatures wrestled, the silhouette swapped the terrain for a gothic church. Plato's class was still nearby, concealed behind a curtain of heatwaves. This intervention left enough time for Sekhmet to bring forth ten thousand rabid cats, all flying in her foe's direction. Somehow, this new stage gave him more powers. With one quick gesture of his left hand, holding the orb with the right, he erased the flying kitties from existence. *He's a Victorian Walker?* Sekhmet thought. She couldn't reflect on all the possible names. She doesn't want a blue flame to Final-Vanish her. The battling magician didn't have time to cast one either, but he did send Frankenstein's monster to do his bidding.

She responded with a black was a lion, just before she summoned a cloak of invisibility around her. Both creatures threw themselves at one another's throat. The lion bit the zombie's jugular, resulting in a splash of blood that covered the walls. The squared shoulders humanoid grabbed the tall cat with a strong bear hug, and he squeezed. Out of breath, the lion dug his claws in his adversary's face, pulled the entire scarred visage off its skull.

At the opposite end of the corridor, past the curtain of wavy heat, Plato felt that something disturbed the Veil. He could have used the orb to investigate. But seeing how the student was well immersed into their current exercise, and how the others appreciated the activity, the wise man preferred to leave whatever was happening to whatever it was. Meanwhile, Sekhmet also acknowledged that whoever showed up to mess with her nosiness proved to be a worthy opponent. She didn't wake up that morning with a desire to fight. She caressed her sphere and reclaimed enlightenment back into her outer reality.

Chapter Seventeen:
How Nempty caught the Wasp

Many an academic assumed that the seventy-two layers of Sophron represent seventy-two periods in one reality's cycle. Truth must be a straightforward evolution. Time travel gets intense when passing from one realm to the other. Skeptics criticize that theory on the basis that various worlds have distinct laws of physics. Differences can sometimes get so extreme, millions of years, even billions of years, would not suffice to support such a drastic change.

Nempty will have his own opinion on the topic. He thinks that each layer represents a shift in time and in space. We must keep in mind that every reflection of Sophron resides in a given Dreamer, with the realms existing as exact copies of one another. When going from one possibility to a new, it becomes evident. Therefore, he does travel in various times of a host's life, and through various stages of that possibility's evolution. He has noted that certain events having occurred in the Avalon layer of one Dreamer did not happen in the same layer of a different Dreamer. Unless everyone agrees to the nature of True Reality, considering common ground remains impossible. Sadly, nobody educated Nempty about the existence of the Beyond, or singularity.

Walking unnoticed in the mountain until he could find an amber tree with the hardest and most translucent resin, the merchant stood in the face of the world. A mining site was right underneath him, at the highland's feet, deeply quiet at this time of the night. He climbed the elevated terrain to reach a nearby cavern. A mirage or some curtain of heatwaves concealed the entrance, mainly an effect of manipulating the Veil. Nempty stopped for a moment. The wasp needed to show enough resilience to survive another trek through and back from a limbo.

With its wings barely agitating themselves, the insect had no strength to escape. Nempty had his hand wide open and could only see the beast slowly moving its head and legs. The bug seemed more numb and dizzier, greatly disoriented, than on the edge of dying. He could wait a little longer to allow it to recuperate, but he decided to give this one last journey through the Veil a good try. Advancing across the heatwave as a ghost passing through the rock, the traveller held his layer-unveiling staff with much assurance. He entered a dimension where the sky, the land and everything in between espoused the appearance of minerals.

The soft texture under Nempty's feet felt like flesh. He walked slowly to avoid axioms from that reality colliding with the wasp's pixels. With a limbo so close to Gaia, the axiomatic friction kept to a minimum, precaution is the key word. The insect seemed to take this friction nicely. It must have inherited the subtle DNA codes that once defined the willpower and courage of this priceless essence it partially carried. The most complex system of tubes and aqueducts ever conceivable pierced the cave. The entire ceiling looked like a highway of long cylinders, some merging, completely hiding every inch of rock we could possibly have seen. These tubes appeared to connect that ground to another.

The room, as wide as a stadium, held a fountain in its centre. It concealed the stairway between this floor and the next. In the middle of the sculptured water furniture was the statue of a dying harpy under Hercules' might. He had one foot against the creature's neck and both arms in the air, about to deal a final blow with a two-edged axe. The fountain formed stalactites and stalagmites all around the icon. At the back of the room were twelve aquariums, each one fed by an aqueduct and supplying another. Inside some fishbowls swam beasts from various parts of Sophron.

Here, Nempty bred animals considered endangered and facing total extinction, knowing very well how select clients could pay fortunes to get one specimen. This is where alchemists, like Nempty, get an edge over manners: The number of axioms available throughout Sophron remains limited. It is possible to handle a certain value and turn this number into an object and or creature. That proportion, drawn somewhere, cannot supersede the pixels. It cannot go beneath this amount either. Cancers, therefore, only manipulate, they do not create. Alchemists, however, can produce new dots of reality and force the Dreamer to compensate by destroying an exact quantity the alchemist designed.

They hold no control over what they form as they do exploit axioms, and their actions can originate an unwanted tragedy. They only experiment with what they have in their hands and wait for results. When it comes to rare items, such as endangered species, most managers won't gather the right power to develop such a specimen. Not as easily as an alchemist will recreate a successful trial. Were the mancer in a position to find such a figurative exemplum, at any given time, in a particular section of Sophron. Then the Walker would be able to summon the beast's pixels from that realm, sending back the same amount and type of axioms from his hosting layer, and leave the Dreamer in equilibrium. But the rarer an objector creature, the more difficult it is for the mancer to accomplish such a feat.

Nempty walked inside his immense laboratory. It seemed more like a warehouse in certain corners, with vaults and boxes piled up, forming ramparts that would make the Great Pyramids into small prisms. He approached the core. There, on a tiny table, an easy system of alembics shares the space with glass recipients. Behind that table was a gigantic wall of shelves. Every known element from all the worlds of Sophron, and possible compound, fill the recipients. We could have counted over twenty billion storage units that covered more than five square kilometres. A simple computer glowed at his feet, something only discovered in the late twenty-third century by Gaia's timeline. Nempty purchased it for mere loose change in the city of para-Angeles, three layers up, in the Dahomey realm.

The merchant turned alchemist stood in front of his computer and summoned a keyboard made of light. He typed a few characters, a mixture of demotic, Coptic, and Chinese, with some Arab numbers, here and there. It originated in a screen made of pure brightness to display these characters before him. There, he pointed at a specific area on the monitor and keyed in a few more figures until he fulfilled his desired sequence. As a result, five mechanical arms, out of a possible legion of forty-two, climbed the countless floors, through the many shelves, until the alchemist's brought back the requested elements at his feet.

Five necessary components could produce the artificial amber he was determined to make: Resin from a pine tree that grows in Nirvana, mixed with one from Avalon. Powdered oxygen that mounts in ethereal mineral states throughout Sint Holo. Liquid diamond from the valleys of Metatron, in Arcadia, loiter the place next to a little bit of Gaian water from the faucets of a nearby motel. The wasp was on the floor, next to his left foot. It tried to stand on all its limbs, greatly disoriented. Nempty grabbed every component needed to concoct the formula.

He mixed the two resins with the powdered air and stirred until it formed bubbles that constantly renewed themselves. Then he introduced the liquid diamond so the oxygen would not die out after a while. He added water to keep the recipe consistent but not too fluid. When the resin was midway between a solid and a wishy-washy state, Nempty swiftly turned to pick the wasp up. He found it flying with more energy than it had the first moment they met, and with this insanely immense room as its playground. Nempty had close to no time before he could expect the formula to form into rock amber, under the action of liquid diamond.

Think fast.

He assumed. Faster. He's not renowned for his ability to reason. Wasps like sugar. Hmm. He requested the arms to pick the most odorant type of sweetness he knows. It comes from a honey-making platypus that populates underground atmospheres in The Open Door. Only one drop of this delicious sugar would destabilize a diabetic's system for months. When he opened the tiny vial, the sweet scent quickly emerged out of its orifice. The insect promptly produced pheromones to attract an entire army, and dove in Nempty's direction. The alchemist grabbed the spoon covered with this drop of honey. The wasp landed on his palm, swiftly charging at the sweet. So much carbohydrate drove the bug mad. It danced like a fool and stung the little guy's wrist. Nempty purposely let go of the spoon.

He used his free hand to capture the insect and throw it in the resin. The beast fought to release itself from the sticky trap until it realized that it could swim. It could just as easily breathe once the resin covered it in full. It almost looked like a prism inside the small spectacle. The wasp seemed to move but couldn't escape. Nempty grabbed the priceless jail, like a limbo made up for size, and put it in his front pocket. He then walked down the stairs that led to his fairy-boat.

Those golems he bought or exchanged in several worlds compose his most faithful company. An advanced android from Patagonia, Lucretia, couldn't discuss beyond the stage of small talk. The other automaton, Jonathan, came from Tabriz. He was programmed more for intellectual interactions. He also knew quite a lot about walking, mythology, religions. Those two couldn't perform housework. Nempty only bought them to communicate with. As for the rest of the constructs, they barely say a word. The only conversation they will have will involve technical issues.

"Get too many of them to think on their own, and you instigate a mutiny," Nempty reckoned.

The little guy saw an advertisement, while visiting the capital of all sins: Vordek of Patagonia. There, a shop could shape the perfect android beauty based on a consumer's dearest desires. Let there be a slave to the submission lover. Let's create a mistress to the flesh addicted. They configured them with a personality that would fit a customer's wildest dreams. They served everyone, from the nymphomaniac to the totalitarian. And so, in a very naive and innocent manner, Nempty decided to purchase the daughter he never had. His paternal instincts collided with the android's program. Where he felt protective and fatherly, she craved exploitation and abuse. In her mind, she desired physical abuse and suffering from other trash treatments. How could cruelty fall over such a delicate flower? Even if she begged him, that would never happen.

Regardless of his accumulated wrongs, righteousness lives in his heart. To the Greater Unknown, nobody might have cared about his choice of behaviour. But any god or goddess will agree: your thoughts create positive or negative energy that carries the weight of your words and action. Nempty knew better than succumbing to his demon side.

She stood taller than him, even for an infant. When he was offered a selection of ages, Nempty kept insisting for a few years younger than he looked. Until he realized that a prepubescent daughter would assist with his desire to act as a mentor. She had black and blonde hair that streamed down to her shoulders, always held in pigtails. They crafted her with a Catholic schoolgirl uniform, very popular in the perverted market. Nempty never thought about the blasphemous symbolism behind this. Besides, she looked cute in these clothes.

"Dad?" Nempty heard her soft-spoken voice through the radio when he stepped onto the boat. Golems were hard at work with some renovations and a great deal of cleaning. The mast had been retracted, until the great wide sea through the Veil would open itself. He walked slowly, then stopped. He sighed, thinking he may have awakened an infirm child. He should have left her in bed. And what if he held his own infirmity? Caring for a sex doll. How insane? Ethics and principles might disagree. To valiant knights out there, he's a hero. "Are you home, Daddy? This you?"

"I'm fine, Lucreatia." he slowly said. He took the amber out of his pocket and observed the wasp. It seemed to dance, with its wings floating like flying ribbons.

"We travel, now, Dad?" He looked at the amber for a long moment. Nempty wasn't a skilled mancer, so there was no way he could manipulate axioms to divide the creature and keep Indra's tiny parcel of the essence. But if there was some Indra in that DNA, then he could sell this artefact intact. There was something else he could attempt, however. He could put the trapped wasp inside a Manchester. It's some twisted technology developed in the realm of Litooma, one layer south of Shun-Yata, in the Logos-Void quadrant. Think of this metal box with half orbs all over it as a computer that links the minds of a million enslaved Walkers. The box allows them to avoid Final-Vanishing, but in return they must do the owner's bidding.

Litooma is known for hosting the greatest number of gifted people in all the worlds, even though they all lack a certain freedom. Perhaps the only layer that will never face an invasion. And it will hardly choose sides in any conflict that doesn't concern them. Nempty opened the metallic box he kept hidden in a special vault, behind a false wall. All the orbs shone at once, and the screams of a million enslaved souls haunted the room. Nempty gently put the amber with the wasp inside and closed the box. He then put both his hands on the many spheres and shut his eyes. "Dissect this organism," he claimed out loud. "Let me keep Indra's essence in that box."

The only problem with having a million slaves doing as you wish is that a weak mind asking a favour may still end up with a direct connection to the Great Entities. It would be like giving access to the launch codes of all US nukes to an illiterate president. But all things would happen for a reason. Many have tried to use this as a means of freeing themselves from their living hell. Nempty understands that every time he wields this cube, he trades his soul with chaos. It's like searching for the most powerful Internet that could, at any time, finds a way to trap your essence and possesses your body. The box seems very safe, keeping the walking sweatshop behind an artificial Veil, like an aquarium. But we never know how creative prisoners can be.

One might have seen an opportunity in having Nempty contact this powerful network. Kitana earned a reputation through her abilities as a powerful Walker. Three hundred years after the Babel Wars, another turmoil shook Sophron, the Ladder Conflict. It is around that time that Litooma's Entity, the Great Ghamqe, almost faced total devastation in Demonee's hands. Gathering Walkers to confront Demonee's army meant the best way of saving his world and avoid finding the same fate as the chimera did, in the palms of Marduk. So Ghamge the Gargoyle made a pact with Tao, Angel Entity protector of Tuurngait.

179

Kitana tried to use this rhetoric against Nempty, whenever she would sense his essence connected to the station. She fought during the Ladder Conflict to protect her village, and she saw the sadistic Demonee burn entire families in front of their siblings, just so he could nourish himself on their terror and grief. She had trained for three hundred years to become the mightiest sophroner of her realm and her time. Still, Demonee was beyond her league.

When Ghamge appeared to her in a dream, he promised her a way to beat Demonee before he could destroy her world, or any other, but that meant to sacrifice her freedom for all eternity. She accepted. For the first three thousand years, mancer technology provided means for many rebellions to overthrow powerful beings and Houses that sheltered ideals of total conquest. That was before Marduk freed himself from his limbo prison and gathered the biggest army, killed an Entity with his bare hands, shook the face of Sophron like never before. For Kitana, that event meant the mancer network had no reason to remain. The millions of slaves expected their release, so they could combat the enemy on the field. Marduk gained from using the mancer network, and bribing Ghamge, so dismantling the system couldn't happen.

Betrayed, Kitana had tried to find a way to evade and break the mancer network. When she took notice of Nempty, an idiot with big influence, who bought a mancer box on the Dark Market, she quickly scanned his essence and possibilities. She saw that her only chance at escaping from this prison was through the awakening of a Sleeper. All she knew was that he went by the nickname Grunt. A certain Seamus Chronenberg intimately joined his connection. This hero would fly with a certain William, who held the consciousness of Indra, and, of course, she knew who Indra was. She had to link Nempty to Seamus. And to William. How could she awaken a Sleeper from her underprivileged position, she had no idea? But as soon as Nempty opened the box and closed his eyes to intertwine his essence to the network, she knew she had to act fast. Otherwise, thousands would find reasons to connect to the smuggler and take it to their advantage.

"Hey, handsome." her essence told Nempty's. "Kitana? You again?" he complained. "You're supposed to be millions, why do I keep bumping into you?"

"We're made for one another, dude. Hey, guess what? Your insect has traces of Indra's DNA in it." She was good. How did she manage to learn so much, so fast? No time to get distracted.

"Of course, girl, even I knew that. I need to know who I can sell this to."

"Nah, Nempty, you need to be told that the wasp evolved on Gaia, and these traces of DNA found their way into a human boy: William Francoeur, he lives in Montreal. We believe that a certain Seamus Chron might act as his best friend. I think, anyway, that's how I see the whole thing." The flow of information froze his brain. *Hold on,* he thought. *Who are these people? How did she know about the wasp? Why is she so smart and she's doing customer service? Over the phone! He's a smuggler who played an extra role during the Babel War!* "Okay." he mumbled. She can't possibly be smarter than him, now.

"Nempty? Are you there?" He should say something quick, or he'll look stupid: "Wow! Damn, girls, this is why we keep bumping into one another. You understand your stuff!" He should have said something else, perhaps. "We don't bump into one another! You do your job, you try to make a living out of it, and I do the same. I just happen to know some things that you and my bosses don't. I'm a smart angel."

"That you are. How do I get to William?"

"Sophron is one big, interconnected mess. I just know my way around it. If I tell you where to find William, can you do me a favour? Like last time?" Kitana inquired. Nempty wasn't sure, but he dared: "I can't give you my body, and even if you tried, Ghamgeis watching. But ask."

181

"I need a happy memory, anything. Can you do that for me?"

"Kitana? You need a happy memory?"

"Come on, Nempty. Give me something. And I'll need something else from you, after."

The dwarf looked at his daughter and smiled. He remembered the moment he bought the android. Only two months old, for an android that looked like she's twelve, and she stayed the whole day attached to his leg, demanding affection. He cared for her ever since. "Can you feel Lucreatia's essence near me?" he asked Kitana. The Walker felt it. If you inquire about her environment, rest assured that her space, while limited, remains somewhat roomy. The best comparison I can offer you, reader, as to her workplace is that of a regular call centre you may find on Gaia. The cubicles stand as wide as a fancy penthouse in a rich hotel, with all sorts of accommodations to ease their living. A tall, pink-skinned angel, Kitana had her wings surgically removed.

She kept the scars, however, and shows them with pride, as she dresses herself in a long V necked t-shirt that embraces her huge breasts and leaves her shoulders and upper back naked. She wears jeans and running shoes that make her look like a regular college student. Her short silver hair almost gave her a tomboyish style. She plays with a pen as she responds to her client:

"She really loves you. I'm overwhelmed by happy memories from her. Why does she desires ill treatments so bad?"

"They sold me a sex doll, or something, programmed to be dominated and abused. I could never find the will to do that. She's my anchor on morals, now. Okay, can you help me or not?"

Chapter Eighteen:
Kitana works in an Office

She decorated her cubicle with images that reminded her of home. Penglai, next to Svarga Loka, shines under a different name: Heaven. It stands only two layers away from True Logos. Some scholars argue that the Beyond reflects opposite worlds from the Below. According to this theory, Hell mirrors Svarga Loka and Thule mirrors Penglai, just as the Open Door lies opposite to Tir na n'Og. The facts, as we poets, prophets, veritas and even mentiones perceive them, speak of a Noesi de Vel made of only numbers and equations.

Zendoria, the world between worlds, serves as a provider of balance, between the Below and the Beyond. When a child, Kitana's essence would play around the Immortal Palace. She didn't know of any other realm, and yet the immense building that overlooked the entirety of Penglai projected haunting sunrises. Of those memories, she kept a small painting that recreated this landscape and the feeling she knew.

To do her job, she had her brain connected to a sphere. Customers would contact her with a Manchester box, and she would produce the spells requested using that crystal ball and her gift. It was limited, of course, and she could have provided more help, if the interlocutor, at the opposite end of the call, had their own orb.

More framed sit next to the sphere. One of them displayed Kitana smiling next to a giant biomech, a bear with metal arms. Another image would show her standing next to a purple bird, with a very dumb gaze. A bronze statue of a junkie getting high on crack stands behind them. Some words were scribbled at the bottom. The writing was that of a child who just started to learn the alphabet. It read: "Thank you for being my friend, Mr. Kennedy. Signed: Your friend: Nunc."

No matter how often she reminded him, he still fails to call her by her name. Whenever difficult times arose at work, she would look at this image and smile. What a true sweetheart. He doesn't seem to understand how rough life is. Even on a battlefield, he wouldn't see pain and suffering. Only beauty get to his mind. She connects with his essence, only to talk and feel less alone.

They met by accident when the purple bird found a metal box and called the mancening network. Somehow, she sensed a strong energy coming from his kind voice. She thought he could become an asset, one day. So, she used her power to keep him always linked to her cubicle, just as she did with Nempty.

That picture came from a dream she projected in Nunc's mind. Those Walkers remain prisoners, but the smart ones will know how to escape. Figuratively speaking. She has other privileged allies, like that, to whom she can rely in case of needs. Ultimately, it will result in her breaking out of this mess. Perhaps she will find a way to grow back her wings. Now, however, her entire focus was on Nempty's call. She used to think of him as a solitary person, as she hardly ever felt anyone's presence. But he mentioned Lucretia.

"Is she the only sentient android you have on your ship?" she asked. "There's also Jonathan." he answered. "But he's a mistake. He's total boredom, only talking about magic and science."

"I see." Kitana kept a few mental notes. She may need to connect with them, somehow. A myriad of awkward thoughts came to her mind. She found that link between Nempty, the wasp and Indra. That also hooked her to William. Someone else attracted her attention. She perceived a dancer. A woman who cared for William, but she had no idea who that essence belonged to. When she stretched her vision further, she could see that William was connected to another god, or maybe a goddess. She couldn't possibly provide that information to her client. He was only looking for the highest bidder. So, let's introduce him to that Seamus Chron person. Then, he'll be led to Sekhmet. Finally, he'll find Varuna, and Kitana can expect a few elements in motion to guarantee her escape. She can do it!

"All right, handsome. I'll take you to a person of interest. Take it from there. If you need me, you know how to find me."

Journey into the Hourglass:
Eight

I didn't enjoy working on the Chronicles of Sophron while Martin stayed in his castle, in Time Square, New York. When he slept at my place, I could tell if he had overdrunk, or if he discussed with me with a sober mind. I didn't worry myself too much with the novel, while I let him write the next few chapters. Martin spent his entire life dreaming about becoming a famous and wealthy author. I never asked for any of my influence, but I got it.

Christine Mai is the barmaid at the Green Simon, on Avalon. That's the bar where we met. She warned me about Martin being a lost cause. Sure, he kept returning to that bar and try to score with her, and she kept rejecting him. Obviously, the connection didn't occur between them. Christine preferred having me around, but I was a happy celibate. The reason why I visited the Green Simon every week was because Martin was there.

Despite all his weaknesses, I felt a strong connection. We were cosmic twins, I think. But while I was aiming at expanding my own self-creation, Martin remained adamant on self-destroying himself. I felt sorry for him, about that. Every day, he would wake up in his apocalyptic world, trying to give meaning to his existence. Only to drown in his own self-inflicted depression. These novels represent his last chance at understanding one simple fact: Enlightenment was never about wealth and fame. It's all about Indra. "Yeah, right?"

Chapter Nineteen:
Nempty meets Seamus

When Nempty opened his eyes, he was in a street, somewhere in Montreal, in the Gaia layer. The wasp seemed to have escaped her jail, but she flew around him like a pet. Grey and motionless, the entire scene felt slow. Kitana brought the dwarf into a limbo, so it appeared. He sat on the sidewalk, thinking how he could blend in, and that's when he saw this good-looking young man, about seventeen years old, with a lunch bag and a packsack. The kid must have a connection with Indra, he pondered. He couldn't possibly hold Indra's self, so menacing was out of his curriculum. A glancer? A dancer? Not a sophroner, that's impossible. Sophroners can't be as rookies as this one seems to be. The kid was passing by him, he had to think of something to get his attention. "Do you have change for a coffee, mate?" he would inquire.

"No, my dad gives me money. Ask him." the child replied, sarcastically. Nempty stood up and looked him in the eyes, but he froze. "Sorry, sir, I have to go to school." the boy complained. The mancer slaves must have found it a right time to strike Nempty's mind with a hit of genius. Of course! A glancer! Not only this, but Ishtar must have visited him, as she tries to reunite with her true love. A name came to him: William. She's looking for someone: William. This boy knows who he is.

"You found her, you son of a bitch!" he expressed, before the kid inhaled deeply to gather the courage to leave. "Get me to him! Get me to William!" he insisted but ran as fast as he could. When he looked behind, Nempty disappeared. He sighed and gathered some time to catch his breath, then he turned right on the following street and walked towards the school, far ahead. Questions floated in the kid's mind. He tried to go past the greyish surroundings, but he was trapped in that strange dream of a world. "It's called a limbo. Sorry I had to drag you into this, but you and I need to talk."

The homeless man came out of the kid's shadow against the street, and it looked as though he turned his silhouette into black smoke. He stood in front him, and he certainly wasn't very tall. He had a hump, but that didn't stop him from standing straight, with his long grey hair falling down his back. He wore denim and an old Hawaiian shirt, yellow with red flowers all over. He didn't have any shoes on. He kept his hands behind his back and observed the kid in the eyes, then he uttered:

"When you see William at school today, tell him Nempty has the boat ready. I could use his mancing skills on board. You should tag along; he will need your gift."

"Where are we going?" he questioned him. "Where am I going? I'm looking for Indra."

"The Indian god?"

"This wasp is linked to him. How did I find out? Millions of enslaved Walkers told me. What's a Walker, you ask, boy? It's you. It's William. It's, well, it's complicated. Somethings the trapped ones understand that I don't. That's because I'm a bit dumb, and I don't know how this jumbo-mumbo."

"Mumbo-jumbo."

"That too, how it works. When you uncover William, make sure he's safe."

"Ishtar talked about a dancer we should look after."

"What does the little girl know about the war we got ahead? No, you go fetch William, and you contact me. I'll take you both to my boat. I'll be waiting."

"How do I contact you?"

"I'm not the glancer; you figure it out!" The limbo vanished and Nempty found himself back on his vessel. He examined the wasp that didn't try to fight for freedom. He observed the bubbles of oxygen that slowly formed around the insect. He sensed his daughter's hand that played with his palm, tenderly, but he didn't pay too much attention. Old memories of tall orchids cloaked his mind. The giant biological robots stood ready for battle over the plains of Babylon. Gaia resembled a tropical forest, around that time, hundreds of thousands of years ago. Politics between Enki and Marduk had gone so tense, Anathema, those decrees of Final-Vanishing pronounced against an individual, House or circle, rained from both sides of the war. The Sapphire Council felt that both were losing their ground on sanity, and that this war, if unstoppable, could leave a possibility on the edge of Death. When a Dreamer dies, the whole Sophron within that possibility disappears. "Kitana?" he asked. "The link is fading, Nempty, but here's my part of the deal."

"Aren't you someone's property? I don't deal with slaves."

"Any one of us could break you to ashes, don't try me. I must find someone. I must connect myself to some essence who goes by the name Grunt. Can you help me with that?"

189

"Yeah, sure, let's see if I get something before. We next bump into one another."

"Nempty, I need you to help me with that!"

He suddenly severed his link to the Manchester box. So many questions, options, floated in front of him. What if he just kept the wasp to himself and let things be what they are? No war! No battle, that he knows. Marduk keeps corrupting circles on Gaia, even though he considered himself imprisoned in a faraway limbo, between Svarga Loka and Tir na nOg.

Marduk's legions invade old strongholds that Enki and, later, when Enki vanished, Varuna held. *Sekhmet is in Tir na nOg.* he thought, then. She's not that much into Marduk. She just uses him. She told me herself. That seemed like a wise destination. When his senses came back to him, he felt Lucreatia's saliva against his index finger. He turned to see his daughter, only a hand, small, gentle, so pale yet so strong. Her wide blue eyes and a long, childish, depraved smile came out of the shadows, into the light.

"If we don't travel, can I have a spunky?"

Troubled, he swiftly took his palm back and left the staircase. "We're going to Tir na nOg. Call the others! We sail."

She seemed a bit disappointed on her way down. A heat wave formed around the Barracuda, and the entire boat levitated from its stand. The blue vehicle gathered a light of its own. Nempty never understood the mechanic behind it, but he knew whom to see for regular maintenance and repair, and he could pilot the thing. That was more than sufficient. He considered that there were other means of travelling through Sophron. Three: Space, Time, and the Ether. None as fast as inner journeys.

It is performed using an orb. It is also best done by fencers, as they can manipulate the Ether. Very advanced glaciers have been seen doing it their way. Space travel requires the longest time, and the knowledge of wormholes. Means of bending space and time until the Veil is pierced, and layers meet. Nempty sailed through the Veil, either by himself with the use of pocket limbos attached to his staff, or with his boat, whenever his merchandise had to follow. This means of sailing would take months, sometimes years, to pass a true world, or reach a paradox. Nempty presented himself as a very patient nymph.

Going through the Veil with such an enormous boat implied the deployment of immense tunnels. Scales that borrowed the same material mancers use to make their crystal spheres cover the vessel. To attain his destination faster, Nempty bought and built laboratories, like the one in Chile, that can produce enough energy to open or sustain a vortex. Those that the Barracuda produced stretched so immensely, limbos had to form themselves only to prevent the Veil from tearing itself while the boat proceeds through it. While in Veil-travelling mode, masts were fully retracted. A roof made the whole boat look like some sort of sausage.

The ceiling seemed non-existent from inside, with screens acting as tiles all over. The world outside could be seen through those screens, and this left an impression that no roof existed. The screens also displayed realms on the way to the vessel's destination, as well as the weather channel and cartoon network. Swirls of blackness and whiteness encompassed the whole tunnel. The boat further engulfed itself into the limbo that would temporarily carry forward. Another tunnel would open and allow the boat to reach the next layer. This would take about a week. If you want to know what happens during that time, just remember the occupants: golems, treefolks and two androids. And there's a selfish captain that can't stand thinking the one being he cares for, the most, only loves him for his body.

After about a month of sailing from one world to the next, the boat reached Avalon. There, they had a rest. Lucreatia couldn't bear the monotone life she was having. She wanted to explore outside. "But you're always in your vault, sweetheart! You like that. Nempty sighed. She ordered the three tree folks that handle the mast and roof to leave. They did and Nempty couldn't even try to stop her. "Dad. You never let me breathe."

" It's because I care for you."

"If you would, then you would punish me when I'm a bad girl."

"I can't!"

She frowned and walked away from Nempty. She always looked for shadows to hide in. "You don't love me."

He advanced in her direction and sighed. "It's precisely because I do. Trust me."

"If you loved me, you'd do what I need."

"I know better, as an adult. As someone who understands how those necessities destroy. Look! I'm sorry. You heard the whole story, and you get why I can't allow myself to be a beast to you."

"I'm not even your real daughter!"

"Stop it!"

"Then let Mon-Shu punish me."

"Treefolks aren't designed for that, sweetheart."

"Fathers aren't either, it seems." She left him behind and returned to her vault. He sighed again and made a quick gesture towards Mon-Shu. "Pray you never get a daughter."

192

"I was not programmed to pray, master." Mon-Shu replied. Nempty signalled him to *do whatever* and left the bridge.

When the boat returned to its initial course, Lucreatia stayed in her room with no light. She only listened to punk songs from the darkest no-name corners of Afghanistan, Avalon. Many days had passed with little news from the rebellious youth that won't get any. She often cried and asked forces beyond her reach about the reason why evil men created her in this libidinous manner. If it is to suffer at the hands of what her father calls morality.
This precious shower of cold water he had the instant he saw this light in her eyes. When he finally decided to knock at her vault's entrance, she hid her face under a pillow. Nempty had to knock.

"Can I come in?" he softly asked. "I'm not here! I died!"

She shouted. He sighed and unlocked the door. Her messy room concealed all sorts of treasures he dug up from all over the known Sophron: Paintings that served as windows to limbos; fake orbs for make-believe manners; A huge hole stretched itself, at the back of the vault. It opened to a moving painting of another world, the most beautiful of them all: Hydaspes. Drapes partially veiled it, but a good look at it revealed a luxuriant river that stretched through a wide valley and lose itself in a dark forest, at the farthest end of the horizon.

Nempty walked through the empty bottles of pop and juice, scattered among socks, bras, and shirts, all over the floor. He approached the small bed and saw her, naked and on her belly, with her head under the pillow. He sighed again and gently covered her nudity with a towel.

"Lucre." He whispered, while he delicately tucked the fabric under her. "I know I told you that story a thousand times. I'd appreciate if you considered it and stop making scenes like that."

He explained, then paused, pondered over a few ideas, and explained: "I never had any form of ethics before I met you. Look at those, designed by gods eager to control those circles of believers, all around Sophron. The only moral I could use was something I called: 'Do as you please and don't pity those you stepover.' Do you understand that?"

She remained silent. Nempty felt like he invaded a layer he shouldn't have. "I am. Okay, I'm your dad. I did very ugly things in the past. To people. I do not choose one side or another in this battle, and I know they're still at it even though Marduk and Varuna stayed in prisons. It's beyond them. But morality, ethics, doing the right thing has no side. It has no bias or preference; it just is what it is: The right thing we should do. And that means I should always respect you. Even when you don't respect yourself." He gently uncovered the back of her head to caress her hair with a paternal and protective intention, and show a bit of affection, without losing sight onto what he was: A loving father. Then he took the amber out of his pocket and observed the wasp.

"I don't know who's doing the right thing on each side. I think they just do what they believe as good, according to them. But we're going to visit Sekhmet, in Tir na nOg. She installed her House there, after she and others from her clan found themselves driven out of Egypt. We'll give her this."

She left the comfort of her pillow to dare a look at the stone. She saw the wasp, and the insect looked at her. She perceived that essence deep inside the bug's eyes, and that glance noticed hers. Intrigued, her eyes, red from having cried too much, she picked the amber and penetrated its light with her curious sight

"His name is Indra. He was a friend of Varuna's. You remember Varuna? The valiant fighter who saved my existence in Agartha. We thought Indra vanished completely, but here he is.

194

Maybe we can find Ishtar. The two were in love. Something big is coming, child. I will have to locate my buddy, the Hindu god of Greater Heavens. I also met young humans, on Gaia. These two warring factions will squash them. This is important, angel. I will require of you that you do as I say. Please, start by existing beyond your perverted program. Can you do that?"

She further looked into the amber and perceived my essence. Something about her felt familiar. Was she someone I called a friend? A sister? I couldn't tell. Nempty took the jewel back.

"When I saw you for the first time, Lucreatia, I assumed why Marduk and Varuna have been clashing so much and so hard, sacrificed so much over a story of godly hormones. You see? I would do the same for you, and more. You made me consider what is right and what is wrong, even though you weren't designed for this purpose. I still don't know if Marduk or Varuna fight for the right kind of love, but I understand what Indra may have gone through. I hope Sekhmet does as well, say?"

"Ishtar..." she whispered. "What?"

"That light in my eyes, the voice in my head."

She looked at her father's pupils through the amber and murmured: "You said her name is Ishtar. I think she's a butterfly."

Nempty didn't seem to understand the meaning of this. I did. Two months later, the boat exited the Veil and entered Tir na nOg. They sailed on that sea of grass for a few more days, all masts taken out. They flew until they reached the city of Arcana, sometimes nicknamed New Heliopolis, after the occupying Houses have brought some Egyptian additions to a somewhat Medieval European architecture.

195

Thoth and Sekhmet wanted to make themselves forgiven for having invaded this world of faerie folks. Sekhmet had convinced her beloved god of wisdom to expand their influence beyond Duat. To confront Marduk, or any other conquering House, it allowed them to intervene, should a new Great War arise. They annexed Tir na n'Og, so they gradually positionned their military between the Archeus-Logos and the Void-Barbelo quadrants. Thoth established a base in the city-state of Wells, while focusing on building a strong alliance with House Guan Yu in the Xuanpu layer. A huge arena stood midway between Sekhmet's capital and Thoth's.

The stadium, twice as big as the palace, pierced the sky at the centre of a forest. Maya designed it, a faerie architect who had taught many from many Houses. From a distance, it resembled a hive with flying bees, but from closer it looked like a cloud of gold and concrete. Different angles on the stadium borrowed different interpretations of Maya's artistic expression. It is important to mention that she grew up in Athanor, a layer famous for its ever-changing background. When Maya was asked to return home to Tir na n'Og, she intended to offer fairies a similar taste. After this masterpiece, building illusions became her best achievement. Nempty stationed his Barracuda after he entered a long canal that divided the city in half. Gigantic ships could rival the immense skyscrapers made of glass and mirror.

Arcana turned into a modern metropolis, after Ossian exited his domain. He reformed a feudal House in the Forest of Flames, vowing to bring Tir na nOg back its medieval glory. Sekhmet and Thoth shared most of his circles, and only a few supporters stayed alongside Ossian. Every other village, all around Sekhmet's capital and Thoth's, remained very rustic. One would think, however, that the advent of modernity in Tir na nOg would influence other kings to adapt or face assimilation. These conservative kings pledged allegiance to Ossian. Sekhmet's temple stood up two streets down from the marina where Nempty's fairy-boat ended its trek. A tall white and silver building with seven towers that stood up and seemed to pierce the sky.

The moment they entered the sacred place, I felt alive. Inside the insect. I knew that place! That wasp, somehow, knew this place. The insect flapped its wings, and I could hardly control them.   I didn't know if my fear froze me mid-flight, my intense apprehension for the unknown I faced. Or if the insect simply flapped its wings as I awakened. One thing I could tell was that.

"Nempty?"

We're already facing Her Grace. She stood in the middle of a garden, observing us as we approached. It was as though she expected our visit.

"Sekhmet, you are a goddess beyond all I've bowed to."

Nempty bowed down much below his actual height, and that's little saying. The nymph really is short. "Quit that, I know you. I have nothing to trade." He stood up, trying to come back from an insult he may have uttered. "My dearest lord. I came to do diplomacy."

"Thoth is the Lord of your House. Speak your business, smuggler. You're no politician." He belongs to no House, but Sekhmet likes to assume that everyone belongs to someone. As far as I can tell, the little smuggler assumed this House as his own, the moment he had to fill out a census paper. But he never really believed it. "I have. Found this insect."The whole world seemed to stop its motion, as though life came to me in an instant that lasted forever. I saw the face of a black panther. She loved mine, some time, long ago. What happened? I did not know. This fragmented essence could hardly reconnect with reality. Mutually aware of one another's presence. I, a subtle piece of a chemical code within a tiny animal, felt this aborning paradigm. If he sensed me, then she could sense me even more. Through the wasp, I managed to imagine the world around me, as though in a dream. The garden room projected intimacy.

197

A golden throne stood at the back, with red velvet drapes all over it, black drapes at its feet, some were suspended against the lustre in the middle of a floating island ceiling. At our back, walls formed an immense fortress. The fairy-boat was parked about two miles beyond the building. The guards that let us in were able to keep an eye on our vehicle, mainly because this world, unlike your planet Earth, is flat, and covered with a dome. Sekhmet's palace was a perfect mixture of indoor and outdoor architecture.

Pieces of armours that represented formidable changelings that Sekhmet's army killed to conquer this world. The shiny golden scaled armour belonged to Freya Die Feen, born of a powerful Norse king from Valhalla and a faerie mother from Avalon, died a hero to save Tir na nOg. The pale red armour's dead owner was Godfrey Le Juste, a French fair folk who grew up in Arcadia and once served as a counselor beyond the Veil to a certain Joan. There was the picture of an American by the name of Joseph. A sprite was drawn next to him, holding golden plates.

She walked through the field of textiles with such sensuality and ease, Nempty could hardly conceal his animalistic attraction, yet he knew he had to. He shut his eyes; I opened mine. On both sides of the throne were two faerie slaves, the twin maidens.

Chapter Twenty:
Marduk's bitter Memories

Every time Marduk finds solace in his private corner, the sum of his existence freezes. A reality he knew, tens of thousands of years prior, haunt him to no end. The thought of Ishtar is enough to disturb his mind, like an earthquake that leaves his skull in shambles. Why did she choose a foreign god? Why did they have to wed under the blessings of an empire? And why are they back in his life? Angered, the Hound Lord of Nibiru threw his orb against the wall! It shattered in billions of pieces, and reformed as it rolled to his feet. While he looked away, images appeared at the sphere's center.

There were ancient ziggurats that once stood tall in what is now known as Iraq. A flock of gigantic eagles patrolled the sky, while two armies battled on the ground. Mitanni was fast expanding around the Euphrates River. Marduk felt insulted, seeing how humans who fought under Indra and Ishtar's love evolved. The worst would have been seeing technologies from his world paired with the wonders of Svarga Loka. There, an archoid the size of the Empire State Building walked with an ax made of pure light.

The projected images showed Marduk sending his giant eagles to dive and eat the flesh out of this gigantesque anthropomorphic creature with the head of a deer. The biomech quickly responded. Slashing one bird in half, the blade cut through the forehead of a second beast. It finished its move against a wall. Further down, against the ground, thousands of humans fought in the name of deities they only knew from tales by the fire. From a wider perspective, however, we can assess that this battle had progressists and conservators vie for their ideals. As it will repeat itself throughout history.

One side dreams of power for himself. He subjugated his followers, cultivating their fear of the mystery. Indra and Ishtar wanted mankind as potent as gods. They sparked mathematics, science, philosophy. In the end, the Mitanni empire proved far superior to any other army willing to invade Gaia. Marduk observed this battle, the last one he fought before retreating to Nibiru. This sight brings him bitterness and anger. The Babel Wars were only beginning, but the Indra and Ishtar alliance demonstrated how powerful two Dominant Groups coming from different worlds can be.

For three hundred years, the Hound-Lord worked out a plan to reinstate his thirst for conquest. While Gaia had powerful dynasties to evoke enlightenment to mankind, Marduk knew that only a display of power would inspire other Houses to bow down and show him the respect he deserved Surrounded with silence, the Lord dared to look into his orb to further collect ancient memories. While Indra taught humans the ways of some secret knowledge, Ishtar brought them the beauty of art. We could have sworn having seen the Golden Ratio hand in hand with the Golden Crafts of old. This, you see, is what the Tower of Babel was always about. That, and a tall building made of bricks and metal. The tower itself hosted a school that could educate millions of classes to hundreds of thousands of students. The human pupils learned everything, from the secrets of Sophron to culinary arts, poetry, theatre. If the House in power knew the subject, then meant to be taught.

On Nibiru, Marduk found shelter under the care of his mentor. The tall and muscular Lady Marl-ures of Alibastat dearly loved her adopted son. On that morning, just as the Hound-Lord recalled, she invited him to join her in a modest meal. Sitting alone at the far end of a wide table, slaves brought her the cooked carcass of a sphinx. Marduk entered the dining room with his head down, unable to face her eyes. Marl-ures didn't turn her gaze his way either. She signalled a servant, and five of them swiftly sheltered and serviced her son. While he planted his fingers in the heart of the winged animal, the mother broke the silence: "Shame? Do I feel shame coming from my doggy boy?" she asked, almost laughing, but she wanted to let him feel her influence.

"I committed one mistake, Mother." he replied. "I allowed myself to fall in love."

She didn't say anything in return. Her attention was focused on nourishing her entrails. Marduk found the courage to add a few words: "But I know of their weakness too!" he proclaimed. The Queen Mother listened, while cleansing her teeth with two fingers.

The Hound Lord added: "They rely too much on teaching enlightenment to those humans. We need to regroup, build a much stronger army. If we wait until they consider themselves untouchable, greater, bigger than they are, and we strike! We exercise a power they will have forgotten about.

We can destroy that Tower of Babel."

Marl-ures laughed: "Don't you think they'll see you coming from worlds away?" she asked. "They can very well build orchids to prevent an attack arriving from anywhere, at any time."She had the answer, but that wouldn't be doing him any service. Her adopted son pondered for a moment. He didn't need to connect himself to her essence to find out what she was thinking. It made sense. "We have to infiltrate their tower. We will get insiders who will invest years of training, aimed at their self-empowerment."

"Empowerment?" she asked, a bit curious. "If they fear our return, they will prepare. If they are taught to forget that we even exist, then we have that edge."

"You will need something more, my son." she frowned. "When you reappear, make sure you have acquired a prowess unlike anything they have ever seen. And then, use the element of surprise to chop the head off! Kill Indra! Make Ishtar your own! And come back to me triumphant, or don't return at all!"

The images faded from the orb. In the centuries that followed, Marduk gathered an army and subjugated many layers. He started his journey on True Archeus. There, he led a civilization of nymphs against tyrannical muses. Fallen Angels, Risen Demons joined the battle. The homonymic Ocorsur guard True Archeus.

Rarely will those Entities of Major Influence choose sides in futile quarrels. The Hound-Lord understood that he couldn't claim this True World as his own. His eyes were elsewhere, anyway. He brought his army to the next realm, Dahomey. The fight, over there, seemed special. Legends have it that Houses who preserved this layer didn't see Marduk's invasion coming. The truth is that they knew, but they had no idea what his plan was. Dahomey, Cibola and Alibastat lay next to each other. Being the first three realms in the Archeus-Logo quadrant, they stuck to protect one another from occupations since times immemorial. We call them: the Three Sisters. Why would Marduk capture the worlds of his own adoptive mother, anyway?

This move made absolutely no sense. Even though Marl-ures left Alibastat long ago, to sit her strength over Nibiru, always welcomed and venerated where she came from. Also, this didn't look like an invasion. On True Archeus, the Hound-Lord came as a violent and bloodthirsty saviour. Once he gathered a unit solid enough to subjugate Dahomey, he just taunted them and did nothing. He bullied the Three Sisters, but he did not arm them.

He did, however, climb the ladders of power until he became intimate to the Great Entities that guarded these worlds. Curiousity, perhaps. Why would a lord play this game? Attacking a city, one day, and rebuilding it the next. Instructing politicians to lie and get away with it, by establishing faith in the heart of emotional people. Pushing an insurrection, blaming another party, and hiding. Just so the entities could notice the strange game he was playing.

Enlil-Bastat, Guardian of his mother's home world, projected a weird aura. When Marduk earned the trust of this mighty chimera, he knew he had achieved his goal. Time came to do the one final blow that would sit his authority and go back to Gaia. One immense blow. Take his newfound army of millions and destroy the Tower of Babel.

Journey into the Hourglass:
Nine

On how Martin didn't appreciate seeing me writing so many stories about so many characters, but it was always just about two opposing forces: selfishness versus selflessness. No matter how complicated we can get with our novels, and if we include parallel universes or possibilities, at the end of the day, we're just telling the story of Og and Om.

Sekhmet knew that when she invaded Tir na n'Og. Back when Egypt dominated the awakened world, on Earth, the panther goddess could hardly compete with the likes of Seth or Osiris, Horus, or Isis. Yet, she knew her worth. She probably understood that ancient wisdom would fall, at one point, when humans would learn to develop their connection with singularities. But for the gods and goddesses of Egypt, that opportunity ended with the rise of Thebes, then Athens.

I'm always losing Martin when we discuss the influence of Noesi de Vel. So, I just asked him: "Can you let me write about Sekhmet invading the world of fairies?" Yeah, right, of course. He replied. I think we're finally getting somewhere.

Chapter Twenty-One:
Sekhmet's Entourage

As the Princess's personal maid, Katrina O'Forgismund acted as the custodian of Her Majesty's secrets. She kept this position for most of her two hundred years on Tir na n'Og, until the Duatian invasion. Like her kindred faerie folks, tall and insanely slim with skin white as snow, her wide-open eyes covered one full third of her face, with a mouth barely visible when shut. Her nose almost only consisted of two tiny holes for nares. Her long blonde hair seemed to stem midway across her scalp whenever she kept her lock falling down her back.

She enjoyed a braid going against the flow to land on her modest breasts. When Sekhmet claimed victory over House Ossian of Arcana, she had entered the throne room and walked through corridors littered with thousands of bloodied corpses. Only a brave young maid, mutilated from the killing of a dozen animal-headed Duatians, stood between her and this victory. She held on to that weapon the size of her very long thighs with vengence in her eyes. "You will not steal this throne while I live." She recalls a loud whisper she threw at this powerful goddess.

Sekhmet walked very gently with the feline grace of an amused empress. Silently, she spun the blade into dust. Katrina reached for the sword that lay near a dead body, but Sekhmet had already cast a spell on the corpse, turning it into a living sarcophagus. She imprisoned the maid and finished her invasion, despite the absence of Princess Anastasia. She had been escorted into an undisclosed safe when the first war boats appeared out of the Veil. If Katrina had known how Anastasia betrayed her own queendom, she would have plotted an assassination.

The retainer served Sekhmet with a mix of admiration and hate. For almost two hundred years, she stood by this gentle despot's side. She had shown, however, goodness for the surviving people of Tir na n'Og. Seas of blood had spilled when she and Thoth took over Wells. A lot more was slopped when she drove Ossian away from any position of influence, but she allowed this world time to heal its wounds.

She became very powerful very fast during these days of peace. For her sense of fairness, her display of moral and justice, Sekhmet soon made the faerie folks and gods and goddesses of Duat forget the royal family. In some way, Sekhmet ruled better than Anastasia, and Thoth seemed wiser than Ossian. Perhaps, now, sprites would fight the nobles were they attempting a return. This made Katrina admire her mistress. Although she kept her memories of the war close to remind her how much she must hate the invaders. Fiona Sullivan, on the other hand, did not experience the conflict. She was born twenty years after, when peace settled down. Abandoned by her parents, royal immigrants adopted her. They had flown all the way from Duat to try their chance at a new world. Her foster begetters decided to preserve her from the Houses' politics. They invented stories and myths to dilute the inaccessible truth and keep it away from their faerie daughter. Truth that had once linked her adoptive father to the command of Thoth's assassins. He has seen the cruelty of the so-called Sophron wars.

He wasn't born at the time of the Babel incident, but what he experienced convinced him of the deeply anchored indecency. A big masquerade in the form of supposed enlightened beings. This is as far as Ghonad said-Sullivan, wraiths and stray fair folks have it right. Power corrupts, and systems nourish it, regardless of the scale or people involved. He married a Sleeper who was taught that animal-headed creatures have always existed in Tir na nOg, unaware of her ancestors' home layer. It doesn't take much for a non-awakened to fall for the gods' illusions: A good residence, a husband, and a job.

Many of those who migrated with Sekhmet thought they colonized a new planet. Then, gradually, Thoth's scholars reinvented history, fabricated myths, and in a matter of only a few generations, we talked of them as natives of this world. Those who could prevent the formation of these circles were killed. Ghonad said-Sullivan chose to leave and pretend none of this happened. He would die with his secrets. Two anti-conspirators sent by Thoth assassinated the king, right in front of Fiona's eyes. They murdered her unsuspecting mother in that same violent motion, but they spared the child's life. Those heavily armed mercenaries provide a difficult battle. Their pristine orders without a conscience: Kill the parents, leave the girl behind. Sekhmet entered Fiona's home, soon after. She lit her glow magnificently.

Tall, with a body that seemed to carry large shoulders and imposing breasts, she concealed her fine attributes under shattered pieces of armour. Half an orange and green flag served as a bra. Her dark skin made her look more African than felines, although her face clearly bore resemblance with that of a panther. The offspring of a Pharaoh, a human being, and a nymph mother from Duat, Sekhmet displayed hybrid features. She kept her long legs behind a short white leather skirt with a brown and black fringe.

She stepped over the corpses of those who once provided a little girl's love and security. She never minded the sea of blood that stained her large charcoal and golden cloak, and she stopped in front of a frightened daughter whose tears shattered her voice. Without a word spoken, without a gesture performed, she stood there. Fiona's terror met with awe. The goddess inspired safety in the infant's mind, and the child felt as if she belonged with her. Fiona shares similar traits with Katrina except for their hair colour, with the former showing lavishly blonde fleece, the latter a more average brown. Their likenesses, paired with matching uniforms, gave them their nickname: The Twin Maidens.

Sekhmet cared for these two slaves. They sometimes acted more like best girlfriends than submitted beings. The two of them became Sekhmet's most trusted anchor onto the world of faerie folks. Upon choosing them to occupy such an important position, closer to power than any other faerie among every circle that supported Sekhmet, the mistress saw complementary elements in one and the other. The palace's librarian performed a simple spell, faithful to the goddess's cause.

And the two fairies had nothing but a deep trust in Mandragora Semmens' abilities to manipulate essences. The idea was to fuse the two so as to having Fiona's loyalty paired with Katrina's skepticism of the Duat establishment. This procedure ensured both a form of security for the mistress and a direct contact with the former queen, Anastasia. She still benefited from a great deal of popularity among the people of Wells. But today, a smuggler's visit promised the beginning of a brand-new saga. Sekhmet approached Nempty. He respectfully bowed down in front of her, almost to the point of kissing the floor, and she observed his offering. He kept the amber and the insect way above his prostrating head. She looked at it, grabbed it, manipulated it. I sensed the perfume that once seduced me. It was good, and I know she felt even better.

"A stone? Sure."

She bluffed, as she gave him back what was to her like an engine of torture. She knew who I was. One glimpse at my essence, and she noticed that I had almost tasted Final-Vanishing, but have fought, and fought to remain existent. She added, with ahead pushed away from my sight: "Leave it here. Should the object be of any value, I'll consider lowering your debt."

A bit afraid, knowing the many influential friends she had, the powerful ones, mostly, he walked towards the table that stood behind her. His eyes scrolled through the room to find some sort of reassurance from either Katrina or Fiona. The wasp intrigued both of them, as though they had seen me before. Nempty stopped for a moment. He realized he would soon entrust her with an object of the most crucial importance.

"My goddess."

He expressed in his thoughts, as he kept with him the most precious discovery of his entire life. He put it back in his pocket and simply said:"My apologies, but can you assure me that this insect will be treated with care, were I to leave it here?"
She struggled not to smile as she responded with a flawed: "Was there an insect in that rock? My goodness, what poor eyesight I must have." Nempty hardly sounded convinced. What sort of bluff did she just play?

"It is, huhrmm. One of its kind."

"Go, sell it to a freak circus, for all that concerns me, Grey!"

"Nymph. From my mother." She turned around and furiously threw him the worst anger he had ever faced: "Sell it to some kids! Tell them they can smash and smoke it, for all that I care!"
She walked towards him. Nempty moved backward until he hit the wall.

"But know one thing, stinky Grey, don't ever come back here to trade or I will have you hunted down, you heard? I will see you sacrificed and torn to pieces! If you think of visiting me and trying to sell me some rock again!"

"It's, not. I'm not."

"Listen to me! I will make you wish your life was only miserable. Don't you dare insult me with your garbage?"

The louder she shouted and the more I felt connected to this scene. Yes, I have had an affair with this temper before. Wasn't it when she gave birth to Cleopatra? Nempty was greatly destabilized. Her chaotic burst of anger made him second-guess his own abilities to tell the essence of a god from crack cocaine.

Okay, that was not it! He shook his head and sighed. "Fine!" he concluded, then turned away. I felt more aware of this existence, somehow. Perhaps, just maybe, if I could gather another fragment, I could strengthen this grasp over reality and properly reincarnate myself. I only need the piece that recollects my knowledge of mancing. As a wasp, I was already more than what that insect's instincts could have ever brought.

"Oh, don't let words get to your lovable heart, pretty boy. You came to me for a reason, my Grey friend." she ushered in a most seductive tone behind these words. "More of a nymph. My mother was a nymph."

Her sensuality troubled him. Greys tend to be among the most pragmatic species of beings throughout Sophron. Nymphs, however, show a more sexually driven life. That has always constituted a complicated issue in Nempty's life. He could never allow one side to control him better than the other. Sekhmet knew exactly which half to manipulate and how.

She undressed herself, piece by piece, finding very well that the dwarf could neither escape nor pretend she didn't exist. "Why, beautiful, did you decide to visit me first with such an expensive present?" Nempty calmed his urges. He shut his eyes and thought of Lucreatia. A strong paternalistic affection comes whenever he thinks of his android daughter. He could give his life for a robot designed as a sex slave. How stupid of him, some would say. One truth he owes his time spent alongside Varuna: when haunted with a sexually active half and a pragmatic one, always give the wheel to reason and dignity. He also vowed to allow nobody to touch her. Keeping his daughter close to his heart provided the resilience that would make him survive a cat-lady's appetite. Sekhmet dropped her bra at his feet and whispered:

"You haven't made love in so long, have you? This is only that son of a bitch's last remaining essence. But it could equal the price a goddess would ask to sleep with a puny traveller, wouldn't it?" She caressed his left lobe with two fingers and purred.

Hormones boiled in him. His entire blood burned like lava. One kiss and he would explode. "Right?" she insisted. By then, he forgot all about Lucreatia. "I, hmm. Yes. That's correct, yes. Affirmative." he calmly stuttered. "There you go, beautiful."

She suavely murmured, while he opened his eyes to face her lips about to land on his mouth. His pupils, however, only had sight for her breasts. All. Hmm. Sweaty. She captured his right palm, approached it over her shoulder, as she whispered "Can you pay up front? I'll bring the bed after." he hesitated. He must have had some pragmatic strength out of nowhere. Ah, those breasts! Tremors took over his cool while he caressed her down her back. She pressed him closer. His left fingers grabbed the amber. All shaky and no longer thinking straight, he gave it to her. The moment she secured the stone into her right hand, Nempty realized the tension over the Veil had vanished. Free to go, he alone occupied the entire room.

Something at the back of his head made him ponder that he must have accomplished the biggest error in his life. The sad truth was that he did hope he could have slept with her in exchange. That error began to show the moment Sekhmet entered along the corridor between Tir na nOg and the core of Sophron. Katrina and Fiona followed her. The passage appeared as a horizontal tornado that simply remained still while axioms spin and twirl. Behind them was the palace, with luxurious artefacts and stone walls. In front was a pitch black that contrasted with the whiteness of the hallway. The further they walked, the more this whole path seemed like a tunnel. Until they finally reached the essence of Sophron. It has the texture of a colourless beat, a pause and a beat, a pause, and a beat. The core of Sophron has no axiom; yet it pumps them in and out like a metaphysical heart.

Consciousness doesn't resemble anything until those pixels provide a certain form suitable for creatures to observe. Void ones yield its element of silence, while Barbelo does so with the flesh. Archeus supports the throbbing movement and Logos adds the sound. As it is in the realm of these four Entities, these four elements are indistinguishable from one another. The essence, thus, simply is.

For Sekhmet, entering the core of her possibility seemed almost sacrilegious. After spending so many years alongside faerie folks: "When you call the Dreamer by any name, you awake him. In enlightenment, he, she or they notice the Entire Sophron. Those can become either gods or authors." They would explain how she learned to leave that essence room for anonymity. She trembled while she signalled her servants to remain behind, as to keep the vortex open. She held the amber and looked at me through the wasp's eyes. She smiled.

"Hey." she timidly greeted the wasp.

"You have no idea how difficult life has been without you. I had to play masquerading card to let everybody know that I never cared, yet I sided with you. For some, I did out of trust and loyalty to a common cause. To Marduk, I did through a hidden agenda. I am sorry I lied to both, and to us too. I did it for you. I did it for me. I always felt left down whenever I was told of this war that scarred the whole pluriverse and wounded the entities."She looked behind and observed the two maidens. "I know you hear me, Indra." I heard her say. Then she examined the core again: "What happened to us?" It didn't seem to reply. I, myself, felt smothered by this immensity of blankness. I wished I could share her memories. Her voice bore the seal of a wounded secret.

"Both our nations, you remember? We were the pride of this Babel project. How strong Egypt and India were. We had this whole humanity thing all figured. No scientific advancement, philosophy or artistic breakthrough missed our influence. Oh, we had this tower in the palm of our hands!" I sensed a smile that betrayed a tear. Waves of poignant visions made themselves felt throughout this core that formed me. Babel. Tremors in her sigh brought the heartbeats to a halt. They resumed when she swallowed her headache. "You trusted me, and I trusted you. What went wrong? Do you really think I was jealous when you married Ishtar?" The pulse got louder. She laughed, timidly at first, but she increased the tone as she tried to cover the pounding. "I felt happy for you! Wasn't polygamy an idea we cherished? Not only for those African royalties, I assure you." The beat intensified itself, stopped for a long silence. Then resumed its volume.

"I was. Indra, I was. Believe me. You think you would have been happier with me? I never considered our association in this whole 'build a humanity' thing involved laws of attraction for ourselves. Besides, you know me. I'd rather give the keys of a civilization to Osiris than calling myself a great goddess. I didn't feel the open love for the aspirations you defended, Indra! I despised poems to chant my glory for eras to come. I just wanted to do my thing and enjoy seasons under your Sun."

213

She gasped, paused for a moment, and added: "See where this lack of ambition brought me? You warned us about Marduk. I always said I would not take sides in your battles. I didn't do it. I might never do it. Since the invasions of Khan-Ro the Red's armies ended, I chose to stop playing war.

Because I appreciate being at peace with you. Perhaps my jealousy and my complete apathy divided me. I hoped that Marduk would destroy you, and kill Ishtar, if only to avenge this scar I have carried on my back ever since I presented myself drunk at your wedding! Maybe I didn't wish to join the one who would murder my only love." She examined the insect. I observed her through the blankness reflecting my jewelled prison.

"Look at you. You are so handsome. I missed you."

She deposited the shiny coffin onto an invisible table, as though she hoped the essence jailed within could reach the substance that roamed without. It just wasn't that simple.

"You know who else rooted for us? Guess." Was I in a position to express myself?

"Melpomene. Yes, really. Whenever I feared for you, I contacted him, and he would veto anything the Greater Council of Bast would vote on, just to protect you."

Heartbeats got more regular as though they sought some sort of rhythm for a melody that begged to be born.

"You never thought the Muses liked you, right? You thought too much of yourself, Indra. Oh, let me face all of them entities! *I know my stuff; I can show you! I'll show you, right?* That's what you thought. We drank your every word, Ishtar, and I! For what? To show these monkeys that women should drool when a male stands strong? Kiss my lion ass!"

214

She turned around and realized that her maidens were about to vanish. She had to make a choice, at this point. Either she stayed here and join the essence as a mere outburst of bitterness, or she walked away from her nostalgia and returned to the system.

"All right, I think you've had enough of me, as always."

She sighed. She forgot about this last fragment of me, right here, close to the centre of the universe my universe, my possibility. Am I the Dreamer of this story?

"I'll speak to Melpomene! Maybe a reason persists. He'll know. He should know. But before I go, I want to assure you that if I sacrifice everything, it is for the greater good. Your essence found its path into a boy's soul. The wasp's genes have served their purpose and should now die." She threw the amber in the True Void and left. I sensed certain congestion in the way axioms floated within me. As though her presence had caused my thoughts, or those I held, to clog until they had gathered a mob. It would reflect a matter. Greedy desires always repel other selfish contemplation. Hear me! I'm here. Come back! Speak to me She left! Talk to me. My Overqueen, do so.

Sekhmet parted from the Core of Sophron, returning to Tirna n'Og. She had a direct ethereal tunnel that linked her temple to True Void. Fiona and Katrina escorted her, while my essence remained in the amber, consumed by absolute nothingness. Perhaps I did disappear, then. Or maybe another player decided to intervene. Void is, at this moment in the story, the only one of the four True Entities currently acting. He will not openly choose sides, simply having his pawns and bishops do his bidding. It was fortunate for him that Sekhmet sacrificed me in the core of my True Existence. Providential also that Void had played a part in freeing Marduk from his exile, while Varuna remained imprisoned in a limbo.

215

Journey into the Hourglass:
Ten

My concern towards Martin grew a lot more, while he stayed away. I would rather see those chronicles fall into Oblivion, rather than not hearing from Martin's consciousness ever again. I would probably lose myself to save his soul, but what do I know? We met in this purgatory we called our creation.

"You do your best, I'm sure."

I sent him that text message; he never replied. Why would characters die to free Varuna? For one, India inspired the maths that put Europe on the enlightened map. But Europe came back with an egotistical scheme to direct politics on Earth. Heck, I'm not from Gaia! Why am I even trying?

Hey. Martin texted me. "Hey! How is it going?" I texted back. He replied three weeks later: *Sorry, I thought you were Candy.* "Who is Candy?" I asked. *Who is Candy? Hello, who is she, anyway?* I'm the one writing these novels. They won't write themselves, right?

Chapter Twenty-Two:
Nempty finds Varuna

Varuna's essence occupied this limbo long enough for the Lord to have forgotten all about his previous existence. The wars, the treason, the hopes, the losses, none of them mattered. Every axiom shone with pure matter, with no opportunity for a manifestation. If it weren't for this godly prisoner, the truth would evade everyone. Yet, Varuna's essence wasn't enough to provide this realm the required pixels of thoughts to reflect upon itself. The Councils, when pronouncing their judgment, chose the right jail for someone who could easily break free. that is

If he could make the world he lived in self-awareness. Then let all worlds taste fire. Varuna enjoyed the peace that seemed to have lasted an eternity in this mindless Barbelo. Nothing prepared him for the arrival of this peculiar visitor, and especially in this very unusual manner. Oblivious to any walking craft, Nempty had to improvise in order to enter this jail. Powerful Entities built it up for size so it would only carry Varuna, one of the most formidable mancers in all the known Sophron.

After having interrogated his contacts, and having his most loyal ones question theirs, Nempty gathered many possible hypotheses as to where the location of Varuna's prison could be.

"The only limbo that could detain a soul as influential as Varuna would have to be like a sponge capable of holding an ocean." Dvorak explained. A twelve-year-old nymph from Patagonia, a world between Mu and True Archeus, he came from along lineage of monk alchemists. Dvorak pledged to invest his entire existence to the path of the Greater Light, or seeing Logos ultimately vanquish Void. His life changed when he met a grey-nymph smuggler, exploring his village of Sutra-Kamal. The dwarf introduced him to the pleasures of board games. And a lasting friendship was born. Whenever Nempty would visit him, Dvorak would welcome him, and they would exchange deep discussions, over bets and losses, and alcohol. But when Nempty would leave, the boy would resume his meditation. "Imprison light in darkness, Mr. Nempty. Which world can act as a sponge to a being of light, such as Lord Varuna?" the infant scholar asked, from the other end of a poker table, holding up a cigar while Nempty poured glasses of whisky. "An ocean has limits, Dvorak. If there is one, Varuna's soul would have found, with time, ways to destroy them."

"What if Lord Varuna didn't want to break free from his prison? Marduk did, out of greed and hunger. Lord Varuna is much wiser." Dvorak grabbed a card from his library, while enchanted hands drew one for Nempty. After leaving the wasp to Sekhmet, Nempty had to think of his next move fast. If she awakens Indra, transposing my essence into another body, then she would have an edge over Marduk. She could downplay their alliance, or she could secure the newborn while she hunts for Ishtar. What else was he supposed to do? He couldn't have given his precious finding to the Hound Lord! "If I inform Varuna that Indra's essence lives, he will want to break free. Indra is key for Varuna's House to regain power and influence." Nempty informed him.

"Marduk's dominance is no longer active in Gaia. My friend Gaia is the key, not Indra. Earth, this is where the Great War took place. The realm that the Great Council protects. Marduk knows that. Varuna knows that."

They played Vendelika, a popular variant of poker across many fair folk worlds, like Avalon, Annwn or Penglai. If I were to explain to you the rules, you would simply assume a mix of Texas Hold'em and Crazy Eight.

"Then, Varuna is either in a hellish layer, or in True Void." Nempty thought out loud. Dvorak smiled. "I can't go to True Void; I don't have the right technology. If Varuna is in the Void-Barbelo quadrant, how can I infiltrate these jungles without bloodshades, talons, or other bloodthirsty demons dismembering me?"

"Look for a llanorfina."

The childlike genius smoked and drank, then bet a few coins. Nempty knew what the boy meant, but he awaited further clarifications. Dvorak continued:

"A sponge that expands to infinity will contain an ocean that swells as much, for as long as the sponge has had an edge in its creation. So, obviously the Great Councils considered Sebekia Pistis as the right realm to imprison Lord Varuna.

Now, llanorfinas also host their enlightened beings through dozers, those floating brains. If you can locate Lord Varuna's Prison, you'll have to negotiate with those mighty creatures to remain alive." Nempty pondered over his friend's logic while he stationed his boat in Sebekia Pistis. Immense rivers of lava cover this layer that stretches to eternity. Worlds that do not evolve on limited surfaces are referred to as llanorfinas, from an old Avalonian dialect, meaning: a land of infinity. We call llanorfinis those domains that usually share borders with a vast area of either Void or Thoughts.

Scholars believe this world carries devotion. Basically, every layer that precedes The Dark Fire Circle, its other name, has too much Void axioms and not enough matter, with life as their dominant form of reflection, as opposed to thoughts. Creatures that populate them bear a state known as chaotic. Just like hollows, they will change their form all the time, or will remain without any. With Sebekia Pistis, and further with The Open Door, Hell and Hades, beasts tend to keep a more static fashion. Axioms of thoughts start to be more and more present with reflections from the Beyond.

Still, their immediate form of awareness mixes with the Great Entities, resulting in worships and devotion by the mirroring lot. This mechanic, then, finds its way among every circle of believers throughout Sophron.

Fourth Intermission:
The Student and Void

For Emerald

Those two words haunted the student, while their eyes could hardly get accustomed to total blankness. The surroundings had no colour, texture or substance of any kind. It was impossible to tell if breathing was of the season since lungs had no say in the process. At the back of their mind, the disciple knew Plato's orb absorbed them. They just had no idea where it took them.

They recalled his stories about leaving a cave to witness a light brighter than any clarity anyone had seen. What sort of radiance involves total annihilation of all senses? Were they freed from the illusion or brought into a different brand? They heard a voice, before appearing where they were. Wherever that was. Who spoke? Hades? Did they enter the land of the dead? No words could have produced that matter. Life remained indissociable from their thoughts.

They didn't know, but I will tell you. This world is called True Void. The only layer without any city, or any sort of civilization. Perhaps a gateway between all Dreamers. You have gathered many concepts since you opened this book, reader. A genderless pupil in ancient Greece imagines the story of a selfish boy from Montreal. Gods and goddesses battle over the fabric of reality. But allow me to show you the magic.

While the student noticed my existence, in every aspect and all its glorious manifestation, grant me time to present you the significance of For Emerald. You have witnessed these two words long before you invested yourself into this weird expression of a fantasy novel. You may have thought: the Author wanted to dedicate his work to a lady who meant the world to him, and maybe something happened to both, or has yet to be. From my vantage point, I see a romantic fool behind his computer trying to vent his dealing with a cruel illusion, and he hopes it will please you.

Emerald. Ishtar to his Indra. In the past, I did invite quite a few of his loved ones to my realm. One of them shared his name, his date of birth, and his demise prompted a desire to craft the basics of this pluriverse. We all exist as prisoners of our individual stories, and we fear what we will never know. Well, the Author expressed the intention to acquaint me. He meant to discover a form of love that had no anchor onto distinct needs or wants. He renounced to many a shape of material happiness to favour the quietness of inner tranquility. I understand a thing or two about the fire within that.

Peace isn't Void. And I am not what you would consider, calm But ever since I allowed the Author to give me a name, he had permission to destroy my serenity. Memories appear to shine like sweet and sour attractions. They keep you back, even in the most precious intents. I hold on to nothing. I project nothing. You are born out of blank, and you spend a childhood learning how to adapt within the illusion. When you fall in love, nobody can tell you which it is. Matter, life, thoughts, or me. You can only do your best to live as a good person, to yourself, others, to those who care.

Then, it only happens at specific moments in someone's existence, you encounter a soul that redefines love's entire infrastructure. This, you see, is Emerald. When out of youth, you may say the wrong things at the right instant, or the opposite, and you will lose your chance to give life to your dreams. You will want to win at life so you may become the one Emerald should have always been with, from the start. But it's too late. Life went on, and so should you.

I'll show you something else if you may. The Author did survive past the pain of non-reciprocity. He learned happiness on his own, and that love wasn't about filling an empty space. It was always full within that empty space. Now, observe him. He's into some role-playing games, with three friends. There's a tall table, you see? They incarnate characters who investigate gods in Lovecraft's Sophron. The bearded bard, here, with blonde hair and thick glasses, that's the Author. If you pierce through his essence, you will see, in his Sophron, the Alibast character he created.

Do you know what they have in common? Nothing. They hold true love out of nothing. When all of this perishes, another Dreamer will carry their essence, nothing will recall the good times they shared. But he lives beyond. Because he chose to write these words, make me the narrator, and dedicate this entire chapter to his friends. He looks at the muses he met and left, and he remembers that the universe is expanding. Fear will make us cocoon until we stand smaller than ourselves. Love, my love, has no frontier. So, am I the villain in this trilogy? Oh, good, your eyes are getting accustomed to my world. Let's continue. You imagined Seamus Chron as a narcissistic prick. Why not as a frightening warrior? He just charged towards the unknown, and he had no idea that he was wounding an old friend. Sure, from your creative perspective, what we read isn't that bad. Seamus reflects you, though. What brought you this spark of enlightenment, students? Why are you here? And why aren't you dead?

Chapter Twenty-Three:
The Death of Nempty

Out of Sebekia Pistis, beyond the oceans of lava and the red rocks, you see the inhabitants. They resemble gigantic brains, at least the size of a large mall, and float freely all over the flat world with no sun. They seem to mirror the orange sky that never sleeps. At the bottom of these beige blobs are twenty-four tentacles that can't grab anything. They drift and gather nutrients into these brains as chance allows. To reproduce, dozers simply wait until two of them bump, again by chance, into one another in such a way that the tentacles of both beings mingle and twist. An exchange of various proteins happens, then dropped. Those proteins will fall on the ground and gradually become young floating dozers that will grow as they will randomly nourish themselves and expand further.

Since the physical world mirrors a metaphysical domain, these giant floating brains could project thoughts. In fact, their realms within are an inhospitable deep sea for any traveller or mancer who would dare picking one as a Dreamer to visit. They illustrate one of the many mysteries that not even great scholars of the Councils can truly comprehend. As though one of them could represent a much more complex Sophron yet depending on the Sophronia laws that everyone knows. Therefore, the creatures that were born out of their collective thoughts are greatly respected.

House of Hotzigardbrinunzigorndz dominates over Sebekia Pristis, also known as the Dark Fire Circle. Hell completes this trio of worlds that precedes the first apparition of life axioms. Nempty is like a microbe, whenever he walks in these layers. Everything stands out so immensely compared to his minuscule stature. Mountains would apparently crumble on him. The sound of lava always leaves a creepy feeling to whomever trespasses over these lands. No wonder past travellers who had made it out of these scary places have reported stories that later inspired theocracies with myths of eternal damnation.

Perhaps because the circle stands the closest to Void. Maybe chaos seems to exercise some sort of influence with axioms, but of the entire triad, many would agree to say that it is the most mysterious and, therefore, most frightening. Nempty has seen it all. He knew better than to fear a layer that's like a vast movie theatre for flying jellyfish. With an axiom reflector, a device that alchemists came up with to peel the Veil and facilitate journey from world to world, Nempty delicately revealed the hidden limbo. This gadget, nicknamed stripper, consists in white gloves made with bits of mancing orbs and quartz, highly energized with anti-ions prior to use. After finding a particular channel, the traveller puts his hands on what looks like a curtain of heat and waits until all that surrounds the dwarf's palms get more and more blurry. His fingers dig through the Veil as though they tried to tear the world apart. After much effort and patience, a vortex forms around the wrists. The Veil is literally peeled open. This represents more work than with the ferry boat. He could then join uncharted domains and limbos. Once a sojourner penetrated a layer, he may store the destination and, using the same channels, re-enter the realm at will.

On the other side of the peeled Veil, flesh got real. It was as if the traveller had put a pinkish block of skin in the middle of the air. He could poke it, touch it, but he could not physically join this limbo. He wondered if he could outsmart an Entity. Especially one capable of such powerful reality manipulation. Will he or not find Varuna on this plane of existence?

225

As he pondered how he could reach the imprisoned god, a cavernous voice reverberated against the mountains and the dozers? "What are you looking for?"

It hissed. Nempty stopped. He recalled the tone. It was that of Manakin. One of the few hellish Neymlisses that meant trouble. A total maniac who had lost contact with any form of reality the moment he realized he had earned the ability to provoke Final-Vanishing. Hot exhorted to have them chained, as he feared this form of threat could force the Sapphire Council to act against the Hellish triad of Demonee.

"I won't stay for long."

He said, but that didn't stop the beast from appearing a few metres behind him. Tall with an egg-shaped head and eyes that easily encompassed three fourths of the face, he had a lizard's mouth and a tongue that could stretch over half a kilometre. His shoulders were four times the length of his scaly back. Insanely muscled thighs, as were the arms. A skin as black as the night, with pupils as white as snow, and a nose carved inwardly.

Powerful chains cover his ankles and wrists, preventing him from moving. Manakin was allowed to travel only among these three worlds. He would have tasted this total oblivion himself, should a Great Entity such as Archangel Michael had learned of his presence beyond Hell. In recent battles that involved these Houses, however, Manakin proved himself a much-needed asset against demon-hunting angels.

"What do you look for?"

He insisted. His speech sounded slow and badly articulated. Nempty understood that he was safe, but he felt deeply unsecured knowing that his existential finality breathed next to him.

"It's all good, Manakin. Everything is good."

"What do you look for? Hey! What?" he shouted.

Nempty can't tell him the truth, he can't risk having entities from Hell discover Indra's presence.

"I have a friend. A dear friend. In a limbo, here."

"Who your friend?"

Nempty had to insist and pursue his quest, but the monster repeated as well. Unarmed, he knew it would be challenging to leave without a fight, and difficult to escape the attention the slow-witted brute would give his masters. He realized, then, why the Councils put one of the most dangerous Babel heroes here. He should have thought of that before he came to this hole.

"Never mind, boy. I will leave, now."

"Hey! Who your friend? Whom your friend?" The monster wouldn't let him go this easily. When Nempty considered the leave-now-leave-fast option, five bloodshades already surrounded him. These creatures looked all the same: Muscular shadows, six feet tall, pitch black, with eyes covering half of their face. Their mouth could stretch over their torso. And teeth. So many of them, you could mistake them for a forest of ivory knives. Having two conversing with one another was confusing enough, five would leave poor Nempty lost in translation. "You his friend?" one asked.

"No, you?"

"You think me his friend? Hey! Me no friend his. He ugly!"

"No, me thinks he the friend of someone."

"He friend of Hot?"

"No, I have only respect for Hotzigard." Think, how to say?

"I have respect for Sir Hotzigardbrinunzigorndz! There!"

"What did he say?"

"He says he no friend of the boss."

"It is not what I said! I swear. I love your boss!"

"He says what?"

"He says he wants make love the boss."

"Gross! I say we kill."

"I say we kill too."

"Boys! Boys! Please! I am a friend."

"He says his friend, now?"

"Me thinks he pees in pants."

"Me thinks too. You pee in pants?"

"If you want me to." Nempty turned around to probe for a sign of life into the limbo: he didn't see any. He turned back to face the five blood shades about to eat him alive. "What are you looking for?" It hissed. Nempty stopped. He recalled the tone. It was that of Manakin. One of the few hellish Neymlisses that meant trouble. A total maniac who had lost contact with any form of reality the moment he realized he had earned the ability to provoke Final-Vanishing. Hot exhorted to have them chained, as he feared this form of threat could force the Sapphire Council to act against the Hellish triad of Demonee.

"I won't stay for long." he said, but that didn't stop the beast from appearing a few metres behind him. Tall with an egg-shaped head and eyes that easily encompassed three fourths of the face, he had a lizard's mouth and a tongue that could stretch over half a kilometre. His shoulders were four times the length of his scaly back. Insanely muscled thighs, as were the arms. A skin as black as the night, with pupils as white as snow, and a nose carved inwardly. Powerful chains cover his ankles and wrists, preventing him from moving. Manakin was allowed to travel only among these three worlds. He would have tasted this total oblivion himself, should a Great Entity such as Archangel Michael had learned of his presence beyond Hell. In recent battles that involved these Houses, however, Manakin proved himself a much-needed asset against demon-hunting angels.

"What do you look for?" he insisted. His speech sounded rather slow and badly articulated. Nempty understood that he was safe, but he always felt deeply unsecured knowing that his existential finality breathed right next to him.

"It's all good, Manakin. Everything is good."

"What do you look for? Hey! What?" he shouted. Nempty can't tell him the truth, he can't risk having entities from Hell discover Indra's presence.

"I have a friend. A dear friend. In a limbo, here."

"Who your friend?" Nempty had to insist and pursue his quest, but the monster repeated as well. Unarmed, he knew it would be challenging to leave without a fight, and difficult to escape the attention the slow-witted brute would give his masters.

He realized, then, why the Councils put one of the most dangerous Babel heroes here. He should have thought of that before he came to this hole.

229

"Never mind, boy. I will leave, now."

"Hey! Who your friend? Who your friend?"

The monster wouldn't let him go this easily. When Nempty considered the leave-now-leave-fast option, five bloodshades already surrounded him. These creatures looked all the same: Muscular shadows, six feet tall, pitch black, with eyes covering half of their face. Their mouth could stretch over their torso. And teeth. So many of them, you could mistake them for a forest of ivory knives. Having two conversing with one another was confusing enough, five would leave Nempty lost in translation.

"You his friend?" one asked the other.

"No, you?"

"You think me his friend? Me no friend. He ugly, you eat?"

"No, me thinks he the friend of someone."

"He friend of Hot?"

"No, but I have only respect for Hotzigard." Think, think, how to pronounce. "I have respect for Sir Hotzigardbrinunzigorndz! There!" Nempty turned around to probe for a sign of life into the limbo: he didn't see any. He turned back to face the five blood shades about to eat him alive. He swallowed painfully as they taunted him. They encircled him. They walked slowly. They had such huge white eyes that covered four fifth of their darkened face. They had more teeth in their open mouth than a shark will ever have in a lifetime. Teeth that went all the way down their throat. Short with a curved back, black blades grew out of their spine, claws for fingers. Saliva gathered around their teeth until they drooled their way closer to his head. Nempty knew it was coming.

"This is no way to treat an intruder." a growling voice made itself heard. Nempty fell on his knees and whispered:

"Thank you, thank you, whoever did this!"

The blood shades walked away to allow a splendid floating throne to enter the scene: Golden and filled with precious stones from all over Sophron. The man, or rather demon, who sat on it looked like an elderly baboon's skeleton, with long grey hair that was braided to form his military uniform. He had an iron armour to give him a semblance of muscles. The throne further floated in Nempty's direction, and stopped while the frightened smuggler stood up, panicking. "Why, why, if this isn't the traveller who said he would stay away from the Houses' conflicts."

Hot uttered in absolute sarcasm. "I did, Mr. Hotzingalooringling. Sir, I did." Hot smiled as he observed the window Nempty had opened.

"It takes a lot of courage to come all the way here. I must admit, you are the last being in all Sophron I expected to see."

"It's a tactic, actually! I don't serve Varuna. And I don't accommodate Marduk. You know that." Adrenaline made him express these words, and it made him speak quite convincingly. "Whom do you serve?" Hot asked.

"I am not at liberty to tell, sir. Let's say I am loyal to me."

"That we were aware."

"And myself is better catered for with prizes. And what top ones can a selfish traveller like me hope to get from the hands of the Great Councils?" he grinned. Hot laughed.

231

"You think I will buy that lie? No, before you die, let me know
what brought you here. Why would you even bother, now?"
Nempty shut his eyes and could only see Lucreatia. Her smile.
Her pupils. That light in her sight. He opened his eyes and
nonchalantly uttered: "Kill me, now." Hot felt deeply disturbed.
He looked away and made a sign to his blood shades:
"Tear him to oblivion, kids."

He vanished while the demons jumped on their prey. Nempty
cursed his name for having forgotten to prepare better. So many
strength-enhancing potions he could have come equipped with.
He's not that bad an alchemist, really. But he's not a warrior.
And he never was. He's a merchant. He shouldn't have decided to
put himself in this mess. He should have stayed home. See where
does altruism takes you? What empathy brings you?
These thoughts haunted him from all over as he tried to escape the
trap that quickly shut around him. He looked at the open window
and knew he had one chance at this: "Varuna!"

He shouted, just as two blood shades jumped on his back and
dug their fingers deep in his flesh. Nempty felt their claws reaching
in for the spine. Agony cramped his nerves, while the demons'
hands closed themselves around his bones as though they meant to
strangle them. The merchant's weak muscles couldn't fight back,
and soon he was overwhelmed with pain. He had just enough
energy to do one thing: Shout! Scream, but make sure everyone
nearby can hear him.

"Indra's alive!" he blasted, and then allowed the monsters to
finish him. They jumped on the poor corpse, eating it like hyenas
getting a meal after days of hunger. With or without effort from
Nempty, they tore his flesh away, shattered his bones, stretched
tendons until they let the limbs break free. Every new charge bore
a greater agony. Hot observed the scene with immense interest.
He couldn't help, however, to examine the open window.
The limbo's membrane tremored softly.

232

He shut his eyes and nodded. He left his throne and summoned an immense axe from behind it. One by one, he decapitated his children to free Nempty. One by one, head fell, monsters died. None ever dared fighting back. Hotzigard looked at Nempty's corpse, and Varuna's limbo. Hot had antagonized Demonee for a long time. When Houses started to invade other layers of Sophron, the Dark Fire Circle and the Open Door realized it was wiser to end their wars and ally against possible conquests. Their worlds stand as the most dangerous, with the most violent cultures, in all of Sophron. In choosing them to hold the exiled souls of Marduk and Varuna, the Great Councils assumed that nobody in their right mind would attempt a move towards freeing the condemned Lords. Marduk found his way out, while Varuna remained trapped in his prison, accepting his fate.

Even a brainless demon like Hotzigard knows that Marduk has gained much power and influence since his escape. The Great Councils have probably ignored this willingly, supposing that as long as one of the two great antagonists stayed locked up, Sophron might not experience danger again. Hot and Demonee thought this as well, and why Varuna's prison remained so well guarded.
But Indra exists. Varuna will desire to protect him, at all costs.
Or find a way to resurrect him. A mere smuggler sacrificed himself to bring this news.

"We don't want you out, Varuna." the demon frowned.
"We have known peace, among the Houses of Hell, we can't risk that peace to see you alive."

"I can free myself whenever I desire, Hotzigard. I'm not requesting your permission. I'm asking for an audience with Demonee. I need both your Houses' allegiance."

233

"Don't you dare?" he warned Varuna.

"You know what that means?" Varuna replied.

"The war was never over." Hot concluded.

"To a god who brought hope, love, light to mankind?
You think, for a moment, that demons, creatures of pain and
despair, will agree?"

"Politics never conveyed those emotions. Let's keep it rational,
no chaos or order to interfere. We must do what's right to protect
the pluriverse. I'm not asking you out of desperation, Hotzigard.
I'm warning you that if I leave my prison, Marduk will invade your
worlds to punish you. You will need my House's protection."

"Yours is destroyed, Varuna! You hold no more influence, out
of your cage."

"When the moment arises, you will have to choose allies.
I let you know, now, that I keep no grudge, hate or hard feelings
towards the Houses of Hell. When the time comes, and should
demons elect to side with me, I will welcome you with my
arms wide open."

"Demons were born to burn and die, god of the sky." Hotzigard
expressed, as he shut Varuna's limbo prison up, and left Nempty's
corpse to rot. He deserted the scene, unaware, as any of this
chapter's protagonists, of its author's identity. But Marduk looked
at the words he brought to this book. He observes you, this very
moment, honest reader, and he smiles. He feels more in control,
now, than he ever was. You want to know why?

234

Journey into the Hourglass:
Eleven

Did we kill Nempty? Or did we just allow the character to do something crazy and? Die? I think we should bypass that part.

Let's say: his soul reincarnates into another character. What do you think? Hello? Martin? Okay, anyway, I'll take care of that one.   But why did he show up in Hell? Did you write that? Martin? Hello?

Hey

Anyway. Maybe Nunc can save his soul! Yeah! He'll do his best, I'm sure. But then, what do I know? I'm just his creator. Unless, Nunc is just one soul, and there's another! Jamieson!

Jamieson Fairfield! Let's work with that.
What do you think, Martin?

"Hello?"

Hello?

Never mind! I gave up. I felt like a failure, for one moment. "Our characters are self-aware!" I tried to warn him.

Chapter Twenty-Four:
Seamus finds his Gift

The next morning, I looked at the old man and I wondered about the day before. Why did I dare car owners into slamming me to death? How would this take me to that strange world where I can see William and, I guess, I don't know? Say sorry? He slept on his bench, and I couldn't disturb him. He seemed so peaceful. I checked my pocket change, and I thought I could leave it to him, and just go back to my family. But what if he made that poutine appear, last night? What if he brought it the one before? Why didn't he just make a meal materialize in front of me when I mentioned my hunger? Damn it, old man! Wake up! We need to talk. He snored. And it's eight in the morning? Responsible people are at work, at this hour.

I played with my pocket change, and I thought I could just go to a nearby restaurant and buy me a nice breakfast. I did. I'm not dependent on that elderly fool. I can return to my family if being homeless doesn't suit me. I don't want that, though. I know things that they don't. Damn it with the old man. I must survive on my own! I felt like I needed his advice, but he remained there, almost dead, maybe dead. On the bench. I can do this on my own.

I walked without looking at the streets' names. I just strolled, trying to scare my filthy ideas away from my ideal. I can do this! I could come back to the park, and connect with the old man, read his entire life, and see where he got this idea about a wasp, or why he opposes Marduk so vehemently. *Why did he disappear after Marduk and Varuna's incarceration?* These weren't my thoughts, but, yeah, I guess. Why?

I looked around, as I felt a bit groggy. People go to work. Others enjoy their vacation. Some happy or worried. Some rich or oblivious. Some hopefuls, many were lost. And what about me? Was I left behind like a country song trying to make sense of its existence in a metal concert? I heard several voices in my head, and I intuited that only I could dictate my next move. Metal makes life felt, but country music, the kind my father listened to, always sounded too nostalgic. Should I be daring or caring? About myself or, what? We all want to be loved, right? I remained tall and proud in front of the unknown. Was I a bishop or a king?

"You're my pawn." I heard. Who said that? Voices in my head, and of course.

The street felt deserted. I saw a few bystanders looking at me, wondering if I could respond to their frightful eyes. I couldn't. A pawn can become a queen. I assumed I expressed, but nobody heard me. *We should be much greater together!* I thought. The voices faded away. I roamed around Sainte-Catherine Street, and I pondered what it would be like if I walked in Manhattan. Would I be chased in central park? Why am I visualizing Time Square? And why is there a Victorian Castle? I hate predators. I need to figure out something else. I had to locate that old man again, but the bench only showed an untouched poutine on which a note read: Don't go to Tir na n'Og. I discarded the note and ate the meal with great appetite. The fries and gravy felt warm, and the cheese curds sounded fresh and squishy. I savoured every bit and bite, licking the remnants afterwards.

I then sat and looked at the paper I threw in the garbage, next to the seat. Don't go to Tir na n'Og. Was the old man trying to protect me from an imminent danger? I have yet to understand how this whole travelling to another world thing functions, so I doubt I will be cruising anywhere, any soon. What else can a runaway young adult do under the sun? I thought I could, perhaps, practise my gift a bit. I closed my eyes and meditated until I could sense essences around me.

After three hours of attempting, I managed to visualize floating emotions sharing the park with me. Some of them carried joy, but I perceived pain, resentment, regrets. I couldn't properly connect to any of these inner worlds, and yet they were there. When I opened my eyes to put a face on these emotions I felt, I saw everybody grinning, even though out of the ten essences I sensed, only one of these smiles seemed genuinely happy.

Another existence roams in the lot. I caught it, a very dark, evil, violent one. Its mere presence brought a deep chill down my spine. I unsuccessfully tried to locate the person hosting this villainy. Until I heard, right behind me:

"Seamus Chron, I was told." I turned around, and I saw a tall and slender ginger with a dirty beard, in which maggots and worms were crawling freely. When he smiled, his mouth showed only so few teeth, but so much putrefaction, I thought I was in the presence of a zombie. His wide eyes looked straight at me.

"My name is Marvin, but you can call me Mr. Marvin. Please, can I sit? My master has sent me over to talk."

"Who told you to find me here?"

"Oh! Where I come from, we have ways of locating people." he explained, while leaning next to me, even though I never permitted it. He then continued:

238

"My colleagues and I are in the business of terminally ending your kind. Just peeps that my master has deemed a threat. We were told that a certain William Francoeur has collective memories with you. Therefore, I travelled here to kill you. Before you lose your last breath, I shall link myself with a possibility that you and William share. Do you understand what is about to happen, Seamus Chron?"

I nodded respectfully, although I wouldn't come out without a fight. I connected my gift to his dark soul. I considered him a more powerful Walker than I may ever hope to become.

"Now, now, Mr. Chron, applying your rookie glancing against me is of no use. Would you like to have a battle, or would you prefer to die quickly?"

"I, hmm." I stuttered, and never continued. I stood up from my seat and ran away. The faster I did, however, the more immobile I was. When I looked around me, everything had stopped. The evil man approached me with a machete that he pulled out of his black trench coat. He walked slowly. I wanted to fight back, but I had turned to stone. My gift seemed like an only alternative, but how? He was about one metre from me, and when I closed my eyes, I saw his essence standing in front of mine, like Goliath facing David.

Maybe I could piggyback away from this spot, I thought. Could I merge with his psyche? I pictured the first thing that came to mind: Scotch tape. I imagined my being as paper, and he was a rock. The sheet grew hands on which it made Scotch tape appear, and I taped myself to him, so that if he hurt me, he would wound himself as well.

239

"A fight, you have chosen, Mr. Chron? Fair enough."
He smiled, before visualizing a pool of blood on which my
wrapping form would float and eventually sink. He remained in
control of his position over me. I can do better! The Scotch tape
transformed into needles that I threw at his balloon self, but he
swiftly turned into a dinosaur. The spikes bounced right off his
scales, as he charged into the scarlet pond to sink me further.
I transformed into a shark, however, a megalodon, waiting to bite
his head off. Just as he approached, he transformed into an ant, got
deep inside my throat, and transmuted back into a giant lizard,
Japanese movie style, tearing my flesh apart, spreading my guts
and blood all over the red water. It hurts. It hurts so bad

I opened my eyes, still in shock, and I looked around me.
He stabbed me with his blade, and he pushed further, piercing my
heart. I was losing blood like crazy. It wasn't over yet. I closed
my eyes again, and I pictured those pieces of my flesh
reassembling into a giant robot that battled the reptile with a
gigantic sword. The Red Sea was replaced with grass. My first
swing missed, and the lizard swiftly punched me down, wounding
my back with its enormous fists. I turned around and threw another
blow, hitting his shoulder. He changed into some sort of blob to
suck in the blade and trap me along with it. He quickly covered my
body entirely.   It was suffocating. I opened my sight again. I was.
Losing energy. Blood. My breath. I won't die! I closed my eyes to
return to this sort of dreamland arena and continue the battle.

From inside the blob, I decided that the robot representing me
would heat up with molten lava, burning him from within. He just
changed into lava as well and floated away, transforming into a
firebird, in midair, and charged at me. Right before hitting me,
I turned into a dark night, holding two bastard swords. I struck the
feathered beast twice and chopped his wings.

240

The apterous body fell on the ground and became a giant snake, rushing towards me with so much speed, I could barely evade this attack. The servant opened its mouth wide and swallowed me in full. That was it. Everything faded into black. I will die. And just as I wanted to give up my last breath, I sensed his presence deeper in me. He was accessing all my memories, and I could do nothing to prevent it. I'm sorry, William. I hope you're safe. And then, the sensation stopped. I could hear him mutter something:

"Leave! This is not your fight, old man." Marvin complained. I woke up from my trance, and I was still in that virtual reality kind of place. Except, I was me. Marvin stood in front of the old man who winked at my sorry face. For the first time, I sensed his essence talking to mine. "Have you ever seen a Walker perform Morphosis Template before?" What was he talking about?

"You made it my fight when you attacked my friend." the hobo replied. He closed his eyes, projecting himself into a pocket dimension within this limbo, and he opened his dirty coat. A dash of light knocked Marvin hard, and while the red-haired glancer turned blind, I witnessed my elderly dude's metamorphosis into a half angel and half werewolf. He charged Marvin. The goon turned into a giant squid with blades in lieu of tentacles.

One such cutter hit the werewolf angel in the face, tearing the flesh and splashing blood all over me. I thought about how I could contribute but watching two formidable Walkers at it proved rather educating. The homeless hero seemed more powerful than Marvin. The winged canine healed its wound rapidly and charged to bite an arm off the calamari. Marvin transferred his essence in the lost limb, transforming it into a dragon, while the body left without any simply turned into dust. Just before the beast bit the wolf angel's head off, the dude changed into a living spear, impaling his opponent who swiftly transmuted into water to escape.

241

The flying lizard's axioms reformed into its draconic shape and dove at its prey. In the blink of an eye, the man upgraded into a rhinoceros, twice the size of an elephant. He charged to gore his assailant against a tree. Marvin regained his initial form, only to find himself bloodied, while a huge horn tore his guts and torso up, leaving a trail of entrails on the floor. This hardly comforts the injured Walker. He turns his entire body into a gaseous crow and flew. He then charged at the rhino. The elderly mage transformed into a white eagle and rammed the black bird. By then, I realized that this pause, aside, allowed me to heal my gashes, simply by visualizing some sort of medicinal factor coming from deep within my inner worlds. I watched my wounds cleaning themselves, and my flesh growing back. Too afraid to open my eyes, I couldn't see if the same happened to my outer shell. Besides, I couldn't leave the action. Not now. The old man might need my help.

Water Marvin formed a gigantic tsunami that surrounded the spear, just as the dude became a mountain. The wave soon was a meteor that struck Everest heavily, shattering its rocks all over the place. Every piece and pebble in the room transitioned into demon fairies. They charged onto the cosmic stone with sparkling blades. That last spell proved very difficult for Marvin, and it demanded of him some time to recover and get enough energy to transform again. The imps hit the boulder hard and repeatedly. They all merged into a titan-sized racoon, with volcanos for hands. Just as the immense furry would blast the meteor, Marvin gathered plenty of axioms to turn into mist and dissipate in the air.

The gigantic cutie faced the fog when it would reform into something tangible and wrestle it, but instead Marvin became gaseous, a toxic cloud, smothering his opponent along the way. I had found the energy to transform, although my very new walking skills hindered my chances. I could only randomly mutate into things, so when I considered the shape of a dazzling sun, I turned into a wooden spoon. "Having enough, old fool?" the fog asked, while the racoon choked to death.

I focused once more. Dazzling sun. Dazzling sun. White sheep, damn it! Marvin gradually solidified his mist, becoming a rock around the giant cute little pup's head. And I thought: *Come on. Dazzling sun.* But no, I was a World War II era tank. So, I shot the steam with one huge bullet. And right then, as I angered Marvin who turned his attention on me, I focused and changed into baby cats. The cloud turned into a giant vampire.

He walked towards me, and I couldn't change. I could only look at him with my cute little kitty eyes. His mouth was dripping with blood. Mine just uttered a "Meow?" The monster, with his floating cape and spider limbs stretching from his back leaned against mine, extending a muscular arm with razor-sharp claws to grab me. I inhaled a deep breath and I tried, one more time, to get this spell on tracks. His hand covered my head, and I could feel the heavy pressure closing in on me. Right before the abomination looked at me with surprised eyes. A spike came out of his chest, hard from behind. A wooden golem stood there, tearing the vampire in half. Marvin turned away to face his other opponent, just as I became. Yes! A Dazzling Sun, ladies, and gentlemen.

Blinded and weakened, Marvin died in the dude's arms. I opened my eyes and saw the red-haired corpse next to me, just as the old man cared for my wounds with light emanating from his hands. He waved me goodbye and left me by myself. Marvin's body loitered in the park. Bystanders watched two drug addicts struggling with their sight shut. A third junkie soon escorted them. He looked away while he joined the fun, ending with one of them having an overdose. They told their children not to make grown-ups' mistakes.

Say no to drugs, kids!

Still shaken, I managed to walk away from that scene. Montreal became a new kind of playground, for me. I could now freely practise my power.

243

Chapter Twenty-Five:
Marduk and Sekhmet

The ghost boat docked in Tir na n'Og after a long trip across the Veil. The fleet landed on a field of white lilies. Other ships arrived later, and they had to find a space to station themselves. Sekhmet expected this visit, and she knew it was important to play the right cards. Nobody wants to anger Marduk, while his House stands strong and undisputed. If only we could resurrect Varuna, many would think. Sekhmet doesn't believe this as the solution to stop Marduk from his path of destruction. It would only bring back the Babel War, or something far more devastating. She prefers staying in his better grace, while doing her things behind the curtains. It implies empowering opposing forces without the Entity Killer's knowledge. Modern warfare means friends and traitors.

This could explain why she avoided telling him about William possessing Indra's essence. Instead, she brought a girl into his life. Her name? Emerald Leone. She acted as her spy and William's bodyguard. When he went rogue, however, Sekhmet faced difficulties keeping this operation on. When she learned that Indra's host passed away, and he is stuck in his personal dying world, she thought about ways to get him out of there.
Now, though, she couldn't do just that without risking jeopardizing her plan while Marduk knows of his existence, and desires to see him ousted from the picture. If only to claim Indra's essence has his very own prisoner.

For Marduk, the landscape differed from that perspective. He wants to remain king of the mountain until he can destroy Sophronas we understand it. Being on top, however, came with its share of solitude. A song made its way into Marduk's mind, and it haunted him since his earliest time. With so many centuries passed, we may call it a pimple he allowed to become a wart, then a square, on the most remote spot of his soul. "Tell of the loneliness." it whispered. Say it! He can never rule alone if he conquers the lands protected by the Greater Councils. Songs of passion for desolated nations.

"Do they think this is just a game? Do some know it is a novel, comic books, a film, a series, or something?" he insisted, just so the voices of lemurs would find the same razors that clammed onto the white fur of his last admiral. He calmed himself, watching his delegation landing on Tir na n'Og, burning down entire civilizations of mushrooms along the way. He looked at the self-preserving waterfall next to his biomech, and then turned his attention to the vast nothingness that populated his chambers.

"How do you want me and how do you aspire to break me?" He asked. He closed his eyes and added:

"Allow me to feel you, I want to be loved. By you."

He missed Ishtar like crazy. When he parted from his boat and embarked on a shuttle that would take him to Arcana, his trusted gold and grey shadow of a spy appeared against the wall.

"Don't be a bringer of bad news, Jarrow." he sighed.

The spy materialized in front of Marduk. He's one of the few privileged who can show up and leave Marduk's chamber at will, since the Lord gave him a direct access from a hidden room, in the Layer Killer. Jarov approached further and whispered: "The bad news I provide? Merely a warning, Lord, as a far worse comes with it."

245

"I listen."

"Mr. Marvin is dead, Master Marduk." the spy mourned.

"Dead? Seamus killed him? How? He can barely use his newfound gift."

"No, my Lord. Seamus Chron didn't kill him. It was Alibast."

That name, again. It brought a moment of fear in Marduk's mind. Why would the monk poet decide to interfere in his quest? And why now? Many things made him question Sekhmet. Thankfully, his shuttle could wait for him. A long and narrow corridor took the warlord to a cabin, covered with gold and silver. A screen shone bright, just like the one in his chamber. It allowed him to look at his surroundings.

That monitor encircled him, leaving the fancy cloak to plate the floor, the only seat, and the ceiling. Marduk sat on the bench and observed the four other shuttles, smaller but with more cargo space, forming a protective square around him. His Squall Squad was dispersed among all four, the only guards he needed. All five ships took off and hovered over the grass, then the desert's sand, until it reached a thick forest. They continued along the way, flying at high speed for an hour until they got to Arcana's gates. A stone gargoyle kept them from joining in, but Sekhmet had been expecting their arrival. She stood in front of the main entrance, surrounded by five of her fiercest female warriors. A lioness, a tigress, an antelope, a praying mantis, and a pink-skinned woman stood guard, ready to fight to their death should Marduk launch an attack. The visiting Lord exited his shuttle and waved his escorting faction to fly away. Just as they did, Sekhmet dismissed her guards as well. "It is a pleasure and an honour to have you in Tir na n'Og, Lord Marduk." she nonchalantly uttered.

"Quit licking my feet, I don't trust you." he growled. "You'd better have good wine, I'm thirsty."

246

She waved the gatekeepers, and the bridge was soon lowered. They entered Arcana, with its great wonders of ivory-white buildings rising to form a mountain, its streets of gold and its community, as diverse as strange, roaming everywhere, like ants. Marduk and Sekhmet walked these roads until they reached her immense palace. She welcomed him inside, and they hastily found their way to her royal chamber, as wide as a city, with only one throne to populate it. Alone in the room, she summoned a cloud and two glasses. The mist poured the most exquisite wine known to any living taste bud. As she handed one glass to her guest, she began the discussion: "Yes, I am aware of William's existence. I ask of you to understand that while we could be allies, we are not under the same House's roof. You have secrets that could compromise my dignity, or my House's sovereign integrity. I also gather that you wish this William individual dead before he can master his mancing skills to become a threat."

"I desire to parlay if you have something that might interest me." Marduk replied. "Don't count me as his protector; the boy means little to me. He's just a card up my sleeve that I hold in case they compromised our alliance. I'm asking you, in exchange for my non-involvement, that you consider Gaia a no-invasion layer."

"I can guarantee no such promise."

"Marduk. Either you comply to this request, or I deploy my Duat army in Biarmaland, cornering Nibiru in a non-aggressive manner. Simply conducting a self-defence offensive, as you say."

"I didn't come all the way to visit you, so we can break our fragile alliance and declare war!" Marduk shouted. Sekhmet remained calm and asked: "Who talks about war? Only you do. I mention compromises, and possible actions if we can't get to terms."Marduk quelled his mood and thought for a long moment. He then diplomatically ordered: "Bring me the boy, and I will delay my plans for Gaia."

"Marduk . Oh, Marduk, are you afraid Varuna will show up to take you down?"

"He rots in the Dark Fire Circle! Don't mention his name again, am I clear?"

"Whose? Varuna's?"

"I warn you!"

"But Varuna can't hurt you."

"Sekhmet don't turn this diplomacy into a mockery!"

"Fair. No more pronouncing the syllables for Varuna. I will accept your decision to delay attacks on Gaia."

Marduk thought for a moment, again, and proclaimed: "I will stay in Arcana for a while. Do you have a hotel to suggest?"

"My friend, please, allow me to offer you my most prestigious and luxurious guest room." They shook hands and kept their knife hidden behind their back, so to speak.

Chapter Twenty-Six:
Sekhmet's Scheme

Long before Marduk learned of Indra's essence thriving alongside William's, just as Sekhmet herself was becoming aware of this fact, she visited someone who would accept to become this young human's guardian and mentor. This chapter takes place the very same day William was born, in Montreal. Sekhmet has been monitoring activities linked to House Varuna ever since the end of the Babel Wars when the sky god was expelled in a pocket dimension. Should his empire rise from its ashes, it would provide her a way out of Marduk's alliance, and her chance at conquering worlds while the two old foes would get into a vile battle.

Sekhmet last visited Hydaspes a thousand years before humans built a cult in her honour. This world flourished with a wildlife that would make enchanted forests jealous. You had more flamboyant phoenix to roam the sky than you would have had seagulls at a Gaian fast food restaurant. Not that Sekhmet would have known what this reference meant. She didn't return to Gaia when her House lost its influence, there. If only the rise of this Roman-Hebrew-Greek coalition represented an actual threat. Nobody expected a human being could become a potent mancer in his lifetime. A powerful Neymliss who left as soon as he came. Maybe just gun powder spark, but that Christ character certainly broke many attachments that Gaian circles had with Houses of Duat.

She assumed everything would perish, forced to die off from the face of Gaia when this Christian empire spread all over. She didn't know that Indra's legacy would remain strong in Asia. She only realized when she saw this fragment of the consciousness that had survived, grafted onto the specie of wasps. *How ingenious.* she thought. Whoever did this possess a strong gnosis, and Indra represented more the warrior type. How could he have succeeded in annexing his essence this way? That made no sense, regardless of how he had managed it, he obviously survived. The danger of this fact signified that she had to warn Marduk.

With the Hound-Lord of Nibiru imprisoned in some limbo, the truce they signed, his vow to protect the interests of Duat, meant nothing. She should have visited more important acquaintances, like Horus or Osiris, she thought, but what do they know? They didn't participate in the Tir na n'Og invasion. They preferred to stay away, in Hades.

So, she met with an unlikely ally in Hydaspes, home of the nine Great Muses. She approached a desert of cinders that stretched to no end. On her way were scattered whitened skulls, spines, and bones. The sky shone bluer than any she had seen in a while, and the absence of clouds promised days with no rain.

She walked straight and proud in the middle of the ashes, with a dark robe that embraced her feline figure and left her long neck out to support her black panther head like an altar. At the far end of this desert stood a tree of glowing dots. Pilgrim moths from all over Hydaspes flew to encounter that tall plant and die the instant they finally kissed the light.

"Melpomene!" she shouted when she stopped near a cloud of night butterflies. "I have humbly come to request your assistance." The tree remained still while the moths gradually formed a face that floated around and over it.

250

"We have no say in your battles, goddess. I desire of you to leave." She challenged this face with a daring glare and penetrating eyes: "Of all the Muses, it was you who wished to join the Sapphire Council. How tragic, a human outdid you? A mere naked ape who only walked as a Neymliss for a short time."
The face looked down for a moment. "It was not my choice."

"It was not even Zoroaster's. Why him? After all you did for the service of this Dreamer?"

"Which Dreamer?"

"Oh, you know how I express myself."

Melpomene grew rather hurt while Sekhmet further penetrated his eyes. She calmed her own anger and explained: "I lost my home in Gaia because of a human who proclaimed himself Son of the. Beyond and saw a conquering religion built around him. You have no idea how quick it gets once these humans find the right keys to usurp our positions in Sophron. The wisest of them, the smartest, could easily take your place before you realize it."

"I hold no more power over them."

"They have stripped off your influence, Melpomene. Which circle do you influence, now? Do you even have a House?"

"I live in Hydaspes and I attract moths to die. Always my reason for being."

"Oh, the enlightenment! Oh, the achievement!

Meanwhile, Varuna and Marduk are back at it. The very war that cost us our hands over humanity has returned, stronger than ever. What are you going to do about it? Nothing?"

"Varuna remains imprisoned. And Marduk isn't a threat. Why do you say the old ways have resurfaced?"

"Because I know it's coming. Gaia isn't safe."

"We're not in Gaia! This is Hydaspes. Entities have allowed me to spend eternity in this plenitude. I do not wish to revert to a mortal form if only to play politics again."

"You consider this a game?"

"Not plenitude either. I would belittle myself, were I to join anyone camp."

"Then join mine. I do not care much about Varuna or Marduk! I care for humanity. I crave having a home and circles of believers. I have found both in Tir na n'Og, and you deserve as much."

"I deserve only peace. Please, Sekhmet. Allow this Great Muse to experience everlasting bliss. And leave."

"Then you have lived for no purpose. You will be forgotten all over Sophron, in the entire pluriverse, until someone sees a weakness in Hydaspes and decides to invade. They will simply chop this tree and burn its wood. Your essence, where do you think it will go? You assume they will let it reincarnate? Oh, no. They will have sophroners to work for them. They will make sure you stay dead. I planned an occupation myself, and I won." she got him pondering. She turned around and faced the desert of ashes, then brought her attention back at him.

"You know why I did not pick this easy a target? Why I did not invade Hydaspes?" He listened further and looked at her.

She concluded: "I always dreamed of fighting by your side."

"By my side?"

"Who allowed these Greeks to learn from Egyptians?"

"They did as much from Hindus."

"Forget Varuna, please. Why do you think?" Melpomene observed the ashes and the bones. He examined the intense blue sky above. He eyed Sekhmet who would not leave without a word from him. "I beg of you."

"Oh, no! It's not like that."

"Good! I couldn't bear a story like those I made happen."

"About so." she uttered, and looked at the ashes and skulls.

"You create tragedy. I scatter deserts." These last words haunted Melpomene. He thought to himself: *Humans liked to believe I inspired them. I am what I am, and that's what it is. Heck, what is it now? They can't get it straight and they usurp my place on the council?* "Indra was resurrected in a wasp, but I fear most of his essence found their way into the body of a young man."

"Where is the wasp, now?"

"You don't have to know."

"If his consciousness shines in an insect as well as in a human, don't you think he could have survived elsewhere?"

"I am convinced that the minute Varuna is told about Indra's miraculous reincarnation, he will seek the greatest fragment. We don't want a full Indra alongside a full Ishtar, and Marduk to vent his jealousy, now, do you?"

253

"Humanity lost from this battle. It was never my fight."

"It becomes your concern when you see how they pushed you against walls of no return. This, Melpomene, this brings us our fight.   It takes our time to get what we are owed, what we deserve. And I suggest that you gather your sisters and brothers to your cause."

A flow of moths shaped a wounded face as Melpomene frowned heavily. He wasn't the youth he once was. Too often throughout his existence did he approach power and never allowed himself the opportunity to taste it. Is the Fates giving him another chance? He thought of all the civilizations he could conquer, and all those believers who would build statues for him, retell his feats in poems for generations to teach those Greeks, like his children. Instead, they chose to divide their circles between Varuna, Marduk and Osiris. As the other Great Muses, Melpomene found in art, science, and philosophy means to unify some influence. It was crucial to avoid more wars among the three great Houses of Gaia. Still, Marduk managed to get the last laugh. Perhaps Sekhmet thought of a good plan. Maybe she could weaken Marduk, benefit from the absence of the other two, and reshape the cultures of Earth. This time, Melpomene's New World Order would prevail. He had to figure out a way to limit the influence and the might that Sekhmet already had. His power may surpass hers in certain aspects, but she holds the upper hand over him with this scheme.

"Do you realize?" he calmly said.

"That you ask of me to come back from this retirement.

You ask my siblings to join us. And you want us to participate in a battle for the resurfacing of an outlaw?"

254

"The council didn't criminalize Indra. They simply imposed restrictions on his influence, as to protect mankind from our greed. Marduk never complied. The entities themselves may have had a reason to bring Indra back, even if in a shattered form. I say we use the confusion that will destabilize Marduk's solid hold on humanity to claim our share. This is all I suggest."

"My concern, Sekhmet, is your own appetite. I will not resurface from this blissful retirement and battle opportunistic Neymlisses and Walkers just so my allies can abuse of my benevolence." She knew she couldn't fair in this war unless she convinced the Muses to fight with her. Heck, she might as well return to Tir na nOg and forget she had ever laid eyes on this object of her obsession. Indra will come back, but this time he will be her pet. She will chain him in her room and play with him as she pleases. Hurt him like he wounded you! Make him crawl and beg for mercy! When he does, she will lower his face against the floor with one heavy foot behind his head. She will have it her way, at all costs.

"I will remain very close to you, and very quiet. You will have all the room to maneuver. It is our fight, but your circles will stand their ground. All I want is to have Horus worshiping me. Bring me that revenge!" Melpomene smiled as he observed the dark butterflies that formed his flesh and skin.

"I ask you one favour in return."

He softly uttered. Sekhmet nodded before he added, pointing at the moths: "Be one of them, oh my secret mother. I will call you Sthenele."She approached the tree, attracted by its gleam. The oak further cast a shine that grew to blast an intense light, as though it gravitated around Sekhmet's presence. She remained motionless for a moment while Melpomene underwent a slow process of re-engineering every axiom that composed his being.

"Sthenele?"

She realized what this meant. She would become a moth queen whose sole purpose in life would be to inspire a poet. Let him find his greatest work and then die. They must find another way. "Hmm. With respect. I will give you total control over this army of ours, including my legions!"

"I am aware of this."

"But Oh, Great Muse!"

"This is my only request, and my final." A moth queen. She lowered her gaze and felt the weight of his condition. This is going to be more frustrating than she expected. "If this is your wish. Your Highness." Her eyes probed the cloud of light, darkness, dust, and air that shaped Melpomene. She observed the whole population of butterflies within his transitional state.

They kept the same urge to become one with the beam, at the cost of their lives, as they had before, unaware of this whole reality changing around them. They had only flight for what burns. Sekhmet remained of stone while her own pixels were called to cement the cloud. A second thought got to her. "Do I want to live the life of an angel with wings of wax?" It quickly brought a third vision, while her detached axioms joined those of disintegrated night butterflies. Their reflections brought mere dreams of a day that dreamed an Egyptian goddess.

"Hold on!" she meant to say. She did! She second-guessed, only to add to the wounds that made her scream from outside in! Silenced. The whole metamorphosis atrociously wounded her. The next phase involved a full merger with Melpomene's only source of worship. She remained silent. Axioms glued onto one another until they became a corpse, then a silhouette. A glow brought life to a cocoon. While in that state of eternal stasis, the goddess caressed her mancing orb. She expected a similar request to come from the Muse. Her ties with an Author provided her insight into her main escape and source of salvation.

Veins appeared at the sphere's core, producing sparks that floated around her. The Ether she held from the crystal ball's centre pierced the Veil that surrounded her body. It was as though she dug a small tunnel from within. When her meditative state looked down this hole, she saw the sweetness of a loving lady. It took only a millisecond for her conscience to swap places with the unsuspecting woman's.

Meanwhile, Melpomene fine-tuned the last touch in sculpting the most fearsome figure he ever had: Muscled, intimidating. What was he thinking before, in Greece? Tragedy should never have held the essence of a woman.

It is important to conclude this chapter with one detail: Sekhmet wouldn't accept the role of a secondary character's tool that easily. She usurped her essence's place with one that would prove to be good leverage, allowing her to roam free, having Melpomene convinced he fooled a House's ruler. And, in doing so, she could continue with her agenda. The lady who inherited her place now responded to the name Sthenele. And Sekhmet could freely return to Tir na n'Og like nothing happened.

Chapter Twenty-Seven:
Kitana meets Lucretia

Her feet walked from one end of the boat to another, but her mind floated somewhere else. Golems cleaned around the cabin, ignoring Lucretia who could hardly conceal her anxiety. Danger happened to her daddy, she thought. Why did he leave like this? He must have landed in a treacherous world. Maybe he'll never come back! The anguish put so much pressure against her forehead, she couldn't find room to ponder. And yet, what could she do to save him? Think, Lucretia, think. You're not just a sex-driven android, are you? She remembered that Nempty would often play with strange toys. One of them must put her in contact with his soul.

She rushed into his cabin, disturbing the cleaning crew, and looked around. Against the wall, she could see a few rifles. Most of them had weird shapes. A long tube on a handle would appear more like a portable bazooka than an actual gun. Some seemed very small, but they had big cannons. Next to them, a table stood with various gimmicks and bizarre items. This one caught her attention, however: a box. She remembered having seen Nempty use it to talk to strangers. Maybe she could get help.

Lucretia walked quickly to grab the black cube. Once in her hands, she manipulated it carelessly, as she had no idea how to operate it. There were carvings and symbols all over, and none made any sense. Is she supposed to speak some magic words? "Open up, sesame seed!" she ushered. Nothing happened. "I command you to open up! Come on! We need to find Daddy!" Silence. Outside these closed perimeters, the boat's botanical staff observed her, all too puzzled to say anything. Lucretia then moved her hands and fingers across the box's surface. Nothing happened.

Sensing a burst of distress, she fell on one knee and could hardly gather the courage to stand up. Instead, she abandoned all hope and crumbled against the floor. At the back of her mind, she imagined the worst that could have unfolded. Did he disappear and will never return? She closed her eyes and turned away, so that the golems wouldn't see her tears. As she sobbed, she heard a voice in her head.

"Welcome to the mancening network, my name is Kitana, how can I help you?"

It came from the box, Lucretia realized. "Hello?" she answered. "Who is this?" Silence. The ghost inside her mind replied: "Nempty? Is that you?" The android quickly jumped on her feet. She screamed: "No! My name is Lucretia! Daddy needs me! I need to find my daddy! Can you help me? Please, madam?" Kitana needed some time to process this weird information, and asked: "Do you know where he went?" The poor orphaned girl shook her head and looked everywhere. "I don't know." she whispered. "What about magic? Maybe we can use it to find him!" The sophroner not only understood what to do, she thought that if Nempty experienced a Final-Vanishing, she would lose her only chance of leaving this painful job.

"Listen to me, Lucretia. This is very important. Can you check in your daddy's things and tell me if you locate a crystal orb, okay?"

It was unlikely that she could find any. Those rare things that only managers and some sophroners will carry. "There isn't, Mrs. Kitana. I'm looking all over the boat!" The poor girl was indeed searching through Nempty's belongings, and she uncovered books, laptops, cellphones, enchanted swords, laser pistols, gold coins, platinum coins, five thousand dollars in small bills, but no crystal orb. "Are you sure? Please, Lucretia, this is the only way we can save your father!" *A sphere*, she thought, *a circle thing made of glass, diamond, whatever. Anything.* She looked, and she looked, and she found nothing. "I'm so sorry. Daddy, I'm so sorry. Okay, let me ask around. Hold on!" She put the box away.

The girl quickly ran to speak to nearby golems. "Hello?" She stopped a young one who looked like a cross between a bodybuilder and a brick. "Do you know if there's a crystal orb on this ship?" The creature shook his head and resumed his cleaning activities. She then rushed to question another, a large boulder with a grin on his face, but he had no idea what she talked about. The next five members of the staff she encountered couldn't understand what she queried, until she heard Jonathan: "You." He explained.

"Your heart is made with an orb. You didn't know?"

"My heart?" Lucretia inquired. "How come?"

"This is what gives you a sentient persona. It allows you to connect to Sophron, and become a true conscious being. You emanate existence, even though you are an artificial toy. I do too, Sister. I am also an android with a heart, just like yours." The wise construct obviously had some experience to tell. He spoke those words calmly, before supervising the rest of the staff. Lucretia fell silent for a long moment. If she tears her giver of life out, she will die. She adored her father dearly. She recalled how he respected her.

Her program aimed at pleasing sexual predators.
She understood that her cruel and evil makers implemented those
urges. But Nempty treated her with the tenderest caring love.
Death? How? What happens when this? No! She can't die! Daddy
can't die too. What can she do? Her head turned faster than a
whirlwind in a teacup. Nobody prepared her for this. And what if
her father left for good? "Lucreatia?" She heard Kitana insisting.
"I'm thinking!" she shouted. He couldn't abandon her. Could he die
for her? What happens when we quit the layer of the livings?

"Are you sure you need an orb?" she asked the voice.

"Listen to me, Lucretia. Your father gave you everything.
He cared about you, even though you were designed to be treated
like trash. Do you understand?" Silence. Of course she did.

"He made pure gold out of you. He pressured Heavens to turn
you into absolute diamond. Now, believe me when I tell you that
he's about to die. He needs you. Please, tell me you found a crystal
ball. Please, Lucretia!"

Silence. Her entire life was all about true fatherly love.
Maybe this sort of ultimate sacrifice matters, for the light that
Nempty cultivated in her soul. "All right." she whispered softly.

She walked slowly towards the box. She looked at it for a
moment. "Lucretia? Are you there?" the voice in her head asked.

"Yes." the android answered. "Did you find a crystal orb?"
Kitana questioned. After a long pause, Lucretia trembled: "I did."
She heard a sigh of relief, and the helping magician added: "Good!
You have to put it against the box. Make sure the two of them
touch. They must be stuck against one another for the entire spell,
or else it will not work. Do you understand?" *Will I feel pain?*
Were the only words that came to the girl's mind. She cried and
answered: "I understand."

261

It took her a lot of courage to act. There, on the table, she saw a knife. She didn't know how hurtful it would be, but it was the only action she could do to save her daddy's life. Her hands trembled with apprehension. She slowly put the box where she found the blade, and then she looked at her chest. All she could think of, while opening her blouse to reveal her breasts, was: "Please, Daddy, be safe." And she planted the knife into her thorax. She screamed in pure agony. "Lucretaia?" Kitana asked. "Hello? What's going on?" The girl didn't respond. Blood filled her hands. The agony felt atrocious, but she had to carry on.

When the wound got wide enough, she dug right into the flesh. Losing blood as fast as she surrendered her breath. She knew she had to act swiftly. There would be a small window of time before her brain ceases to function. Thankfully, her artificial frame would convey sufficient energy for her to complete her mission. With one daring set of fingers, she grasped the orb. It produced an intense light that blinded the curious golems who showed up to watch. Lucretia held the sphere. She grabbed the cube with her freed hand. Losing her life, she allowed her entire body to fall on both.

And she died.

Jonathan closed the cabin door and told his peers to get back to work. Meanwhile, the orb and the box fused into one another. On the opposite end of that existential phone call, Kitana couldn't see what had just happened, but she quickly acted to activate the mancing sphere. Fortunately, Nempty's essence was all over it. Connecting her own reality to the orb allowed her to sense his presence. "What are you doing in Sebekia Pistis?" Kitana wondered. "It's okay. Stay with me. I'm sending you some help."

Chapter Twenty-Eight:
Nempty is Reborn

Nempty's corpse was getting colder by the minute. His skinny frame embraced the position of a fetus that had yet to tell masculinity from femininity. The farther from its anchor on a substance the essence went, the more the body became one with the surroundings. The background was filled with axioms of Void, like maggots born from the flesh's lack of thoughts. Void, until atoms themselves could no longer reflect anything. Then came a dozer, just one. Like a melody without a tune. A tiny pup who had lost its parents. The closer to the carcass, the more distinct from its surroundings went. The warmer the dozer got, as it neared the cadaver, the fewer Void axioms exited out of the dying dwarf.

And the pooch advanced until the silhouette of a fat phoenix took over. It appeared the dozer projected the bird's presence.

"Hey you." the chubby feathered one said, soon after his shadow stopped next to Nempty's corpse.

"Hey, buddy, you, okay?"

A purple-plumaged hand gently approached the dead body. Time remained still, as though the flaming beast had managed to act upon the entire universe within Sebekia Pistis.

The mountains at the far horizon beyond the bird's point of view appeared flattened as though the landscape turned into a two-dimensional painting. Nempty's corpse carved into the picture, like a concave depiction of himself. The purple phoenix further focusedboth his hands over the body, then raised them closer to Nempty's forehead.

The bird's sight seemed blurry. Nempty appeared to stand out from the background that surrounded him. Though he did not move in any form or manner possible, his skin lost its colour, until the nymph's entire flesh became translucent. Nempty's blood had dried out. His bones turned to dust that flew inside what appeared like a humanoid-looking aquarium. And the shelter floated above the magma river. "What we got, here?" the obese purple beast interrogated the corpse.

"Your essence does not look fine, friends. What is troubling you?" the phoenix added.

"Don't ask questions, Nunc. Get him out of here." a voice in his head seemed to insist.

"Yes, Mr. Kennedy, but I need to know he's okay." the bird replied. "It's Kitana, silly. If he's fine, get him out, and, please, find the three teenagers!"

Several membranes formed within the translucent body, resulting in an onion-like flesh, the more vitreous as we voyaged deeper. Each coating died and vanished in dust while new ones pushed old layers farther away from a tiny orb of light. In the middle of Nempty's frontal lobe, a disc of gloom and glory arose. A similar blueish ball emerged in the solar plexus, and a connection gradually appeared between the two. A sphere of darkness pointed out at the back of his head, right under the cerebral cortex, where the skull once sheltered a cerebellum. "You were given the touch of Ishtar, say?"

Mancers manipulate reality from the outside in, stemming axioms to maneuver essences, known as thesis. Glazer's manage reality from the inside out. They fashion the essence to control the pixels. They call this craft gnosis. Sophroners do a little bit of this and a little of that. This bird knew Varuna. They developed a good friendship, for as much as they never had to discuss philosophy.

"Me, I'm sorry if I say to you she's gone. And me, I'm here because they need you, they said. Well, Mr. Kennedy, he said it louder than the others, but I like Mr. Kennedy! He gave the moon to the one he loves, you know?"

And while Nunc further kept his focus on Nempty's essence, dozers gathered behind him to observe. Demons examined the scene through the beasts' fantasies. They witnessed spectacles that rarely happened in Hell, or any of the other two hellish worlds. Resurrection was a practice that sophroners prefer to keep to themselves.

"Your boat, they left it in Anirniit, so that nobody they'll see it, okay? And, quid, I'll call you quid, okay? Find the children, they said. We find the three teenagers from Gaia, the girl. The two boys are special, right? Special, quid! It's okay I call you quid?"

The carcass resembled that of beings inhabiting most worlds in the Logos hemisphere. Creatures of light reflecting matter, just as here in Barbelo, we get the opposite view on the spectrum.
The other quadrants end up as mirrors of what their contrasting pole is not. Nempty's consciousness spent its entire existence within the body of a nymph, with grey DNA. This curiosity happened under the miraculous act of a sophroner. A more potent one than Nunc, however. The essence remained pristine, as it is throughout every being of all the worlds, and Dreamers. As pure as beauty in the form of a harmonious attraction.

"Alibast, he talked to Mr. Kennedy, I think. They said: We need this one reborn. And so, you're dead, but I'm the one he'll get you reborn. Alibast, he said to Mr. Kennedy, and she said to me, hold on, that's not what happened. Anyway, and they said: I need to speak to Mr. Kennedy. And I said: Can I take a message? Mr. Kennedy, she's always busy, say? She works on the phone, all the time."

A beauteous sphere of light engulfed both tiny dots and the darkness. Soon, that sphere would cover the membranous flesh until it mutated into an orb, like those that dancers carry. It transitioned into an egg, while the glow intensified. The spark and the blank merged into a single cell, became two, then four.

"But Alibast he didn't say to me you were touched by Ishtar. She's sweet, say? He said to me her name it was Emerald. But I know it is Ishtar. Emerald is in Tasmania. You know why I know that? Vanessa, she told me. Vanessa, she tells me all the stories. You follow, quid? You take your boat, you find William, you find Emerald, and the new guest, he is a shameful king or a prince, I call him Shame, and we all go to pick up Emerald, but you know what? It's not emerald! Guess she is who!"

Demons watched the powerful sophroner's silhouette transport the fertilized ovary away from their realm, beyond the Veil. Big question marks haunted those who dared trying to figure out what he talked about. And the tall purple phoenix walked through the core of Sophron to enter a vortex that led him into the enigmatic world of Athanor.

He carried the egg with immense care as he crossed an ocean that stretched to no end. Blue algae filled it, imprinted with a stench so vile, it was impossible to consider any form of life in this area. Far to his left, Nunc could see a unicorn the size of a skyscraper. The beast had nine mouths, with one visible on a giant hump near the donkey's neck. Water around the creature flowed as clear as crystal and as pure as it seemed incorruptible.

266

Nunc seemed very tall, himself, with broad shoulders he kept under a very tight white cloak. So minuscule was it, it made the muscularly obese bird look like a fat kid with a tiny shirt. His belly overlooked the lower half of a robe. Perhaps it was more of a miniskirt, at this point. The cloak's hood was equally funny looking. It was so small that it could hardly cover his neck. Nunc's gigantic yellow bird feet, with shades of ochre around every scale, stretched beyond ruined tennis shoes. His big eyes bore a very silly gaze. A beak stood midway between the shape of an eagle and a seagull. Some feathers harboured signs of eternal flames, hence the obvious conclusion any onlooker would have about his specie.

Can you hear me, Daddy?

When Nunc approached the shore, a storm formed itself. Wild waves menaced his trek, but Nunc never strayed from his focus. He kept the egg firmly against his chest, both arms around it to provide a much-needed warmth and protection. He braved the small tsunamis with every breath in his body. Unable to use his hands to manipulate axioms with his conscience, Nunc could only hold on to this spell to walk on water. He channelled his essence through his feet, pushing his substance against the surface. He hoped that no wave would make him lose his concentration.

When one such torrent crashed against him like a shattered piece of porcelain, Nunc had to shut his eyes, grab his breath, and stay focused. Another one hit him from his left side. He got off balance for a moment, as he tried not to fissure the egg in any way possible. The third one made him rattle and tremble. More of them smashed against his back and threw the bird and his prized ovary against a more monstrous wave that slammed him up front. *Do not lose the egg.* he thought. *Do not break it.*

267

A freshly resurrected psyche is always very fragile. Axioms all over try to smother it and leave it dead, and only well-equipped essences can oppose pixels and earn its right to exist. Usually, a consciousness that has undergone several reincarnations find the adequate tools to force their organisms towards an efficient adaptation. But for Nempty's being, at this point, so soon after his demise, and on the verge of a Final One, Entities would easily get a final say on his reality.

When another gigantic wave pushed Nunc down, the egg fell in the ocean. Nunc swallowed too much water to breathe properly. Much bigger walls came and knocked the sophroner good until he lost consciousness, almost. He battled. Fought to remain awake. Blue algae surrounded him, blurring his vision under an intense opaque sight. Meanwhile, the egg further fell down the ocean. Focused, Nunc gathered his essence behind his nostrils and kept them shut, while a few gestures allowed him to form a substantial bubble of air around his head. It grew to cover his entire body.

The madam said I could save you.

The ovary finally reached the sand, at the bottom. Among the dust, no colour. The storm hardly produced any sound. The water was still. Life was harsh, except for tiny shrimps with wide monkey eyes. Some fish swam around the precious egg. The oval-shaped heart stood there on the dune like an alien shell in a foreign world. Strides emerged on the surface, with blue algae attracted by these crevasses. Down here, rot appears in a matter of minutes.

Hence the precipitation that Nunc had. He looked all over for a sign, anything. He was miles away, unable to tell a rock from an egg. He wandered like this for hours and hours, those that flirted with a full day until desperation came to him.

He could absolutely not find a grey egg at the bottom of a same-coloured ocean. Unless. The unicorn, he had seen was the one he encountered. Karkadan: Zoroaster's mount during the Babel Wars. An archoid designed not to attack and destroy, like most, but rather to collect axioms and reassign them. He was more of a menacing tool than an actual vehicle. The pressure that thousands of trillions of inner universes do against one single enveloping pluriverse force pixels to break, and fragments to join others, leaving Sophron in a highly chaotic state. Cancers channel these parcels, as they fracture and reshape reality.

I think we are together, now. With Karkadan's natural design that seemingly purifies, Zoroaster would battle the authority of Ahriman and counter any mancing spell his nemesis would cast on him. After the war, Karkadan retired. The unicorn was posted here, in Athanor, one of the most chaotic worlds within Archeus, to regulate fluxes of chaotic axioms. He's the most powerful biomech ever created, and a rare one who has its own essence. Archoids, usually devoid of a sentient affirmation, walk, swim, or fly like cells in a bottle. The scarce gems of his kind feel, reflect and express themselves. When the pilot's soul bonds with the organic robot's cockpit, the two existences become one. Karkadan continues to function, live, walk, howl at the open sky. His essence allows him to make his own choices and decisions. All biomechs will hold actual conversations with their host, but only a handful of them will question or argue. Therefore, he's very picky with his bonding.

When the Babel Wars ended, Zoroaster left all planes of existence, and we believe he had joined a world within the Beyond. Karkadan remained behind, and occasionally he would choose a new pilot, and allow him, or her, them, or it to share his being, for the duration of a battle, a mission, or a war. Karkadan was one of only twelve orchids with their own gifts.

The beast was able to project its essence through copies of itself in other Dreamers, gather these copies to fight by its side, or change its appearance and size. Intrigued, Nunc projected a good glimpse at the monster in the middle of the ocean, like an immense horse-like Titan, the height of three skyscrapers, filtering the water to feed on axioms. But Nunc was on a mission. He must find that egg and save Nempty.

For Nunc, it meant to have this whole portion of the sea cleaned until it was clear enough to locate his prized treasure. He waited underwater for the storm to calm down. And he waited. Leopard-goblin sharks swam in hordes near him, and went away, as though repulsed by this anomaly of an intruder. Chameleon rays appeared in their flamboyant lavender with shades of fuchsia, thus attracting the predators' attention towards them. They hunt like wolves.

I love you, Daddy.

The weakest will chase the prey until the leaders may come out from behind a rock and go for the kill. One thing these beasts will never get is that chameleon rays scavenge.

Whenever they allow their emotions to display flashy colours like that, they attract stupid predators into the mouth of a clumsy whale dragon. The lizard will simply open its wide mouth and snap a few sharks in half, leaving huge pieces to fall on the sand, near a curious-looking egg. The rest of the pack will swim for their lives. The surviving rays will, then, enjoy their buffet. When the storm finally vanished, Nunc resumed his quest for the missing treasure. This time, he resurfaced and observed the horizon. To his right: Water. To his left: more water. A bit anxious, he swiftly looked behind him: Water, and water and more water. The other way?

Here he assumed that a huge unicorn could, at least, stand still for a few hours. How can it leave its place like this? The perfect plan, but he should have thought about it before. Well, before the storm he had that egg secured in his arms. What spell can he do to find it before it hatches then drowns in the coldness of this harsh environment? As he considered every option, he realized something. The water seemed more polluted behind him than it was in front. That could be a trail. Or. He thought. He could summon a tornado in the ocean, right about where he had lost his precious and have the egg part from its danger zone. What if he'd cast winds too powerful?

Every time Nunc considered spells that required connecting himself with the substance of inanimate objects, it always ended in total disaster. Should he risk killing his new friend by his own doing? Or should he go for his first idea and abandon his buddy in intense cold until he could locate Karkadan, the agent of purity? *Think fast.* he slowly thought. And thought, until shivers and spasms made him expedite an alternative:

He calmed down, joined both his hands together and channelled his essence. He raised both his index fingers to bring the inner energy towards the tip of his nails. He focused his presence, in the same manner, and, finally, he connected himself with the very substance within Athanor. He levitated, pulled by a complex series of threads that made a web, with atoms, particles, every molecule around him shaping the strings. He channelled chill and heat from his immediate surroundings and allowed his body to act as their vehicle. Then, he faced the sea. He slowly, carefully, extended both hands as if to carry warmth. He lowered himself down to touch the surface, but he forgot he had an arm shorter than the other. And so, he channelled all the heat into the ocean. He fought the elements he had awakened to bring his prize closer, but the heaviness was overwhelming. By the time Nunc finally got both hands to reach the oval orb, he gathered more than enough heat to boil the water in a ten-kilometre radius. "Oh no." he muttered in a sorry voice.

Steam formed around him, huge walls of steam. Any attempt to channel the essence of cold in his immediate surroundings ended up fruitless. If this weren't sufficient, he had already opened himself as a channeler and could hardly close this down. Now he remembers why it was a bad idea to play with the elements like that. More heat was projected into the ocean, and more thrown back in his entourage, resulting in more heat projected in the ocean. Every creature boiled within this ten-kilometre radius. And the egg? Just as bad. "No! No! No!"

He kept repeating like a goofy kid who didn't want anyone to see his maladroit act. When he finally managed to push himself away from his doomed position, the channel broke up. The water kept on boiling for five hours, or until a shadowy giant unicorn sensed that something, around here, was awfully wrong.

Three plane carriers piled up on one another would hardly cover half the size of this Titan. When Karkadan decides to move, every creature in the ocean knows about it. His sole purpose, on Athanor, was to regulate elements to avoid pollution, as any other agent of destruction, to prevent life forms from enjoying a healthy environment.

When Zoroaster retired from his position as a knightly mancer, he gave his mount to the people of Athanor to thank them for their loyalty towards his cause. Karkadan hasn't involved himself in a fight for the last two hundred thousand Athanor years. The beast enjoyed his new role and the peacefulness of this ocean. He considered this his blissful eternity. So, when it came to his awareness that something had just turned a portion of his ocean into a gigantic ragout, Karkadan decided to act promptly.

Meanwhile, Nunc also decided to act very fast. Fortunately, the water was now clear, conveniently distilled. While the suns were at their zenith, it was time to dive in. Nunc swam among the deliciously cooked wildlife until he could find the spot he occupied when he last held his fried. He observed around him carefully, then opted for an ideal spot to dive deeper, until he reached the bottom. After a few more nervous looks to his right, to his left, there he saw what seemed like an egg-shaped pearl. He approached the object and recognized the strides. It was his friend, all right. He swiftly grabbed it and swam to the surface. He wasn't prepared for this heart attack! The mice faced Everest about to squash it.

"Hey, hmm. Hi!" he uttered, hoping the mammoth of all mammoths would listen.

The horse's white body covered the size of three large stadiums, covered with very fine hair half a millimetre thick. The horse's head had all three mouths wide open. From Nunc's perspective, three skies seemed to fall on him. Panicked, he whistled like nothing had happened and walked away, carefully, before he could fly and escape a first attack. Despite his immensity, Karkadan was impressively agile. Nunc had no choice but to trust in his magic once again. So, he channelled heat and cold to give his wings enough wind to dive away from here at the speed of sound. Karkadan didn't bother a chase. He simply cleaned after Nunc's mess, refurbishing this ocean with algae and life.

After almost an hour of flight, it was time for Nunc to walk on the water, again. Sustaining his obesity in the air was already enough of a challenge. Walking was much better. And when he finally reached that shore, he had little energy left to go very far. He settled for the first cave he encountered. There, he let his sophroner magic redecorate the place. He built a nice nest for his friend's egg, even though he knew how, sadly, the inevitable happened. With the sunset piercing through a small crack in the eastern wall, Nunc knocked on the egg's shell

It was cooked solid, all right. He tried to probe for a sign of essential life. A small pulse, very faint but present, carried a sign of life. He sighed and threw his arms away in abandon. Alibast, he wanted me to save him, he thought.

He left the egg on the nest and walked outside the cave. *I failed*, he thought, realizing that he should have stayed in the Circle, at the very least, or choose his entry into Athanor more carefully. He should have left Athanor and re-enter! Why didn't I think of that? All hopes had left when a cute little kitten came out from a bush with a dead frog in his mouth. Nunc didn't want to be bothered, but that little thing was so cute. The kitten played with his prey, licking the frog. Kitty threw his meal at Nunc's feet, then jumped on the frog, gnawed a leg, licked its back, loved to lick its back, so much, kitty had to lick even more. Then stopped, a bit dizzy. Kitty looked at the giant bird. Kitty felt vertigo but resumed playing with the frog.

"If only, boys, if only I could find more life. I could maybe save him. Where can I find life close by?" Nunc looked down and saw the frog and smiled. *Of course.* he thought. He grabbed the frog and checked for a pulse, despite the possessive kitten who just jumped on his arm. He entered the cave with both animals and put the frog next to the egg. Kitty jumped on the frog and laid down to sleep in this comfortable nest. Nunc probed the egg again. The signal was as faint as it was earlier, like a kid who'd expect a symphony out of a guitar and got nothing but noise. He then began a long ritual to merge Nempty's essence with the cat's life, and the cat's life with the essence. A kid places his fingers, somehow, and strikes the chords with a melodious sound. The cat's essence will move into the frog, he calculated, but the kid simply kept on placing his fingers and strike chords. This way, the essence would regain a stronger pulse. Then, a very nice sound filled the space.

The kid simply stroked the instrument like that, drew some figures to remember where he put his fingers, and played again. The fetus could, in no way, feed on a boiled source of nourishment. So, Nunc crafted an umbilical cord from the frog's flesh and connected it into the fetus. The kid was onto something. He tried a few more accords. For that, he had to pierce the egg, dig through the white, reach the yoke and connect the frog to the yoke. Once Nunc felt a satisfying pulse of life, he let nature do the rest. The kid worked at it for days, weeks, months, and finally got the best song ever made.

The thought of this question increased the blood flow in his brain's amygdala. His heart palpitated. Fatigue, mild nausea, chest pain. His breath was shortened as he grew more and more worrisome. It caused a shortage in matter axioms to turn into life, and Nunc produced wild axioms of thoughts that twirled in his mind and left little space for void. Within his Dreamer self, it was harvesting time for Houses thirsty for axioms of Logos, regardless of how pessimistically tainted they were.

Nunc left the scene, just as he heard a voice in his head:

You did great today, Jamieson.

The voice congratulated him. "Please, Mr. Kennedy. Do not call me Jamieson. Never call me Jamieson, please."

The bird flew away, trying to cope with the stress he just faced. How in the world did he find the strength to show up in the most dangerous layers of Sophron? He did it to pick up a body, put it in an egg, face the most powerful archoid, boil the egg. And just because some voice in his head said he had to? He should just fly, now. Just fly.

275

Journey into the Hourglass:
Twelve

Our characters are alive! Even if we manage to glue a few concepts and a few ideas together! The moment order comes out by itself, leaving chaos like a dried-up cocoon, we, authors, lose our grip and control. I may just be a poet, and he may be a dust-up screenwriter, but we're in too deep. We've lost it. From this point forward, the characters live on their own.

It sounds scary, but then again, I'm a poet. Maybe authors exist, in all layers of Sophron, and in all possibilities. Maybe Martin and I are characters in someone else's universe. My own fears and my own pride show up to guide my thoughts and my actions, but their strings attach my soul to a Dreamer I never met.

Being in control of the narrative, does it mean to let it go? Accept that illusions speak to our animal nature, while, what? Intelligence isn't a nature? So is Void! I lost contact with Martin, at this point. I connected with Seamus, and that felt right. Marduk is after me. He wants to see me vanish for good. Maybe I will.

Fifth Intermission:
Written by the Author

New York City, in the post-apocalyptic possibility of the Victorian Prince. Ruined buildings loiter the streets. Human corpses rot alongside those of humanoid animals, while a bloodied mist covers the sky. A flock of giant bats with vulture heads patrol the air in search of decayed meat they can call a feast. And then there's Time Square, with its immense palace overlooking the gloomy city. Three towers surround the building, like columns framing a cube. At the central one's summit, a balcony draws shades over the dying trees scattered around. Standing up like a lonely dictator, the Author observes his domain. Martin keeps his face concealed behind a grey hood, with both his arms behind his back. He seems preoccupied. His mind wanders over a thousand ideas, many of them are frightening. How could he have lost contact with William? Why can't he further his narrative?

Behind thick brown glasses, the Author's blue eyes contemplate the horrors that shape the landscape. The Dreamer above him must go through a very unpleasant life to imagine so much ugliness. Martin didn't ask to grow up in this environment. He never expected, even when awakening, that he could escape. More beautiful manifestations of Sophron must exist, out there. But he must attend to more urgent matters. Of course, he can travel through portals, visit his friend, Alibast. Why would he? His life belongs in this torpor.

He couldn't alter William's life. He can control a character in the boy's entourage. And how did he end up in his own inner Sophron? Understanding this meant Martin achieved a higher level of enlightenment. So far, all he managed to write about involved the story of a Greek student who discovers this pluriverse. Even that seemed compromised, with the presence of Plato. He had to find a way to write about the philosopher's vanishing, so he could bring his version of a wise man guiding a protagonist. Sekhmet's intervention demonstrated that other awakened beings could make him lose control over his own creation.

He gazed at a red light, struggling to remain bright, at the far end of a long corridor. The weight of his apprehension felt heavy over his shoulders. He's ill-equipped to challenge gods and goddesses. What if the Egyptian Lady of the Night decided to follow his assassin all the way here? The balcony seemed to disappear behind him, as Martin approached the source of the red gleam: a huge beating heart on top of a wooden door. Just as it is with the overall décor, blood dripped out of the gigantic organ. He opened the entrance into his throne room and looked at the glare that came out of his laptop, sitting on a small table.

The Author stopped midway through the room, observing the breathing lungs that formed the tapestry. His thoughts sprinted around his mind, like a thousand million billion atoms about to detonate. This Book One was almost finished, and the Author had to consider writing the sequel. Perhaps he was looking at it from a wrong angle. What motivates the student to travel across Sophron? It was too late for him to contemplate another rewrite, but they will have to develop this in the second book.

The sound of the refrigerator broke the silence. Martin walked past a river of blood and opened its door to grab a beer. He hurried up behind the bright screen, reading the last words he typed:
Chapter 14: The Order of Muses.

If Sekhmet threatens to interfere with his storyline, then he won't make her ambition any easier. He may have lost contact with William. But he can get another pawn on the table. The Author looked at his laptop for long minutes, drinking his beer as though injecting some magic potion that would grant him inspiration. *What about them Muses?* he thought. If Marduk rose, powerful enough to annihilate an entire world, and if Sekhmet suddenly seemed interested in the aftermath of the Babel War, then stronger players need to rise.

He closed his eyes and let his fingers type: Euterpe existed as the head of a House that had grown interested by the prospect of thoughts this musician Dreamer can produce.

The Great Muses reflect themselves as Orphaned Entities.

When the Library of Alexandria fell, they found shelter in Hydaspes. Soon after the initial Big Bang, when matter, life, thoughts and void first expanded into myriads of chaotic illusions, the Muses became the first beings to develop a form of sentience. Back then, the creation of planets, suns shone as nothing more than excited electrons. Sophron flowed like a vast soup of energy. Out of this total blankness, Void gave birth to itself as the first element to manifest itself. If the universe, at the time, were able to feel anxiety, Void would become the force to exercise it. The expansion couldn't be.

Everything had to return to its initial state of absolute blankness. Then matter appeared, with atoms and electrons shaping it up. With astral bodies turning into planets, moons and stars, Void could no longer stop this expansion from embracing form. So, the champion of Gaia spoke the first word. It sounded like What the. Just as stars provoked the formation of gravity. Having realized that it could reflect on its own existence, he forced this newly born universe into a state of absolute sterility.

279

Billions of years later, Barbelo had the same confused reaction towards realizing its humble existence among the great unknown. Seeing how Void swiftly prevented other beings from achieving a state of consciousness, Barbelo allowed for its reflection to bring life on billions of planets, across the expanding universe. Void got quick to bring an end to this miracle, but some planets managed to transcend this purge.On those giant rocks, life evolved to the point of creating entire universes within themselves. Big Bangs, as thoughts, ideas, stories, concepts, philosophies, all existing in the minds of billions. Void remained the one most active agent trying to bring those movements to an end. Just as Logos was born, the Great Muses came to be.

Suddenly, Big Bangs happened a billionfold! In the soul of beings who shape their inner worlds, those entities of greater ideas helped influence the nature of thoughts, shaping the matter around, influencing the lives out there, chasing Void away. Martin knew all of that when he wrote this chapter to enhance his Chronicles of Sophron. He thought he could inspire one of them to participate in his written odyssey. He stopped his typing after the phrase: *What if nostalgy could breathe outside of Tragedy,* she thought? *Tragedy*. Muses are non-binary. They are essences that transcend the very notion of biological identity. Why did the ancient Greeks picture them as women?

"Are you having another writer's block?" the voice said.

"I don't know how to express the idea of genderless identities." Martin replied.

"You don't." the voice answered. "Existence is genderless. What you make of it, in the shape that makes sense to you, that's the illusion putting pressure on what never was."

"I'm thinking about bringing Melpomene in our story." Silence.

All the axioms that formed the words floating around the Author gathered to illuminate the white and orange painting above him. It looked like a purple door opening. The red vanished, leaving the blue to form the silhouette of a beautiful woman. A princess born out of amazing fairy tales. She floated above the Author and walked next to him.

"Tragedy? Martin, are you sure about that?"

"I am Ishtar. I think they're the most eloquent Muse for what we want to achieve." The goddess put a hand on his shoulder, reading the words he hadn't expressed yet.

"Almost as powerful as the Veritas that populated the True Worlds or the Mentiones of the Paradoxes." she recited.

"I'm creating a universe for my novel." the poet explained.

"Martin, do you really think this starts and ends with you writing a novel? What about those who will read it? What about those who won't but will drink the honey or venom coming out of those   who did read it? You can't just invent words like that!"

The Author thought about it for a moment. He couldn't possibly publish it in a possibility where zombies are everywhere and finding one enlightened being is akin to looking for the Holy Grail. "I still think Melpomene should be a warrior of some kind, in this story. Maybe he'll find the essence of Indra, who knows?"

"And why should Melpomene be a man?"

"Because. Come on, Ishtar, how else do you want to save your beloved Indra?"

"By having a man warrior do the job? Damn! I should have given that simple task to Simone de Beauvoir."

"Where did you get that?"

Feeling aggravated, Martin binged his beer and stood up. Bats got scared and agitated all around the room. The Author calmed down. "Okay, I get that." he grumbled. "But I don't think we should keep the old shape, like. Why did the Greeks picture the Muses as fragile maids? Give me just this one, Ishtar, please." The goddess smiled for a moment. "You're the poet. I'll leave that to your capable hands." She vanished just as she appeared. Attacked in his manly pride, Martin regained his seat once more. He opened another beer and installed his fingers on the laptop's keyboard. For the next chapter, he will be a metalhead poet trying to rewrite Beethoven's lost symphony.

Chapter Twenty-Nine:
The Order of Muses

Euterpe sits as the House of Great Muses' leading Entity. Those that this musician Dreamer can produce. Some would call the Dreamer god, but she calls him friend. In a previous incarnation, she used to listen to humans play instruments, and think that Logos axioms could mate with Archeus axioms through arts. She lived as a brainless student protesting the Babel Wars, back then, but she evolved. She never wanted to be like her incarnation's parents, though. She always said her parents gave up their dreams so that powerful nymphs could govern. Dreams live in their acquainted instant. *Life serves the dreams of thoughtful beings*, she thought.

Her parents had no idea. What if Nostalgy could breathe outside of Tragedy? Her sisters never listened. Melpomene did, though. She knew something more than feeling good would emerge. Youth is a breath, not an ideal. "Is it time to inspire?" A firefly would sometimes question, but Hydaspes would remain silent. Euterpe would remain even more silent. "Not now, please. I beg of you, not now." She would remind the voices in her head.

She looked within herself and remembered why the Great Muses left their people to die, so they could reflect upon their own enlightenment. They never participated in the war that brought Babel to mankind, but they remained faithful to the light that mankind sought. She could look at the fireflies and smile, thinking: Mankind is getting more and more enlightened, daughters. Let them breathe. The fireflies would leave Euterpe. They don't know what mankind looks like.

In Hydaspes, the nine Great Muses harvested and consumed every axiom the layer had ever produced. They did it to grow, placing them as very powerful entities, almost as powerful as the Veritas that populated the True Worlds or the Mentiones of Paradoxes. At the bottom of a great volcano, a lonely wind sang the best of Edith Piaf. The diva's voice sounded better with an Arctic's intense coldness and the centre of Hydaspes' soil propelling a very faint depression against the rocky walls. The volcano was Euterpe. Its entire structure collapsed and formed an organic gramophone. The melody, then, unable to hold on to the note for too long, became a rocky alembic. The magma underwent a complex travel through its tubes, ovens, vaults, and fridges until the rock turned to snow. The Muse filled the world outside, until the Muse could breathe once more and resume its volcano form.

On the other side of Hydaspes, a whole continent left blank carrying no particles. Every axiom at any given time, in any given space, reflected themselves through this Dreamer's Sophron. They remained reduced to fill a one on ten googol scales, yet they stood up to turn this entire continent into an oily display of gaseous colours. Reality as a soap bubble, and then some. Upon much closer scrutiny, an alert observer would see these dances of colours as quadrillions over quadrillions of different flowers. Each one appeared as unique as a snowflake, with a unique scent and texture, each and all born, bloom and die in a millisecond. Polyhymnia loves to carry this chaos to find a common melody to a Dreamer's plurality of being.

284

"My sisters!"

Every particle in the entire layer soon carried Melpomene's voice. He aimed his call at every one of the nine Great Muses. He hoped, above any other, that Clio would listen, but only Euterpe and Polyhymnia seemed to pay attention. These three words conveyed fear in the minds of eavesdroppers. Tremors could be felt all the way to the Great Councils. Another war? Can't they put an end to those quarrels and accept that peace is the only way towards higher awakenings? And this happens at a time when the Great Muses accepted their eternity as giant symbols and obscure metaphors.

While the Councils noticed, only the Muses gathered around Melpomene. He stood tall and strong at the summit of a windy mountain. Sthenele crawled at his feet like a feline slave lavishly chained to her master's thighs. An immense sword pointed out of his bare-naked back. A bronze ceremonial armour shone against his tanned torso. Tattoos covered his body from face to toe, although he wore boots that sometimes vanished to reveal the feet, sometimes covered his entire legs. Clio breathed sand in and breathed timeout. She convinced herself to avoid any of these schemes. Maybe, perhaps, somehow, if a Sleeper, much an Author, an occult Dreamer, could have reached her. She would have allowed his thoughts to carry history, his story to give birth to a culture. Her symbolic form came as less eccentric than that of her brothers and sisters.

On top of a crystal sphere was an amber castle that constantly built itself in a breath in and destroyed itself in a breath out. Civilizations of ants gathered at her feet when her metaphysical lungs attracted amber sand to form a hill. The ants grew in numbers, in organizations, developed technologies. They waged wars, imposed cultures, destroyed cultures, enslaved others, until their own greed, their selfish natures, their blindness caused the whole amber castle to fall, and them to fall and die with it. Then, it was time for Clio to breathe out.

285

"What makes you think this is the same Babel that cost us our native world?" Clio asked. Melpomene observed a mount of sand at his feet. He saw ants that laboriously carried pieces of plants into a hole.

"Gaia was never left alone after the judgment. I know because, for a time, I have participated in the exchange of information between Marduk and his agents, in the Nomicon. I knew that Varuna's influence was present on Earth as well, and someone had to balance these influences! The Councils wouldn't see it from my angle, so I acted alone. That was before I decided to join you in this last rest. As you can see, I have decided to fight once more."

The ants looked at him. One of them, a soldier, sighed and frowned. "You will never learn to humble yourself, Melpomene. Our state among the community of Veritas is as much an accident as it is our own design, but we can never be of them or with them unless we let go of our previous states."

"We have a responsibility to assume. We have altered the course of Sophron, and we must be accountable for our actions."

"The Councils would have punished us long ago. There is no need to seek redemption now."

"Clio! I beg of you to hear my plea. Babel is reborn, and this time the war will be subtle, yet deadlier than ever before."

"What will our participation bring? You have carried Marduk's influence on Earth, maybe elsewhere in Gaia, so he could benefit from his circle's axioms. You have allowed Varuna to harvest axioms as well, and you now face charges of conspiracy. Yet, you expose yourself and ask for our help. You ask of us that we join your machinations. But I would rather lose a brother to the Councils' decisions. I will allow myself to miss true awakening."

"Clio."

"Do you know how many rebirths? Do you know how many painful rebirths it took this essence to be where I am, now? You should because we were all in this together. You have grown too attached to the flawed reality of circles and gods; you have never allowed yourself freedom from karma. Why are you at the head of tragedy? Because you are the essence of failure, Melpomene. You worship disaster! And now you wish us to participate in the boldest failing scheme in our history."

"You are not attached to these creatures? Speak frankly, Clio. Since when is history supposed to be selfish?"

"It has always been subjective, brother."

"History, Clio, History!"

"Who's the story?"

"This one!"

"Oh, this one, Melpomene? Who is reading it?"

"Who is living it? We are!"

"Memories have nothing that existence can envy. I build memories. Existence builds itself." At this point, Melpomene looked at the gorgeous conqueror he kept attached to his ankles. As Sekhmet, she faced her own leaders, broke free from her circles, formed new circles and convinced dangerous Houses to join her invasion. As Sthenele, she is useless, harmless, and she is all his. His toy. His everything. Right now, he wished Clio was attached to his ankles as well, but he already felt beyond lucky when Sekhmet begged for his assistance. Someone of her magnitude and power. This Babel War will be different.

This Babel War will be different. This Babel War is the one that will allow the Great Muses to amend and adjust the errors of their past. This one is it. He must convince his siblings to sleep, even if only for a moment. Just a moment, just. Maybe for one book! Or two, or just for now. He looked at the ants. They resumed their lives. Sthenele had only sorrowful eyes to offer when she placed rocks on these ants' path as though her deity's influence humbled that game. Melpomene observed her with all the disdain he wished to project on his sister. He calmed down, closed his eyes, and deeply inhaled.

To his right, Euterpe projected himself as a tall and slim humanoid deer, under a beige and blue coat. Polyhymnia joined him in the form of a dove's shadow. Calliope, the eldest and most respected, joined them, behind Melpomene. She espoused the forms and colours of a membranous shield and a flesh sword. Erato stood next to her, and she embraced the beauty of a moon reflected through a cello. Descending white stairs, under the traits of an angelic Charlie Chaplin, I present you, Thalia. To complete this circle that formed around Melpomene and Sthenele, I show you a flock of ballerinas that almost looked like foam: Terpsichore. The sky closed itself to form a dome when all six other Muses closed the world around him. They formed walls. Urania formed a ceiling. The ants and the sand further shut this sphere.

For a moment that stretched far into eternity, the Muses felt the struggle of two Authors struggling to tell a story. That was unheard of. There could only be one, but who? Obviously, the Author in charge mastered enlightenment beyond the scope of a Buddha. Unless they cheated. Oh! They created an entire universe, sold it as a series of novels, made videos and songs, and convinced their readers that they were the true access to Great Awakenings. That didn't explain how the Great Muses found themselves entrapped in this storyline. Who was the protagonist? Who cares? Melpomene didn't stay behind and let the entire Sophron swallow him. He became a man! He made a goddess fall! She's now his pet! All those Muses should man up and wake up!

288

Silence. They want liberty, but traditions bring solid grounds. Ideas exist only to die in the arms of oblivion. Those gods and goddesses who carried their nasty ordeals, only fought for themselves. The Great Muses had humanity's best interest at heart. Melpomene knew better. How can he convince his sisters to join his take on a brand-new gender? Or sleep and let him work on their behalf? He thought about it for a moment, and he calmly said: "We can make a difference this time." He looked at Calliope, as though he wished to hear her approval.

"The war will take place on metaphysical grounds. We are at home on these soils. I say. Polyhymnia, Euterpe and myself will infiltrate the Author's mind. We will have direct interaction with his characters." He felt Polyhymnia and Euterpe's nod.

Melpomene will get to act as a general, and that thought made him feel confident. He added: "I say. We will have his lead character seek you, while Erato influences his romantic feelings. You will direct the head and she will direct the heart." Erato's face appeared against the sphere. She had the traits of an infant girl with deep purple eyes.

"I want to meet the Author. Please, allow us to discuss."

She is a very shy lady, and she has always had difficulties imposing herself against her siblings' influence. Melpomene looked in her eyes and borrowed a paternalistic tone. "At no time! Must the Author know the forces at work behind his inspiration? At no time, Erato."

"I sense a strong distress in his mind. What you consider a great conspiracy in the making, a. A war, a battle. To him, it's a cry for help. I sense a heart broken beyond repair. Please, Melpomene. Let me speak to the Author." He ignored her and looked at the floor. There, ants formed the fierce, yet highly attractive, face of Clio.

"I demand that you hear my plea, Clio, because we will never gather another opportunity to amend our past and correct our errors. Never a better time than this one to make things right and prove to the Sapphire Council that we are worthy of playing their games, on their scale. Worthy of our last awakening." Erato didn't like the role she received. She thought to herself and came up with the conclusion that if a place exists for love in this conspiracy of his, then let love speak for its acts. She kept these thoughts to herself but swore she would do what she felt was right, and not what she would be told. Clio appeared in front of Melpomene, in the form of an ant lady, and said: "We simply influence an Author's mind. We direct his inspiration, lead the development of a novel."

"Or a play, an opera or, maybe, a film. Regardless, we do it like in the old times when we were in Greece." he pleaded. Erato paid attention when Clio nodded and agreed:

"Very well. Leave the mind and the emotions to Erato and I. Urania will supervise from here, and we will keep Thalia nearby and ready to act swiftly. If the novel doesn't unfold itself the way we plan, we'll use a bit of comedy to break free from the harshness of drama. And we all return here and leave this battle to those who chose to fight. We do not fight. These are my demands."

She turned towards Calliope and waited for a nod. The Muse of heroic poetry smiled candidly and said: "Let Melpomene, Polyhymnia and Euterpe fight. Let them form an army, but let's make for a certainty that both the Author and his main character will face a heartbreaking choice. They'll have to choose an allegiance that will decide both their faith and Sophron's fate."

"With respect, Calliope." Clio interjected before her elder interrupted her. "There is no heroism in easiness, Clio."

"I do not intend to fight, but I wish my presence to be alongside Melpomene and Polyhymnia."

Euterpe expressed his desire in the form of a breeze that caressed everyone's cheek. Euterpe then manifested himself under the traits of a fragile university student. "This is the form I will employ. I will personify a fragile thinker, with as many flaws as he has curiosity. This way, the Author will have less pressure over his main character." Calliope, Clio, and Melpomene all approved of his suggestion. This is when Erato decided to manifest herself in the form of a highly attractive Ki-Rin, lady. She walked three steps forward and stopped short from seductively embracing her brother.

"Let me encounter the main character too! If I cannot directly reason the creator, let me comfort the creation." At this point, Melpomene sensed it was a big brother's duty to remind a little sister of her place in the family. He looked at her and smiled.

"No." He sighed. She felt weak and humiliated. Sthenele looked at her, and in an instant the two bonded. Urania was the last to speak before this secret meeting adjourned: "Once again, we will stray from the course the Sapphire Council has imposed on us. We put our very awakening on the edge of never happening. We have inspired this humanity, on Earth, in Gaia, in silence after we were asked to leave these circles to specific Houses. It is my understanding that outlawed Houses are also back on that layer and ready to break their hell loose. I say we go according to Melpomene's plan, and we follow Calliope and Clio's judgment and decisions. As for you, Erato, you will do as you are told. This is no time to inspire another Romeo and Juliet. Now we close a dangerous issue we started long before our current state."

Erato frowned while Polyhymnia and Euterpe embraced mortal forms for themselves. She wanted to join them. She wanted to be there, meet this character! A love triangle triggered the last Babel War. A conflict emerged between Marduk, Ishtar and Indra. Or was it William, Emerald, and Seamus? What if romance also affected this one? She inspires passions! She should know. She should take part in this saga!

291

She looked at Terpsichore and Thalia. Both Muses stood behind others in this so-called family business. Nobody took her seriously. Even back in Greece, it was always either tragedy or comedy that required a presence by the House of the Great Muses. Oh, sure, romance was there, in all of them. But never to the point of considering Erato as a poem's architect. This time, she will show her siblings just how important love is. Not only in art, in telling stories, but in binding beings together. Even if at the cost of a loved one's own life.

It pained Erato to remain on the side. They talk about war when the very fabric of this story spells out love: her specialty! *All right!* she thought. I know exactly who to bring to your chessboard. With Book One about to end, Erato knew that new characters would soon be introduced. She closed her eyes and revisited an event that took place between the first two parts of this ongoing trilogy. Her elderly people think she can't play her part? Wait until they see her wildcard play his. She smiled, as she built walls in her mind. It's a bar, somewhere. She sits there and drinks, alone. Whoever sits next to her will play a major role in their war. He only needs to respond to a poem that inhabits the Ether, right this moment:

When you can be so detached as saying I love you without a fiesh that aims at being viral. And when you can be so in love, your soul is the universe to all plus the one you care for. Then you may plant that seed and let it grow enlightened. Or die forbidden.

Erato would think of a firefly, and the pretty insect would dance around the projected image she gathered. She was either a naked youth or a reflecting crone. A swan or a dove. A peacock or a hummingbird. She was poetry, she thought. She wanted to recollect that night at the bar, right before the House of the Great Muses voted in favour of participating in the next Grand Battle.

Erato would simply guide Dreamers of Gaia into creating beauty. Why didn't they fight, like the others? Erato always assumed that Muses had a role to assume in the last Babel War. Love! We need more love! They shied away, when Amazons allied with Spartan warriors, fighting Persians. What was wrong with inspiration? Why should they retreat because politicians decided to educate in their image rather than elevate beyond their greed?

She looked at the fly and smiled. *Take me back to my love.* she thought. Her cowardly warrior, with a big flying boat. I've never seen you in the Lonesome Crone, but your eyes make me swear you've seen me before.

These were the first words he said to her. She stood behind the bar, sipping her Logos-Daiquiri like she didn't want to be disturbed, but she felt he had to disturb her with the right attitude.

"I usually go out in a nexus naos we find beyond True-Archeus, towards Void." she explained. The handsome delinquent sat next to her and ordered a beer that smelled like blood.

"Regulars in those bars tend to overthink, and I can't stand that." he complained. "You should hang in that side, beyond True-Archeus. This is what life is about." She just then realized they were in Hades. She smiled, pretending she knew all along, forgetting she visited this world to reject the decision they made. No. She won't spend eternity as an immobile object in Hydaspes!

"And what do you like about this place?" she asked the traveller. He kissed her hand and said: "Random encounters. We never know who will sit at the bar, thinking they're alone. Everyone has a story worth a reader's attention. But I admit, I like to hear stories that carry my essence forward."

"You're a boy looking for a girl? You want to feel more masculine in your conquest?"

"Who said conquest had a gender? I want to grow. Without losing my ground." The firefly landed on Erato's flesh. She smiled and looked at it. She looked at Melpomene, standing up and proud as a warrior. *An essence has no gender,* she thought. Maybe she should find that bad boy and see. There's more to what she'll bring to this story than just a quick glimpse. "I want to grow as well, but you don't seem like the type I would marry. Why should we keep talking?" she asked the nameless intruder, at the bar.

"I don't want to marry you either. But we have needs. Tell me yours, and I'll share you mine. If we can find an optimal option, then let's create something and call it love."

"Then, I'll return to my phantom frigate and find another bar." He has a phantom frigate? Was he an admiral in a big battle or did he steal it? How could he steal it? Spectre boats have souls of their own. Did he seduce the boat like he's trying to seduce her? She's one of the nine Great Muses! She's not that easy, obviously. She looked at him, alone on his table, playing with a smartphone. She could discover so much from this other side of Archeus. Why couldn't she get it all at once, tonight? With this earthling who pilots a god's frigate. She pretended she was unimpressed by his burst of manhood. But she knew he was into her. Somehow, he was into her leaving the Archeus-Logo quadrant, just so she could have a beer. *And he's into sci-fi classics!* she thought, as she looked at him and smiled, timidly. He didn't even smile back.

He looked at a Ki-Rin waitress, passing by, and he felt like he had a chance with her. He wants to have fun. And he wants a family. Why can't he put his cards on the table and stop play a game? "Why do you all play games?" she shouted! Melpomene looked at her and sighed, like an ant at the feet of Mount Olympus. Erato calmed down and breathed. She did her best, but now. She breathed.

294

Epilogue:
Void is having a good Time

"Does it mean I'm dead?" the student asked.

"What do you know about death?" they heard coming out of the absolute blackness surrounding them.

"I guess I just have to wake up and realize that I tried too hard." "Open your eyes? Look around and see that you are still in your bedroom? Oh, it's getting late. You should go to the Parthenon and talk to Plato, right?"

"Something like that."

"And do you feel like you are dead, now? You didn't fall off a bridge, or anything."

"I don't know. I thought I created you, for some reason. And William, and. I need to wake up. I just. I have to wake up."

"Nobody's forcing you of anything. Just open your eyes," When the student complied, they found themselves in a gigantic cave. They quickly realized that they were brought back to that room where they saw the orb for the first time. A sigh of relief got to them. It would only be a matter of time before Plato and the other disciples would show up. Walking around, they thought about inspecting the room a bit.

It was as empty as the last time. The same blue light gleamed all over the gigantic chamber, but the student stood where the orb used to be. They gathered impatience to be reminded that a comforting illusion could come back and make sense.
"Hello?" they shouted. "Teacher? Are you there?" Nothing. "Sir? Are you still there?"

"Why are you calling me sir?" Void distastefully answered. The student was unable to reply. They looked around and tried to fathom the face of their interlocutor. It felt as though it was their own, and yet it was foreign. They saw a table, they recalled, when William discussed with Void for the first time. Where is it? "Quintilian will say: Grammar and arts are one. Maybe not with those exact words, but the meaning is there."

"I know who you are."

"Of course, you do. Okay." A door opened through the wall that faced the student. Through it, a longer tunnel emerged. The student found the courage to walk inside, leaving the room and its comforting warmth behind. This new corridor seemed to stretch towards a greater unknown. The student could easily take the other tunnel and leave this place. Perhaps they could end up in their bed, or at the Parthenon, but they preferred exploring this new place, as though a white rabbit took them along. Darkness awaited the Walker, leaving this blue light behind them. Coldness got the best of them, but why should they turn around? Whatever they would find, at the end of this corridor, would certainly be worth more than what they would have gotten, should they have elected to leave Plato's cave, the old-fashioned way.

The corridor appeared to grow larger, but the student felt smothered under a burden of mystery. Ideas and words came to them: What should have I done? Why did he do this. Where is he now? They stopped and looked behind. The door remained shut. Did Void leave them to this total uncertainty?

The orb should be within their grasp, but all they could ever see was. Void. "My name is Marvin, but you can call me Mr. Marvin. Please, can I sit? My master has sent me over to talk."

"Who told you to find me here?" the student shouted. Silence replied. Anxiety took the stage. Who just talked to them? Where did the voice come from? It was impossible to comprehend the surroundings. They could breathe, they could realize that they were breathing, but all their senses stayed silent, gone. As time went by, their memories also faded. Is it too late to walk out? To where? Their mind could barely grasp the reality that now defined their presence. A sigh. A deep sigh. Breathing in, holding it, and breathing out. That was it. Perhaps they could abandon themselves further to this state of being. The only true reality is that of the moment when air goes to his lungs, and his brain realizes that air must now get out.

"A sigh." they whispered. "A deep sigh." And light reappeared. They could have pictured themselves in a coffin, buried under a ton of dirt, and that would have been quite the terror. Instead, they didn't picture themselves at all. Was this the ultimate test that Plato had in mind? The student slowly walked towards this dimmed light. It was yellowish as though someone imprisoned a dying fire inside a small prism. When the student approached the source, they heard a strange music. Someone must be scratching metal, for some reason, while a cat would screech under a pillow. The whole process behind those noises was too alien for the student to start to understand what was going on. They walked closer to the source, only to see various books loitering on the rocky floor. They knew about papyri, and they understood the concept of collecting pages under two hard covers, but the images on these artefacts were unlike anything they had ever seen. They walked closer to the source of light, and this is when they saw the orb. It floated behind a blonde bearded man. He was naked behind some sort of book, with a window that displayed two white pages and words. When the student approached further, they could read: *When the student approached further.*

The Author froze. He closed his eyes for a moment, feeling a presence that frightened him. The student walked across this new cavern, looking around, trying to make sense of what they saw: An open window on the other side of the room. They walked to look outside, only to witness a dead city. It used to be New York. Now, it's a Victorian cemetery.

Some sort of book stood atop a small table, displaying moving pictures of a wide field with gigantic mushrooms made of rock and metal. They grabbed a magazine that loitered the floor and observed the glossed painting. Some words sounded intelligible, but it felt as though the cover mentioned Sophron's Mimes. They opened it at some random page, and there it was, in an approximate Greek they could make sense of: They put the magazine away and walked next to the frightened Author. On a piece of paper next to him, words were scribbled along nonsensical doodles. When they focused, the student could figure out one intelligible sentence:

For Emerald.

When he opened his eyes, he looked at his computer screen and read: He looked at his computer screen and read.

"You're not here."

The student felt the meaning of these words, but it hardly complied with their interpretation of what was going on. Should they reply out loud? Are they imagining this scene?
"Hi." They smiled. "Can you teach me?"

Teach what? Storytelling?

"I mean. About Seamus and William. I have to find the right story for them." It burned from your inside, right? Oh! What is this thing doing here? You can't even tell if it's a he or a she! Damn, Author, why are you pissed? Was it something I said?

298

Shut up.

The student walked away, frightened. I laughed. You will never get her, Martin.

Shut up! Shut up! Shut up!

Both the Author and the student suddenly felt like reality meant nothing. If they closed their eyes, they faced a long corridor that separated a state of darkness from one of enlightenment. If they looked behind, they would see lifetimes of regret and error. All the people hurt, and those who did them wrong. Every reason they ever had to end their lives and forget their hopes for a better tomorrow. The lungs breathing against the walls seemed keen to undergo the same stress. Blood flew across the room, pumped by a broken heart. If the building had eyes, tears would flood its floors. The Author had only focus the lit screen facing him. Words he was about to write dwelled in the Veil between his mind and the medium waiting to fossilize his thoughts. Who brought this visitor to his lair? Was one of his characters suddenly awakening and taking charge?

Was it William?

"Don't narrate my part, Void!" he shouted. The unwanted guest looked at him. Their eyes were wide and filled with fear. The horror that came with those living organs in lieu of a tapestry was enough to haunt them for the rest of their life. How did they get here? How can they leave? And this madman behind a glowing box. Would he torment them in the name of Hades?

Martin closed his eyes again and frowned:

"You're not supposed to be here." The student realized this very weird *something* was only the beginning.

299

"Are you with Plato?" the disciple asked. The Author thought for a moment and said: "It depends on what your Plato thinks of Sophron." Martin returned to his novel, trying to forget their presence. The pupil looked at the lungs that fought for their life, and they weren't certain if they had to smile or be worried. What if someone read these lines and thought: *Martin Poirier is asthmatic?* He wrote this to symbolize how.

"Hey!" the Author shouted. "Leave my orb alone!"

They weren't even conscious that the mancing sphere had appeared in the palm of their hand. Their heart was beating so fast, their ears went shut. Despite all the excitement, they just had a WAIT A MINUTE moment. The student didn't realize they were caressing the floating crystal ball. "I'm sorry, I just. Your room is a mess." they argued. At the same time, they attempted to reproduce the exercise their teacher taught them earlier. *The Author was grumpy, trying to ignore the presence of the lovely Greek tourist.* they thought to themselves. The orb shone in approval.
Satisfied, they left the bringer of reality on a small table and walked around the room.

"Who is Sophron for you, sir?" they asked. Martin had difficulty concealing his irritation. "He wrote mimes, back in your time. Only fragments survived. He was admired during the Hellenistic period, but he fell into near oblivion. Your mentor may have kept many of those texts intact. Did he teach you his poetry?"

"A bit." the genderless interlocutor replied. "I don't think my purpose was to know about his texts, however." The poet cleansed his mind and tried to return to his craft. Of all the characters in his book that he expected a visit from, this one was rather unusual. Whoever decided to play with his inspiration, he or she or they wouldn't get away without a fight.

"Sit here." he instructed his new friend. "This is a laptop. I'll show you how to use it. We can discuss it later but let me write that book on my own. We'll figure your place in the greater scheme of things to come."

A few hours ago, the student had no idea there existed worlds beyond their modest Athens. Now, they met their new teacher. They gladly grabbed a stool and sat next to the bearded blonde beauty. So many characters claimed existence inside their mind. Martin opened a drawer and installed his backup computer in front of his guest. The sun set over New York City. Inside the immense palace that overlooked Time Square, two minds collided in front of empty pages. Zombies crawled around the desert streets, vampires flew into the sky and mummies gathered in parks. A novel was about to be written from scratch. I observed what was going on, and I thought to myself: *I did well, so far. I can't pretend that I have it in me to direct the course of events, but my brothers and sisters will have to agree. Void isn't devoid of resources.*

Throughout the seventy-two layers of Sophron, gods and goddesses prepared themselves for a grand battle. Sekhmet took notice of Marduk's plan. She realized soon enough that an Author was involved. Perhaps the Hound Lord of Nibiru would leave her beloved Tir na n'Og alone, but she had to be proactive in her next moves. Whatever the reason that prompted him to reacquaint himself with his ideas of conquest, she won't stay on the side until it's too late.

Melpomene was also getting ready to show his might. Just as he left Hydaspes to return in his quarters, down on Athanor, he thought about this young boy. He reflected on that essence of a god inhabiting William's soul. The Muse was glad they incarnated themselves in the body of a muscular warrior. He felt the coming of a storm, a war like none had ever occurred before. Finally, he could leave poetry aside and wave that big bastard sword in the face of an enemy! Now that's tragedy!

301

End of Book One

All I could hear was: "William committed suicide, this morning. An ambulance found his body down a high path. With a bullet in his head." And that didn't feel right.

Maybe it was murder.

I'm sorry, what?

The student was reading those lines above my shoulder. I may have had too much to drink. I guess it's only good if I don't do drugs. I had no idea what to tell them. Hi! Did you just leave Plato's cave? That wasn't the right formulation, I guess. You know that for some teachers, this allegory justifies the use of hatred against the unknown? At least they get that they don't understand a thing, I guess. I hope! Okay, now the student walks around my lair and they touch my stuff. Yeah. My walls have lungs. That wasn't my idea. Don't poke them!

"Hey! Stop it!" I shouted, hoping to make them disappear.

"It may have been a murder, what do you think?" they asked.

"According to your own narration, I'm the one who came up with the story of Seamus and William." they pondered, in an approximative English.

"Dude!!" I complained. A thought, here, is this considered a non-binary word? Who cares! "Dude. Like you came up with Montreal as an imaginary city. Come on, now! Think, for a moment." And they did. After a while, they confronted me with an unexpected conclusion:

"Yes! You obviously came from my imagination since I came up with this. Montreal word. But I don't know how travelling across the pluriverse functions."

Neither did I. Well, I may have had an idea since I invented this entire fantasy setting. Heck, even Alibast admits that he uses my voice and my entire body to do his videos or talk with people from my world. I may as well have created his entire life! Although not quite. Okay, so the student has a point. I can't deny seeing them. Even if I close my eyes, I can still hear them breathe.

Someone's loss is another one's gain. Who said that?

"I sensed Seamus' existence." they whispered. "The more I would force his story, and the less it made sense. When the teacher instructed me to abandon myself to the will of the orb, this entire story came up."

"I bet you want me to acknowledge your existence, now?"
        I grinned. If this gets published, I'll probably be cancelled, but there's no way this student doesn't have a gender! I mean, come on, Alibast! Are we doing this? I bet you would say: Which gender would you have them be? I don't know. I should have cast you out of my life the moment you made me write this crap.

"I was thinking." The student disturbed my anger. "Maybe the old man, in the park, could be a god."

"Are you still talking about Seamus Chron?"

"We should write the next book together."

"I already have a partner, and he's a total douchebag."

"Just let me try."

I sighed. Sure, whatever. I would rather get drunk, anyway.

"Be my guest!" I shrugged, right before giving them my seat.

They looked at the keyboard for a very long moment. I wanted to burn their entire world! Get out! Don't you tell me to calm down, Alibast! This isn't about us! You don't even exist. Like I gave you a spotlight, with those videos. Come on! I'm not bitter. You are! "Mr. Martin?" The student disturbed me again.

"What?" How did they get to know my name?

"Can I write something?"

"Suit yourself, kid."

How come they don't know how to work with a laptop? "I would prefer writing the story with your orb."

"It's just a stupid crystal ball I bought to impersonate a stupid character and sell my books! Well, hopefully." They ignored everything I said. They grabbed the orb and caressed it. I need another job. The sun rose over Montreal. Seamus found himself sleeping next to that homeless person, under a bench. His head got heavy on top of the old man's belly. A cocktail of warmth and bad body odour gathered next to the youngster's nostrils. Why is he still with him, he wondered? He left his home to wander around the world, and he's stuck with a delusional hobo. When he left his uncomfortable posture, Seamus saw a piece of paper oddly installed under the man's makeshift pillow. He looked at it with a sight swamped in amazement.

Where did that yellowish letter come from? It looked like a piece of cloth filled with urine. Curiosity was threatening the cat. It didn't look like any piece of paper. For some reason, Seamus felt the presence of an essence coming out of it. Yet, he still couldn't connect with his new friend's psyche. Was the parchment alive? Was it sentient in some manner or another? Intrigued, Seamus found the courage to grab this little piece of mystery from underneath the homeless' head.

ELECTRIC SHOCK!

Or kind of. The runaway youth wasn't prepared to deal with billions of existences linked to his mind at once. How could they exist from his fingers touching a piece of garbage? He was best leaving it under the old fool's head, he thought.
What just happened?

The old man remained asleep. There's no way he could have heard the young boy's scream. Maybe another attempt at grabbing that piece of paper could happen. Seamus took a long time to recover and gather the bravery needed to grab this. Whatever that is. From underneath the slob's heavy head. He could hear the voices within the mind of billions of voices within. It was just white noise, by the time he ran away with the fragment of an old papyrus in his hands.

A few words were written on it, with a question mark in the end. He couldn't tell anyone's identity from this amalgamation of absolute nonsense. But one manifestation seemed clear to him.

"Did you find William?" she asked.

"No, but I think I know how to get to him."

"Seamus, please! Stop fooling around!"

"I know Ishtar! I think I met someone who can help us."

"Who? Tell me his name."

"I don't know, but he got into my life at the right time. I think he can help me practise my gift, or at least point me to the right direction."

"Seamus, I need to know who that is!"

The old man woke up at that moment. He smiled at Seamus and didn't say a word. When he closed his eyes, Ishtar's voice disappeared. Nothing happened; the homeless man resumed sleep.

Silence.

Seamus was left with nothing but the piece of paper that stole his sanity. He walked away, like a shameful child who got away with mischief. He found solace under a sole light pole. He took a deep breath and read the fragment:

Hello, Seamus. My name is Alibast Page. Welcome to your redemption arc. We'll see you in our next book called:

The Chronicles of Sophron: The Saviour Squad.

www.ingramcontent.com/pod-product-compliance
Lightning Source LLC
Chambersburg PA
CBHW072121020726
47501CB00003B/922

* 9 7 8 1 7 7 8 1 1 2 2 2 5 *